QUINN OF CYGNUS:
LIFT OFF
QUANTUM FOLD

AM SCOTT

Something is wrong at Adzari Net Academy.

Really wrong.

It all seemed so right—Quinn's big chance! She'd leave the mud, giant lizards and back-breaking labor behind forever and gain so much more: skills, connections, a job, a real life.

Then Quinn arrives to find the academy under new ownership and everything's changed. Mean girls, strict schedules and tough teachers aren't a problem. Quinn's got the brains, discipline and training to beat them at their own game.

But the new owners raised the stakes and the house always wins. Quinn's big adventure has become a fight for survival. Light years from home, with no power or backup, how can she endure?

Some might give up and fail. But not Quinn. She's determined to not just survive, but escape and do a little damage on her way out.

They'll never know what hit them.

DEDICATION

To my readers! Thanks for your patience—I know this took way too long. Thanks for buying my books, which allows me to write and publish more. I really appreciate it!

CHAPTER ONE

Sweat poured down Quinn's body like a Cygnus Secundus afternoon thunderstorm, and every muscle in her body trembled. She wouldn't break—she'd never break. But holding this y'ga stance—standing on her right leg, bent forward, with her left leg raised behind her and her arms out to the side— was agonizing. As it should be—there was a reason the Sisters of Cygnus called these punishment poses.

"Release," Sister Lashtar snapped.

Quinn gratefully dropped her left leg to the floor, pulled her arms into her sides, and stood upright.

"Recover. Ten minutes."

Slowly, Quinn sank to the floor, folding her legs below her body and lowering her forehead to the mat. *Ah.* Eventually, she got up the energy to turn flat on her back. She breathed, slowly and evenly, concentrating entirely on her breathing. The fading remains of resin-laden incense was sharp in her sinuses but soothing all the same, as was the silence.

"Penitents are released to drink and eat. In silence." Sister Lashtar's voice was as cold as a Cygnus Gliese winter night—

Quinn didn't remember a lot about Gliese, but she remembered those frigid, starry nights. Cygnus Secundus was warmer but far wetter—a clear night was rare. "Quinn, my office after the meal." A faint sigh followed. Poor Sister Lashtar, stuck with all the tough cases, like Quinn. Lashtar led the Sisters for more than one reason, but her tough love approach was a cornerstone.

Quinn heard the rustle of clothing and the pad of bare feet. She knew the others were gathering bev-tainers and y'ga mats, more than ready to leave the Sisters' meditation room, but if she moved, she'd have to think, and she didn't want to do that yet.

Something hit the bottom of her foot. When Quinn ignored it, the tapping continued, getting harder and switching feet randomly. Quinn sighed and opened her eyes.

"Finally," Nat hissed, brown eyes scowling at her. She held out a hand. "Come on. We need water and calories." She glanced at the door, obviously hoping Sister Lashtar didn't hear her.

Quinn took Nat's hand and let the taller, older girl pull her up. Head swimming, she focused on a single spot on the wall and clung to Nat. Finally, she let go, pulled the rough-spun Sister's robe Nat handed her over her head, and gratefully accepted the bev-tainer Brin handed her. Drinking slowly, she followed the two young women out of the meditation room, down the hall and into the dining hall. They lined up at the kitchen window, muttering, "Thank you, Sister," as they took trays with stew, bread, and water and then headed to the front of the huge room. As usual, the scent of baking bread permeated the huge dining hall, and the clatter of hand-thrown clay pottery seemed loud in the silence of the Sisters of Cygnus's orphanage. Quinn put her tray on the small table and turned to face the leadership table.

Sister Navarr stood and intoned, "May the Mother bless the food we are here to share. May the Mother bless our efforts to praise her. May the Mother bless us."

"May the Mother bless us," echoed back from every corner of the high-ceilinged room, Quinn joining in. She was blessed to be here, but sometimes boredom drove gratefulness and common sense right out of her head. Then, she'd find something she wasn't supposed to see, and her anger wiped out every thought, including gratitude, like a lightning strike shattering a tree.

Sitting at the small punishment table at the front of the dining hall full of her fellow orphans, Quinn concentrated on eating her simple stew slowly. Why bother looking up? She'd only see the rest of the girls pointing and laughing at them, a practice the Sisters ignored, hoping peer pressure discouraged further bad behavior.

Too bad for the Sisters that it didn't work. Quinn smirked. She could care less what the "good girls" thought. She ate, trying not to think about what she'd found. But it was hard to concentrate on a negative. Still, she did so until she finished eating. She stared down at her bowl, watching the head table out of the corner of her eye.

Finally, the leaders stood, bringing everyone to their feet, and they waited while Sister Navarr announced the work assignments. The leaders left, then the long table with the teenagers caring for babies and toddlers, another teen shepherding the young children, then the pre-teen table and finally, the few remaining teenagers without childcare jobs tonight. Most of them headed to the kitchen to pick up hot boxes containing their midnight meal—something to warm them during night watch. Quinn wished she was headed out with them. A boring night watch over the Sisters' compound would be far preferable. For that matter, a terrifying night watch defending their fields and flocks against the huge, dinosaur-like wildlife would be better.

Quinn reluctantly followed the leaders out of the dining hall, Nat shooting a half sympathetic, half accusatory look at her as they split, Nat and Brin going to clean the kitchen. Quinn trudged up the stairs to Sister Lashtar's office and knocked quietly.

"Come in."

She sighed and entered the dragon's lair, standing in front of Sister Lashtar's desk, looking straight ahead.

"Well, here you are. Again." Lashtar's voice was dismissively disappointed. "Despite defining your limits, you insist on exceeding them, prying into things you have no right to know. Why?"

Why? Isn't that obvious? Or is this a trick?

"I asked a question, Penitent Quinn."

Well, she had little to lose. Why not give her the real answer? "Yes, Sister. After Ferra's betrayal for credits, how can you ask any of us to trust you?" Their home destroyed, friends dead, fleeing Cygnus Gliese as refugees, all because of one woman's greed.

A sharp inhale followed by silence. Quinn risked a glance. Sister Lashtar's eyes were closed, mouth clamped shut. *Uh oh.*

Sister Lashtar exhaled ever so slowly and took in another deep breath. Her eyes opened, their icy blue pinning Quinn's. "Penitent Quinn, we have outlined the processes and procedures we have put in place to ensure no one person has control of the Sisters ever again. *Full* Sisters are given full access to everything. You are not a Sister. I sincerely doubt you will ever be a Sister of Cygnus."

Quinn gasped. Not be a Sister? What else would she be? She'd lived with the Sisters her entire life. She closed her eyes.

"Look at me."

Quinn did so, examining Lashtar's expression. Quinn found nothing on her pale, freckled, hollow-cheeked face.

Lashtar said, "I didn't say that to hurt you, Quinn. But the women who become full Sisters aren't prone to constantly breaking the rules, questioning every word. Nat and Brin tried to talk you out of this, didn't they?" It wasn't really a question.

"Yes," Quinn admitted.

"I thought so. Nat is a natural leader, as are you. But she's a leader by the book. You are not. The Sisters who thrive here need rules and consistent leadership according to those rules. Survivors of violence, disaster, and poverty require safety to heal and grow. Fairly enforced rules provide that safety. If you stay, you and Nat will clash constantly. You will stress everyone in leadership. *You* will be more stressed than anyone because you'll never really fit in here, Quinn." Lashtar said the last in a surprisingly sympathetic, gentle voice.

"And besides that, your talents aren't well suited to the Sisters. We have an agriculturally based, subsistence lifestyle. We teach net skills, y'ga, and other security skills, so those who choose to move on can support themselves in the wider universe. We have more than enough net expertise here already. You'll be bored. And a bored Quinn is a dangerous Quinn."

Quinn clenched her fists at her sides and clamped her lips together. She wasn't sure if she would laugh, scream, or cry, so she didn't say anything at all.

"Again, Quinn, I'm not saying this to hurt you. I'm telling you this because you already know it's true. You just aren't willing to admit it." Lashtar tapped a work-roughened finger sharply on the desk once. "Or maybe you aren't ready to admit it. Either way, the restrictions of the Sisters chafe you, like a too-tight set of boots. Even though you're physically younger than Nat and Brin, you've outgrown this place." She swept an arm, clearly indicating the entire compound of orphanage and farm, not just Lashtar's office.

Quinn swallowed hard and bit her lip. Where would she go?

"At fourteen, you're younger than I'd like to send folding across the universe, but the net academy Katryn attended has a partial scholarship available." Lashtar snorted. "And this is where your rule-breaking will come in handy. The scholarship's upper age limit is thirteen standard years. You're not a big girl, and I don't think you'll ever be big, not with your obvious heritage. You can easily lose a couple of years." Lashtar's mouth twisted. "And you are much more mature than your physical age."

That was all true. It was hard to stay a little girl when you'd experienced war and you did the job of an adult. She'd been Sister Ani's net security deputy for over a year. But she still looked like a little girl. Quinn had more in common with her predecessor, Katryn Phazeer of Lightwave Fold Transport, than her net talents. They were both tiny, with hair so black it was almost blue, big, slightly tilted brown eyes, and pointed chins. She looked like Katryn's little sister or an anime action figure.

Quinn bit her lip, trying to hold back her growing excitement. Katryn was almost legendary—raised as an orphan by the Sisters of Cygnus, she'd left for school, got a great job on a core-system world, fought Galactica Corporation, found the love of her life, Tyron, while running from Galactica's wrath, and ended up with a net security position on Lightwave, since Tyron was Chief of Security. Most of the girls here prayed for an adventure and rescue like Katryn's. While Quinn desperately wanted the schooling and job, she could do without the battle against a giant corp or being tied down to some man. Or barely making a living on a small fold transport, folding passenger shuttles across the universe without a schedule or guaranteed income.

Lashtar continued, drawing Quinn out of her spiraling thoughts. "The age requirement seemed suspicious, but the academy assures us they are trying to reach disadvantaged girls before they are trapped into a life of servitude and poverty. Katryn attended the same academy at the same age and Adzari doesn't appear to have changed at all. Katryn did very well and had no problems." Lashtar shrugged. "Well, until she went out on her own and decided to go up against Galactica Corporation. So, part of your punishment detail is this: you will investigate the academy, make sure it still is what it says it is, and you will create documents supporting your new age." Lashtar snorted again. "Not that you will have any trouble with that, since none of you have real documentation by core standards."

Quinn took her first real breath since arriving in Lashtar's office. Off-world? To a net academy? It was a dream come true. A slightly scary dream but so exciting! She'd get away from all these ridiculous restrictions, the religious trappings, the steamy, sodden jungle of Cygnus Secundus, battling the wildlife for every meal. And she'd be on the net all day, every day. No more weeding, shepherding, building fences, clearing jungle, none of that. Learn more and more about the net, and how to infiltrate it and secure it, and—

"Quinn!" Lashtar snapped.

She jumped.

"Don't skimp on this research. Don't assume you're better than a school full of net experts. Your life is at stake, and you should know by now there are worse things than death." Lashtar pointed a finger at Quinn. "Even though there are no indications Adzari Academy has changed, Katryn attended a long time ago. And there's no way for us to come to the rescue if everything goes wrong." She narrowed her eyes. "We'll be sending you with a list of codes and phrases. You *will* check in. If you don't, we'll be asking Lightwave and others we know to check on you, but there's no guarantee anyone will have the time or the ability. You will be alone and unafraid out there on a world halfway across the known universe in Canis Major. Do the work." Lashtar's expression was an odd combination of worry, pride, and sorrow.

"Yes, Sister, I will." Quinn would do the research all right— she'd heard too many horror stories of slavery from the Sisters not to—but she wasn't going to squander this opportunity either. Even if this school wasn't the right one, there had to be another one out there. Net talents like hers were rare and she knew it.

Plenty of beings wanted someone with her talent and would pay to see it grow.

Sister Lashtar was right—Quinn didn't belong here.

"And Quinn?"

"Yes, Sister Lashtar?" She kept herself from bouncing around the room with joy, but it was hard.

"The research is part of your punishment." She smiled a slow, rather evil smile, her pale brows arching. "You are still obligated to all the others, including kitchen duty." The smile grew. "You're late. Go!"

Quinn spun and sprinted out of Lashtar's office. Even though the nasty job of cleaning the kitchen's grease traps waited for her, she was too excited to walk. Off-world! To a net academy! All day, learning net skills.

She couldn't wait.

∆∆∆

Brin squeezed her tight. Too tight. "Can't breathe." Brin's arms loosened but didn't let go.

"We'll miss you." She set Quinn away from her at arms-length, hands on her shoulders, and shook her a little. "You'd better write."

Quinn smiled. "Of course I'll write. I'm going to a net academy. I'll have way better connections to communications than we do here. Getting it here, to Cygnus Secundus, will be the problem."

Nat pulled her away from Brin and into a slightly gentler hug. "I'll miss you, Quinn." She let go. "I won't miss the trouble you cause, but I'll miss you." Her smile trembled.

"I'll miss you too." She looked around the group of girls and women. "I'll miss all of you. Stay safe."

Sister Ani walked her to the shuttle's short stairs. "Safe folds. You're always welcome to come back."

Quinn laughed. "Thanks, Sister. I'll be fine. How could I be anything but fine? You trained me." She forced a chuckle. Now that her foot was on the first step, climbing up seemed to take far more effort than it should. She blinked back sudden tears and bowed. "Thank you for your teaching and patience." With effort, she smiled. "I'll succeed and make you proud."

Ani nodded deeply in return, her black curls bobbing. "I am proud, Quinn. Whether you succeed or not, I'm proud of you. Don't you be too proud to come back if you need to. This is your home, and you truly are more than welcome to return. May the Mother bless you and keep you from harm."

Quinn sniffled but couldn't say anything or she'd burst into tears. Ani gripped her shoulder, nodded with clamped lips, then turned Quinn's body to the stairs and urged her up. She climbed, turned back, and waved at the hatch, unable to see through her tears. She forced herself inside.

"Come, Gentle Quinn, all will be fine." The co-pilot, a Grusian named Keyser, led her to a seat and strapped her in. "It's always hard leaving home." Keyser turned away, strapping into her chair. "Ready for launch."

The pilot, another Grusian named Hout, looked over his shoulder, "Small surge, then normal gravity. Sit back and enjoy the ride, Gentle Quinn. It will be approximately seven hours and ten minutes before we arrive at Fold Transport Frederick." He flicked something in the holo in front of him. "Initiating thrust now."

Quinn's body pressed into the seat and she gasped, but the pressure let off before she even finished the breath.

"Do you want to watch?" Co-pilot Keyser asked. Her dark blue skin, bald head, and big eyes marked her as alien, but Grusians were essentially human, DNA-wise. Or humans were Grusian—nobody knew why human-type bipedals were so common across the universe. "Once we've reached space, you can move around the cabin, use the galley and the sani-mod—but be ready to strap in if necessary." Keyser chuckled. "I doubt it will be necessary—there's not much traffic here."

She nodded. "Yes, I'd love to watch our flight." Quinn wiped the tears away with her hands. She didn't want to miss any of this.

"Once we reach our folder, we'll show you to your cabin and around the rest of the transport. You're our only passenger so far, but we'll fold space to at least three constellations, perhaps more, for cargo drop off and pick up." She shrugged. "Maybe another passenger or two. We'll make your fold to Canis Major and Omicron in six to ten days."

Keyser pushed a screen over to her, and Quinn accepted it into her e-torc's public holo. It was a navigation display, showing their shuttle's orbit in relation to the planet and a view of Secundus, receding rapidly. Before long, Secundus was just a marble of blue and green. Quinn sighed and swept the visual of the planet away, concentrating on the shuttle's flight path to the fold transport.

All the Sisters said she was welcome to come back, but Sister Lashtar was right—Secundus and the Sisters of Cygnus held nothing for her. She'd look forward and move forward. Be bold.

With great risks came great rewards, and Quinn was determined to earn her share of rewards. With the net skills she'd develop at Adzari Academy, she could find a job anywhere in the universe, and she wanted to see all of it!

CHAPTER TWO

Purser Tre said, "I understand now! Captain, our net is more secure, and we are much safer. We owe Gentle Quinn Cygnus a debt." The brightness of her white teeth against her dark blue skin was dazzling and clearly displayed her happiness.

Quinn smiled and shook her head. "No debt. I'm happy to help. I was bored." Doing nothing was great for the first few days but after that? Dead dull. Folding space should be exciting, but it wasn't. Without the announcement, she wouldn't have even known they'd folded. She was thrilled to have something real to do.

Captain Vaness looked up at the screen Quinn and Tre shared in the living area of the big cargo fold transport. "I agree with Tre. That," he pointed at the screen, "is all tlhIngan Hol to me. We owe you a fold." He walked away.

Quinn noticed the Grus didn't like to argue—if they couldn't resolve a disagreement, they simply dropped it. Sometimes, they'd discuss the point again a few hours later, but if they couldn't agree, one of them did the same thing Captain Vaness just did—they left. Quinn had looked the oddity up—scholars said this was true of the entire species.

Evidently, the Grus had a massive war in their system thousands of years ago, and a fold clock was destroyed. The Time Guild, as the fold clock owners and maintainers, were ruthless when one of their clocks was attacked. Everyone on both sides of the conflict had been annihilated by the Sa'sa, the only species in the Time Guild. The Sa'sa were a cold-blooded, hivemind species, strictly divided into task classes at the equivalent of their puberty. Warriors were the largest Sa'sa and the only ones who fought. Clock maintainers did just that—fixed the fold clocks. Humans found all the Sa'sa rather terrifying—they looked much like Old Earth dinosaurs. They were extraordinarily difficult to communicate with—they were always in groups of three, usually more, talking about a dozen different things all at once. A human had to somehow pick out the thread of the conversation they needed from the cacophony.

Supposedly, the Grus lost something else during the Time Guild action, something critical to the Grus psyche if not their physical beings. No one but the Grus knew what the thing was, but Grusian mourning pairs still traveled the universe, dressed in dark, layered rags covering their entire bodies, warning others of the consequences of war. Or at least war involving a fold clock. They were almost a pacifist species; they would defend themselves when attacked but only if they couldn't leave and destruction was certain.

"I am glad the captain agrees we owe you a fold," Pilot Hout said. "If you have more to do, please continue, but be aware we'll make our fold into Canis Major in a few hours. Immediately after we check with the fold controllers, we'll make the fold to Omicron and your new school." He bowed and walked away, probably to the folder's control center, someplace she hadn't been. Co-pilot Keyser followed him.

While Quinn no longer found the anticipation of fold thrilling, she was excited and a little nervous about the new school. Before she could say anything, Purser Tre also stood. "I must do my checks as well. Will we continue later?"

"Of course. It would be my pleasure." After Tre left the folder's common area, containing a kitchen, dining table, and some lounge chairs, Quinn stood and stretched. They'd been sitting for quite a while, working on the net, and it felt good to move around. She'd thought about asking if she could watch the pilots, but she'd looked up fold planning—it required a lot of higher math. Of course, most of it was done by net programs, but Quinn understood good pilots checked all the factors and the calculations.

The most important was the destination designation. A pilot had to specify a fold destination in space and time. The time part was critical—she'd discovered that if the time was wrong, the fold transport never arrived. Speculation was the folder was destroyed or changed planes to an alternate reality because time travel didn't seem to happen. Thus, the Time Guild fold clocks ensured the destination's time was precisely known and tuned to a universal standard available only to the Time Guild.

If she hadn't helped the Grus secure their net, someday, some evil being could have interfered with their navigation and sent them folding to some unknown destination—or oblivion. Quinn shivered. She could only hope her relatively inexpert help was enough. The Grus had suffered enough over time and timing—they didn't need more trouble. And the Grus on this folder were wonderful, friendly people. She'd hate to see anything happen to them.

She spent the time before fold in her cabin, memorizing the code phrases the Sisters gave her, along with the message designations for Lightwave, this folder and a few other fold transports the Sisters knew were reliable. Lashtar was surely overreacting—the latest information to make it all the way to Cygnus Secundus showed Adzari Academy was the same place Katryn had attended—but Quinn had promised Lashtar she would, so she did.

"All stations, we are go for fold to Canis Major." Quinn pulled the harness over her body. The security seemed unnecessary—she'd never felt any movement during fold—but Purser Tre asked, so Quinn complied. Pilot Hout continued, "We will fold in five, four, three, two, and fold. We've arrived safely in Canis Major."

Quinn sucked in a startled breath. That fold kind of ached. How odd.

"Report any issues or problems to the captain immediately. Pilot out."

Releasing her harness, Quinn stood and stretched. She didn't feel bad, but she felt a little...squeezed. How very strange. Humans didn't feel fold.

Purser Tre messaged her, asking for status, and she sent back a "status normal" message. The sensation was fading, so there was nothing to report. Maybe it was some sort of wrinkle in the space-time continuum? In a parallel universe, Quinn Cygnus was passing through the same spot? Quinn laughed at herself and headed back to the common area, ready to teach Purser Tre more net tricks.

△△△

"Safe folds, Quinn Cygnus," Co-pilot Keyser bowed deeply. "We've enjoyed having you onboard. Thank you again for your help in securing our net. You have travel credit with us."

Quinn returned her bow, just as deeply. "Thank you for making my first fold transport so easy. I enjoyed working with you and hope to do so again. Safe folds." She turned away and hopped down the stairs, enjoying the slightly lighter than standard gravity. Quinn followed the arrow in her holo to the arrivals lounge. Thank the Mother she'd spent a lot of time studying tourist guides to Canis Major and Omicron or she'd be sprinting back to the shuttle right now.

Even though she'd immersed herself in a tourist simulation, nothing could have prepared her for the reality of a major spaceport in a big city. Quinn didn't want to blink—she might miss something. Shuttles of all sizes and types waited on the port, and the port itself was surrounded by tall buildings, with huge holo displays showing advertisements for a dizzying array of products. She had no idea what most of them were or did. And under all the new sights, smells, and sounds was the terrifying realization that she was completely on her own.

Quinn stumbled and looked around a little wildly. She should probably pay attention to where she was going rather than trying to see everything all at once. But it was hard to focus with everything going on around her—and the fear. Forcing herself onward, Quinn strode to the large, low plain beige building marked "Arrivals" in Trade and entered. A long line of clear booths waited, green circles with "open" on some of the doors, and beings of many species occupying the ones with a red square. She entered the first green one she came to, tugging her small luggage float into the tiny room behind her. The sudden quiet and empty off-white room was soothing after the bustle of the spaceport.

"State your name and business on Omicron, and put your hand on the DNA sensor," a female voice said. "You will be scanned."

A square on the wall in front of her flashed stripes of white, red, yellow, and blue. She put her hand out, wincing at the bite of the sampler. "Quinn Cygnus, Academy Adzari student."

"Do you have anything to declare?"

"No." And she didn't. Clothes and her e-torc were all she owned.

"Proceed." The door clicked and slid open. "Welcome to Omicron, enjoy your stay."

"Thank you." Quinn left the small room, entering a huge, high-ceilinged space filled with hundreds of beings all hurrying somewhere, the chatter and hum deafening and the clashing scents slightly stomach-turning. She backed to the wall, waiting until she got a little more accustomed to the noise and bustle. Then she reengaged the navigation program and looked at her route. She had to go straight ahead, then take a slight left to the local pickup zone. A reminder pinged, and she messaged the Academy she'd cleared customs.

A reply came almost immediately. "Pickup in five minutes. Look for Adzari lift van. The driver is Gentle Vincenz Coll. Human. Ask for his identification." A pic of Gentle Coll followed. A heavy-browed, olive-toned round face, with small, deep-set dark brown eyes, topped with short dark brown hair, sat on top of a thick neck. A rather thuggish face but no one looked good in identifications pics.

Quinn sent back an acknowledgment and took a deep breath. Blowing out, she stepped into the noisy, slightly chaotic crowd and wove her way among the beings. With the crowds, she was extra grateful she wasn't wearing one of the Sisters' rather bulky robes; even the simple pants and shirt she wore were pulled this way and that by beings brushing against her. Most of the beings were human, but there were a substantial number of other species. The ones that stood out the most to her were the RRs. Short, bright orange cylinders with big goggles shading their eyes and high, squeaky voices, they seemed to travel in packs.

"Out of the way, station scum," a large, dark brown fur-covered being rumbled, mowing down a couple of the RRs.

"Hey, leave them alone!" Quinn said, helping one of the RRs back to their feet. Or whatever it was that propelled them below those cylindrical bodies. "Go around."

"Mind your own business, human," the hulk of fur bellowed, pushing her aside with the back of its paw.

Quinn stumbled but kept her feet. What a rude being.

The RR she'd helped bowed to her and skittered off to rejoin its pack, meeping and beeping madly. Quinn smiled and got back on her path to the pickup zone. Finally, she left the massive transit room and stepped out to a bewildering plethora of roadways and walking paths. She followed the green arrow in her holo, grateful to have a guide—this place was huge and confusing. At least it wasn't raining. She glanced up—rain wouldn't matter; tinted, translucent panels covered every walkway, probably to alleviate the impact of the dazzling blue-white sun.

Vehicles of every kind waited and drove or flew past, and beings of many species traveled the walking paths, some towing huge trains of luggage. Or maybe trade goods. The air still smelled of dozens of perfumes and strange scents, with a dry, dusty undertone that reminded her of the deserts of Cygnus Gliese just a little. Even with the shades above the walkways, the blue-white light was very bright, but her holo darkened it enough she didn't have to squint. The shadows seemed very dark, and everything had a slight bluish cast, but her holo gradually adjusted for that as well. She peered past the roadways. What seemed to be vehicle parking structures and office buildings blocked any view of the city beyond. Eventually, Quinn reached her pickup point.

Only a few moments later, a lift van with the Adzari Academy logo on the side pulled up and a tall, bulky human with olive-toned skin and dark brown hair, dressed in all black, stepped out, towering above her. "Quinn Cygnus? I'm Vincenz Coll," he rumbled. He flicked something to her from his holo.

Quinn pulled it up in her public space. Identification as Vincenz Coll, employed by Academy Adzari, and an Omicron registration for the lift van too. It could undoubtedly be fake, but the name and face matched the ones the Academy sent her. "Yes, thank you, Gentle Coll."

"Just Coll. Is that all the luggage you've got?" He pointed at her small case.

Before she could answer, he was tugging it away to the van. Quinn hurriedly released the luggage to him and followed him into the van.

He put her luggage in a bin. "Strap in." He pointed to the seats behind the enclosed driver's area at the front. "It's an hour or so to the Academy, depending on traffic. There's guides to the city waiting. They can answer all your questions. Once we're out of the city, we'll be crossing a protected forest area. Use that time to look at the Academy introduction so you know what to do when we arrive." Coll swung into the driver's seat and closed the door, leaving her alone in the big van.

Okay then. Quinn sniffed. Guess she'd do what he suggested. She pulled up the guides and picked one that allowed her to select specific sites, rather than a general narration as they traveled. She'd studied the tourist guides, so she knew all the basics, but specific, detailed information about some of the sites might be interesting. She also needed to watch where they went, so if she had to get back to the spaceport, she'd know how without relying on her e-torc.

They joined the stream of vehicles leaving the spaceport, traveling crowded roadways packed with every kind of vehicle, from single-seat lift bikes to massive bulk transports, all of them within a meter or two of the next. Since Coll didn't have his hands on the controls, the traffic here must be all net controlled, something Quinn knew about but had never seen. Every time a new vehicle appeared next to theirs, Quinn jumped, sure they would collide. But they never did, and gradually, she relaxed. About the time she did, the bulk transporters mostly swung away to other roadways, and the huge buildings became smaller, so she could see the astonishing city.

The spaceport was on a huge, flat plain below the city; the city enveloped the small mountain in front of her. The buildings alongside the vehicle way became smaller and shorter, finally becoming what must be houses for one or two wealthy families, surrounded by flowers or gardens. As the city ascended the hill, the buildings became bigger and taller, crowning the mountain and lancing up in crooked, angular spires of translucent plas and cerimetal like demented, shiny metal and glass stalagmites or hoodoos. They seemed to defy physics, but maybe the lighter gravity allowed that? According to the guide, they were lit with bright colors at night. Quinn couldn't imagine what that would look like, but she hoped to see it someday.

The lift van seemed to head straight into the center of the city, but as Quinn watched, they turned left, merging onto a major roadway that encircled the city. She stared, mesmerized by the huge structures holding millions of beings. Suddenly, they turned left again, and the city was behind her. The buildings became smaller and smaller, gradually turning into houses for the wealthy again, with lots of security surrounding them.

Then, the dwellings stopped and dense, dark growth began. Quinn brought up the entry from the guide. Tetzlaff Forest, the only remaining native growth within five hundred kilometers of Omi city. Contact with the indigenous flora and fauna was risky and potentially dangerous—humans were allergic to much of it. Dangerously so, for some humans. Access to Tetzlaff was restricted and controlled. Researchers were required to wear isolation suits; most opted for soft armor because some of the wildlife was vicious and apt to attack upon sight or smell. Stunners didn't work on most of the fauna either. The road twisted and turned, going around critical habitat, so the travel time was much longer than the straight-line distance would imply.

Sister Lashtar's warnings in mind, Quinn brought up a map. Tetzlaff Forest lay between the Academy and the spaceport, extending for many klicks in all directions. If something went wrong and she needed to escape, she'd need a vehicle and/or armor. That was a complication she hadn't considered when she did her research—she'd been reassured by the relative proximity of the school to the city. Quinn's fingers itched to immerse themselves in code, allowing the fear to fade away, but her training wouldn't let her do anything that stupid. She had to discover everything she could about her surroundings so she could escape if necessary.

After staring into the tangled growth for ten minutes, Quinn quickly decided it wasn't a good use of her time. If she had to travel this on foot without armor, she was dead. The driver said there was an Academy introduction document she had to review, so she should do that. Quinn scrolled through the public offerings on the lift van's net and found it immediately—it was marked as important—and she pulled it into her e-torc.

A vid started, and Quinn groaned. She hated sitting through

these ridiculous things. A simple document was so much faster and easier. As an aerial view of the Academy appeared, with orchestral music, Quinn searched for a way around the vid but found nothing obvious. Hmm. This was a net school. Was she really supposed to sit through this or hack her way around? She smiled. Why not start now? Discovering what she was up against now was smart. And a lot less boring.

As the vid continued to play—a campus tour—Quinn tried the obvious net tricks first, looking for root access and backdoors. Unsurprisingly, everything was well secured. Quinn wrinkled her nose. Maybe come at the vehicle's net from outside, rather than in the Academy's file system? She brought up a new window, trying various tools. Again, she got nowhere.

The vid flashed, a bunch of bright-colored blanks screens accompanied by a hooting, blaring noise bringing Quinn's attention back to it. A human female's face appeared, dressed in a plain black top with a severe decorative jacket over it, also black. The woman's hair was the color of black coffee, her skin was tan with olive undertones, her eyes also dark brown, surrounded by lush lashes. Her lips were a dark red, and her teeth blindingly white, rather like Omicron's sun. She could be thirty standard years old—or body-modded to look that way. "Now that you've made your predictable attempts to break into Adzari Academy's net, please pay attention to the rest of this presentation. We expect a certain level of respect from our students. That includes respecting the instructors and staff and the rules and regulations of the Academy. The first rule is: you are not allowed access to any net except the student net." The woman's eyebrows pinched together slightly. "Any attempt to access the instructor or household net will result in termination of the student's enrollment and immediate expulsion. There are no exceptions to this rule, no second chances. You will be dismissed from school. I hope this is very clear."

The woman's lips turned up, but it wasn't a smile. "I am Academy President Rias Bel. As a student, you will not see me often." The non-smile twisted. "If you do, neither of us will be happy. So, follow the rules. Obey your instructors. Behave with dignity and pride. Study hard. If you do these things, you will be successful here and in the future." Bel's non-smile showed again. "Academic classes, other than introductory sessions, are taught on a rotation basis, so students can enter a class at any time, learn those lessons, then continue the class and complete the rest. Net skills are almost exclusively learned in a lab. You are set a problem and expected to find a way to complete it. Both cooperation and competition are encouraged here. The very top students will be given the best positions, so study hard. I now turn you over to Adzari Academy's House Managers, House Mistress Vormer for the girls, and House Master Jonstew for the boys. You will meet your instructors as you begin your classes."

Quinn shivered. Whatever she was, Rias Bel wasn't a pushover, and she meant business. Quinn's next net access attempt had to be successful—and it probably would not occur soon. She had a lot to learn. More importantly, though: who are these people? These were not the same names or faces she'd researched. She bit her lip and kept watching, hoping to see one of the people she'd investigated.

A human male and female appeared on the vid, sitting side by side but not close like a couple. They had the same complexion as Rias Bel and Coll, dark brown hair, tan olive-toned skin, and brown eyes in oval faces. They also both looked older, maybe fifty standards with stern visages, rather prominent noses, and also dressed all in black but with plain white shirts.

The man spoke first. "Greetings, students. I am House Master Jonstew. You will address me as Master Jonstew. This is House Mistress Vormer. You will address her as Mistress Vormer. We are here to ensure the safety of all students. If you have a problem with another student, you must come to one of us—me for the boys, Mistress Vormer for the girls. Do not go to an upper-class student." Jonstew scowled. "In the past, the upper classes were allowed to govern the lower classes. This led to abuse. We will not tolerate such. The upper-class members know this but sometimes have trouble remembering. You will be assigned a room with one to three other students, which you must keep clean. The bathrooms are shared, and all students share the responsibility to keep them clean. The dining hall has posted times for breakfast, lunch, and dinner, and there are healthy snacks available at all times. Students take turns cleaning the dishes and dining hall." He turned to the woman. "Mistress Vormer?"

She nodded regally to him. "Thank you, Master Jonstew." Facing the vid, she continued the lecture. "Good manners are a must here. In the past, net students have been allowed rudeness because of their talents. This is unacceptable. All beings must exhibit a basic level of consideration for others. The proper address will be used at all times, as will the words 'please' and 'thank you.' Timeliness is required as well. We keep strict hours for classes, recreation, and sleep. These times will be enforced." Vormer's lip curled for a second. "Proper hygiene will also be enforced. There is plenty of water on Omicron, so daily bathing is required, along with bathing after strenuous physical activity. Students will be clean and your uniforms will be clean and neat. You will be issued uniforms and those are all you will wear. Accommodations may be made for non-restrictive religious garments. Your rooms will be kept neat and tidy. Inspections will occur daily and randomly. Physical activity of some kind is required. Team sports are encouraged, but solo pursuits are acceptable. Strong minds require strong bodies. If you do not participate in a physical activity, one will be assigned. Master Jonstew?"

Jonstew sneered into the vid. "Upon arrival, your possessions, including your e-torcs, will be placed into storage and secured. You will be issued everything you need for success here. Do not attempt to hide any private net gear. It will be found. Punishment will be severe." A smile flickered.

Quinn shivered. This man enjoyed punishment. What kind of punishments did the Academy use? What had she gotten into? Good thing she'd already memorized the code words and phrases Sisters Lashtar and Ani insisted on. And net addresses for them, Lightwave Fold Transport, and the Grus folder. Both Jonstew and Vormer spoke about past allowances and rules—was the academy's leadership new? Quinn was relieved she hadn't missed something critical, but the relief was overwhelmed by the fear that whoever these people were, they weren't going to provide the safe, comfortable environment she'd thought she'd found.

"You will also receive several inoculations against local diseases. There is just enough overlap with our basic Old Earth DNA that humans are very vulnerable to both viruses and bacteria here. Please inform us of any allergies you have when you check in with the Academy Medicos."

She didn't have any allergies. Well, except for a bunch of Secundus native plants, but all humans did. Should she fake one? Probably not. She wouldn't be able to research what to fake without giving it away because the only net available was the Academy's on the lift van. A shiver ran down her back. Quinn would have no way to know what they were really injecting into her body. Unfortunately, she knew they spoke truly about the diseases—she'd found that out during her research.

"You will be allowed to send messages to your home." Jonstew's lips lifted in a parody of a smile. "It's mandatory, actually. We want your parents or guardians to know you are thriving. We are sure you will thrive here. We'll make sure of it." He sniffed. "Mistress Vormer?"

She repeated Jonstew's non-smile. "The lift van will drop you off at our Administrative Center. We will assign a student to escort you through the onboarding process. They will also mentor you for the first week. Again, if there is a personality clash or the mentor oversteps, come to one of us immediately for reassignment. We will not allow any physical or mental abuse from other students."

Vormer didn't say anything about staff abuse, though. The shiver down her spine became an electric current. Well, guess the

Sisters prepared her for just about everything, didn't they? Quinn would keep her head down, be obedient, just a little dumb, and very, very naïve. The Sisters just became a more remote, cloistered, and strict society than they'd ever been, even under Ferra's control. She'd learn what she could survive, and when she got the chance, she'd escape. But until then, she'd have to act far more obedient than she'd ever been in real life.

She snorted softly. She'd wanted a challenge—she got one. Quinn desperately hoped it was worth it.

CHAPTER THREE

A notice flashed in her holo: "You are leaving the Tetzlaff Forest. We hope you enjoyed your stay. Report any health changes occurring over the next week to your local Medico."

And that wasn't ominous at all. Quinn shuddered again.

The straps around Quinn tightened momentarily as the lift van made an abrupt turn to the right. A narrow road appeared in front of them, cut off by a solid black gate. High fences stretched left and right from the gate, razor wire glinting at the top. The lift van slowed, and the gates swung open.

Another vid appeared in Quinn's holo, and she selected it immediately, rather than delay as she wanted to. "Welcome to Adzari Academy," scrolled across the vid, showing the view she had now, only the gates were fancy, decorative things with the Academy's name and the fencing had no razor wire. Orchestral music began, with an overhead view of what she assumed was the Academy.

A pleasant, female voice said, "Welcome to your new home away from home. We know you will love it here! Adzari Academy is a large campus with many amenities. First, a short introduction to the grounds. The roadway you are on parallels the Tetzlaff Forest. While it is fenced, if you choose to walk or run along this roadway, please keep an eye out for native animals. If you see one, do not run. Back away slowly and notify a staff member immediately. This is a rare occurrence because the fence is charged, but it does happen. Do not touch the fence, or you will receive a severe shock. We will travel several kilometers into the grounds before the Academy appears. You are free to use this area at any time for recreation. It, and the rest of the Academy, is planted with human-safe vegetation."

Tetzlaff Forest was to Quinn's right, a large, open field with scattered trees to the left. The vid's voiceover had odd jumps and stutters, like it had been badly edited. What was edited was telling—they'd taken out all specific distances and possibly the shock level of the fence. And fences that kept things out could keep things in too.

"The Academy's campus is spacious and mostly self-sustaining. Food for the Academy is raised on-site. Many of the farm and ranch workers are local students learning their trade. Thank them if you have the opportunity—the food here is delicious! Allowances for dietary restrictions are no problem; you will find a pleasing number of choices for every meal. You may eat as much as you like, but please don't take more than you need. We are conscious of the environment here and try to minimize waste." Pictures of gardens, greenhouses, and pastures came and went, all with smiling, laughing workers.

"We have two dormitories, split by the dominant human sexes and separated by year level—three, nominally, although some will stay longer or shorter periods as necessary. Students may self-identify as either sex. A warning: sexual relations are strictly forbidden for students, including between students."

The dormitories appeared to be four stories high, in some sort of native stone with a chalky appearance. The windows on the ground level were tall and wide; the three stories above narrower and shorter but still generously sized in rows of six. Quinn did some math; they could house twelve to twenty-four students per floor.

The warning about no sex was another bad edit, so this was another recent change. The Sisters themselves were chaste but didn't enforce the restriction on their charges or associates, instead relying on extensive education about sex in general and emotional relationships. Quinn paid attention to the lectures but had no interest in romantic entanglements. From what she saw of her classmates and neighbors, romance and sex caused a lot of problems and often kept people from reaching their goals. Quinn's only concern here at the Academy was to become a net expert. And it looked like she had to become the very best or she might not leave this place.

"The dining hall is right behind the two dormitories. Mealtimes are strictly enforced, but there is a selection of healthy food and drink available at all times." A long, single-story building, in the same stone, also with lots of windows. The vid entered the large, double doors, flying into a large open area with rows of long tables and a cafeteria-style serving bar at the end. There were seats for at least a hundred people, maybe more.

"Classrooms are in the Academic Building, located beyond the dining hall." Another four-story building, the same chalky-white stone, lots of windows. The vid flew through large, auditorium-style rooms, more familiar classrooms with rows of seats for twenty or so, and small rooms with one or two larger tables, chairs around the outside. "As you can see, some classes are lectures and some are more participatory. Once you become an upper-class being, you will have the opportunity to lead projects. The meeting rooms can be reserved by students for these projects."

The vid swept out of the Academic Building and over to another building, almost the same size and type, but labeled as the Net Lab. The vid flew inside. Two rooms with rows of desks, students filling those seats swiping away at holos. The upper floors had smaller rooms, mostly set up as classrooms. The very top floor contained three large, open areas with a variety of seating options and what appeared to be a small kitchen.

"The Net Lab building is set up for practical training. Some will be done in a group setting, some in smaller groups as projects, and some individual efforts. You will find the latest and greatest net programs and tools available to you! Adzari prides itself on producing the very best net technicians. Because intelligent, quick minds require fuel, healthy snacks are always available on the third floor. Also on the third floor, underclass beings will find Third Year beings willing and able to advise them on individual and group projects. Mentoring lower class members is part of the graduation requirements."

The vid flew out of the building and up to a bird's eye view of the area beyond the classroom and lab. "As you can see, there are many recreational opportunities. Gymnasiums for athletic training and team sports, pools for swimming, fields for team sports, and running tracks are all available, as are other enjoyable outdoor pursuits. Explore these options at your leisure. We hope you enjoy your time at Adzari Academy!" Orchestral music crashed and swooped again.

The lift van halted in front of a building helpfully named Administration. Two stories tall, the same chalky-white stone as the rest, with wide windows. The driver exited his compartment and grabbed her luggage float. Quinn hurried to unstrap herself and hop out.

Coll pointed at the Administration building. "Go through the doors. They're expecting you." He turned away and entered the lift van without waiting for her reply.

Quinn took a deep breath, re-engaged her electronic luggage leash in her e-torc, and walked up to the doors. One opened in front of her and she walked in, fully aware her life was about to change forever.

She just hoped she survived this change as well as she survived the Sisters' evacuation from Cygnus Gliese, the building of the new compound on Secundus, and the reorganization of the Sisters' religion. But she suspected this one would be much harder, especially since she was all alone.

Quinn entered an open area with plush seating in beige, accented with blue and green. Soft music tinkled and a light, flowery scent wafted to her. A girl, a few years older than she was, waited. Taller by a good ten centimeters at least, she had blonde hair, blue eyes, and a blandly welcoming expression. She wore what must be the Adzari Academy uniform—black pants with a bright green sweater and what seemed to be a white shirt underneath. A single red and white stripe slashed diagonally across the forearms of the sweater. The very idea of wearing something so pretty was shocking. No one wore white at home— it got too dirty.

"Quinn Cygnus?"

"Yes."

"I am Freya Helmi. I'm your mentor for the next week. Welcome to Adzari Academy. Come, let's get you checked in." She turned away and crooked a finger over her shoulder.

Quinn followed. Freya's tone was machine-like; was she a real person? They passed rows of offices, all separated by clear plas walls, men and women working on holos or talking to them. Everyone wore predominately black clothing, although there were touches of bright colors in scarves, shirts, and, in one case, a hat. At the end of the hall, a door labeled "Student Administration" opened in front of them. They entered a room with a long, chest-high counter running the length of it. A woman stood behind the counter, also dressed in black, dark hair pulled back tight against her skull, a look of disdain plastered across what might have been a pretty face if she'd smiled.

"Logistics Mistress, this is Quinn Cygnus," Freya turned away and walked to stand at the end of the counter.

"Your luggage and e-torc, Student Cygnus." The woman held out an imperious hand.

Quinn swallowed hard. "Can I keep my pics in some form? A few hard copies?"

The woman glared. "No. Students and rooms will be neat, tidy, and standardized. Now, Student Cygnus." She pushed her hand toward Quinn.

Biting her lip, Quinn disengaged her luggage leash, pushed it to the woman, and then pulled off her e-torc and handed it over. Her luggage float rose over the counter and disappeared behind it.

"Any jewelry or other adornments?"

"No."

A hand smacked the counter. Quinn jumped. "That's no, Logistics Mistress. Understood?"

"Yes, Logistics Mistress." Quinn stumbled over the title. How awkward.

"Proceed to the dressing booth," the woman pointed to Quinn's right, "take off all your clothes, and stand inside the circle on the floor. Your measurements will be scanned and the appropriate uniforms delivered. Additional uniforms and physical fitness uniforms will be delivered to your room shortly. Understood?"

"Yes, Logistics Mistress." She turned and walked to the door, opened it, and entered a small room, only a few meters square. Quinn swallowed again and took off all her clothes, standing in the circle as ordered.

"Scanning," a male voice said. "Raise your hands over your head." Quinn did so. "Lower your hands, separate your feet by at least ten centimeters." Quinn followed that direction and the rest. "Scan complete, stand by for clothing delivery." A small hatch slid open in front of her and Quinn pulled out the clothing. It included undergarments and shoes. "Place all your clothing, including shoes, into the hatch. These items will be stored with your luggage."

Quinn did as she was told, feeling ice-cold even though the dressing room itself was warm. She pulled on the garments she was given, shivering slightly because the clothes were chilly. They were so much nicer than her old ones, though, made of a smooth, slightly stretchy material that fitted her almost perfectly. The shoes were better too, with firm soles that almost cradled her feet and stretchy uppers. She looked at herself in the mirror—she looked like a whole different person! A net worker, a student. Amazing. Even the scary Logistics Mistress couldn't keep her from smiling. Quinn left the dressing room and returned to the counter.

"We understand you are a child from a subsistence farming world. Is this correct?"

Close enough. "Yes, Logistics Mistress."

"You will have enough clothing to change every day. Do so. This uniform is for classes and net work. You will receive athletic gear for sports, a more casual version of this uniform for after class hours, and sleepwear. You will keep all of it clean and in working order. There are autocleaners on each floor. If you tear, stain, or damage the clothing, you must return here for replacements. Depending on how the damage occurred, you may be charged for these replacements. If you outgrow the clothing, return here for a new scan. Is this understood?"

"Yes, Logistics Mistress."

"Good. Here is your student e-torc. Do not lose it." She turned to Freya. "Take her to House Mistress Vormer for a room assignment."

Freya bowed her head. "Yes, Logistics Mistress." She turned and exited the room without waiting for Quinn.

Quinn slid her new e-torc around her neck and stumbled after Freya, who immediately turned left, striding down a long blank hall and out a door at the end. Quinn squinted against the bright sun but couldn't stop to adjust her e-torc or she'd lose Freya for sure. Freya turned left again, following a plascrete walkway, and one more left, bringing Quinn to the dormitories.

Freya entered the dormitory on the right. They entered a large, high-ceilinged room with soft seating in shades of brown, with accents of pink and yellow. "This is the women's dorm. Mistress Vormer's office is right here." She motioned to the right. Clear plas walls created a small room. Two chairs, a desk, and Mistress Vormer waited, seated behind the desk. Mistress Vormer looked exactly the same as she had in the Academy introduction vid, strict and humorless. Freya stopped at the door and entered when Mistress Vormer beckoned with a sharp hand gesture. "House Mistress Vormer, this is Student Quinn Cygnus."

"Thank you, Student Freya. Return to your studies for now. I will have Student Quinn message you if necessary."

"Thank you, Mistress Vormer." Freya bobbed her head again and left, leaving Quinn alone with Vormer.

Vormer scanned her up and down. "You are tiny. Did they not feed you?"

"The Sisters fed me sufficiently, House Mistress Vormer. It may be genetics." Quinn tried to find the line between defending her family and not offending her…keeper. Captor? She'd have to wait and see what Vormer really was. Despite the nice new clothes, the chill in her spine was spreading.

"Did you watch the introductory vids, Student Quinn?"

"Yes, Mistress Vormer."

"Good. Do you have questions right now?"

"Only when do I start, Mistress Vormer?"

A slight upturn appeared on her lips. "Excellent. You start tomorrow—I have sent your schedule to your e-torc. You are on the upper floor, in room six. As of right now, you do not have a roommate. We anticipate further arrivals soon, and you will receive a roommate or perhaps two. With your background, I am sure this will not bother you. Neither will the shared bath, two on each floor. Since you are in room six, you are responsible for cleaning Bathroom Two, along with the students in rooms six through ten. If any of the students are unwilling to fulfill their responsibilities, I expect to be notified. Is this clear?"

"Of course, Mistress Vormer." *Right.* Because that's the way to make friends so they'll help you with projects. Quinn kept her face impassive.

"For the remainder of today, you should explore your new home. Do not enter any of the classrooms or intrude on any organized activity unless invited, but you may watch, both visually and on your e-torc. If you wish, the student net has a tagging feature you can enable. This will ensure you know everyone's name and address the instructors and staff appropriately." The smile that wasn't a smile appeared again. "Infractions against other students and especially the staff are not tolerated. There is a rule book in your e-torc, I suggest you study it carefully. Punishments run from mild to severe. None of them include any kind of physical damage, but some of the more severe will be painful. Do not make me administer any of these. I do not enjoy it."

That might be true. Her distaste was obvious. It could be fake, though. Quinn didn't know this woman's tells and quirks. She'd have to tread carefully. She was pretty sure the boys' house master enjoyed the pain of others.

"We expect you to write or vid home now, with news of your safe arrival, and at least once a week while you are here. We want your family to know you are healthy and happy." Now she did smile, but it looked painful. "All messages are sent from a central Academy message center. Just send your message there and it will be forwarded. Now, if you have further questions, ask Student Freya. If she cannot answer, message me for an appointment. If you have issues with another student, message me immediately. We cannot have anarchy at this academy. It has an impeccable reputation, and we will maintain that. Do you have any questions?"

"No, Mistress Vormer. Thank you."

"Excellent. You are dismissed." She turned away to fuss with something on the shelf behind her. Quinn took the opportunity to leave the dragon's lair immediately. Pulling up a directory on her e-torc, she searched for a map of the building and found one immediately. Here on the ground floor, there was the common area, a small kitchen, two medico units, and two stairways to the upper floors. She headed for the closest one and started climbing.

The stairway was brightly lit, and her footsteps echoed slightly. The next floor was marked, "Third Year Students Only," the following, "Second Year Students Only," and the final one, "First Year Students." No exclusivity here, which meant the other classes could bother them at any time. Having lived in a similar environment all her life, she knew it was almost guaranteed.

Quinn walked down the hall looking for room six, her assigned room. It didn't take long for her to find it—the walls were plain beige and the doors plain brown wood so the large, silver numbers on each door stood out. Room six was at the very end of the hall. There were twelve rooms on this floor, but, as she suspected, two of them were bathrooms. So, if there were two students per room as Mistress Vormer implied, then there were twenty students per floor, which meant up to sixty female students and sixty male students.

Of course, they could shove more people into each room and Mistress Vormer said they might. Quinn opened door number six, her new room, and entered. Again, the room itself was very plain. Beige walls, beige blinds on the windows, two narrow beds, one on each side of the room, and a large storage cubby on each side of the room, presumably for the issued uniforms.

Both beds had pillows and linens piled on them. One of the beds also had a stack of the same uniform Quinn wore now, plus many other clothing items. So, the Logistics Mistress had already delivered the clothing she was promised. Quinn walked the few steps to the bed. Underneath, shoes waited, similar to the ones she wore now. Plus, sandals, probably for the shower and for swimming, and athletic-type shoes. There were also two kinds of boots. One appeared to be plain black plas, presumably for muddy conditions, and the other appeared to be dress boots, the shiny black uppers rising to just below her knee.

Quinn sorted through the clothing. The athletic wear included long tights, shorts, and both long and short sleeve shirts, along with a hooded, heavier-weight shirt. There were also rain jackets, both a sporty one and a more formal plain gray one, probably for the class uniforms. The uniforms, four more of them, were the same as the one she wore now. There were also five sets of clothing in the same colors as the uniform but more casual; the sweater had buttons, the shirt was a plain white T-shirt, and the pants were a little softer and stretched more. Probably the after-class uniform the logistics Mistress spoke of. There were also thin long pants and shirts, presumably for sleeping in, and a stack of towels.

Moving quickly, Quinn placed the uniforms in the cubbies on "her" side of the room. When she got to the bottom of the stack, she noticed one of the Academy uniforms was fancier than the others. A dress uniform? She looked for and found a narrow area for hanging items, and carefully hung the dress uniform and the jackets.

She made the bed, making sure the corners were crisp and sharp. Then, wanting to explore a little more virtually before venturing out on the campus, Quinn pulled up her new e-torc menu. There was indeed a student guide. Would it be updated for the new Adzari Academy or was it still using the previous owner's version?

But first, Quinn looked at her new schedule. Breakfast was at a local time of zero-seven-hundred, lunch at noon, and dinner at eighteen hundred. There was a note that athletic wear was not allowed in the dining hall for dinner. Good to know—she'd hate to run afoul of the rules before she even got started.

Tomorrow, her entire day was assigned to testing. They must want to test her level of net expertise before entering her into classes. Why did she do all the tests back on Secundus then? But despite the test results, her classes the day after tomorrow were already assigned. Her first class was at zero-eight, an introduction to the local net. That was scheduled for two hours. The next class was an Introduction to Net Security. Then lunch, followed by a History of Omicron and Canis Majoris. Oh boy, history right after lunch. Quinn's nose wrinkled. Whose bright idea was that? Hopefully, the instructor was good, or she'd fall asleep. Then, Introduction to File Structure and Co-Working, whatever that was, followed by Introduction to Viruses, Malware, Net Riders, and Other Tools of the Trade, and at the end of the day, Math for Net.

When was she supposed to do the required physical fitness? Quinn looked at the following day's schedule. Oh, different classes, and the afternoon was dedicated to athletics. She was assigned a testing period for that too.

Which made her think. She knew a lot of self-defense through her study of y'ga. But if she needed to physically defend herself at some time, which seemed likely, she'd be better off pretending she knew nothing about martial arts. That way, her reaction would be a surprise to any attacker. The first time, anyway. She'd been trained to react rather than think, but she'd try to remember to use the minimal force and skills possible, so she could claim a "lucky hit" or something. After two or three, though, it would be obvious she wasn't just lucky.

Well, she'd have to do what she could to avoid confrontations. And if she didn't want a confrontation with House Mistress Vormer, she'd better leave this room. The woman told her to observe, so she'd better. Her stomach growled. Quinn snorted. She should feed herself something before that.

Leaving her room, she noticed it secured with her e-torc. With a school full of net experts, that probably wasn't very secure. If she ever had something to hide, she couldn't hide it in her room. She'd be on the lookout for a good hiding spot, just in case. It would have to be somewhere she could get in and out of quickly because she was sure the e-torcs had trackers. The instructors and staff undoubtedly had access to visuals from their e-torcs as well. She'd be careful not to vid herself or others when they were undressed or in the shower. Quinn shuddered. That could be misused so easily.

Hopping down the stairs, she found the small kitchen. Bev-tainers for water waited, a couple of pitchers of some sort of fruit juice in the cold storage, along with what she assumed were fresh fruit and vegetables, although the colors were unfamiliar to her. Because of the blue-white sun, perhaps? On the shelves, plas packages of various kinds of snack and meal replacement bars, tea and coffee packs, packaged soup, and dried fruit. No sweets of any kind. Quinn wasn't used to those, but she'd heard stories and had hoped to try some. Well, a protein bar and fruit would probably be her best bet, since she'd missed lunch.

She picked two at random and had started to walk away when her e-torc buzzed. Bringing up the notice, she shivered slightly when she read it. "A reminder—students may not have food or drinks other than water in their rooms or the classrooms." Also a reminder they were watching. Or maybe it was an automated message? Quinn sat in the lounge area, finished her snack, and carefully checked to make sure she didn't leave so much as a crumb. House Mistress Vormer was sitting right there. She gave no sign of noticing Quinn, but she could be watching on a vid someplace and Quinn would never know.

Taking in a deep breath, Quinn forced herself out of the dormitory. Since class was in session, she'd go watch. Walking outside, she winced when her e-torc didn't respond to the bright sun. Stepping to the side of the walkway, she found the settings and changed it to automatically adjust for brightness. Wonder what else she'd have to adjust with this new e-torc? She walked to the Academic building and let herself inside. The auditoriums on the first floor didn't have plas windows, so she walked up to the third floor, thinking the smaller sessions might be easier to watch.

Enabling the "display location" setting in her e-torc, she saw the first class was an advanced net security class. Quinn selected the "live classroom feed" option but quickly swept it away. The class was working on some sort of project, and it was well beyond anything she knew. She put a hand over her stomach—the bar wasn't settling well. The next two classrooms weren't any better. Quinn found a chair and breathed, trying not to panic. Here she was, trapped in a strange place, with beings who were definitely not on her side, and she'd just learned how pitiful her hard-earned skills were.

How could she survive this place when she knew nothing?

CHAPTER FOUR

"Student Quinn? Student Quinn—"

Quinn jumped up and out of her chair, almost colliding with the person who'd called her name, but he'd stepped back just in time.

"Are you all right?" The boy's face showed concern with an undertone of fear.

Quinn swallowed hard. "Sssorry about that. A little jumpy."

A smile flickered. "That's okay, I understand." He huffed. "We're all a little jumpy these days." The boy grimaced. "Do you need help?"

He seemed genuinely concerned, but Quinn wasn't sure she could trust anyone. The boy was only a few centimeters taller than she was, with short hair the color of toasted bread, eyes a shade darker, and cinnamon-brown skin.

Quinn shook her head. "No. I'm just…a little overwhelmed. This is all new to me."

"How new? I mean, I know you just arrived today, but what part is new?"

"All of it." Quinn spread her hands out. "I'm not used to big cities or any cities. Or fancy uniforms. Or net at that level." She tossed her chin to the classrooms.

He snorted. "You're new. Those are Third Years. If you knew that stuff, you wouldn't be here. Speaking of things you don't know, did you enable the tagging function in your e-torc?"

She looked at him, chagrined. "I forgot. Thanks." Quinn scrolled through the settings, found the right one, and toggled it on.

"No problem," First-Year Student Tiber Rios said. "I'm not much further ahead of you. Got here thirty-two days ago. The recent change of ownership has been a bit…chaotic." He glanced around, clearly wary.

So, the bad editing of the welcome vids was a good clue. The takeover wasn't that long ago. "I can tell. I'm sorry you had to experience all that…chaos."

Tiber widened his eyes and put on a very fake smile. "Oh, it was fine. So much better now. All good. Perfect."

"Of course. So, why are you out here?"

"I'm moving to my next class. I've only got a few seconds left. Look for me at dinner. I'll introduce you to my roommate and a few of the guys, okay?"

"Sure. Thanks."

He jogged away, a hand raised above his shoulder.

"Oh, look, the new girl's got a boyfriend already."

Quinn turned slowly to face the group of girls she'd attracted. Mean girls, she was sure. They seemed to be a fact of life, perhaps of biology, because they were always some. The Sisters didn't let them get far at home, but from the stories some of the older girls told, that wasn't the case in most schools. Lucky her, to attract their attention on her very first day. She didn't say anything to them, knowing they'd pounce on anything.

One of the three girls towering over her wagged a finger in her face. "New girl, it's rude not to greet your betters. Rudeness isn't tolerated here at Adzari." She was tall, with the same dark brown hair and olive-toned skin the administrative staff had, and she was beautiful. Long, flowing hair, big, heavily lashed eyes, a small pert nose, and a wide generous mouth gave her the face of a siren. Her body was the same—she'd clearly matured early and was proud of it, wearing a sweater a size too small.

The auburn-haired girl standing next to her snatched Third Year Student Gianna Ricci's hand out of the air and pushed it down. As she whispered in Gianna's ear, her nasty smile flattened. Gianna pulled her hand away and sneered at the redhead, but she didn't say anything else to Quinn. All three of them turned and sauntered away.

Maybe showing up right after the takeover wasn't such a bad thing. The mean girls were just as worried about the new rules— and rulers—as the rest of them. Quinn decided one close call was good enough and retreated to the second floor. Listening to the classes there, her lack of knowledge was thoroughly confirmed— she officially knew nothing. She was totally and completely unprepared for this school, even without the threat of the new owners. Quinn glanced at the time and decided to check out the athletic facilities. Maybe there was something there she could be good at without giving away her background in self-defense.

On her way to the athletic training facilities, she noticed small areas of trees or flower gardens were scattered across the campus. Depending on vids, those might be good hiding places for things—or herself. On one of the big fields, students played some sort of team ball game. They threw the odd-shaped ball from person to person but didn't run with it except away from what must be the goal. The referees kept stopping play, but Quinn couldn't figure out why—the rules seemed byzantine.

Quinn kept walking and found the swimming center. Entering, the sharp scent of chemicals made her nose wrinkle. Following the signs, she made her way to the viewing stands. There was only one person in the pool, a dark-skinned man swimming laps. It was a huge pool and had a separate, smaller pool, evidently for diving, and an even smaller pool that bubbled next to that. She would like to learn to swim, more so she wouldn't drown than a desire to exercise that way. Perhaps there were beginner swimming lessons?

She left the aquatic center and turned back toward the dormitories, detouring to enter the gymnasium. Inside, her virtual campus guide offered directions to the locker rooms, the large ball court, smaller ball courts, weight room, aerobic machines, gymnastics, martial arts, and something called the Atlas Challenge. The last option was intriguing, so she followed the guide upstairs. On the third floor, she found clear plas walls keeping any passerby from intruding on the athletes but allowing a clear view. There was a martial arts and boxing room, the gymnastics room, and finally, the Atlas Challenge. Lucky for her curiosity, someone was using the Atlas Challenge equipment.

Quinn watched the woman, tallish and thin but with muscles

like the fiercest Sisters, throw herself from obstacle to obstacle. She climbed tall walls, swung from ring to ring, ran along a rolling log while avoiding big, padded arms swinging at her, and did a dozen more challenges. Now that—that looked like fun. She might even be good at it. Quinn pulled up the person's tag: Fitness Instructor Katherine Switz.

Well, Instructor Switz had finished her run, so maybe she could ask? She opened the door and the woman's head turned her way. A scowl formed. "No Academy uniforms in the fitness rooms, Student! You should know this!"

"I'm sorry, Instructor Switz. I haven't read all the rules yet."

Switz marched to her. "Do so. Quickly." Her accent made her a little difficult to understand, but that was crystal clear.

"Yes, Instructor Switz, I will. I just wanted to ask if I could learn to do this?"

Switz stopped abruptly. "You want to learn this? There is no fame or fortune here. Many years ago, the Atlas Challenge brought both things. Today, the Gravity Games are everything. This is old-fashioned." She motioned to the course behind her.

Quinn shrugged. "I don't care about fame and fortune. I have to pick a sport, and this looks challenging and fun."

A lopsided smile started to form on Switz's face. "I see. Well, then, perhaps. You are…ah, Student Quinn Cygnus, arrived today. Interesting." She sniffed and mopped her forehead with a towel. "Well, then, Student Quinn, we will see what the results of your fitness tests say. Do you have a background in fitness?"

"Not anything like this." Quinn shook her head slowly. "This is amazing."

Switz examined Quinn from her head to her toes. "You are in decent physical condition, especially for a net worker. But this," she motioned to the apparatus, "takes strength, flexibility, reflexes, speed, balance, and a good sense of timing and depth perception. It also takes fortitude; the ability to keep going even when it's painful. The ability to push your limits. You have to want it very badly to be successful." Switz examined her again. "You are very petite. You might be good at gymnastics too. There's a class starting now. You should go watch. I will see you in two days. Then, we'll discover if you can be taught." Switz turned away, returning to the apparatus.

Quinn watched her for a few more moments, then walked down the corridor to watch the gymnastics class. Girls and one boy in tight athletic wear worked on skills at various stations. There were parts of these kinds of events in the hardest y'ga routines, so she might be good at it. But, the reason for performing these motions were entirely different and had different timing. In a crisis, Quinn didn't want to sit back and wonder if she'd picked the right reaction. No, the Atlas Challenge looked like a much better idea. There was nothing there that would trip her up, make her second guess when she needed to act, and no skill level to hide.

She wandered the rest of the facility, but nothing else really interested her except the martial arts studio. And she didn't dare train there or her only advantage, surprise, would be gone. Well, now that she'd looked at everything, Quinn could find a quiet corner and read some of the student manual and the rules and regulations while she waited for dinner. She walked back down the stairs, thinking about the boy she'd met.

Quinn hoped Tiber Rios's invitation was for real, not a cruel joke. She didn't get that impression from him, but she'd been wrong before. Look at everything that happened at the Sisters of Cygnus while they were still on Gliese. She was totally clueless about evil "Mother" Ferra, Nat's willingness to attempt a hijacking to save her friends, the men on Lightwave's crew being nice rather than evil, Chef Loreli, all of it. Sure, most of the Sisters were blind to Ferra's machinations; who would have thought the stalwart defender of the faith and orphaned children would try to sell them out for mere credits? Still, Quinn's judgment was worse than most of the Sisters. She had to get better, fast, or she might not make it out of here.

Needing the wide-open, Quinn blew through the doors and ran for one of the small gardens she'd spotted earlier. Surrounded by tall trees, it looked like there might be someplace to sit inside. She found the narrow walkway into the group of trees and abruptly stopped, her troubles forgotten.

Beautiful. Flower beds sported colorful flowers, the colors not matching but harmonious, the plant heights increasing further back in the beds, so each type could be admired while pollinating insects buzzed about them. Several sweet, flowery scents wafted to her. Birds hopped in the trees, and some little animal scurried away. In the center, a small pool with a fountain, the edge of the pool the perfect height to sit on. Quinn walked to the fountain and around it, enjoying the slight spray in the bright sun. She reached a shiny plaque: In Memory of Allana Adzari, Co-Founder of Adzari Net Academy.

How sad. Quinn shrugged. Or maybe it wasn't. Gentle Allana may have lived a long and wonderful life. She probably wouldn't be happy with what was happening to her Academy now, or maybe she wouldn't care. No matter what, Quinn was grateful to find this quiet refuge. It probably had vids like the rest of the Academy, but at least it was out of sight.

Quinn set an alarm for ten minutes before dinner and pulled up the Student Guide. She had to learn everything about her new environment—her survival depended on it.

ΛΛΛ

Her head spinning, Quinn entered the dining hall and got in line with all the other students. Unfortunately, she'd timed it all wrong and was surrounded by third-year students. Fortunately, they studiously ignored her.

Without Quinn requesting it, a tray with a plate of some sort of pasta and red sauce was dropped in front of her. So much for the "wide variety of eating options" the vid talked about. But she wasn't used to variety, so it didn't matter. It smelled decent and rather like some of the herbs the Sisters grew. She picked up a few other items that looked edible and a layered dessert that seemed downright delectable. Filling a glass with water, she picked up her tray and searched for Student Tiber Rios.

A hard shove sent her stumbling forward. She managed to keep her feet and save her tray from falling, but her water splashed all over her food.

"Move out of the way, first-year," a low voice snarled.

Quinn didn't look back. She kept walking as if nothing happened. She checked the student tagging function in her holo and selected "find"—Tiber was at the far end of the room. Keeping her head high, she skirted the tables, not getting close enough for anyone to trip her, and watched her rear holo carefully. No one else approached her. She carefully avoided Jonstew, stalking the edges of the room, glaring at everyone. She stopped next to Tiber.

"Hey guys, I mean, fellow students, this is Student Quinn, the new girl," Tiber told his small group of friends. He smiled up at her. "You're welcome to join us."

"Thanks." Quinn put her tray down and sat next to Tiber.

The boy across from her had long bright red hair, tied at the back of his neck, and pale, freckled skin. "Hi. I'm Bran. Nice save with the tray. You're fast on your feet."

She smiled. "Thanks. Guess I'll get plenty of hydration with my food."

The boy next to him, with black coffee skin and ebony curly hair, snorted. "I'm Ekon. You'll need plenty of water to choke it down and it won't change the taste, that's for sure." Despite that, he shoveled the food in. But he seemed to be twice the width of Bran and Tiber, so he probably needed the energy, no matter how bad it tasted.

Tiber said, "I'm sure you read we're not allowed to talk with our mouths full, right?"

"Yes, thanks." Quinn spooned up the pasta and sauce. Watery tomato, gluey pasta, and some sort of ground meat or meat substitute. Well, she'd had worse on Cygnus Gliese. None of the food was particularly good, but it was filling. She ate what she needed and left the rest. Expecting disappointment, she took a bite of the layered cake. "Oh!"

The guys chuckled. They'd already finished. "Yeah, that stuff is good," Ekon said. "But they'll only give you one piece."

"Most of us can't eat more than one," Tiber replied.

"But they serve it every. Single. Day," Bran moaned. "Tira is good, but so is variety."

"You're not complaining, are you, Student Bran?" a voice sneered above Quinn's head.

Bran jolted and jumped to his feet. "Of course not, Master Jonstew. Just missing home."

Jonstew sneered. "What, exactly, do you miss, Student Bran? Starvation, destructive weather, solar flares? Do tell."

"Just my family, Master Jonstew." Bran dropped his head.

Jonstew snorted. "Well, don't bite the hand that feeds you." He walked away.

Quinn figured her eyes must be the size of moonflowers. What a horrible man. All three boys gave her narrow-eyed looks of warning and she nodded. "Can I ask where you're from?"

Bran's mouth twisted. "I'm from Dschubba. Our sun is going supernova." He shrugged. "It hasn't gone yet, but the solar flares are intense, and everyone who can is leaving. My family applied for this scholarship—one less person to find transport credits for. But I miss them."

"I'm sorry. That's horrible."

Bran shrugged. "I hope they can all find a way off-world soon, but if not, I hope they can hold out until I can get a job and send them the credits. Where are you from?"

"Well, I'm from Cygnus. I was from Cygnus Gliese, but

Galactica Mining Corp kicked everyone off the planet, so now I'm from Secundus."

"Oh, the giant tunnel worms!" Tiber said, his eyes wide. "Did you see one?"

Quinn snorted. "I saw bones, like everyone else. A real tunnel worm has yet to be found."

"She's part of a religious cult. A weirdo, just like you three," Gianna sneered, peering down on them.

"The Sisters of Cygnus aren't a cult, Student Gianna," Quinn said evenly. "They are reclusive, and women only, but women are allowed to come and go as they please. And they take in lots of girls who would otherwise be homeless."

Gianna sniffed. "A cultist's spawn, that's all you are."

Quinn shrugged. "What you call me doesn't matter. I know who I am."

The boys were wide-eyed, giving her little headshakes.

"Oh, it matters. When no one will partner with you for projects, it will matter a lot." Gianna sauntered away, her followers on her heels, giggling.

Quinn scowled at her. "There's always one."

"One what, Student Quinn?" Jonstew's nasty voice said behind her.

"One student who's too beautiful to be a net worker, Master Jonstew."

Quinn felt the breeze generated by his turn. The boys gave her big grins and subtle head nods, but all three sobered quickly.

Ekon glanced around the area. "Be careful. She's one of *them*."

Quinn gave him a puzzled look.

"Familia," Tiber hissed, then immediately held up both hands, with a warning look. Much louder, he said, "Do you have your schedule already?"

"Yes, it's mostly testing the next two days." Quinn tried to keep her face impassive, but inside, she was terrified. Everyone knew Familia was evil, dealing in slavery, drugs, extortion, and murder. They had so much power in so many systems. Mostly core systems, where there were lots of credits to be stolen.

"Those aren't fun but necessary." Bran shuddered, bringing Quinn's attention back to his words. "You don't want to get into the wrong class. Failure is *not* an option."

Quinn nodded slowly. She could understand that caution. When in doubt, play dumb—better to be bored in class than be overwhelmed.

"Well, Student Quinn, it was a pleasure having dinner with you, but we," Tiber motioned to the three boys, "need to do our homework. Also, you're aware boys and girls aren't allowed in each other's dorms, other than the lounges on the ground floor?"

"Yes. Thanks for asking me to join you, Student Tiber. And yes, I read about that restriction."

"Good. So, if you partner with a boy for a project, you'll need to use a public area for work outside of class time." Tiber raised both brows.

Oh, good warning. "Understood, thank you." In other words, partnering with another girl was better because they could work after official curfew hours, until lights-out. Quinn grimaced. She'd better get to the dorm and see if she could meet some of the other first-year students.

"Most of the girls have been here for months, too, so you might have to partner with one of us," Bran said.

"Thank you for the invitation," Quinn told him.

"You're welcome. See you soon, Student Quinn."

"See you soon," she replied. They split outside the dining hall doors, her for the girls' dorm, them to the boys'. A curfew at twenty-hundred and lights-out at twenty-two hundred seemed awfully early to her, but those were the rules. She could stay outside for another hour, but she had to meet some of her year mates, or she'd be fighting off a giant Secundus lizard without a rifle. Right now, she'd feel a lot better if she had a rifle. Or just a stunner.

Familia. Suddenly, it dawned on Quinn—that's why the administration all looked the same. Dark brown hair, olive skin, brown eyes, oval faces—all common characteristics of Familia. And the boys said Gianna was Familia. What had she gotten herself into?

Quinn entered the dorm and trod slowly up the stairs, her footsteps echoing. She should practice walking quietly—she had a feeling that skill would be important in the future. But right now, everyone was aware of the "new girl" so she didn't want to raise suspicions. She passed the third-year floor and breathed a sigh of relief.

Turning the corner on her way to the second-year floor, Quinn learned her relief was too early. Gianna and her friends— including Quinn's "mentor," Freya—appeared in front of her, while others thundered up behind her, hemming her in. She bit her lip. Nothing to do but survive this—even if she went on the offensive, she couldn't prevail against ten or more girls.

Her e-torc was yanked off her neck and they all stared at each other. "Clear!" a voice said from behind her. Gianna punched her in the stomach, hard.

"Oh!" Quinn doubled over, gasping for air, not faking it at all.

"New girl, this is your only warning," Gianna said. "I run this dorm. You do what I say when I say it, or there will be a terrible accident. It would be so easy to send you flying down the stairs right now. Or, I could simply push you out your dorm window — oh, so sad, little Quinn couldn't handle the pressure. Is this understood?"

"Yes," Quinn gasped.

Hands grabbed her hair and pulled her up. "That's yes, Third-Year Student Gianna, cult scum."

"Yes, Third-Year Student Gianna," Quinn said, feeling hair ripping from her skull.

Gianna dropped her and she collapsed to the stairs. Girls left, some of them kicking or hitting her on the way, all of them careful to only hit uniform-covered body parts that would bruise, rather than break. Quinn cowered and survived. Finally, her e-torc dropped in front of her. "Don't lose it again, Student," a different girl's voice sneered.

Quinn waited until the footsteps and laughter faded, then she used the handrailing to pull herself up. She'd be a mass of bruises, but nothing seemed broken. Slowly, she climbed to the first-year floor and entered the hall. Closed and locked doors greeted her. Obviously, the rest of her fellow first-years were told to ignore her.

She entered her room, finding that, as expected, anyone could enter. All her clothes were strewn about, the bed was torn apart and the frame turned over, and one of the sheets had been torn right down the middle. She sighed and started picking up the mess. Some of the clothes had mud and possibly other things smeared into them, so those she piled to the side. Quinn moved deliberately, trying to stretch a little as she cleaned up, hopefully minimizing the muscle damage. Some of those hits had been terribly hard. She made her bed as well as she could, placing one of the sheet halves in her pillowcase, using the other to "make" the bed. A half-sheet was better than no sheet. She'd be in trouble for damaging school property, but that was the way things went.

Picking up her soiled clothes, she found the autocleaner closest to her and set it on the highest setting. She'd be cutting it close, but the cycle should finish before lights-out. But only if the other girls would leave her things alone. Quinn started a stretching routine, keeping her movements a little awkward and slow, carefully not using more advanced y'ga stretches. Hopefully, this would help. She'd set her alarm for extra-early tomorrow, just in case she needed the medico station. Although, by the time she made it down three floors of stairs, she might have loosened everything enough to walk.

Finishing her stretches, she pulled up the rules and regulations. If everyone was against her, she had to know the rules perfectly, so she could use them to her advantage. Since Gianna and her girl-gang were third-year students, they might not know the new rules or be inclined to study them. They'd have more leeway with the instructors, Quinn was sure, but using the rules against them was the only real advantage she had. Right now, this was more important than net work—it was her life.

CHAPTER FIVE

Quinn woke to her alarm—a harsh clanging from her e-torc—
and swept it away. *Ow.* Moving that quickly was a mistake. She
put her arm down and took stock of her body. The outsides of
both arms were bruised and achy. So were her legs and buttocks.
A few other, lesser bruises too, but nothing critical. She could
sleep another half hour, but she was awake now, so she'd be
better off getting up and using the bathroom before the other girls
showed up.

Rising slowly, she ran through a series of gentle stretches and a
warmup, then took clean clothes with her to the sani-mod. Quinn
entered cautiously, but there was no one else inside. She picked
the very last stall and put her clothes where she could see them,
just in case someone decided to try and take them. Fortunately,
she was finished and dressed before anyone else entered.
Returning to her room, she studied the rules until ten minutes
before breakfast. Exiting her room, she found all the other first-
year students were also leaving. None of them would meet her
eyes. Despite that, Quinn greeted every single one of them by
name, determined to show them she had no hard feelings and that

she wouldn't be cowed so easily. They all walked to the dining hall together, lining up for food in a group. So, lesson learned, first-years went through the line first, letting the upper classes sleep in. Would third-years eat first or last for lunch?

She got her food—some sort of egg pie with root vegetables—and looked for Tiber, Ekon, or Bran. She found them at the same table at the back of the room and walked over, unsure if she'd be welcome. As she neared, they gave her tight-lipped glances and small shakes of their heads. *Message received.* Quinn sat at a table by herself and ate quickly. Even though she could feel the hostile gazes, she refused to cower or scurry away. She knew displaying weakness made bullies bolder and more persistent. But Quinn also knew that sometimes, bullies got worse no matter what. If she was going down, she'd go down swinging.

Finished with her food, she pulled up her schedule and walked to the testing center, which was on the first floor of the lab building. Quinn didn't try to enter the room, not knowing if that would violate some protocol or not. She found a small area outside the rooms with hard chairs and sat, studying the rules.

Many of the rules were unfortunately contradictory. That was undoubtedly on purpose, so the instructors could twist them whatever way they chose.

Quinn chuckled to herself. Weirdly, she had to thank "Mother" Ferra and the evil Inquisitors for the idea. Ferra, as the former leader of the Sisters of Cygnus, knew the rules inside and out and twisted them to make dissent almost impossible. The Inquisitors, the vicious exploratory miners supporting themselves by pillaging the surrounding communities, had no real rules except the strong survive by force and caring about anyone else was a weakness. Those final weeks before they escaped Cygnus Gliese were terrifying. At the time, she was too young to understand fully, but later, the Sisters made sure they all knew exactly what happened and how people could manipulate and abuse others, both subtly and obviously. Ferra's machinations were a study in expert-level abuse of power.

If Quinn had come to Adzari Academy straight from her previous, comparatively sheltered life with the Sisters on Gliese, she'd be completely overwhelmed and bewildered. But now Quinn knew, in a place where the rules were everything, knowing them inside and out was her best defense. Knowing she was utterly alone, she had to maximize her defenses. Offense would have to come later, when she discovered Gianna's weak points.

She also had to remember Gianna wasn't her only enemy. Some of the instructors, and certainly the house master, possibly the house mistress, might be enemies, or at least not fair advocates. Quinn was sure they were all expert manipulators. And they made the rules and wouldn't hesitate to change them if necessary. They'd have all this down to a science, Quinn was sure.

Would she be better off just leaving? Feeling so abandoned and alone made it hard to think, but she had to fight past that feeling. She didn't know if everyone was against her; she only *knew* Gianna didn't like her. She might be blowing all of this out of proportion. Being dumped with the Sisters as a baby predisposed her to assume she'd been discarded, but she knew the Sisters cared and her friends there cared. She might make friends here too. Maybe it would just take time.

She studied the rules and regulations until five minutes before the testing period, then tried the door. It opened, so she walked in, hoping that was the right thing to do. The rule book wasn't clear on testing protocols—or anything else.

In the room, two rows of desks, all separated by clear plas dividers, waited, empty. There was no one in the room at all.

"First-year student Quinn Cygnus," a man's voice said. Quinn looked around the room, but there was no one there. "You will test in cubicle one. Once you start the test, you will be given a break every hour for ten minutes. Work as quickly as you can, but do not guess; wrong answers will count against you. This test will last all morning, possibly longer. If it goes longer, lunch will be brought to you. You cannot leave this room until you are finished. There is a sani-mod in the corner. Is this all clear?"

Quinn said, "Yes, Instructor."

"Time will start when you hit the start button inside the cubicle. Use the facilities now if you need to."

Quinn did as the voice suggested, then entered the testing cubicle, closing the door behind her. It snapped shut with an ominous click. She sat, pleasantly surprised by the supportive comfort of the chair. In front of her, a curved one-eighty view screen, a keyboard, and a stylus. *Interesting.* Good to know they allowed manual input as well as virtual. Or maybe it was required, in case they were at a facility where virtual input wasn't allowed?

Well, it didn't matter now. It was time to start. Quinn adjusted her seat and desk so her feet were flat on the floor and the input devices at elbow height, then she reached out and hit the start button. A vid began, "Welcome to the Testing Center. Remove your e-torc and place it in the drawer below your work table." She did so, then a long list of rules appeared.

Quinn took a deep breath and concentrated. She planned to do well but not great. Whether the testing protocol would allow that remained to be seen, but she'd try.

∆∆∆

A chime sounded, and the screen went dark. Quinn blinked, then shook herself. That was intense. She had no idea how she performed or even what the scale was. The door to the testing cubicle unlocked and she suddenly realized her bladder was painfully full and tummy was rumbling. She walked quickly to the sani-mod and took care of business. When she exited, she started walking, swinging her arms gently, trying to warm her stiff, bruised muscles.

A person dressed in all white entered and put a container on the plain desk at the front of the room.

"Thank you, Gentle," Quinn said.

The man said, "Please, Student Quinn, have a seat. Eat. Testing will begin again in no more than thirty minutes."

Quinn did as he suggested. Opening the container, she found it held a much better-looking meal than dinner. There was pasta and sauce but with some sort of breaded protein patty; a salad, a vegetable, and a roll, along with more Tira.

She started eating and thought about the testing. She'd found out her so-called net expertise was pretty slim and her knowledge of events important to the universe at large—by the standards of this academy—was very small. She hadn't even heard of half the historical and political events they asked about, so she definitely didn't know the answers to any question about them. She supposed some of the events might be fakes, to see if she was guessing after being warned not to, but they couldn't all be phony. Those after-lunch history classes might not be so boring after all.

After she ate, Quinn walked around the room a little more, then went back to the testing cubicle. Three rest periods later, Quinn was thrilled to see the "Test Complete" banner on the screen. *Thanks be to the Mother!* The drawer with her e-torc opened, and she put it back on, then let herself out of the test cubicle. A message waited for her: Report to House Mistress Vormer immediately.

Heart sinking, Quinn took her e-torc, noted the summons, and left the testing center. Fortunately, it was right in the middle of a class period, so there weren't any other students around. She passed a few workers on her way back to the dorm and greeted them on her way, a little dismayed their names weren't displayed on her holo. The workers nodded in return but said nothing. Was that natural inclination or instruction from the new owners? None of the staff looked happy.

Quinn made her way to Mistress Vormer's office and stood at the open door, waiting for her acknowledgment.

After a good five minutes, Vormer looked up and motioned for her to enter. Quinn walked in and stood in front of the desk.

"Student Quinn, did I not say you would be partially responsible for one of the bathrooms on your floor?"

"Yes, House Mistress Vormer, you did."

"Then why does that bathroom look like this?" She pushed a vid over to Quinn's holo.

The vid showed towels and toilet tissue strewn everywhere, puddles of water on the floor, and something smeared on the walls. Quinn swallowed hard. "I don't know why, Mistress Vormer. When I left this morning, it was clean. Who did this?"

Vormer scowled at her. "It does not matter who did it, Student Quinn. The schedule shows that you were responsible for cleaning this bathroom today. You should have stayed to make sure it was clean before going to breakfast. You will clean it now, and you will keep it clean for the next seven days. If it is spotless every day, then the regular rotation will start again. Is this clear, Student Quinn?"

"Yes, Mistress Vormer."

"Good. Dismissed."

"Thank you, Mistress Vormer." Quinn turned and walked away. She wanted to sulk, whine, and curse, but she wouldn't give that awful woman or those horrible girls the satisfaction. Stopping in the kitchen, Quinn shoveled down some protein bars, fruit, and juice, then ran up the stairs to make sure she made it to the top floor before class got out.

As she ran upward, she realized—the school had vids in the girl's bathrooms! *Eww.* Who could see those and what did they do with the vid? From the angle, that lens must be right over the entry door. Hopefully, they didn't have vid of the individual stalls. Quinn shuddered violently. While she cleaned, she'd be checking very carefully and figure out a way to block the vid lenses casually.

For the next seven days, she'd also be eating breakfast from the kitchen downstairs because she'd need to leave last. She only hoped she could grab something and not be late to class because she wasn't sure which option would be worse. She'd also have to go to bed late, or someone could destroy the place after she went to bed and raise a fuss in the morning. *Hmm.* What if she took vid when she was done cleaning and posted it someplace public?

Quinn snorted at her ridiculousness. She was surrounded by net experts. They could alter the vid and the timestamp without her knowing. Quinn would record what she did on her e-torc, but she wouldn't bother posting it anywhere.

One way or another, if the upper-class girls were determined to make her into a target, she'd be one. All she could do was minimize the impact and the amount of work she had to do. Walking into the filthy bathroom, a wave of homesickness washed over her like an afternoon deluge in the jungles of Secundus. Cleaning the bathroom, even the mess they'd made, was nothing in comparison to mucking out stalls or doing a dozen other unpleasant chores at the Sisters' compound. But none of the Sisters would have tolerated this kind of nasty, cruel behavior.

She got the cleaning supplies and went to work.

ΔΔΔ

That morning, Quinn slept in until forty-five minutes before breakfast. She left all her things in her room, went to the sani-mod, grabbed cleaning supplies, and stood just inside the door but out of the way. She greeted every girl that came and left by name, with a cheery, "Good morning! Lovely day, isn't it?" followed with a fierce look. Most of the girls looked ashamed or guilty. Quinn knew it wasn't fully their fault; the upper-class girls made them do it. One or two of her classmates tried to leave a mess, but Quinn stopped them in their tracks.

"Oh, Student Suzette, I'm sure you didn't realize you accidentally smeared feces all over the toilet, did you?" Quinn stepped into Suzette, pushing her back into the toilet enclosure by stepping on her toes. "Since it was clearly an accident, here, I've brought you cleaning supplies to help you." She shoved them into Suzette's stomach hard, pushing her onto the toilet, right into her own mess. "Oops. So sorry. Here you go."

"Gosh, Student Quinn, thank you so much," Suzette said through gritted teeth. "I'll be sure to repay you adequately."

"I'm sure you will try, Student Suzette, but there's no need." Quinn bared her teeth and snapped them together.

Suzette shrank back. Quinn heard snickers beyond the toilet cubicle. When she slammed the door on Suzette, no one remained in the bathroom and it wasn't destroyed. Quinn got to work sanitizing it to the stated specifications. When Suzette slammed out of the bathroom, her toilet stall sparkled as well. Quinn grinned. Hopefully, this would put an end to her own class ganging up on her, but probably not. She knew many of the girls had no choice: make Quinn's life miserable, or someone would make all their lives miserable.

Quinn did her cleanup, dressed, and ran down the stairs, grabbing two protein bars and some milk. She'd eat them on the way to class and hope it was enough to tide her over until lunch. She was looking forward to this class and hoped the instructor was one of those left over from the old academy. Entering the auditorium-style classroom on the first floor, her heart sank. No such luck. Instructor Stefano had the "Familia look" that was too familiar by now.

A notice popped up in her holo. She was assigned to a seat right at the front and center of the room. *Lucky her.* Pasting a smile on her face, she entered and stood by her seat. She noted Tiber, Ekon, and Bran were also in this class, seated at the back.

"Have a seat, Student Quinn," the boy next to her sneered.

"Oh, thank you so much for the invitation, but you know I can't do that until the Instructor says so."

The boy glared. Someone behind her shoved her between her shoulder blades. She took one step forward but stopped herself on the desk.

"Student Marco, that was rude and potentially dangerous. Report to me after class," Instructor Stefano snapped. "Students, have a seat."

Quinn sat.

"Now that we have our final student, welcome to the Introduction to the Adzari Academy Student Net," Instructor Stefano intoned. He glared around the room. "Do not attempt to access any other net, here on the grounds of Adzari or anywhere on Omicron. Your attempt will be discovered, and you will not like the consequences. Is this clear?"

"Yes, Instructor," Quinn and everyone else replied.

"You will use only the net storage you are assigned. If you need more, request it from any instructor. You are forbidden to access other students' net storage areas. There are shared file systems for joint work. You will not use the skills you learn here to get around, counter, or change any Academy policies, procedures, rules, regulations, or security measures. This includes intruding on, harassing, or harming other students. Is this also clear?"

"Yes, Instructor," Quinn and the class agreed. The stipulation against attacking other students via the net was obviously not followed, or whoever trashed her room would have been caught.

The lecture on rules and regulations continued for another twenty minutes. Quinn kept herself upright and engaged by attempting to guess what the Instructor was going to say next. Some of the other students didn't—Quinn learned Instructor Stefano was fond of slamming his open palm on the desk of drowsy students, jolting them awake.

"All right, now that the official rules are over, let me tell you what I expect." He glared at each of them. "I expect you to act like decent beings. To the instructors, the staff, and *all* the other students. You will not use your skills to attack anyone on the Academy or the planet in any way, shape, or form. You will use your skills for good, not evil. You will be helpful and kind. Is that clear?" Another glaring survey.

Quinn nodded but knew the instructor was either willfully blind or purposefully misleading them. She'd have to wait and see which was true.

"And if you decide to be otherwise, remember that everything you do on the net can be seen by the instructors and academic staff. Attempts to hide such things are futile." He sniffed derisively. "For example, I know that Student Quinn's dorm room was broken into yesterday and her room disturbed. I know who did it. The attempt to hide such a thing by a third-year student was truly pitiful. I've recommended, based on this poor attempt, that this student be held back a year."

Quinn listened with growing horror. Instructor Stefano must want her dead. Gianna would not take that well, even if the staff ignored his recommendation, which they probably would. They had to be aware of Gianna's predations and might even be encouraging them. Not only that, but there were vid lenses in her room? She got dressed in there! She shuddered.

Instructor Stefano glared around the classroom, his glare turning to puzzlement, then realization. "Ah, no. Your rooms are not under vid surveillance. The hallways, however, are." He returned to glaring. "Any attempt to take advantage of the lack of vid surveillance in your room will be one, punished, and two, rewarded by the installation of surveillance. Is this clear?"

Quinn nodded a little frantically, seeing everyone else around her doing the same.

"Let us get to the real intent of this class: an introduction to the local net. Many of you have been using it already, in some cases, extensively. Nonetheless, pay attention. I'm going to show you some things you haven't discovered, and some tricks and tools to make your daily lives easier." A twist of his lips. "Don't fall asleep."

Quinn pulled up a note-taker, determined to push away her personal problems, at least for now. She'd do everything she could to learn, hopefully, more than the Academy realized. It might be her salvation.

CHAPTER SIX

Quinn leaned wearily against the sani-mod wall. Although her first-year classmates hadn't made further coordinated efforts to sabotage her, they studiously avoided any contact with her. So did all the other students. Tiber wasn't even apologetic anymore. No one talked to her—she was a pariah. Between the worry and the work, she wasn't getting much sleep. The only bright spot in her life was training for the Atlas Challenge. During that, she could work her body so hard she no longer had room to worry or even think. Instructor Switz's all-business approach was a welcome relief from the subtle and not so subtle barbs from some of the other instructors. Over the last month, Quinn had become stronger and faster than she'd ever been. And Switz ordered the kitchen to provide her special nutrition, so her food was better too. Quinn sighed. She'd be happy to share if anyone was brave enough to be her friend. But no one crossed Gianna.

Every time it was Quinn's turn to clean, she made it very clear she wouldn't tolerate vandalism. Her classmates finished their morning routines and turned to stare at her. Quinn gripped the mop tight, ready for an attack. She wouldn't survive if they all seriously ganged up on her, but she'd make as many of them pay as she possibly could. All the showers turned on, and one of the girls, Lise, jumped up and slapped something over the vid lens above the door. Lise tried to step into her personal space. Quinn blocked her with the mop handle.

Lise scowled and held up both hands. "Just talk, okay?"

Quinn nodded. But she kept the mop handle between them.

Lise came in close and whispered in her ear. "Look, none of us, except maybe Suzette, want to do any of this. But Gianna runs this dorm. Our failure to make your life miserable is making all of us miserable. We can't take her down—she's the daughter of some important person in…the organization that runs this place. So, let's work together to make it look like we're beating you down, okay?"

"As long as it's not real."

"You'll still have to do the work, but we will *all* help, I promise. We'll just be careful about it. Tomorrow, get ready and leave early. We'll mess up the place again, just towels and water. You'll get in trouble and have to clean tomorrow, but we'll clean the rest of your punishment time. Then, on the last day, we'll do it again."

"We can't do the same thing again or the staff will catch on. We'll have to do something else next time."

"You're right. We've got at least seven, maybe fourteen days to figure it out. We'll make sure you get some sleep and decent food too. Okay?"

"Okay. But if you are doing this to set me up, you won't like the results."

"Understood." She jumped up and pulled the cover off the vid.

"You're so pathetic, little girl." She shoved Quinn lightly, but Quinn stumbled back like it was an all-out effort. Lise winked at her and swept out, followed by the rest of the girls, all sneering at her.

Quinn leaned against the wall, emotionally exhausted if not physically. She hoped this was a genuine offer because she couldn't take much more. She started cleaning. Maybe she should just give up and go home. She could contact the Grus and get a ride. They'd been happy with her work, and she might even find more work from their friends. But how long could that last?

But she probably couldn't leave. All messages were routed through the central messaging system. The academy might not let her message go through. Besides, what would she do on Secundus? Lashtar was right—she didn't fit in there any more than she did here. The Academy might be a hostile environment, but she was learning real skills.

What Quinn didn't understand is why Gianna was targeting her. Gianna was finishing her final year, and she probably had a guaranteed position because of her connections, if not her skills. So why pick on poor little Quinn? Just because she was the newest? It didn't make any sense at all.

Quinn started mopping again, aware of time ticking away. Could she ask? Should she ask? The students wouldn't know, but an instructor might. Maybe Switz? Would she be sympathetic?

No matter who she might ask, she'd have to find a non-obvious question, a way to lead the conversation that way gradually. She couldn't afford to raise suspicions.

She finished cleaning, cleaned herself, and ran down the stairs.

In the kitchen, a warm box waited for her with a note "for Quinn" on the top. Could she trust it? They might make her sick or poison her. Well, at least she'd get out of the work. Or die. Then it would all be over. Quinn shrugged. What did she have to lose? Quinn opened the box. An egg sandwich. She pulled it apart, but it looked and smelled normal. Good even. She gobbled it, grateful to have real, hot food but aware she was cutting the time close. She left the box in the autocleaner and ran to class.

Getting to her seat just before Instructor Stefano entered, she breathed a sigh of relief. That relief was short-lived. Stefano entered, glaring at her. What did she do to him? Quinn couldn't take much more of this. The next two hours passed like eight. Every question was aimed at her and Stefano's biting wit was on full display. She'd cry, but she refused to give him the satisfaction. Even the students who hated her the most seemed sympathetic.

"Student Quinn, stay. The rest of you are dismissed."

The other students ran out the door, jamming it up in their hurry to leave the tower of anger and impatience the normally even-tempered Instructor Stefano had become.

Quinn stood by her desk, straight and tall. She wouldn't let this man intimidate her.

"My office, Student Quinn."

Uh oh. She followed him out the back door of the classroom, almost jogging to keep up with his long strides. She'd never been back here—it was off-limits to students unless escorted by an instructor. Stefano marched down the narrow hall, passing many closed doors, all with nameplates of classrooms, then instructors. He opened one door, motioned her inside, and slammed it shut behind her. Quinn stayed by the door in case she needed to make a quick escape. She'd never gotten any truly creepy feelings about Stefano, but some people were better at hiding than others.

Leaving her standing there, he walked behind his desk and sat. "Student Quinn, I do not understand what you are doing here. You seem to be incapable of answering the simplest questions or studying enough to answer those questions. You are wasting my time."

Quinn stared straight ahead, unwilling to let this man see her pain. Catching glimpses of him sweeping through screens and doing something on his desk as he ranted at her, she tipped her head down slightly to see better.

"Ah. Prerecorded vid in place." Stefano's voice was calm. "Have a seat, Quinn. Sorry about that. Had to make it clear to the administration that I was falling in line with their plans."

Quinn sat but considered him warily. It could be a trap.

"Yes, this could be a trap. But at this point, what do you have left to lose?" He quirked his lips and brows.

"Nothing."

"Except you do. Your life and your freedom." His face and voice were grim. "You must be wondering why everyone is targeting you, right?"

"Yes, Instructor Stefano, I am."

"Unfortunately for you, you arrived at exactly the wrong time. As I'm sure you have guessed, a Familia organization bought this school about two months ago. Since your arrival, you have attracted the attention of two powerful individuals. One is Gianna. She's not just a student here but the daughter of a very high-ranking individual in Familia who spoils her. She's a terrible person. You're much better at everything net related than she'll ever be, and you're pretty in a way she will never be because you're kind, and that gives you inner beauty. Also, you don't back down. All of that makes you a perfect target for her." He snorted.

Stefano shook his head. "You have a much bigger problem, though. You've attracted the attention of Familia's Head Enforcer, Enzo. He has a lot of power. In disputes between Familia, he's the one who punishes the loser. In many cases, that means death, for a lot of people, and the destruction of businesses and organizations. He's told the staff they must test you, push your limits, so he can see what you're made of beyond your Atlas Challenge performances."

Shock jolted through Quinn. People were watching her train?

Stefano scowled. "I hate to tell you this, but your determination is your downfall. You'll do much better if you whine and cry and carry on. Enzo hates crying women. If he sees you like that, he'll leave you alone. And if Enzo isn't interested in you, then Gianna might not hate you quite as much either." He shrugged. "Or so I hope. Either way, at this point, you have little to lose by trying the whining and crying route because your fortitude is backfiring. Quinn, you must break down. Whine, cry, sob. Do it all and often. Then, they might leave you alone." He shook his head, glowering. "Maybe. It's your only chance to survive."

Quinn bit her lip. "If I do, it might become real."

"I'm so, so sorry. You're smart and you're good at net work—really good. I know this situation is horrible, and under normal circumstances, I would never advise you to take this course, but it's the only solution I can see for now." He sighed. "And to make everything worse, this is the only time I can do this, Quinn. If I try to talk to you in private again, I'll probably end up dead."

Stefano closed his eyes and dropped his head, rubbing his forehead for a moment. Then he looked up at her, gaze stern. "If you get the chance to leave this school, such as a trip to town, do it. Don't hesitate. Run, far away, and don't come back. Don't return to Cygnus either. You need to hide, somewhere Familia can't find you easily. Do whatever you have to do to survive. I'll make sure you get extra lessons, so you can get ahead, and if I ever hear that you are going on a trip outside the Academy grounds, I'll do my best to get a clean e-torc and a credit chip to you, but I can't promise it will happen."

He swallowed hard and stood. "Now, leave. Break into tears and run. If you run to the end of the hallway, you'll end up outside, near the dorms. You're already late for your next class, so just run to your dorm room. Tell them I said you were terrible at this, you have no talent, no drive, no ability. Cry and whine when you get in trouble. Understood?"

Quinn dropped her head and sniffled. "I don't want to, but I will." She looked up at him again. "Thank you. May the Mother bless you."

"Take care, Quinn. Safe folds." He swallowed hard and blinked rapidly, then turned away, doing something on his holo.

She squeezed her eyes shut, thought about how she felt today during class, and let herself feel the fear and despair. A sob broke loose, surprisingly loud. Quinn fell into her emotions and bawled. She stumbled to the door, opened it, and ran down the hall, one hand on the wall because she was crying so hard she couldn't see. By the Mother, she hated everything about this place.

Scrubbing the tears away enough to see, she ran back to the dorm and up the stairs, slamming into her room and plopping down on the bed. Quinn cried, wailed, and sobbed until she was dehydrated.

Her door hit the wall with a bang. "Student Quinn Cygnus, you have class," House Mistress Vormer snapped. "Why are you here? What is this unseemly display?"

Quinn ignored her and kept blubbering.

A hand clamped on her shoulder and rolled her over, then shook her. "I asked you a question, Student Quinn."

She blinked up at Vormer. "Why?" she wailed. "Why bother? They all say I'm terrible, I'll never succeed, they all hate me, so why?"

Vormer dropped her and stepped back. "Why? Because you have a duty and a debt. You are here, you are a student, you will go to class, study and do your chores, or you will not like the results."

"What debt? I'm here on scholarship and the Sisters paid for half of my school." Quinn wiped her eyes and blew her nose.

Vormer snorted. "Your scholarship is repaid by service. You owe three years of work for every year here. The tiny amount your precious Sisters paid is nothing. It doesn't even cover the cost of your food."

"What?!" Quinn stared up at Vormer with real horror. "That's not true. I read every word of the paperwork. It was a scholarship, not an indentured servant contract!"

"That was under the old owners. The updated terms are right here, in your files, Student Quinn," Vormer sneered, sweeping a link to her e-torc. "It's stated very clearly. If you didn't bother to read these, that's not my problem."

"I read everything! This wasn't here!"

"It certainly was. Student Quinn, calling me a liar will not end well for you." The narrow-eyed glare promised retribution.

Quinn stared up at the harridan. Suddenly recalling Stefano's advice, she dropped her head and started wailing again.

"Student Quinn, stop this nonsense immediately. You will control yourself, clean up, and go to class. Now."

Quinn kept crying and wailing. She wasn't faking it—indenture was one step up from slavery. In most cases, it was slavery because, somehow, the terms of the contract were never completed. How would she ever get out of this? Especially with Familia.

"Totally unsuitable." Vormer turned on her heel and spoke over her shoulder. "You are confined to quarters. A meal will be brought to you. You will keep both bathrooms and the public areas on this floor sparkling for the next seven days." At the door, she turned back. "After that, you will conduct yourself properly, or the next punishment will be worse. Do you understand?"

Quinn just cried harder. Now, she wasn't faking it. All alone, no hope of rescue, enemies everywhere, nothing but a cleaning drudge, and the possibility of worse? Why not cry? There was nothing else left to do.

∆∆∆

Quinn stood in the girl's bathroom with her mop. Suzette

sneered at her and shoved her, hard. Making it look like part of her stumble, Quinn whacked her ankle with the mop handle with a loud crack. Suzette wailed.

"Sorry," Quinn muttered from her half-collapsed position against the wall. "It was an accident."

One of the other girls helped Suzette limp out and the others glared on their way out.

When they were gone, Quinn started cleaning. Most of it wasn't too bad, but it took a long time. Probably because she just didn't care. Why go fast? She was stuck here all day, doing nothing but cleaning. Her access to everything else was cut off. The only things that came over her e-torc were school-wide announcements and messages directly to her—assignments she couldn't complete because she wasn't allowed access to the student net.

She finished that sani-mod and started on the next. When she got back to her room, her only meal of the day waited—a plain plas package with a single emergency ration. She wasn't hungry, but Quinn swallowed a glass of water and ate it slowly. She'd learned if she didn't eat it all, the rest disappeared. After she finished, she drank another glass of water, hoping to stop the renewed rumbling of her partially satisfied stomach. Then, she started cleaning the hallway. She wanted to sleep, but she wasn't allowed to. Even at night, she only got an hour or two at a time, alarms ringing at unpredictable times. After six days of cleaning, the entire place sparkled. And her head swam if she stood up too quickly.

Polishing the baseboards with a cloth, she stopped when a pair of feet appeared. Looking up, she saw the face of Fitness Instructor Switz. "What, by all that is holy, are you doing?"

"Cleaning, Instructor Switz."

"Why?"

"Because that is my assigned task."

"Stand up!"

Quinn climbed slowly to her feet, putting a hand on the wall when black dots spun around her.

"What in—Vormer! What are you doing to this child!" Switz yelled into her holo.

It must be in privacy mode because Quinn couldn't hear Vormer's reply.

"She's about to pass out, you idiot," Switz snarled. "She was muscle and bone six days ago, now she's just bone. She was an *extreme athlete*. She's cannibalizing her muscles to stay alive. You could survive such a thing just fine, but she cannot. She was a growing child and you've just set that growth back, significantly. Stupid woman." She swept the holo away, glaring. "Come, Student Quinn, let's get you to the medico." Switz wrapped an arm around her and half-carried her down the stairs. "Stupid, stupid, stupid."

Quinn wasn't sure if Switz meant her or Vormer. She didn't care. Finally, they reached a medico station, the sharp smell of disinfectant rousing her. Switz settled her on the med float. Appendages appeared and attached themselves, including a clamp around her arm, followed by a needle and fluid. Switz waited until the diagnosis appeared, read it, and stomped away.

Quinn read the diagnoses on the holo above her. Electrolyte

imbalance, sudden weight loss, muscle tone atrophy, possible sleep deprivation, poor physical condition overall. Without treatment, death by starvation was possible. Assess for eating disorders.

Quinn tried to laugh but couldn't. Was not being allowed to eat considered an eating disorder? Unintelligible, strident voices penetrated the medico walls, growing from two women to a third and a couple of men. She didn't feel sorry for Vormer, not one little bit. Vormer deserved verbal abuse and more for her stupidity.

The medico chimed. Electrolytes and glucose would be administered slowly in a warm solution, to avoid shock. The patient was counseled to sleep, but medication wasn't recommended due to possible unintended side effects. Quinn closed her eyes against the pain of sudden hope. Not willing to consider a foolish notion, she concentrated on her breathing and prayed to the Mother for oblivion.

A chime sounded and Quinn woke. Blinking, she tried to wipe the sleep away from her eyes, but she couldn't move her arm. She looked down her body, seeing her right arm was clamped to the bed, an IV flowing into it. *Oh.* Now she remembered. She was in the medico—she'd gotten up to use the sani-mod a couple of times, then dropped right back into sleep. She looked at her left arm; it was free. Quinn swiped at the holo above her for her patient status. Electrolytes and fluids back in balance, feeding protocols prescribed, bed rest for another day, then a slow return to activity.

The question was, would the Academy actually allow her to

slowly recover? She probably shouldn't have taken Stefano's suggestion to such an extreme. Quinn snorted. Like she'd had a choice. But she'd learned a valuable lesson: she was vulnerable in a way she hadn't previously considered. And reasonable reactions sometimes created unreasonable reactions.

"Ah, Student Quinn, you are awake." Despite her medico-green clothing, the woman who entered had the Familia look and Quinn's heart sank. "Excellent. Since you were deprived of adequate nutrition and rest for a relatively short time, I think your recovery will be relatively short as well, and you'll be back to normal activity soon. I've put together a schedule for you, based on your previous student schedule." The woman's heavy dark brows formed a deep V. "I have reviewed your records and many vids of your experiences. Changes are being put in place to avoid further issues between students. This kind of harassment is not appropriate. Additional staff training has been mandated as well."

She held up a hand. "I understand you may not think this will be in your best interest since others are bound to blame you for their poor behavior. I have recommended you be enrolled in a different school, but I hear this isn't possible. So, I have made it clear the medico community here at Adzari will be monitoring you often and at random times. I believe some of the administration will also be monitoring you. While I would normally tell a student to ignore bullies unless physical harm results, in your case, you will notify me immediately of any and all issues. Is this understood?"

"Yes, Medico…" Quinn winced, knowing she couldn't name the woman.

"Medico Lucia. You'll get your e-torc back shortly." Lucia did something and the needle in Quinn's arm was withdrawn, a sealant sprayed on, and the clamp withdrawn. "Your clothes are there, on the chair," Lucia pointed toward Quinn's feet. "Let's get you up, slowly, and then you can get dressed." Lucia helped her sit up and get out of the bed, waiting until Quinn was steady.

The room didn't spin, nor did black spots appear, but she did feel weak. "Medico Lucia, how long have I been here?"

She chuckled. "About forty-eight hours. Most of those, you were asleep. Trust me, you needed it. Follow my prescriptions, Quinn, including the full amount of sleep, and you'll be back to athletic pursuits soon. Then Switz will get off my back." The last was muttered.

"Thank you, Medico Lucia."

"You're welcome, Student Quinn. By the way, Student Gianna will no longer be a problem. Her family found they needed her at home. Hopefully, she'll be doing something better suited to her talents." Lucia's nose wrinkled. "Most of her instructors tell me she won't be missed. Student Suzette has been moved to a different school since her inclinations seem to run more to business than net. I'm sure she'll do well there. Take advantage of this time, Student Quinn. Try to forge some connections here so you're not alone when the next bully pops up because you know one will. Oh, and try to avoid the third-years, boys and girls." Lucia scowled. "Gianna was quite popular."

Great. Like she could do that easily. But maybe with Gianna gone, some of the first-year students would be friendly. "Thank you, Medico Lucia, for your care."

"You are welcome. Don't waste it." The door shut on Medico Lucia's frowning face.

Quinn got to her feet and left the small medico facility. If she remembered correctly, the rest of the academy wasn't too far away. She set off down the path at a slow walk but had to rest at the next bench. A float bike zipped by her, then turned back. "Student Quinn, what are you doing?"

"Going back to the dorms, Instructor Stefano." She stood, unwilling to give the man who, unwittingly or not, engineered her downfall any kind of advantage.

"I am certain you are not supposed to be walking any great distances yet, Student Quinn."

She sighed. "Well, I have to get back to the dorms somehow, don't I?"

"You should have called for a ride."

"I don't have my e-torc."

His head dropped to his chest. "Of course." He huffed and raised his head. "Because it's on my desk for reprogramming. Your health will now be monitored continuously." His mouth twisted and he shrugged. "Get on." Stefano pushed his thumb over his shoulder. "I'll give you a lift and bring your e-torc to you after that."

"Is that allowed?"

"I don't care, Student Quinn, because I'm not letting you collapse and relapse. Get on." He looked straight ahead.

Quinn sighed and climbed on the lift bike. She had no choice but to put her arms around the instructor, so she did, lightly.

He started forward gently and gradually gained speed but not much. Riding along the paths, it was only a minute or two before they reached the dorms.

"Thank you, Instructor Stefano, for the ride."

"You are welcome, Student Quinn. I'll send your e-torc over shortly." He zipped away without a glance. He didn't like being near her but wouldn't leave her to stumble along either. Maybe this is what having an older brother was like? Stefano was probably as close to it as she'd ever come.

Taking a deep breath, Quinn entered the dorm. No one in sight. She started up the stairs, resting at each landing, and made her way down the hallway to her room. Entering her room, she was relieved to see nothing had been touched or moved. Good. She didn't feel like cleaning, that was for sure. She didn't really feel like staying here, either, but right now, she had no choice. She laid back on the bed and stared at the ceiling.

A knock sounded.

"Come in."

Lise stuck her head in. "Can I come in?"

"I said so, didn't I?"

She shrugged. "Yes but…" Lise flicked her fingers. "It doesn't matter. Here's your e-torc." She held it out to Quinn. "Instructor Stefano asked me to give it to you."

"Thanks." Quinn took it and slid it around her neck. She didn't feel the relief she'd normally feel. No, she felt trapped.

"Quinn?" Lise asked plaintively.

"Yes?"

"Can we start over? Now that Suzette and Gianna are gone, I'd like to see if we can be friends. We all would."

Quinn forced a smile. "Sure, we can try."

"Oh, good. Why don't you come to dinner with us tonight?" Lise's relief seemed real.

"Okay." She nodded. "Thanks."

"Of course. I'll come get you." Lise shut the door quietly.

Quinn pulled up her e-torc interface. A medico alert waited, so she brought it up. Oh, her recovery schedule. This didn't look too bad, except asking for special meals at the dining facility was bound to bring unwelcome attention. Nothing to be done about that, was there? Something seemed different about her interface. She swept through the screens and files. Well, it was faster for one. And…interesting. A privacy mode? She never had that before. Quinn bit her lip and pulled it up. It appeared to be memory, with a password. Storage for private notes?

Quinn took a breath, hope lightening her thoughts, but it crashed quickly. It was a trick, that was all, just a mean trick. She swept it away and decided a nap before dinner was a better idea than using something that would just get her in trouble. She locked her door and slept.

ᐃᐃᐃ

Lise set a tray down in front of Quinn. "Yours looks better than ours."

"Thanks. Trust me, you don't want to do what I did just for better food."

"No, I suppose not," Selena said. "Besides, I'm not an athlete. If I ate that, it would go straight to my hips." She giggled softly, drawing the attention of the boys at the next table. Not that she needed to giggle—she was beautiful. Warm tan skin, long, thick, dark brown hair, big milk chocolate eyes, and lush lips, curved in a secretive smile, Selena was a boy's favorite dream. "I have enough trouble with the fitness instructors." She frowned at her salad.

"You have good reflexes, Student Selena. You should try tennis or handball," Zara said. Tall and thin, with espresso-dark skin and eyes, Zara was elegant and ran like the wind.

Selena shuddered. "Balls whizzing at my face? No, thank you."

"When you put some effort into it, you can dance," Issa said. Isabella was Familia; she claimed it proudly. She had been a competitive dancer until an ankle injury prevented her from serious training.

"That's my only saving grace," Selena said. "I shake my hips and they all lose their minds." She laughed and wrinkled her nose.

"They're sexy hips," Tai said. "I wish I had hips or any shape at all." Tai's heritage looked similar to Quinn's: black hair, tilted dark brown eyes, and umber skin. Tai was a little taller than Quinn, but not by much.

"Me too," Quinn told her.

"You two are tiny," Mariah said. She was tall and broad, light-skinned with pale blue eyes. A powerlifter, she'd been ranked at the constellation level but decided she hated it when she hit puberty. Her parents weren't happy with her decision and shipped her off here, but she loved net work, so it had worked out well from her perspective.

"They might grow still." Amaya shrugged. "They're still young." At sixteen, she was the oldest first-year student.

Cinnamon-brown skin, dark chocolate eyes, heavy, dark brown hair, and eyebrows, with a rather beaky nose, Amaya wasn't conventionally pretty, but she seemed nicer than most of the girls. Maybe because she knew what it was like to be shunned. She said her family sent her here over religious differences.

"I doubt it," Tai replied. "I look like my aunts. Student Quinn looks a lot like some of the other families on Hiro, so I doubt she'll grow either."

"Shh. Don't say that," Issa hissed.

"Why not?" Lise asked. "It's pretty obvious."

Issa shook her head almost violently. "No, it isn't. So, Student Selena, why not dance for your fitness?" she asked in a much louder tone.

"Because they all lose their minds!" She flung her hands up. "Dance is supposed to be fun. They make it work." Selena pouted.

Quinn and the rest laughed. Switz and the other fitness instructors did have a way of sucking joy out of their workouts. It seemed odd to Quinn—they were in a net school, not in some university where they could compete at a constellation level. But everything was odd here and it was getting stranger by the day. When she went looking for the documents Mistress Vormer told her about, committing her to repay her schooling with service, she found nothing. Quinn was sure they'd spring it on all of them right before graduation.

Don't think about that right now, Quinn! She pasted a happy smile back on her face.

"Students should be eating, not chatting," Vormer sneered. "Especially you, Quinn. You must recover quickly."

"Yes, Mistress Vormer," Quinn said meekly, the others chiming in. Quinn ate, trying to enjoy the unusually good food, but it was hard with Vormer glaring at her. Vormer blamed Quinn for the mess she'd created with her starvation work plan. Quinn wanted to glare back, but her life was miserable enough. She didn't need to make it worse.

"After dinner, Selena, you will accompany Quinn while she does her prescribed walking. You need to exceed your step count requirement." Vormer stomped away.

"Cow," Selena muttered. Lise punched her arm and Selena rolled her eyes. "She needs the exercise more than I do." She huffed, exasperated, at their attempts to shush her. "It will be my pleasure to accompany you, Student Quinn."

"Thanks, Student Selena. I'll be happy to have company." She kept shoveling food in her mouth until she couldn't eat another bite. "Ugh. Too full. You guys have the rest."

"Are you sure? You're supposed to eat all of it," Amaya said.

"I really can't. I'm stuffed."

After casting a few glances around, the girls made short work of the rest.

"Oh, that is good," Selena moaned. "Good thing there isn't more."

Quinn smiled. They might be forced to include her, but at least she could sweeten the deal a little. "Are you ready to get the mandatory walk done?"

"Sure. May as well get it over," Selena said.

"We'll see you back at the dorm," Lise said.

"Sure." Quinn got up and Selena joined her, walking out of the dining hall and down the path away from the dorms.

"How far are you supposed to go?" Selena asked.

"Just a kilometer today, two tomorrow, three the next. Then I can add in some jogging." Quinn grimaced.

"Ugh. That sounds horrible."

"It's depressing. I could sprint a kilometer and easily run ten before all this."

"I don't understand why this hit you so hard and so fast," Selena said. "I know you're thin and small, but still…"

Quinn grimaced. "They said it's because I was under so much stress and training at a very high level. Most people would be just fine after five days of almost no food, but not me. Aren't I lucky?"

Selena shrugged. "Actually, you are. You could be dead. It's a good thing Instructor Switz came looking for you because all of us were too scared to say anything." She sighed. "I'm really sorry about that. We were scared, but that's not a good excuse for letting someone almost die."

Quinn sighed. "I get it. I really do. I think we're all scared. If I wasn't so scared, I would have confronted someone or asked for help. Instead, I convinced myself I was worthless. I know I'm not, but after weeks of being told that…"

"And I get that. I am truly sorry."

"Don't worry about it." Quinn scanned the area. "Hey, the Adzari garden is right there. Want to come with me for my mandated rest period?"

"Ugh. I have two more kilometers to walk than you do. How about you go rest, and I'll walk and come back and pick you up? You have plenty of study materials to catch up on, right?"

"Yes. Great idea. See you in a bit."

"Half an hour or so," Selena said, sauntering off.

Quinn snorted. At the pace Selena was walking, it would be more like an hour. One of the second-year boys jogged up to her, then fell in next to her. A giggle floated back. Quinn chuckled. Maybe even longer.

Quinn walked into the Adzari garden, looking around. It was beautiful, but it would be very easy to hide multiple vids in here. Quinn sat on a bench and brought up some of her net homework. Working through it, she finished it quickly and started the next. She might be stuck here, but she was determined to learn as much as she could, no matter what happened. Her life depended on it.

ΔΔΔ

Quinn laughed with Selena. Poor Mariah was so easy to tease. Unlike Selena, who would keep a joke going long after it ceased to be funny, Quinn couldn't stand to see anyone unhappy for long. "We're just kidding, Mariah," Quinn told her, sweeping the real net program she'd written into the shared student space.

"Oh, you two!" Mariah glared. "Why did I save your ungrateful hide?" She looked shocked for a moment and clapped both hands over her mouth.

Quinn stared at her, astounded. Mariah was the one who told Switz Quinn was in trouble?

Selena laughed long and hard, with her entire body, and then got up and danced around the room. "Fooled you! Hah. You'll always save my sexy self, Student Mariah. You just can't help yourself because I'm that awesome."

Quinn laughed with Selena, her laughter sounding far more

forced than Selena's. Thank the Mother for Selena because her quick reactions had saved them from unwanted attention several times.

Mariah glared at her. "Yeah, yeah. This better be perfect, *Student* Selena." She turned back and started working to incorporate their parts of the program into her framework. "I know I don't have to worry about Student Quinn, but you…"

Quinn let her laughter die and went back to working on the documentation for the program. Documentation was the worst. So boring. But she knew it was important because part of their lessons was attempting to use the net programs the other groups designed. Sometimes, that was practically impossible because the instructions were so bad. A clever interface couldn't make up for everything.

They'd been warned that, in future lessons, they would need to incorporate all the small group efforts into a larger whole, which meant finding and correcting the mistakes of others. None of them wanted to make that difficult because their class rank depended not only on their individual efforts but also on their leadership skills and willingness to be team players.

Quinn concentrated on her task because she knew her face gave away her thoughts too easily. If she let herself think about Mariah's statement, she might cry. She'd always wondered who tipped Switz off; Switz herself told Quinn she'd been left a written message saying Quinn's life was in danger and she had no idea who wrote or delivered it. Mariah made sense because she used the same part of the fitness facilities Quinn and Switz did, but Quinn had always thought Mariah barely tolerated her, let alone liked her enough to risk disobeying Vormer.

But Mariah's sense of right and wrong was very black and white. She followed the rules until she thought they were wrong, then she fought them long past any hope of winning or even stalemate. She'd been threatened with expulsion several times, but it didn't seem to bother her much. Probably because her parents still loved and supported her, despite Mariah crushing their hopes and dreams of making her a Universe-wide sports star. Mariah had brothers who were already stars, and she planned to support the family business with her net skills. She didn't need to graduate for that; she was good enough right now.

Quinn dropped some hints, but it seemed most of the other first-year students hadn't been threatened with the changed school contract. Whether that was because President Rias Bel was going to spring it on them later, just before graduation, or because some of them had powerful parents, Quinn didn't know. She did know that Lise, Zara, Tai, and most of the first-year boys were in the same boat she was; poor and dependent on scholarships, mostly directly from Adzari Academy.

She didn't trust any of the students fully. Any one of them could be reporting on her to the administration, willingly or not. Quinn finished off the documentation. "Done."

"Good," Mariah said. "And great job on the program too. Student Selena, you're a pain but when you actually work, you do a good job. I've integrated all of it, and it's running smoothly. If you two want to test it, I'll review the documentation."

"Of course, Student Mariah."

"Sure," Selena said. "Then, it's dinner time! Finally."

Quinn laughed. Trust Selena to concentrate on the important things.

ΛΛΛ

"Come on, Quinn, you have to have some fun," Selena said.

"Student Selena, that's Student Quinn to you," Vormer's unpleasant voice said.

"Oh, of course, House Mistress Vormer. It won't happen again," Selena blinked up at her innocently.

Quinn kept her face straight with some effort, but she managed it. Selena said, "it won't happen again," time after time, but the Administration's efforts to change her were useless. Last time she'd been punished, restricted to her dorm room, her father, a popular politician here on Omicron, showed up for a visit and took her away for three days. When Selena came back, her family brought a big party along with them: food, drinks, and a dance band, setting up everything in a big tent on one of the sports fields. They also brought local media along to vid Selena's father making a big donation to the Academy's scholarship fund—President Rias Bel's jaw was so tight, Quinn thought she might break teeth.

No one knew how Selena was getting word to her family, but Quinn suspected code words similar to hers. Every week Quinn sent a message back to the Sisters, including the code words telling them not to send anyone else. She had no idea if her messages were getting through—she'd only gotten one back from the Sisters shortly after she got here. Quinn wouldn't even bother sending more, but the Administration insisted.

"Well, Student Quinn?" Selena asked archly. "What else are

you going to do? Sit in your room and study? So boring. Come on, it's not like we're going dive hopping in the spaceport; we're going to my family's compound on North Island. It's very safe and secure." Selena tilted her head and tapped her lips. "I know! What if I let you talk to the security guys on the compound! You can ask them all kinds of questions and stuff. But!" She held up a finger. "You have to make time for me and enjoy yourself. You only get an hour a day with security."

Quinn bit her lip. "Two."

"One and a half." Selena raised a single brow.

"Deal."

"You're so ridiculous. This shouldn't even be a discussion!" Selena threw up her hands. "Who else turns down a chance to relax someplace beautiful?"

Someone who won't be allowed to leave the Academy? The question was, how badly would it impact Selena's family?

"But…"

Selena scowled. "But?"

"Only if the Administration allows it. If they don't, please don't fight it. Please?" Quinn widened her eyes pleadingly.

Selena narrowed her eyes in return. "Agreed. I understand. My father has fought the Administration enough lately."

And she was sure Selena understood more than Quinn knew.

∆∆∆

Unfortunately, Quinn was right. At the shuttle pad, Selena hugged her. "Get out of your room, girl, even if I'm not here to drag you out." She stood back and took Quinn by the shoulders. "Take care. Best of luck." Her expression was mournful and

Quinn knew Selena wasn't coming back. Selena hugged her tight again, then let her go.

"You too, Selena." Quinn forced a smile. "May the Mother bless us both."

Selena walked to her father, sliding an arm around his waist, and he pulled her in close, his arm around her shoulder.

What would it be like to have someone care that much about you? Someone willing to fight Familia for you? Selena and her father waved at her from the hatch, then the Quinn had to leave the area. The shuttle took off, taking her best friend with it.

Well, at least she had other friends here. Selena was the most fun, but the rest of them still had each other. And she knew Selena was safe—that was worth the pain of losing her.

CHAPTER SEVEN

"Student Quinn, you've made good progress. Keep it up." Instructor Stefano walked to the next desk.

She sighed, feeling ten times lighter. Praise from Stefano was hard to come by, but she'd worked so hard on her first-year capstone project. At least all her efforts to learn every bit of net expertise she could and the Atlas Challenge kept her too busy and tired to brood.

Despite that, with every class and project she completed, the confines of Adzari Academy seemed to grow smaller, like someone was watching, waiting to pounce, and she had nowhere to run. Which was unfortunately true. There wasn't anywhere for her to run. Vehicles were restricted to instructors and administration, and messages went through a central hub. The Academy was physically isolated, so even if she managed to escape the grounds, her chances of making it to a spaceport were just about zero. The Sisters should know there was something wrong—Quinn used the right codes and phrases to tell them—but that wouldn't help her. It only kept them from sending anyone else to Adzari.

Selena kept sending them gifts full of delicious food, little games, and pictures of her high-society events, but after the initial joy, it just reminded all of them that an entirely different life existed outside Adzari. That life felt very far away.

They were starting their second-year studies soon, but the feeling of entrapment grew faster than the feeling of accomplishment. Especially when Quinn knew their class wasn't being taught some critical net skills. She'd asked for clarification and additional information on several net techniques and was told those were advanced-year concepts. But they weren't. Some of the friendlier second-year students confirmed it in casual conversation. Quinn watched and learned what she could from them, but she couldn't just come out and ask without those students getting in trouble. She did receive extra tutorials from Instructor Stefano, but they stuck to the same subjects they were being taught now. Not that she trusted him—it was his advice that got her in trouble. Although, she was sure he hadn't foreseen those particular consequences.

After Selena left, her class was no longer allowed to do group projects either. All their work was done alone. Sure, they all helped each other, but that wasn't the same as learning how to work as a team. They didn't even present their projects in class— the instructors graded them and gave them written feedback. The leadership and management courses the second- and third-year students got—before the Academy changed ownership—weren't taught to them either. Quinn overheard enough conversations to know that.

Someone was keeping them in the dark, trying to deliberately limit their skill sets. From the little she knew about Familia, it made sense. They didn't want their net techs able to stage an effective rebellion or takeover. No, they would compartmentalize their skills and permissions, confining them to a subset of abilities to keep them under control.

Well, they could try. Quinn sniffed. She had excellent spying skills; Sister Ani had taught her well. She'd learned more than most of the Academy instructors intended and once she got out of here, she would learn more still. The one thing they couldn't keep from teaching was *how* to learn. And even though they weren't taught leadership and management, she'd learned the basics at the Sisters. She had plenty of good and bad examples right in front of her. She'd keep watching and learning. Quinn smiled. And spying. She was good at that—people underestimated her all the time. They looked at her and saw a little girl.

Instructor Stefano returned to the front of the room. "Students, you have all done very well. I'm pleased with your projects. The other instructors agree: all of you are ready to move on to your second year." He scanned the room but didn't meet Quinn's eyes. "It's been a pleasure working with all of you. You have been excellent students. Thank you for the opportunity to teach you. I wish you all luck in the coming year." He cleared his throat. "However, many of you must speak to the administrative staff about the state of your accounts before continuing your studies. I don't know the particulars, but it seems there are some payment issues. Stay here. You'll be called out individually." He whirled and stomped out of the room.

And there it was, dropping like a rock into a Secundus mud

puddle, splashing nasty muck everywhere. After House Mistress Vormer told her about the new contract for studying here, Quinn looked for that contract in every single one of her student files and official messages from the administration. She found nothing. But she'd expected the Academy to spring it on them at graduation, not at the end of their first year.

Quinn bit her lip. This couldn't be good. She sat and listened as name after name was called. All her friends except Issa and Zara left and didn't return.

"Quinn Cygnus, report to Conference Room Ten," a voice said over her e-torc. Conference Ten was on the third floor; they were on the second.

She sighed and rose slowly. Turning slightly as she walked from the room, she waved to her friends and they waved back. Trudging up the stairs, she wondered how she could get out of this. Exiting the stairwell, she jumped at the presence of personnel in soft armor. She hadn't seen someone armed and armored like that since the evacuation of Cygnus Gliese. What was the Academy expecting?

Taking in a deep breath, she walked down the hall to the right room and entered.

"Ah, Quinn Cygnus. Have a seat."

A woman with the too-familiar Familia look sat at the end of the table. She was pretty, but Quinn was fairly certain she was older than she looked. She wore an expensive-looking shipsuit in a vibrant fuchsia, with big green gemstones around her neck and ears, and a sweetly flowered scent drifted through the room. A huge person in soft armor stood just behind her, clearly a guard.

So, this was someone important. Quinn sat, leaving a chair between the two of them.

"I am Trevi, an investigator for the organization that owns Adzari Academy. We have recently completed a review of the accounts here at the Academy and found several serious issues." She smiled, but it was a threat, not happiness. "Your account is in arrears. The few payments that have been made are completely inadequate."

Quinn had to object, even knowing it would do little good. "Investigator Trevi, that isn't correct. I have the receipt from Adzari Academy, sent to the Sisters of Cygnus before I left, showing my schooling paid in full after the scholarship was applied."

Trevi sniffed. "Unfortunately for you, all scholarships were canceled when the Academy was purchased. Not only that, but it was only an academic scholarship. It did not pay for your uniforms, food, or athletic training. You also have a significant medico bill."

"The medico bill is the Academy's fault. That is not my bill to pay!"

The woman smirked. "You'd think so, but unfortunately for you, it's not so. No, you owe a significant number of credits, and your Sisters have refused to pay. Therefore, you will be working off your debt. You have a term of three years. You will accompany me now to *Indomito*, your new home for the foreseeable future."

"But—"

"Quinn Cygnus, do not fight me on this. You are going. You can go on your own two feet, or I'll have Nunzi here stun you."

Trevi tossed her head back toward the armored figure and smirked. "I don't care about you or your little friends here. No one is coming to your rescue." She got up and sauntered to the door. "Come. Now."

Quinn swallowed hard and followed the woman out. She had no choice. In the hall, the second and third-year students stared, eyes wide, and jumped out of their way. Her friend Amaya, pushed back against the wall, mouthed, "good luck," and waved, but it was clear there was nothing she could do. If only Quinn could say goodbye to her friends…but it wasn't going to happen. At least Amaya could tell them she was being forced to leave. Quinn waved back but couldn't smile.

They walked down the stairs, Trevi muttering about backwater planets without proper grav lifts, out of the building, and into one of the administration's small lift vehicles. Quinn was pushed into the back seat, squeezed in next to the huge guard.

They practically flew down the roads to the farthest reaches of the Academy grounds. A shuttle waited there, hatch open and ramp down. Trevi left the lift vehicle without a word, and Quinn followed Nunzi, the guard hulking behind her. They entered the main cabin of the shuttle, a pilot and co-pilot already strapped in. Trevi sat in a seat right behind the pilot and pointed at the seat next to her. Quinn sat and strapped in. Nunzi sat behind them.

"Ready for takeoff, Enforcer Trevi," the pilot said over her shoulder. "Just need final clearance from Omicron control." He swept what appeared to be their flight path up to the display screen in the shuttle.

"Let's go," Trevi replied. She glanced at Quinn's body,

checking the harness. "We're ready."

Guess Nunzi was expected to take care of himself. Quinn's mouth twisted. What was an enforcer? She almost heard the pilot capitalize the title.

Some muttering from the pilot and co-pilot, then a muted roaring, and Quinn's body grew heavy for a second until the grav generators kicked in. Quinn sat in silence, watching them fly and glancing around the shuttle. This wasn't cheap plas and cerimetal like the Grus shuttle or her faded memories of Lightwave's shuttles. This was a luxury transport. The cocoa-colored cover on her seat was soft and smooth and the padding cradled her in a firm cloud. The tan floor was soft and springy, but smooth. The walls of the shuttle were slightly textured and colored a warm beige. The kitchen was outfitted with expensive automated appliances. Even the hardware on the emergency hatches looked expensive, and the labels were understated, in an elegant script. It even smelled expensive—a combination of coffee, warm spices, and citrus. On the big screen in front of them, a representation of their shuttle crossed into orbit.

The co-pilot, an older man, turned to them. "You may now walk about the cabin, but we prefer you stay strapped in when possible. We're not anticipating trouble, but you never know. The cabins, sani-mods, and galley are available for your use. We'll prepare a meal in a few hours. Your seats recline fully if you'd like to sleep here. We will arrive at *Indomito* in nine hours and ten minutes."

Trevi's lip curled. "That long?"

"Sorry, Enforcer." He shrugged. "We were instructed not to

draw attention to ourselves. Omicron is crowded. Outgoing is always slower."

Trevi sighed. "I need to speak with Quinn in private. I'll use Cabin One."

"Of course, Enforcer." The co-pilot said.

Trevi unbuckled. "Come, Quinn, let's go."

Quinn unfastened the straps and followed Trevi to the hatch marked Cabin One. She noticed hatches to the right marked Cabin Two and Crew Quarters. Once inside Cabin One, Trevi shut and locked the hatch and pointed at the bed on the right. The room was long and narrow, with two beds, a narrow aisle separating them, and a hatch marked sani-mod beyond. Quinn sat down, and scooted back, leaning against the wall. No reason not to get comfortable.

Trevi did something with her holo and then exhaled with a little "ah" sound. She sat on the bed opposite Quinn's, also so the wall supported her. "Isn't this cozy." She sneered at the space, which seemed rather large for a shuttle to Quinn. "Ah, well, in nine hours, it won't matter." Trevi frowned at her. "From your records, it's clear you aren't stupid. I don't think you're very attractive, but nobody cares what I think. Pay attention, Quinn, because this is your only chance to get some real information. Don't waste my time with useless protests, or I'll stop talking. Capisce?"

"What?" Quinn swallowed. She didn't understand any of this.

A heavy sigh. "Capisce is a question. It means, 'do you understand?'"

"Oh. Yes." Quinn understood Trevi's words but the real

meaning? No, she didn't understand anything. But Quinn knew she was lying to herself—she understood far too much.

Eyebrows raised. "Yes, Enforcer."

"Sorry. Yes, Enforcer." Now the Academy's emphasis on calling everyone by a title made a lot more sense.

"Good. So, here's the bottom line. You're in debt to Familia. Not only that, but Head Enforcer Enzo has also taken a personal interest in you." Trevi scanned her from head to toe. "I don't know why, but he has. You are fourteen standards now, correct?"

"Yes, Enforcer." Quinn's breathing sped up, and she bit her lip.

"Your medical records show you are generally in good health, but you might be older. Why is that?"

"Because I was abandoned as a small child, Enforcer. No one knows exactly how old I am." Quinn shrugged. "No one cares." She tried to regulate her breathing. Panic did no good.

"Ah. Well, either way, Head Enforcer Enzo has no interest in children, but he is waiting to see what you look like when you are older." Trevi smirked.

Quinn mashed her lips together to keep from screaming and clenched her fists.

"Ah, I see you guess what this could mean. Let me tell you how to make this as easy as possible, for us and for you." Her mouth turned up on one end, and she shrugged. "Not that any of us care about you, particularly. Do your job and do it well, no matter what they tell you to do. Don't complain. You can make friends, but any hint that any of them, male or female, might become a lover will end in their death. And your life will become significantly worse. No sex for you." Trevi held up a finger and wagged it at her.

"Do whatever Enzo requires and do it quietly. And, as you've probably guessed, those three years of repayment for your Academy schooling are only the beginning." Trevi jabbed a finger at her. "You're Enzo's until he says otherwise. If anyone on the ship ever touches you with sexual intent or intent to harm, report it to me or another enforcer immediately. If it's an enforcer, go straight to Head Enforcer Enzo. Everyone should be smart enough not to mess with you, but there's always a few who think they can get away with stupidity. Even on the head Justice's ship." Trevi tilted her head. "Capisce?"

"Yes, Enforcer." Quinn's forehead hurt, and her mouth and eyes were dry. She blinked and rolled her shoulders, trying to relax. Fight or flight were both useless here and now.

"Good. Now, a little background. *Indomito* is Justice Fatima's ship. The Justice mediates disputes between Familia. Enzo is her Head Enforcer and my boss. Enforcers carry out the Justice's orders, which are quite often fatal, for people and businesses." An ironic smile flashed. "In other words, you're on a ship of killers. Capisce?"

"Yes, Enforcer." She couldn't escape the Academy; her chances of escaping *Indomito* were even worse. Quinn gulped.

"I'm sure you'll be put to work as a net tech. Don't snoop. You'll be caught. Do your assigned work and nothing more. There is a fitness facility on *Indomito*. You'll be assigned a time slot. Continue your current training. Fitness Instructor Switz will send you training plans. Vid from the fitness facility will be sent to her. It's not ideal but the best we can do." Trevi snort-chuckled. "We all train, but not for those skills. Do not ask to learn our skills." She sneered. "Don't try it on your own, either. You'll fail, spectacularly."

"Yes, Enforcer." At least she'd have that outlet to burn off stress.

"Anyone who says they want to help you is lying. Don't believe them. They're only out to help themselves. Familia works on favors. Do someone a favor, they owe you one." Trevi snickered. "But anyone who asks you for a favor is really asking for a favor from Enzo. Do not put him in debt. Likewise, anyone saying they'll do a favor for you is actually doing one for Enzo. Again, don't put him in debt. Every time you do something he doesn't like, life will get worse for you. It gets worse for the rest of us too. So just don't do it. And anyone who says they can help you escape is lying. No one escapes Familia, except through death. Capisce?"

"Yes, Enforcer."

"Good. Now, I've done what I can for you. Behave. Do not make me punish you. You will not like the results." Trevi stood and again did something to her holo. "I suggest you get some sleep. The *Indomito* is on a different schedule from the planet, so you'll have to adjust." Trevi shrugged. "I have no idea what schedule you'll be assigned to either. It's not my problem." She glared down. "But misbehave and you become my problem. Don't. You will not like the results." Trevi turned on her heel and left the room.

Quinn slid down the bedpost to lie flat on the bed. The covering was slightly fuzzy, warm, and soft. The mattress was heavenly. A message flashed above her bed: "Strap in before sleeping," with a diagram. She felt along the edge of the bed with her left hand and found a bar. She lifted it across her body, and it snapped into place on the right side of the bed near the aisle. The straps were a slightly stretchy net, loose now, meant to hold her in place in case they lost gravity or had some other emergency. Quinn released the bar, letting it retract, sat up, and took off her shoes. Then she wriggled under the covers and put the net back over her.

She brought up her e-torc interface, but it wouldn't connect to the shuttle's net. Quinn bit her lip. She couldn't get it to connect manually either. She could dig further, but Trevi just warned her not to snoop. Well, sand fleas. With nothing else to do, she may as well nap.

Composing herself, she monitored her breathing and relaxed, knowing she'd feel better if she slept or at least meditated. She'd still have plenty of time to process all this information when she woke, and the meditation would calm her panic.

∆∧∆

The pilot and co-pilot talked softly as they neared *Indomito*, then both put their hands on their armrests. Quinn watched as the shuttle docked, the almost imperceptible thunk of the shuttle clamps not as loud as the thunk of doom in her heart. On the planet, she had a hope of escape. In space? On this ship? None. She swallowed hard.

The pilot turned. "Enforcer Trevi, we're securely docked. Medico staff are waiting for the girl."

"Excellent." Trevi turned to her. "Let's go, Quinn." She walked away, obviously sure Quinn would follow her. If she didn't, Nunzi loomed over her, ready to pick her up and carry her away. She'd managed to ignore the man until now, but it was no longer possible.

Quinn unbuckled and stood. "Thank you, pilot, co-pilot, for the meal and the flight. Safe folds." They both seemed rather startled but nodded in return. Quinn followed Trevi into the airlock, which opened into another airlock. Nunzi at her back, the hatch closed with a thunk, and the final hatch slid aside. Biting her lip, Quinn stepped into *Indomito*.

Trevi faced two people in medico green shipsuits. "Medico Marcello, this is Quinn Cygnus. Did the Academy send her medical records?"

The man, with the now-familiar espresso-dark hair and eyes and olive-toned skin, said, "Yes. I will give her a thorough examination immediately."

Trevi raised a brow. "And the other matter?"

Marcello grimaced just slightly but said, "Of course, Enforcer Trevi. As Head Enforcer Enzo specified. Technician Natali will take care of that." He nodded sideways at the woman who stood slightly behind him. She had the same hair, eye, and skin color as the man, but her smile seemed genuine. Like most people, both were taller than Quinn was.

"You don't approve."

"It's not my place to approve or not, Enforcer. I will do as I am required to do. But such things can cause health problems in some people."

"I'm sure Head Enforcer Enzo understands that."

"I'm sure he does. Do you have any further instructions, Enforcer?"

"No." Trevi turned and walked away without saying anything else. Medico Marcello walked the opposite direction. Before Quinn could wonder, Medico Natali said, "Follow me, please." She turned to follow Marcello, walking quickly until she was right behind him. Quinn trailed along, aware Nunzi was still shadowing her.

They trod a long corridor with dark wood-look plas flooring and roughly textured beige walls, art hanging on them. The pictures appeared to be real paintings, not simple prints or screens—pretentious still-life and fancily-dressed humans. Eventually, they reached a lift tube and went up three levels, stepping off into another luxuriously appointed corridor. They immediately turned and entered a room with a few chairs and a small beverage station. They didn't stop there but kept walked through a hatchway and stopped in front of a closed hatch.

Marcello said, "Let me know when she's ready." He walked away.

Natali motioned to the hatch. "This is a changing room. Take everything off and put the gown on, opening in the front, then come out here."

Quinn nodded, put her hand on the hatch, and walked in after it slid aside. As the hatch closed, she heard Natali say, "I'm sure we can handle her from here if you have other duties."

Hopefully, Nunzi did because Quinn didn't like the thought of being practically naked around the thuggish guard. Or anyone, but she didn't have much of a choice. She peeled off her school uniform and put on the gown. The gown wasn't horrible. The material was substantial cloth, not cheap veg plas, and it overlapped and tied securely. She left her clothes behind in the tiny room.

"Good," Natali said. "Follow me."

Quinn did, happy Nunzi had found something else to do. His lack of expression made her shiver. They trod down the hall and entered a room marked "Exam One" with a large, white medico bed. Usually, these beds had mechanical arms hanging all around them, but this one didn't. They must be stored away until they were needed, so they didn't freak out the high-status patients. Although, with a ship this large, Quinn wouldn't be surprised if they had separate medico beds for crew and passengers. Maybe she wasn't entirely considered staff? She bit her lip. She'd rather be a nobody.

Natali poked something in her holo, and privacy shields popped into place between the door and the medico bed. "Take the gown off and lie down on the bed, face up. The medico will take your vital signs and do blood analysis." She tilted her head with a wry smile. "It's also going to do a full pelvic exam, so when it tells you to put your legs in the stirrups and hold still, please do so. This medico is top-of-the-line and very gentle, so don't worry. It will be over before you know it." Natali sniffed. "Trust me when I tell you it's much better than a person doing it. Just hop on. I'll be just beyond the privacy screen. If you have questions or need something, let me know."

"Okay." Quinn did as she was told. As soon as she was settled, a holo appeared above her face, asking if she wanted no information, normal patient information, or full medico information. Quinn selected the medico version, figuring she could always ask for clarification of things she didn't understand. She also assumed the programming was smart enough to start with the simple patient version and then give more details as the patient wanted. Once she made the choice, various arms came out of the machine, doing all the things she expected. Medico Natali was right—the pelvic exam was gentle—Quinn hardly felt anything. She lowered her legs back to the bed, relieved that part was so easy.

Then straps snapped around her waist, thighs, ankles, and wrists. "By the Mother, what's going on?"

Natali came through the privacy screens and sighed. "I'm sorry, Quinn, but this is part of our instructions. You're to be marked and tagged. Please don't fight the machine. It will be far more painful if it has to be redone." She poked at her holo and retreated.

Quinn squeezed her eyes shut. Marked and tagged like a herd animal? Sand fleas, every one of them. A stunner buzzed and a spot just above her left buttock went numb. Then something stabbed her, hard enough to jolt her against the straps. It wasn't painful, exactly, because the area was numb, but she felt the force and the size of the thing. It wasn't small. The probe retracted and she heard a hiss—probably sealant. That was going to hurt later.

Another stunner buzzed across the stretch of skin below her belly button, covering the area between her pelvic bones. An arm came out and a fine needle stabbed her, over and over, leaving a line of black across her skin. Quinn watched in horror as an elaborate scroll pattern appeared, the name "Enzo" emblazoned in a fancy script in the middle, all in thick, black lines. It was ugly.

Quinn sniffed but blinked back her tears. She was not going to let these people see her cry. Then she remembered what Instructor Stefano said, the only person who had treated her kindly at the Academy. "You'll do much better if you whine and cry and carry on. He hates crying women. If he sees you like that, he'll leave you alone."

The tactic backfired with Vormer, but Stefano still might be right about Enzo. Besides, Quinn was scared and alone—she couldn't hold the fear back. She sobbed, letting all her terror, anxiety, panic, and dread out. She cried during the rest of the tattoo, not even looking at the finished product, and continued to bawl as the machine cleaned the blood and excess ink from her skin. A sprayer hissed and she glanced down to see some sort of shiny medical sealant being applied. She kept crying even after all the medico equipment and straps released.

Natali appeared again, frowning. "Stop crying. You'll dehydrate yourself and have to stay here longer. Get the robe on." She spun on her heel and walked back through the screens.

Quinn did as she was told, putting the gown back on. The privacy screens disappeared. Natali handed her tissues and she blew her nose and wiped her eyes. She kept one, intending to keep sniveling wherever they were going next.

"Sit there. Medico Marcello will be in shortly."

Quinn plopped down in the chair, acting like the sulky teen she wasn't. The younger she could make herself seem, the longer she'd be left alone and underestimated. Hopefully, she'd learn more too. Enough to escape this place—a folder. Now, she had to learn piloting along with net skills. Suddenly, she wasn't acting anymore. How was she going to do all that without any help at all? Because she couldn't trust anyone.

Medico Marcello entered and sat. "Net Technician Trainee Quinn. I see in your records that you are a high-level athlete, and you were treated for malnutrition due to mistreatment by staff last year. Your recovery seems adequate, but I do not approve of your previous medico's treatment. The return to intense athletic training was far too fast for someone of your stated age. I am ordering strict limits on your training and ordering time for sedentary recreation, such as net games. This should allow your body sufficient time to recover while you are maturing. Young humans should not be over-trained. This can delay maturation and cause medical issues later in life. Do you understand?"

Quinn swallowed hard and allowed her lower lip to pout. "But training is the only time I had any fun. You're mean!"

Marcello sighed. "Didn't you hear me? I'm prescribing fun for you. You will have at least two hours a day when you can participate in non-physical fun. Games, net simulations, and no work of any kind. Do you understand?"

"Yes, Medico." Quinn lowered her eyes and stared at her lap, wiping her nose. "Is there anyone else on board my age?"

"Not as young as you. You will be allowed to participate in some net simulations and games with the adults on board, and if we're near an approved station or planet, on the net there. Only approved games, Trainee Quinn. Nothing for adults only, capisce?"

"Yes, Medico." She kept her eyes down, carefully remaining meek, and sniffled.

"Technician Natali will take you to your assigned compartment. You will remain there until tomorrow. I suggest you read the care instructions for the tattoo you just received. Failure to follow these could result in infection and scarring. When you are done with that, study the folder's layout, so you understand where you are allowed to go and what levels you should avoid. Pain meds will be dispensed for you and food brought to you. You will meet your supervisor tomorrow morning; they will escort you to breakfast. Do you understand all this?"

"Yes, Medico."

"Good. Pay attention and obey your orders. I do not want to see you here again." Marcello stood and left the room, Natali coming in before the door shut.

"Let's go."

"But what about my clothes?" Quinn whined.

"You'll be issued new ones. They'll be in your compartment. Come."

Quinn followed Natali out of the Medico area, down one level on the float tube, and into another corridor with the same dark wood-like plas flooring and sand-textured walls, a shade lighter than the first corridor they'd entered. The artwork here seemed more amateurish, but it was displayed in pretty frames, similar to the ones she'd seen before.

At the very end of the corridor, Natali stopped. "Put your hand on the sensor and stare at the eye sensor. You'll get an e-torc from your supervisor tomorrow. Follow Medico Marcello's directions and you'll be fine." Natali grimaced. "Good luck."

Quinn followed the directions and the door slid to the right. Fancy. She entered the room and stopped, surprised. She'd been expecting a dorm room with bunk beds and a tiny closet, but that wasn't what she saw here. It wasn't a big room, maybe four meters by three, and the bed took up most of the space. But there was also a comfortable-looking velvety green plush chair near a fold-down desk and a sani-mod at the back. She walked in, and the door slid shut behind her. She sank into the dark brown carpet under her feet, so she kicked off the flimsy slippers. Soft and plush, it cradled her slightly swollen toes. Too much sitting on the shuttle she guessed.

She sat on the edge of the bed. Somehow firm and cushy, the sage-green cover was soft, poufy, and light. It was probably nice and warm. Quinn was tempted to just curl up and sleep, but she needed to check out the rest of her cage. As she put her hand to the sani-mod door, it slid aside. *Very fancy.* Inside, the floor looked like some sort of natural stone tiles in swirls of beige and brown. She stepped in. Warm underfoot, it was probably plas, but expensive plas, and heated too. The sink was set in a meter-long cabinet, with storage underneath. She opened the main doors to find plush brown towels, with shampoo and other toiletries that looked expensive. Above the sink, there was a mirror and a cabinet. The cabinet contained something called a "Beauty in a Box" and a "Style-Net 2500." Neither one seemed to have a control interface, so she'd need an e-torc to use them. A large shower enclosure stood next to the sink. Quinn opened the frosted plas door to find multiple showerheads and an option for a sonic shower. A small door beyond the shower revealed the toilet. Her brows raised—super fancy and super pricey.

Behind her, the wall was covered with more cabinets. Opening them, many were empty. But there was one with plain, dark gray shipsuits, another with workout clothes, including the kind she needed for the Atlas Challenge, a smaller one with underthings and sleepwear, and a lower cabinet filled with various boots and shoes.

The last cabinet contained a bewildering variety of fabrics and colors. Biting her lip, she pulled out a hanger with something pink and sparkly. It seemed to be a dress, but it wasn't like any dress she'd ever seen. The top was sheer and long but had a bra-type thing built-in that wasn't see-through. The skirt was short and fluffy, with lots of layers—it looked a little like a flower. *Ew.* Quinn's lip curled. She wasn't wearing that. She pulled out hanger after hanger, seeing fancy clothing that covered very little of her body but in a very childish style.

These outfits were a huge danger sign.

The Sisters taught them about the various kinds of human predators across the universe. Some of the worst went after children, girls and boys who should be too young for any kind of sexual relations, but those horrible beings didn't care—they only cared about themselves. The Sisters warned them about people who gave extravagant gifts, especially gifts that were too mature for their age. Quinn took in a deep breath and let it out slowly. She shouldn't show her revulsion—there might be vids in here. Too bad she hadn't considered that earlier. She carefully hung the clothes back in the cabinet and closed it firmly.

If there were vids in here, where could she change? Maybe the toilet? Quinn sighed. If someone was absolutely determined to watch her, there was little she could do about it right now. She'd be patient, learn the net, then figure out how to fool the vids in her rooms. Until then, she'd change her underwear in the toilet, and do her best to believe no one wanted to watch her pee. She didn't have any other options that wouldn't give her away.

The safest thing she could do was make them believe she was ignorant and naïve. Otherwise, they'd start wondering if she was trying to escape. She couldn't take any stupid chances at escape either. She had to lull them into complacency, make them believe she was compliant and grateful for the opportunity to live like this.

It was luxurious and far better than anything she'd expected. But a gilded cage was still a cage. Quinn wondered exactly what songs she'd be expected to sing. Especially for Head Enforcer Enzo.

CHAPTER EIGHT

Quinn woke to a chiming sound. Without an e-torc, she had no idea what time it was or when she was expected to be ready. After a remote delivered her dinner last night, she'd inspected her entire room but found no way to control the large viewing screen or anything else. After discovering the door was locked, she'd spent a very boring evening fruitlessly searching for control panels and singing kids' songs to herself. With nothing to do, she'd finally given up and gone to bed. Despite the extremely comfortable bed, she hadn't slept well.

For one, the topical painkillers applied to her tattoo and tracker insertion point wore off, so her only comfortable sleeping position was on her right side. And that wasn't particularly comfortable either. Quinn pleaded for pain relief pills in the sani-mod but got nothing. Either no one was watching, no one cared, or she was missing something.

The most obvious thing she was missing was an e-torc. Quinn desperately hoped she'd get one today, as Medico Natali claimed.

The chime kept ringing, so Quinn said, "Acknowledged." That didn't help. "Understood." Nope. "I'm getting up already!" She sighed and rolled out of bed, gasping at the pain and grabbing her lower belly, making the pain worse. She wiped away the tears. "Ow."

The stupid chime just kept going. Was it the door? Quinn took the few steps over and opened it. A woman stood there. She had the too-familiar Familia look—dark brown hair and eyes, olive-toned skin, and a slightly beaky nose. Medium height and girth—much bigger than Quinn but who wasn't—she was dressed in a dark gray shipsuit similar to the ones in Quinn's sani-mod and seemed to be young but not a child. She wore subtle makeup.

"Why aren't you dressed? It's time for your orientation, Trainee Quinn," the woman snapped.

"Because I have no idea what time it is or what I'm supposed to be doing!" Quinn whined. "Nobody's told me anything!"

"It's on your schedule."

"What schedule? I don't have a schedule!"

The woman's gaze finally narrowed in on Quinn's neck. "Oh." She sighed. "An e-torc was supposed to be delivered last night with your dinner."

"Well, it wasn't." Quinn stomped her foot like a little kid.

"I see that. Go shower and dress. Wear one of the shipsuits and black shoes like these," she pointed at her feet. "I'll send a remote with breakfast, and I'll return when I find your assigned e-torc."

"Thank you," Quinn said, truly grateful. The woman turned to go. "Hey, what's your name?"

"I'm Net Technician Paola. You can call me Tech Paola."

"Thank you, Tech Paola."

Paola nodded and closed the door between them. Quinn didn't

bother to check; she was sure it was locked. Instead, she did as she was told, showering and dressing. But rather than the black shoes, she wore black boots. She wasn't armed and had little hope of protecting herself against anyone larger than she was—which was almost everyone—but the boots gave her a small edge.

She finger-combed her hair to the best of her ability and brushed her teeth. At least the shower and toothbrushes weren't net-enabled. Although, she suspected the shower controls could be adjusted with an e-torc. She hoped so, because being blasted by every nozzle in the shower at full strength was a bit much, especially on her stomach and the insertion site on her back.

Quinn slumped in the chair, trying to wait patiently. It was the only thing she could do—moving hurt too much.

The door chime sounded, and Quinn forced herself off the chair. Tech Paola was there, holding out an e-torc.

"Thank you!" Quinn said, placing it around her neck. She immediately spun through the menus, looking for her room controls.

"Come now, Trainee Quinn. We're late."

"Wait!"

Paola turned back. "What?"

"I need some pain meds."

"I can take you to the medico."

"They said they'd prescribe me some."

"Ah, then into the sani-mod you go." Paola shooed her that way. "When you enter, your e-torc will automatically bring the controls up. Look for the medico menu and select 'my medications.' It will dispense inside the cabinet above the sink."

Quinn hurried into the sani-mod, watching her e-torc. Sure enough, the controls appeared, and she selected the ones specified. When she opened the cabinet above the sink, a slot opened, and a pill waited. She pulled it out and took it. Her e-torc sent her an alert and she selected it. Another medication? She looked at the slot. A small tube this time. The instructions said, "Apply topically every eight hours." Quinn shimmied out of the top of her shipsuit, letting it drop, and pulled the cap off the tube. It was a spray, so she sprayed the tattoo and the insertion point for the tracker. *Ah, relief.*

A gasp sounded loud in the sani-mod. Quinn looked up to see Paola's eyes wide, staring at the ugly tattoo, her hand covering her mouth. Quinn pulled her shipsuit up and fastened it. When she looked at Paola again, the technician's expression was neutral.

Quinn scowled. "I didn't ask for this and nobody asked me. They just did it."

"I see. Well, Trainee Quinn, let's go. We're behind schedule." Paola turned and marched away, Quinn scrambling to keep up with her. Paola stopped just outside the door. "Your e-torc should bring up your compartment menus when you near the hatch. But if it doesn't, you're looking for 'My Compartment Controls.' Is that clear?"

"Yes, Tech Paola." This was a ship, so it made sense they'd call the rooms compartments.

"Please review all emergency procedures by tomorrow morning. If there's an emergency, stay in your compartment or workspace. If you're in the dining hall, fitness facility, or a lounge, follow the instructions on your e-torc. All personnel compartments are vacuum-rated. If a compartment is holed, that means the shields have been breached and it's unlikely any of us will survive." Paola flipped a hand. "That's extremely unlikely. The Chief Justice's ship has never been attacked. Nobody wants to offend the Justice. That's a quick trip to a big black hole."

They came to the lift tube Quinn used yesterday. There were a lot more people around this time. Most wore plain shipsuits in subdued colors, but some wore bright patterns or jewel tones. Quite a few wore mostly black, but the shipsuits also had barely noticeable vertical white stripes, and the tops gaped open. Bright white shirts showed beneath, with an odd, thin strip of material hanging from their necks down the center of the shirt in many different colors and patterns. Everyone stepped aside for the black-suited people, so Quinn assumed they were Enforcers.

"Come, we are rising to level seven. You're on four. Most of us are housed on level six, but you're a special case, I guess." Paola stepped into the lift tube and Quinn followed, hoping she timed it so she didn't run into anyone. She wasn't used to these things.

She followed Paola off the lift tube and into another corridor. This one looked much like the rest, with wood-like plas flooring and neutral walls, art hanging on the walls. The paintings in this passageway were modern, much of it abstract, but it still looked genuine, not like mass-produced prints. Although Quinn didn't know enough about art to know if that was true.

They passed doors—no, wait, they were on a ship, so they'd be hatches—all unlabeled. "There's a map on your e-torc. We don't put visible markers on hatches, just in case attackers board us." Paola shrugged. "But of course, no one would dare." Finally, they stopped at a hatch just before another lift tube, the corridor continuing beyond it. This ship was huge!

The door—hatch—slid open and they walked in. The room—no, compartment—contained five workstations, all but one occupied. Each workstation had a very comfortable-looking chair, three, four, or more screens in front of each chair, a side table with bev-tainer holders, and a set of cabinets below the seat. Each workstation had an oval canopy above it, the screens mounted on a pole coming out of the canopy; it was rather like a chair sat inside a giant egg with a hole in one side.

Paola turned to her. "This is the net trainee's room. The empty workstation is yours. On the left is a sani-mod; on the right, a small galley with drinks and snacks. You'll see you have two bev-tainers and a keep-warm mug in your storage area. You are responsible for cleaning those. While there is a cleaning staff, everyone is responsible for keeping this compartment tidy. If you leave a mess, expect to be assigned to cleaning the dining room for a week or more."

At Quinn's skeptical look, Paola sniffed. "This room is under surveillance, and your fellow trainees aren't good enough to subvert the vid. Whoever makes the mess will clean. We expect you to focus on your assigned training. You are all assigned to different subjects. If you have questions, ask your mentor—that's me—not your fellow trainees. We do encourage you to have meals together and other recreational activities. Hazing is not acceptable. We all have one goal on this ship—help the Chief Justice to perform her mission. Anyone attacking others, physically, mentally, or otherwise, is not contributing to the mission and will find themselves assigned to other, less pleasant duties, off this ship. Don't do that. Report any attempts to me immediately."

Paola turned to Quinn and stepped close. "And I do mean immediately. My comm is always open to you, Quinn." She stepped back again. "Trainees, this is Quinn Cygnus, a new trainee. Introduce yourselves on your next break." She lowered her voice. "Take a seat. Your training will start with properly configuring your workspace, then you'll be tested on various subjects. Do your best, but don't randomly guess. Informed guesses are allowed, encouraged even. We need people who are willing to extrapolate when an unknown situation occurs. Once your testing is complete, which will be a full day or more, you'll be assigned to an area. You'll work with me and other mentors, but you will be doing very basic work. If you're good and patient, you'll be assigned more interesting jobs. Do your job. Don't snoop. Capisce?"

"Yes, Tech Paola."

"Good. Get started. If you need me, call." She turned and walked out of the compartment.

Quinn scanned the other trainees, but they were all immersed in their jobs. Or pretending to be immersed. She walked to the empty seat and sat down. Immediately, three screens lowered from the top of the egg and lit up with a "Welcome, Trainee Quinn" banner. A button with "Ready to get started?" appeared, and she shrugged and selected yes. It would be nice to have some breakfast, but she guessed that could wait. Hopefully, this introduction would tell her what was available and where.

Two hours later, Quinn swept the screens off, and they slid up and away. Her stomach rumbled unhappily, so she pulled her bev-tainers out of the cabinet below her seat and took them to the small snack area. There was a sink, so she washed them all thoroughly, filled one with water, another with a fruit drink, and the keep-warm with coffee. When she turned back, she was surrounded.

She stepped back, so her back was against the cupboards, dropped her containers on the counter, and faced them.

All the trainees smiled, took a half-step back, and the one right in front of her held up both hands, palms out. He had the typical Familia coloring, but the wrong face shape, with a round face and wide nose. "Don't worry, we're just introducing ourselves. We're not going to attack you. None of us want any trouble. Just tell us who you are, and we'll reply."

Quinn nodded but remained wary. "I'm Quinn, I'm from Cygnus Secundus. I was at Adzari Net School, but they brought me here after just a year." She wanted to make sure her fellow trainees underestimated her skills.

"I'm Giovanni. Call me Gio. I'm from Valenti, but my family isn't important in Familia. I got here after I finished Valenti Net School on scholarship."

The second boy said, "I'm Mario and the same deal." Mario had the Familia coloring but, like Gio, the face shape was wrong. His was more of a heart shape than a long oval, and his nose was short and upturned.

"Hey." The only girl in the compartment waved once. "I'm Aurora. I was at Adzari too, but I graduated last year. Had a family emergency but that's," she swallowed hard, "over now. So, here I am." Aurora didn't look like Familia. Her skin was deep espresso, her eyes almost black, her hair curly, shorn short on the sides, and waving in a five-centimeter long strip on top. She was striking but not classically beautiful.

"I'm Fabriano, and I'm from Sirius. Net school there, got picked up for a job here."

Quinn didn't believe him for a second, and from the side-eye from the others, they didn't either. He had the classic Familia look and an unconscious arrogance that said rich kid. She'd seen enough of it at Adzari to know the mannerisms. All her fellow trainees were older than she was by at least three years, but Fabriano was probably ten years older than Quinn.

Gio said, "Since you're new, we'll give you the quick version. We take a ten-minute break every hour and an hour for lunch, kind of like school, but if you need to use the sani-mod, just go. Nobody's watching that close. They don't care what hours you work but how much you work. You know, can you get your work done and done right, or do you need more training, or are you a goof-off?" He held up a warning hand. "Don't be a goof-off, you won't like the results." He shivered slightly. "Don't forget where you are. Ever." He smiled, and it was like a supernova, bright, and blinding. "But you won't, I can tell."

"Don't expect to do anything exciting, even after you finish training," Mario added. "You'll be doing basic-level stuff for a long time. After a while, someone will mentor you in their specialty. Paola is our mentor's supervisor, so you must be a special case."

Quinn grimaced. "Yeah, special. Lucky me."

All four snorted or laughed ironically but said nothing.

Aurora said, "Are you a net gamer? We play most evenings."

Quinn grinned. "You bet! Which games?"

"It depends on everyone's mood and what's been released recently, but there is a nominal schedule. Search for the Net Tech Gaming Schedule, and you'll find it all laid out. You can bounce between the groups and games or stick with one." Aurora shrugged. "Whatever works for you. Be aware, it's not limited to just net techs." She raised her brows. "Anyone can join. Some of the first-person shooter games, like Fringe War 300, are very popular with the Enforcers."

An obvious warning. "Cool, thanks. I'll look." They were way over ten minutes. Quinn picked up her bev-tainers.

"Hey, don't forget snacks," Fabriano said. "You're skinny. I'll bring you some."

She forced a small smile. "Thanks." She returned to her workstation and settled in.

"You're welcome." Fabriano shoved a stack of five different packages and some sort of fruit between her bev-tainers on the little side table.

Her stomach growled, and Fabriano grinned. "Thanks again," Quinn told him.

He nodded and returned to his workstation.

Quinn chose a protein bar of some sort, ripped the veg plas open, and shoved it in her mouth while she continued watching the orientation. Maybe this wouldn't be so bad after all.

∆∆∆

"You want me to do what?" Quinn kept herself from

screaming, but it was close.

"Tech Paola." She tapped a toe.

"What?"

"You forgot my title, Trainee. Don't forget it again." Paola glared.

"Yes, Tech Paola. Sorry, Tech Paola."

"You aren't, but you should be, and you will be in the future." Paola turned and left.

"What's the big deal, Quinn?" Fabriano asked. "Too good for inventory?"

"No." She stamped her foot. "But I just finished checking every built-in console to make sure they were automatically updating firewalls and anti-virus. I could have done inventory then!"

"You had to document all that, right?" Gio asked. "So, why not use the same tracker and just reorder the columns?"

"Because she wants the model numbers too, and the identity trackers have to be scanned. Argh!" Quinn threw up her hands.

"Hey, at least it gets you out of here," Aurora said. "I'd love to be doing something other than checking firewall logs—again."

"Maybe you can trade?" Fabriano said slyly.

Quinn and Aurora snorted. "Right." Neither of them was dumb enough to do that. Refusing an order got you some nasty tasks. Trading was considered a refusal.

Quinn filled her bev-tainer and grabbed the net tech cart. She'd learned it was slow and a little wonky, but it was better than carrying everything. Sure, she should be able to scan everything with her e-torc, but, in reality, her trainee-level e-torc got over-tasked quickly and slowed to a crawl, especially when interfacing with any other net program. Quinn leashed the cart to her e-torc and walked out the hatch, waving at her friends.

Aurora was right, though. Walking busy work was better than sitting busy work. She'd had plenty of both over the last month. Either way, she'd almost kill to get down on a planet's surface, feel the wind and the sun. Or even rain. Both were preferable to the perfectly controlled atmosphere of *Indomito*. She knew it wouldn't happen, though. No one would ever let her off the ship.

Quinn looked at her list. She started with the closest consoles, those in the lounge level, open to everyone on board. Hardly anyone ever used them. Why would they? Everyone had an e-torc. But the e-torc net could go down, or a local net could be temporarily overwhelmed, so the physical consoles stayed. She started on Alpha side, working toward Bravo. This huge ship was built in a square, with the four sides labeled Alpha, Bravo, Charlie, and Delta, and each level was numbered, so you could generally find your way around, even without any labels on the hatches.

By the time she got halfway through Bravo, she was wishing she'd taken Gio's suggestion. Maybe Paola wouldn't notice the missing model numbers? *Right. Sure, she wouldn't.* Quinn sighed and moved to the next console, halting abruptly. A woman sat at the console. She was using it, even though she wore an e-torc. Quinn blinked, unsure what to do, then realized she was being silly. She'd simply go to the next console and leave this one for later.

"Did you need something?" the woman asked her. She seemed very old, with a wrinkled face and gray hair. But her eyes were lively.

"No, Mistress. I'll come back later. I have plenty to do."

"Nonsense. You're here. I will get a cup of tea." She stood with some difficulty.

Quinn, worried the woman might fall, asked, "Can I get you that cup of tea instead? You can stay right here."

"That's all right. I can do it and leave everything open for you."

"No, no, I insist. I'll get the tea. How do you take it?"

"Lemon, please. Get yourself a cup too."

"Yes, Mistress." Quinn hurried to the auto-bev, selecting quickly. She couldn't spend too much time here, or Paola would be on her like a sand flea on a desert rat. She trotted back and put down the cup in the slot on the console.

"Did you get a cup?" she asked.

"Mistress, I can't stay. I have a job to do." She smiled. "I'll come back and get this console later."

"No, no. I insist. Pull up a chair and join me. I'll let your supervisor know you're with me. What's your name, child?"

"Quinn, Mistress. I'm a net technician trainee."

"You seem a little young to be working. Who's your supervisor?"

"Net Technician Paola, Mistress."

The woman very obviously looked up Paola. "She doesn't have any real authority. How did you come to be on this folder?"

"Enforcer Trevi brought me from Adzari Net Academy, but I don't think it was her decision either."

"No?" The woman's head tilted. "What makes you say that?"

"I don't think she was very happy about the trip, Mistress, but

I might be wrong." Quinn shrugged, putting a clueless look on her face. Making an enemy of Trevi might be very bad.

"I see." The woman nodded. "Well, I am Kathe, that's an 'e' on the end, not a 'y' or an 'I,' and I am pleased to make your acquaintance."

Quinn smiled. "Pleased to meet you, Mistress Kathe. I apologize for not knowing who you are. My e-torc isn't authorized for facial recognition or tagging."

"Really? How odd. And none of this 'Mistress' nonsense. I'm just Kathe."

"I don't think I'm allowed to be that informal."

"I just said you were. Don't contradict me, Quinn."

"Sorry, Mis...Kathe."

"Give me just a moment..." Kathe held up a finger. "Ah, yes. Tech Paola, I require Quinn's company for the rest of the day. I'm sure you have others who can do whatever ridiculous task you have her doing right now. Traipsing about the ship looking at things? What kind of net do you run? Don't answer that. And don't bother the girl for this. I told her, she didn't ask." Her finger swept to the side, clearly sweeping the connection to Tech Paola off and then came back, pointing at Quinn. "You tell me if you get in trouble for this. I won't have it."

"I'm sure it will be fine, Mi—Kathe. Tech Paola is smart."

"Good. Now, tell me about yourself. From birth to now."

"I'm not that exciting."

"Neither is my usual life. Talk. Wait." She turned the seat around. "Let's sit over there on those nice soft chairs. This thing isn't comfortable." Kathe rose, slowly.

Quinn bit her lip. "Can I assist you?"

"No, I'm fine, just slow." Once she started to walk, Kathe wasn't slow for long. Quinn grabbed her teacup and followed. They settled in soft chairs set at a slight angle toward each other, so they mostly faced the main walkway but could also see each other easily. "Now, tell me all about yourself."

"Okay." Quinn shrugged and told Kathe her life story. She left out some details of the attacks on Cygnus Gliese, but she hadn't known those until later, and who transported them to Cygnus Secundus. Lightwave didn't need attention from Familia. She simply said lots of folders responded to the crisis and she was on one of them. Which was true. Quinn really didn't remember most of it. She remembered hiding in the Sisters' compound from the armed attackers, escaping on a shuttle, and being on a huge fold transport in very crowded conditions for what seemed like a very long time. Then living in crowded, muddy conditions for an even longer time while they built the Secundus compound. Kathe didn't seem to care about the lack of details, and much of it was public record, thanks to the tunnel worms.

"Did you go into the tunnels?" Kathe asked.

"No, I was too young." Quinn shrugged. "I didn't know a lot of this until later."

"You're still very young." Kathe frowned at her. "Stay that way." She tilted her head, her eyebrows raised in the middle. "But not as young as you look. You're smart." Kathe sniffed. "Don't tell anyone. You're safer being young and dumb."

Quinn bit her lip and her heart rate sped up.

"I'm not telling anyone either. I like you." Kathe nodded her head slowly. "When I need a companion, you're it. I'll send appropriate clothing and shoes." Kathe sneered slightly at Quinn's boots. "Those are practical but not fashionable. Now, what do they have you doing?"

"I'm doing inventory, Kathe." Was being a companion good or bad? Or both?

"Inventory? Aren't all these terminals on the net?"

"Yes, Mistress Kathe. Sorry. Kathe. But sometimes things happen, I guess. I don't ask questions."

"Discouraging questions about work is a poor supervisory technique." Kathe grimaced. "I knew our net leadership wasn't great, but this is ridiculous. Hmph." She shook off her frown. "Other than net work, what do you do?"

"Well, I play a lot of net games."

"And?"

"I train for something called the Atlas Challenge."

Kathe scanned her up and down. "It's hard to tell under that ugly shipsuit, but you do seem to be in excellent physical condition. I'm not familiar with that particular competition."

"They're not terribly popular. It's easier to show you than tell you. I have a vid of my instructor if you'd like to see it?"

"Excellent. Let's go back to the terminal."

"Um, Kathe, I don't want to overstep, but why do you use the terminals when you have an e-torc?"

"E-torcs make me dizzy, and I can't see them. They're too small." Kathe shuddered in revulsion. "I leave mine on voice only."

"I can adjust it for you and show you how to adjust it further."

Quinn did lots of adaptations back on Secundus. The Sisters cared for lots of kids with brain and eye injuries, either from abuse or the dangerous environment. Or both.

"I've had people try to explain, but I just don't understand it." Kathe scowled.

"It's not the easiest thing to adjust sometimes, but I've done it a lot. If you'll give me temporary access to your settings, we can work on it together."

Kathe tilted her head, inquiringly. "Well, then, let's see what you can do. Tell me how I give you access."

Quinn walked her through the process, but Kathe didn't give her temporary access. No, she made it permanent. Quinn took a deep breath. This had to be a test. "Kathe, you should select the time-limited option. We'll be done in less than an hour."

"No. I don't want to do this again, and I'm sure we'll have further adjustments. Now, let's get started."

"Okay." Quinn brought up her e-torc's settings and took control of Kathe's. "Close your eyes for a minute while I put some initial settings in, please."

Kathe did as she requested, and Quinn went through the laborious process. If she only had a decent e-torc.

"Why is this taking so long?"

"My e-torc is slow. There's a lot of security and not enough memory." Maybe she shouldn't have said that?

"Well, this is unacceptable. Authorized for Quinn Cygnus, by my authority." Kathe took her e-torc off and handed it to Quinn. "Make your initial adjustments, then I'll test it."

Quinn removed her e-torc and placed Kathe's around her neck.

She closed her eyes at the sweep of screens. "Wow, something is really set wrong on this thing." Quinn put her hand up and made very slow, very small movements. She reset all the visual settings to standard, then made some initial adaptations for normal aging and the protocols they used for brain injuries. Using those, screens didn't shrink and sweep away to the side when no longer needed, they simply disappeared. There were a few other adaptations as well. Quinn handed the e-torc back to Kathe. "Try this."

Kathe put it back on and raised a hand. She seemed uncharacteristically tentative.

Quinn held back a smile. Funny how quickly she'd placed Kathe in a certain category. She had to watch those kinds of assumptions. She hadn't forgotten Enforcer Trevi's warning—Quinn was on a ship of killers. Kathe might be old and a little slow, but she might still be an enforcer. There had to be a reason she was on this ship. Maybe being elderly was a good cover story? She could get very close to a potential target without being suspected.

"Ah, I see. This is much better. Thank you."

"Of course. Yours was set very oddly. If you go into the setting menu, you can adjust the brightness, size, and speed on your own. Or, if you need more changes, I'm happy to do them."

Kathe glared at Quinn's e-torc, still on her lap. "Not with that thing. I'll fix that too. Hmph." She smiled slightly at Quinn. "Now, let's see that vid. I want to see one of you, too, Quinn."

"Certainly, Mis—Kathe. Whatever you want." Quinn brought up the vid of Instructor Switz's last competition and swept it over to Kathe. She was happy to sit here and talk, rather than traipse about the ship doing inventory. She could learn a lot from this woman.

But what was Kathe learning about her?

CHAPTER NINE

Quinn bent over, gasping for air, and tried not to collapse. She imagined Instructor Switz saying, "Better, but not good enough." It was true. She had to be faster and stronger than most competitors to compensate for her lack of height.

"You are very athletic, aren't you?" Kathe said.

Quinn popped up so fast her head swam but still automatically yanked her tight fitness shirt down. They were a little short in the body and tended to ride up. Her poor stomach was scratched up from scraping over the obstacles.

"Careful." Kathe shook her head disapprovingly. "You need to be aware of your surroundings at all times. Never rely on technology to keep you safe."

"Yes, Mis—Kathe."

"That's Enforcer Kathe to you, Trainee Quinn," a female voice said, the tone like ice on a methane moon.

"Fatima, I told her to use my name. Mind your own business."

Now the woman appeared from behind Kathe. *Justice* Fatima. Quinn was in trouble now. She bowed, jerky with fear.

"This is my business. Workers use proper titles at all times,

Mother."

Sand and sun. Quinn did not want to be in the middle of a family dispute, especially one with Familia's Justice, one of the most powerful humans in the universe. Quinn rose out of her bow and stepped back, using the argument to fade away.

"Where are you going?" Kathe snapped.

"I need to cool down, please," Quinn said as humbly as she could with her heart rate and breathing thudding at double-time.

"Ah. Yes, of course. Please do so. Come, Fatima. We'll leave Quinn to her training." Kathe bustled away.

Fatima stared at Quinn, while Quinn stepped back slowly, carefully not looking Justice Fatima in the eyes. She was a predator. Challenging predators was a bad idea. They'd all learned that on Secundus. After what seemed like forever, Fatima turned and strode away. Quinn started to sag but stiffened immediately. You didn't show weakness to a predator either.

Quinn walked around the Atlas Challenge apparatus. Once her heart rate slowed, she started stretching, but she didn't use her full y'ga stretch routine. Showing that to the Justice didn't seem wise, despite the fact it was already on vid if someone went looking. Eventually, her muscles loosened and her sweat dried.

As she left the Fitness Center, Quinn looked around, but Justice Fatima and her *mother Kathe,* by all the suns, were nowhere to be seen. Why would they stay here? The ship was theirs, along with everyone in it. If they wanted her, they'd call for her. Quinn jogged along the corridors of the ship, wanting a shower in the worst way. If she was getting a lecture or punishment, she wanted to be clean and dressed.

She'd expected Kathe—*Enforcer* Kathe—to show up and watch her train someday, but not immediately. For one, she wasn't that good. Since arriving on *Indomito*, she'd failed to fully complete the standard course; she had to reduce the difficulty of several of the elements. All these months later, with good food and plenty of rest, even with the restrictions Medico Marcello insisted on, she should be matching or exceeding her previous records.

Instructor Switz remarked on her lack of performance and wanted her to speak with a sports mental coaching medico. But Quinn doubted one was available on *Indomito*. Familia didn't seem like the kind of organization that encouraged success through anything but fear of failure.

Back in her compartment, Quinn relaxed a little, but she wasn't safe anywhere on *Indomito*. As she showered, she wondered again: why did Enzo want her? There were quite a few women on this ship with her heritage; many were prettier than she was and probably more willing.

She impatiently washed her hair, regretting the time it took. No matter what she did to the Style-Net, it wouldn't do more than trim her hair. She suspected someone, probably Enzo, wanted it long, even if she didn't. It also wouldn't let her dye her hair to anything but dark brown, which was so annoying. She wanted cool stripes like Aurora wore, but no, she was stuck with plain, boring dark brown. *So boring.* Her natural color of almost black was better, so she didn't bother trying anymore.

She dressed in another dark gray shipsuit and her usual boots. What should she do now? Normally, she'd join one of the net games or go to a lower level lounge with her fellow trainees, but she didn't want to be around others if the Justice was going to call for her. She also didn't want to waste her day off. Maybe just a walk through the garden level? Quinn bit her lip. Wait, she could go to the observation deck.

Before she consciously made the decision, she left her compartment and took the float tube to the upper levels of the gigantic ship. There, she made her way to the best part of *Indomito*. The center of this deck was covered with a thick layer of clear plas and multiple layers of shielding, so anyone could lie on a lounger and stare out into space. If there was an emergency, a cerimetal blast door slammed into place, but who would be stupid enough to attack the Justice's ship? Accidents were unlikely—asteroids and other space junk were blasted out of the way.

Quinn walked around the outside of the observation area, the part open to everyone. The inner part of the deck was separated into smaller areas, some containing ten or more lounges, some just one or two. The center areas were reserved for high-status people, like Enforcers and the ship's officers. Quinn's favorite lounge chair was on the outer ring, furthest from any of the entrances, and separated slightly from the other loungers, as if a row had been removed at some point. She turned the corner and stopped.

Kathe waited on her lounger. When Quinn jolted to a halt, Kathe frowned and beckoned with an impatient finger.

Quinn started walking, carefully keeping her expression neutral. So much for relaxation.

"Join me, Quinn," Enforcer Kathe said imperiously.

"Of course, Enforcer Kathe." Quinn took a seat on the lounger next to her.

"Just Kathe when we're alone. I really don't enjoy titles being thrown at me."

Quinn said nothing. Eaten by a giant lizard or giant bird, either way she was dead.

"Never mind. My daughter is right, but I don't have to like it." Kathe scowled. "I watched your run this morning and compared it to one of the vids from Adzari Net Academy. You are slower. Why?"

"I haven't fully recovered yet." Quinn winced, remembering.

"Recovered from?"

"It's in my records, but essentially, I almost starved to death." Quinn tried to sound like she didn't care, but she couldn't fool herself. She sounded scared and desperate, as if she were still there. She'd been here, safe, for two months. She should be over all this drama. The problem was, she knew she wasn't safe on *Indomito*.

"I see."

When Quinn looked at Kathe, she was busily swiping through screens. Quinn sagged a little before she caught herself. Why would Kathe care? Kathe was important, Quinn was nobody.

"There. Medico Marcello will ensure you see our mental health specialists. There is no reason you should continue to suffer the effects of abuse. Hmph. I can't believe no one has seen to you before this. Unacceptable."

"Thank you."

"You are welcome." Enforcer Kathe turned away for a moment. "I also have something for you. Here." She held out an e-torc.

Quinn took it from her, gingerly.

"Go ahead, it won't bite." She chuckled. "The configuration is exactly the same as your current e-torc. The new one has enough memory and speed to do what you need to do." Kathe frowned. "You have sufficient patience already, there's no need to test it."

Quinn pulled her old one off and put the new one on. Before she did anything else, she stood and bowed deeply to Kathe. "Thank you so very much, Enforcer Kathe. I appreciate this more than I can express."

"You're welcome. They have plenty of decent e-torcs, they're just hoarding them for no reason. Typical supply people, they want their inventory safely on the shelves. They don't understand good workers require good tools and decent support, not stupid harassment and power games. People who want to play power games should be far more subtle." Kathe shook her head, with a twisted frown on her face. "Play stupid games, lose."

Wasn't that phrase, "Play stupid games, win stupid prizes?" Well, Enforcer Kathe could do whatever she wanted, including changing common sayings. Quinn wanted to play with her new e-torc, but that would be terribly rude.

"Well, go ahead. Take it for a spin." Kathe rose and held up a hand when Quinn jumped to her feet. "Relax, enjoy the view, play with your new e-torc. I have other things to do today. I will see you later."

Quinn sank back down on the lounge and watched Kathe walk away. Kathe started slow but sped up and was quickly out of sight. Quinn lay back on the lounger and stared up at space. Not much up there right now, but that was okay. A black background was perfect for reconfiguring an e-torc. She spun through the menus and settings, but Kathe was right. They'd cloned her old one perfectly onto this top of the line model. That was so nice of her.

Or was it? What did Kathe really want? Quinn had no idea.

△△△

Checking her calendar for the day's activities, Quinn noticed she'd been on *Indomito* for six months. She felt stronger physically and mentally, but despite that, she couldn't stop watching for traps, ready to squeeze in around her. Some days were worse than others; like today. Probably because of tonight's big Familia anniversary—Quinn was ordered to attend. The Majordomo told her what to wear—a snug, stretchy, dark-blue floor-length gown already in her closet.

Quinn grimaced. Initially, she thought it was modest, covering her completely, with long sleeves and a wide band around her neck. But the back was basically non-existent, and there was a huge, heart-shaped cutout in the front, displaying the ugly tattoo, and the heart's point was cut too low, showing her underwear. She shuddered, remembering her first sight of the mark of ownership framed by the too-sexy dress. Why her? It was an unanswerable question.

She closed her eyes and breathed deeply. Kathe demanded her company, so she still had a chance to get out of wearing the horrible thing. If she reached Kathe's suite early, Kathe would insist she change into something more age-appropriate. Enzo wouldn't publicly fight Kathe. But was that a fight Kathe should take on? Quinn noticed Kathe tired quickly and the shadows under her eyes deepened daily despite the makeup she wore. Kathe insisted there was nothing wrong, but Quinn knew better. Kathe was aging rapidly or ill. Or being poisoned. Or all of the above.

So, did she want Kathe to fight this battle? Or should Quinn embrace the pain? What could she do without offending Enzo? Quinn had no idea what he found attractive. He didn't talk to her or watch her, at least not in person. If it wasn't for his name on her body, she'd have no idea he was interested. Which might mean he wasn't interested in little girls. Quinn bit her lip, considering her face and hair in the mirror.

What if she braided her hair on both sides, high on her head, and twisted the braids around themselves, forming a big knot on either side of her head? She'd look like a child playing dress-up.

Then she'd wear sparkly, light-pink lipstick and blush, which looked terrible on her skin and made her seem even more like a little girl trying to look like an adult. Then she'd wear a pair of flats with a sparkly bow on them to round out the impression.

That was all she could think of for now. Maybe something else would gel in her brain during the day. Quinn hoped so because that look could backfire. There were a lot of sexual predators who found the sexualized little-girl look very attractive. She was betting everything on guesses, but it was all she had.

But right now, she had time reserved at the Fitness Center. Quinn pulled on her athletic gear and jogged up to the fitness facility. To her surprise, her normal compartment was modified into a public court with tiered chairs. Quinn looked at the stands. She didn't even know they could do that!

"Ah, Quinn, there you are." Fabriano bustled up to her. "I didn't think you'd miss your training time. Good. Get warmed up, you need to go first."

"What's going on?"

Fabriano grinned, a big self-satisfied grin. "Oh, just a little friendly competition. Don't worry, I'm sure you'll do well."

"I didn't sign up for a competition!"

"I know. I designed one around you. You do the run, then everyone else's scores get compared to yours. Anyone can bet on how much better or worse a score may be than yours." He smirked. "I get a small cut of the action, of course."

Quinn frowned and folded her arms. "And if I refuse to participate in this little scheme of yours?"

Fabriano snorted. "You won't. Your life will be miserable."

Quinn snorted back. "I've lived through miserable. You're nothing. An empty threat." Quinn turned away. "I'm not doing this. Non-sanctioned betting is illegal. I want nothing to do with it."

Fabriano grabbed the back of her T-shirt. "Oh, yes, you are doing this," he hissed in her ear. "No one's going to know, I fixed the vids. You'll do this or you and Aurora will start having a lot of problems. And I'll take this." He yanked the e-torc off her so hard it scraped her skin. Hopefully, it wasn't bleeding.

She stomped on his foot and pulled away. "You're an idiot. Did you not hear about this?" Quinn pulled up her shirt and pulled the front of her pants down just a little.

Fabriano stared, wide-eyed, and the color drained from his face. Security personnel entered, sending the would-be spectators and competitors running, but the hatches slammed shut. One of the black-armored people grabbed Fabriano's arms and wrenched them behind his back. Fabriano dropped her e-torc, and Quinn took a chance, stooping to grab it before it was crushed. She looked up to see a stunner pointed at her, Fabriano sprawling to the side.

"That wasn't smart, Trainee Quinn," the armored man said.

"Sorry, I just didn't want it crushed. I didn't think how it would look to you."

He holstered the stunner. "Think next time."

"I'd rather there wasn't a next time."

"That would be best. You're free to go. I recommend you stay in your compartment for the rest of the day."

"Yes, sir." Quinn walked as fast as she could without running. One of the security people opened the hatch for her, and she sprinted from there. Rather than suffering the slow, crowded lift tube, she took the stairs, jumping down them like they were part of the training course, and ran to her compartment, almost crashing into her bed.

Why did these things happen to her? Why did everyone think she was an idiot? Evidently, her efforts to look childlike were effective. Too effective. She rolled to her back and started breathing slow and easy, trying to calm herself. Fabriano would pay for his stupidity, but was he pulling others down with him? Fabriano wasn't just another trainee, either. He was the son of someone important. None of this was her fault, but she was sure his family, maybe others, would blame her, regardless. Why did he decide to pull this level of stupidity today, of all days?

Maybe he'd gotten away with similar things before? He obviously didn't know she was "special." Now, everyone knew. She'd be a pariah again. All the friendships she'd developed were gone.

What an awful, horrible day. Quinn gave up on meditation and cried.

∧∧∧

A remote brought her lunch, but it sat uneaten. Quinn knew she had to eat, but her stomach was too upset. Finally, she threw off her pity party, got out of bed, and ate. She forced it down quickly, not taking the time to taste the food. As she finished, she realized there wasn't much taste—the meal was bland but perfect for muscle recovery. Maybe someone on the cooking staff heard what happened? She was always nice to the cafeteria and cleaning staff—their job was difficult enough and they deserved a lot more than the basic human decency they rarely received.

By the time she finished eating, she felt better. She followed the meal with a gentle y'ga recovery and meditation routine and felt almost normal. Well, what passed for normal these days. Maybe tonight wouldn't be so bad. Fabriano wasn't the most popular person—he used his family/Familia connections too much. Nobody trusted him. She'd known he was heavily involved in the underground betting schemes, but she hadn't realized he was the leader. If Enforcers were participating, she might be in real trouble.

Except she wasn't, because of the tattoo. Quinn would be protected and avoided. Only more so than before. With the security folks swooping in to "rescue" her, it was obvious they were watching her constantly. Quinn sighed. Little she could do about any of it except survive. And learn enough to escape. Despite the endless warnings to not exceed their assigned tasks and limits, Quinn was determined to learn everything she could.

Since she had access to all the learning modules, she'd started doing her fellow trainees' lessons in the evenings while she simultaneously played net games. Since she stuck to the easiest games, she was able to split her attention enough to learn. She'd stumbled a few times in the games, earning a reputation as a poor player, which suited her fine. Being underestimated was good.

Usually. Obviously, Fab completely underestimated her.

Well, all this moping wasn't doing any good. Quinn took a shower, did her hair and makeup, and shimmied into the poor excuse for a dress. Surveying herself in the mirror, she snorted. This thing didn't do her any favors. To pull this off, she needed a curvy figure. Quinn was built like an active teenage boy; skinny muscles and hardly any shape. With her obvious heritage, Quinn doubted she'd ever be curvy. She looked a lot like Lightwave's Katryn—tiny frame, gold-brown skin, wide-set, slightly tilted dark-brown eyes, and almost black hair with a bluish undertone. Katryn's sex appeal came from her confidence and intensity, not her body shape. Quinn hoped she could learn how to pull off Katryn's tricks, but on *Indomito*, that probably wasn't smart.

If she looked too confident, Enzo would think she was happy about her position. But if she was parading through *Indomito* in this ridiculous dress, she'd need every bit of surety and pride she had to survive. This thing clearly marked her as property. She wouldn't allow anyone else to treat her that way. She was a person, an individual, not a thing or a remote.

Her hatch chimed, and she crossed the compartment to greet Enforcer Kathe. Why had she come down here?

"What are you wearing?" Kathe asked, her lip curling. "That's horrendous."

"What I was told to wear, Enforcer Kathe."

Kathe pushed past her and marched into her sani-mod. "Who told you to wear that thing?"

"The majordomo, Enforcer Kathe. She messaged me directly, telling me the navy-blue dress was appropriate."

"If you were twenty-two and looking for a liaison, yes. Fourteen and a child, no." Kathe was pulling out dresses and dropping them on the floor, each on accompanied by a sound of distaste or disgust. "None of these are suitable for your age. I don't know what those people are thinking. Enzo isn't a child molester."

"Maybe one of the design team is," Quinn muttered.

Kathe spun and scowled at her.

Quinn held up both hands. "My apologies. I spoke out of turn, Enforcer."

"No, you didn't. It's an interesting thought." She sniffed. "It could even be true. Or not." A wry smile. "But I'll find out."

Great. More people who would hate her.

Kathe turned back to the pile of dresses. She stooped and pulled a particularly hideous sparkly silver shipsuit off the decking. Quinn hadn't really looked at it. The first time she pulled it out, she'd almost dropped the thing because it was ridiculously heavy, with lots of silver chains all over it. "Ah hah. This will work." Kathe pulled it off the hanger. "Get me a pair of scissors."

Quinn tried to think of where she'd find such a thing. The laser on the Style Net?

"Never mind. Hold this," Kathe said, handing her the silver monstrosity. "Hold it stretched out."

Quinn did so and barely held herself in place when a long, thin knife appeared in Kathe's hand, apparently out of nowhere.

"Excellent." A few slices and Quinn was holding the remains of the jumpsuit. "Drop that mess on the floor with the rest of it. Junk. Nothing but junk." Kathe handed her what appeared to be a wide belt made of fine silver chains. "Put that on."

Quinn flipped it over, pulled the fasteners apart, and snapped it into place around her waist. The belt of woven chains rested on the top of her hipbones, with more chains draping below. It completely covered the cut-out on the dress, falling to her upper thighs. It was quite heavy, even though it was now apparent the material was plas of some sort, not metal. Thankfully, it didn't ring like metal either. That would be annoying.

"Much better, although still not young enough for you." Kathe motioned. "Turn." She harrumphed. "Thank the big black hole of Andromeda the belt isn't made of big chains, or you'd look like something else entirely. Pick that thing back up." Her finger pointed down.

Quinn stooped to get the shredded silver suit.

"Just the top."

Quinn held it out by the shoulders.

"Turn it around…yes. That will work." A few more slices and Kathe held a wide circle of chains. She dropped it over Quinn's head, on her shoulders. "Not bad. Turn."

Quinn did, the odd necklace heavy on her shoulders.

"Yes. It covers down to your shoulder blades, and the belt covers your waist. Much better." Kathe grabbed her waist and turned her around again. "Yes, garish, but modest. Much better. Let's go." She pushed her around again and out of the sani-mod, through her compartment and out the hatch. Kathe towed her down the corridor and up the lift tube to the Justice's level.

Quinn had never been on this level. She never wanted to be on this level. But she had no choice. She followed Kathe into a small area with a closed hatch, two armored guards waiting. One motioned and the hatch slid open. Quinn followed Enforcer Kathe inside. The hatch slid shut behind them—they were in an airlock. A luxury airlock—that was real wood on the walls—but still an airlock. *Interesting.* After a few seconds, the next hatch slid open.

A woman in a severe black shipsuit bowed low. "Welcome, Enforcer Kathe. Thank you for bringing Trainee Quinn. But what is she wearing? This is," the woman's face wrinkled like she'd eaten something awful, "bright. This was supposed to be a sophisticated dark blue dress."

"Your idea of *sophisticated* and mine are far different. Below all that silver, the dress shows too much skin. It is too sexy for a young girl." Kathe said, her tone slightly menacing.

"It is? It's supposed to be modest." The woman's lips clamped together momentarily. "Unacceptable. I will fix this, Enforcer."

"All her formalwear is unacceptable. Fix all of it. And fix the idiot who thought dressing a little girl in sex worker clothes was a good idea."

"Yes, right away, Enforcer. Aperitifs are almost finished. You may go straight to dinner, Enforcer."

"Good."

Quinn followed Kathe through a large compartment filled with luxurious soft seating areas in charcoal and maroon, surrounding low wood tables. Taller tables waited around the perimeter with a few stools. It looked expensive. Smelled expensive too, a faint, pleasant scent of citrus and cinnamon.

The next compartment was a dining area. About twenty people, all with the Familia look, stood around a massive, dark brown wood table, with matching cabinets along the sides of the compartment. The people were older than her by ten or more years, with an equal number of males and females. Most of the women wore long, tight, jewel-toned dresses and the men fancier versions of their daily pin-stripe shipsuits. So, the whole table was probably Enforcers other than her. *Won't this be fun?*

On the table, silver candlesticks with candles, real flames flickering, long, low floral centerpieces, and cream-colored china plates with gold and maroon patterns. There were also several wine glasses and lots of heavy silver utensils at each setting. Chandeliers sparkled above them, and the walls were a deep burgundy red. The scent of roasted meat and baking bread hung in the air. *Wow.* This was really something.

"Quinn, you are there." Kathe pointed at a seat on the other side. "I'm across from you."

"Thank you, Enforcer Kathe." She rounded the end of the table, the chair empty. Quinn started to sit, then noticed everyone else was standing. She waited patiently, despite the side glances from the rest of the diners.

The man standing to her left turned to her. "Well, hello. Who are you?"

She looked up, way up. He was tall and very thin. "I'm Net Trainee Quinn Cygnus. Pleased to meet you." She bowed, unsure how deep to go.

"Ah. I see. I'm Corto. I am also pleased to meet you, Quinn Cygnus. Across the table, next to the lovely Kathe, is Trevi."

"We've met, Corto." Trevi surveyed Corto like she'd found something on the bottom of her shoe. "I retrieved Quinn from her school."

"Ah, my memory. So terrible." Corto shrugged one shoulder and tossed his head.

"Oh, yes. So awful." Trevi said dryly.

The hatch at the other end of the room opened, and a man and a woman entered. The woman was Justice Fatima. She wasn't pretty, but she was still somehow beautiful, with the typical olive skin and espresso brown hair of Familia. She looked quite young, but Quinn knew body mods were easy to get in most parts of the universe. Probably right here on this ship, if you were an enforcer. The man also looked young, with the Familia resemblance, but Quinn knew she didn't want to cross him. Head Enforcer Enzo was dangerous. He trod down the table, his eyes fastened on her. Quinn held herself stiffly to hold back a shiver and stared at his chin.

After Enzo reached the seat next to hers, he looked away, at Justice Fatima. A man dressed in a plain black shipsuit, evidently a server, pulled out Fatima's chair and pushed it in behind her.

The other men at the table did the same, Corto pulling hers out. It seemed very awkward to her, but everyone else seemed to manage just fine.

"Well, Quinn, we finally meet in person." The man at the foot of the table said to her. "I am Head Enforcer Enzo."

She lowered her upper body as far as she could without hitting the table. "I am pleased to meet you, Head Enforcer Enzo."

"Good. I see they failed to follow my directions." He frowned as he scanned her from head to toe and back.

"Enzo, I'm fixing it," Kathe said imperiously. "They dressed her like a strafiga, not a little girl. Disgusting."

"She's not a little girl, Kathe," Enzo said. "She's a teenager."

"Hmph. Barely."

"She has a little girl body," Trevi said. "She should wear clothes that make the most of what she's got." She shimmied, the thin straps on her tight red gown almost falling off her shoulders.

"She will not dress like a puttana," Kathe growled.

"Of course not, Kathe. But she will wear whatever I want," Enzo said, very slowly.

Kathe just stared at him. Neither looked away until the woman at the head of the table spoke.

"Gentles, let us eat!"

Servers rushed in, bearing pitchers, trays, and bottles. Water and wine poured into her glasses, a small plate set in front of her, another above. The one above had a tiny loaf of white bread, with a rosette of butter flecked with green herbs, and the one in front of her appeared to be…something in a red sauce.

While she was examining it, one of the servers asked her,

"Parmesan, Mistress?"

Quinn glanced around; most were accepting some. "Yes, please, and thank you."

The woman used a small grater with a block of something in a napkin, sprinkling little bits of something a light yellow over the red sauce. "Would you like more, Mistress?"

"No, thank you."

Thankful Adzari Academy had a few formal dinners as part of their employment training, Quinn picked up the small fork furthest from the plate and slid the tines through the sauce, picking up some sort of meat? She ate it, tasting salt and smoky oil in a small fillet of some sort of fish. The sprinkles tasted like an aged cheese. The dish was okay but not her favorite, so she left the rest. With the number of utensils around her plate, this was a big, elaborate dinner and sure to have too much food for her, so leaving some behind was a good idea.

Her plate was removed, and another plate replaced it, with a salad of multi-colored leaves, ribbons of dark, slightly purplish brown dressing layered over it, and small cubes of dried bread on top. Colorful bits of what she assumed were vegetables were also sprinkled in. She forked up a bite, enjoying the crunch of the veggies and the tangy but sweet dressing.

During this course, Quinn shot glances at her fellow diners. Many of them engaged in quiet conversations but some just ate. Enzo appeared to be one of the "concentrate on the food" types; Kathe spoke quietly with Trevi. No one spoke across the table. Since Quinn had nothing to say to Enzo or Corto, she stayed quiet and kept reminding herself to relax her shoulders—they kept rising to her ears.

Everyone at the table drank their wine, each course a new and different wine, but Quinn refrained. She didn't like wine and she did not need to lower her guard.

A pasta course followed, this one in a bright green sauce, then one with breaded and fried poultry and one with some sort of red meat. Another red-sauced pasta course, then a small dish of something icy, slightly sweet and lemony. She took a bite or two of everything, but with all this food, anything more and she'd be stuffed to the point of pain.

At this point, Enzo and Kathe started a conversation that escalated into heated hissing, but never got loud enough for Quinn to fully hear. Trevi appeared to add fuel to the fire with comments to Kathe, while Corto watched avidly.

Finally, they reached the end of the meal. Or Quinn hoped that's what the last utensil, a dainty spoon, meant. A tall, fluted glass with a pedestal was placed in front of her, bright, colorful layers interspersed with creamy white and spongy yellow.

"Coffee or tea?" the server murmured.

"Neither, thank you."

"You don't drink anything but water?" Corto asked, his nose wrinkling.

"No. I'm an athlete."

"Oh, yes. The unpleasantness." He sniffed. "Terrible."

"I didn't know anything about any of that," Quinn told him, very quietly. "Fabriano didn't ask me."

"Shh. No names," Corto whispered back.

Quinn nodded her thanks and spooned up some of the dessert

to avoid saying anything else stupid. Sweet fruit, fluffy creamy stuff, and light cake combined into a delicious whole. She didn't have to work at eating this one—it was wonderful.

The other courses weren't bad, just different. The heavy sauces covered the taste of the ingredients. The texture seemed odd to her too, smooth and oily, but she wasn't used to fine dining. Plain food was good enough for her. Except for this desert—she could happily eat this every day for the rest of her life. Quinn scraped the bottom of the glass and sighed.

Kathe chuckled. "Would you like mine?"

Quinn's cheeks felt like she'd spent an hour in Cygnus Gliese's noon sun. "No, please go ahead. It was delicious."

Enzo twitched a finger, and a server placed another glass in front of her. "Go ahead, Quinn. Enjoy."

Quinn swallowed hard, not sure she could eat. She looked at his chin. "Thank you, Head Enforcer Enzo." She took a spoonful, intensely aware of his eyes on her, trying not to feel like a mouse freezing when the shadow of an air hunter swept over. She ate steadily and hoped it would stay down, but her stomach churned uneasily. She finished, and feeling his eyes still on her, said, "Thank you, Head Enforcer Enzo, it was delicious." Then she sat back and stared into the distance, carefully not meeting anyone's eyes.

Applause started and Quinn jumped a little. She turned to look at what everyone else was looking at and clapped too, not wanting to draw attention to herself. A man, slightly heavyset, dressed in white, stood there. This must be the Chef. He bowed deeply, turned, and exited through what Quinn assumed was the kitchen hatch.

"Gentles, let us return to the gathering room," Justice Fatima said.

Everyone stood, and Quinn scrambled to her feet, jumping a little when her chair was pulled away. Corto smiled and nodded toward the foot of the table. Quinn followed his gaze to find Enzo waiting, his arm crooked. Quinn swallowed and slid her hand around his elbow, resting it on his forearm, as she saw some of the other women do. It wasn't comfortable—her skin practically shrank from the contact and Enzo's height pulled her arm uncomfortably high. She held back a shudder. He led her to the couches in the very center of the room and motioned for her to sit on one end of a short couch. He sat next to her, taking her hand between his.

Quinn clamped a closed-lip smile on her face and somehow managed to not pull her hand away. She couldn't show emotion, especially fear, but she felt trapped.

"You need to grow up," Enzo stated.

Quinn blinked at him, accidentally meeting his beady eyes, unsure what to say to such a strange statement.

"Enzo, she's a little girl," Enforcer Kathe said, taking a seat across from them. "She's fourteen standard years old. She'll be grown up in about three years. You should have left her at the Academy."

Enzo flicked a derisive look at Kathe. "She's not fourteen, her medical records show it." His hand clamped down on hers.

"Did you notice the part about her being almost starved to death? No matter what her true age is, her body will need time to recover. It's clear in her athletic performance that she hasn't."

Enzo's eyes narrowed. "And that's why it's stopping, today."

"What?! Stop? Why?" Quinn exclaimed, unable to help herself.

Enzo turned his glare on her, flinging her hand away. "Yes, it stops. No more Atlas competitions. Your body needs time to heal and mature. I spoke with the medicos. High-level training can delay proper growth. I will not have this. Am I clear?"

"Yes, Head Enforcer Enzo." Quinn dropped her eyes to the floor. The only thing keeping her sane, the one thing she looked forward to, was gone. Taken by these evil people, just like everything else.

"You may continue mild exercise. Healthy exercise. The medico staff will prescribe it. You will follow the prescription precisely. Is that clear?"

"Yes, Head Enforcer Enzo."

"Good. You are excused. Return to your compartment."

Thank the Mother for small—and big—favors. Quinn rose, bowed, and walked away as quickly as she could in the ridiculous dress.

"Well, at least she's obedient," Enzo said behind her. Quinn slowed a little. "Kathe, if you want to mentor the girl, fine, but she must grow into a woman. Little girl bodies are not attractive. She will grow into an obedient and lovely woman, capisce?"

"That's all I'm trying to do, Enzo."

Their voices faded as she neared the airlock. The severely dressed woman still stood there. Was that her job? To wait at hatches and greet people? Maybe Quinn's life wasn't so bad after all.

"Trainee Quinn, you will have new formal wear later this week." Her lip curled. "Don't wear this again." She flicked a hand up and down in front of Quinn's body. "And color your hair brown. The color is programmed in the Style-Net already."

"Yes, Mistress."

"It's Majordomo."

"Yes, Majordomo. Thank you, Majordomo." She scampered past the woman and into the airlock. It closed behind her with an ominous thud, then the next hatch opened. She was free of the pit of sand vipers. For now.

Strolling to her compartment, Quinn pondered. She'd escaped this time, but what about the next? And the one after that? She was on a folder in space controlled by some of the most important people in Familia. There were only so many places she could go and nowhere to hide. And the next steps in her unwilling transformation had started—no more competitive sports and forcing her to change her hair color. He'd make her do body mods next. She shuddered. Why her? Why not someone already built in the Familia mode? It made no sense to her.

But it did to Enzo and that was all that counted on this ship.

Quinn entered her compartment and sani-mod, stripped off the ugly outfit, and threw it all in the recycler. She noticed someone had already hung all the formal clothes back up except the shredded silver jumpsuit—it was gone. She put on some comfortable athletic wear and collapsed into her lounge chair, burying her head in her hands. But she wasn't going to cry. No, she'd save the tears for public performances only.

She had to escape, but how? The only way off this folder was on a shuttle. She could research shuttle schedules and manifests and maybe find a way to hide on one, but she was pretty sure they were inspected before leaving and guarded while docked. She could study piloting, but she'd probably get caught. Piloting a shuttle wasn't that hard, though, with autopilots. It was getting a shuttle, with permission to fly away from *Indomito*, and then getting away to someplace big enough to get lost in that was the problem. So, she didn't need to study piloting, she needed to study who flew regularly and why. Which might not be so hard. She'd noticed the shuttles from the observation deck; basic information about each shuttle was publicly available unless they were Enforcers, just like it was for other folders, stations, planets, and the occasional comet.

Then she'd have to study comms and how to fake the comms between the shuttle and *Indomito* and the stations and planets. Or convince a pilot to take her somewhere? *Hmm.* Maybe those awful dresses would come in handy after all.

Quinn nodded to herself. Assuming she could convince a pilot to take her to a station, then she'd have to break into the station's surveillance and make sure she wasn't seen. So, she had to learn to do that first; she'd already started learning how to break into nets as part of the net maintenance courses, but she had to become a real expert. She also had to break into *Indomito's* surveillance and loop a vid of her in her compartment. She'd have to start planting those doctored vids on real net techs, not just her fellow trainees'. This would be difficult because she didn't have access to those nets, workstations, and compartments. Or she'd have to find a way in through the net, which she didn't quite have the skills to pull off yet either. Quinn bit her lip. At this rate, her lip would start bleeding soon.

Then she had to steal and break into someone's e-torc to get credits to buy passage on another shuttle to another folder, far away. She couldn't go back to Cygnus Secundus. She'd have to find a job somewhere else. Fortunately, good net technicians were always needed. She could find some fringe world with no records, similar to Cygnus Secundus, and get lost.

Hmm, maybe not quite that fringe. Not enough people to hide among. Someplace outside the core, but not fringe. There had to be plenty of worlds like that. But she couldn't openly research that, either, because her search history was undoubtedly monitored.

She'd need weapons too. She never wanted to be caught again. She had to be ready to fight off anyone and everyone. Quinn played the first-person shooter games just to keep her skills sharp—back on Secundus, fighting off predators was a never-ending chore—but she could learn the strategy and tactics games too.

In short, she had to become Katryn, Lightwave's net Security chief and y'ga expert. So, Katryn she'd become, no matter what it took. Quinn would do this, and she would escape. There was no room for doubt.

CHAPTER TEN

Quinn watched the shuttle fly away from *Indomito*, desperately wishing she was on it. But if wishes were shuttles, she'd be long gone. Lying back on her favorite lounger on the observation deck, she brought up the shuttle schedule. There was little available other than the shuttle designation and destination, which meant an Enforcer was on board. Possibly even Justice Fatima or Head Enforcer Enzo—either one she'd happily wish a quick trip into a black hole or a mysterious collision with a comet.

She'd wish that on any or all of the enforcers. They were vicious, nasty people who treated everyone else like dirt. Unfortunately, they were also clever and quick; the stupid and weak didn't last long. Quinn bit her lip and brought up her hidden, secondary window. Designed to hide what she was looking at from those watching her on the net, she used it only when she was alone in a public place.

Watching her watchers, she'd discovered those observing her via the net, like Tech Paola, didn't usually bother watching real-time when she was in public. Those tracking her in person, usually via security vid, didn't watch her while she was in her work compartment or living compartment. Both were fooled by her apparent age and meek compliance with rules, regulations, and demands, both reasonable and unreasonable.

"Can I get you something to drink or eat, Trainee Quinn?" a man's voice asked, making Quinn jump. "Sorry, didn't mean to startle you."

Quinn put a hand over her heart and swept away her holo entirely. "That's okay, Angelo." She smiled at the gray-haired man with the heavily wrinkled, tired face. "I should be more aware of my surroundings. But no, I'm fine." She shrugged. "I'm just enjoying the view."

"Very well. Please let me know if you need anything at all. I'll come by later if I don't hear from you. I know you forget to eat sometimes." Angelo leveled an admonishing look at her.

"Oh, please do. You know I just don't think about it. Thank you."

"Of course, Trainee Quinn." He bowed slightly. "It's our pleasure to serve you." He put a little emphasis on the pronoun, bowed again, and walked away.

Quinn sighed. She didn't understand why people, especially "important" people, couldn't be nice. The servers, the cooks, the cleaners, all of the "working" class worked so hard; they deserved to be treated with dignity. But no. She saw Enzo shove one of them so hard he fell and broke his arm. Then they docked poor Roberto's pay because he couldn't do his job until he healed, which meant his family back on Velorum was on starvation rations for a while. But Familia didn't care—Roberto should have gotten out of Enzo's way.

By the Mother, she hated every one of them. Quinn snorted at her blasphemy—the Mother expected love for all beings. But Quinn wasn't too sure enforcers counted as sentient beings—they were more like soulless machines. Maybe artificial intelligences entirely focused on their own survival and well-being, and the rest of the universe could fold into a black hole.

Looking around, Quinn cautiously brought up her holo again, setting an alert for anyone passing within three meters of her. It wouldn't catch everyone—enforcers and security were often incognito on the net and active surveillance would be noticed—but it was better than nothing. Then she used her hidden window to listen to *Indomito's* traffic control communications. Slowly, she was figuring out *Indomito's* shuttle missions and who came to visit via shuttle. She already knew getting on a visitor's shuttle was practically impossible. Those airlocks were guarded by security remotes, real people, and vid backup in a special section of the shuttle docking level.

Most of *Indomito's* fifty-plus shuttles were docked on a dedicated level of the fold transport, except four used by *Indomito's* captain and his staff. The single, "public" entrance to *Indomito's* shuttle-docking level was guarded by a remote, a person, and vid. There were several emergency accesses to the shuttle docks, but those hatches could only be opened by activating explosive bolts, and the alarms were routed on a dedicated net and watched by security vid.

But, watching the common dock entrance guard post, Quinn noticed security there was slightly lax. The remotes weren't the best ones, often weren't fully charged, and the security team in charge of the remotes expected the in-person guard to do the work, while the guards relied on the system too much. It seemed Familia's security was convinced it was too hard for most people to steal a shuttle and get away. Or they had everyone so downtrodden they wouldn't try. To some extent, the carelessness was understandable—even if someone succeeded in stealing a shuttle, *Indomito's* weapons could pulverize them with a single blast.

Regardless, Quinn had found several ways to escape on a shuttle. Finding a pilot to blackmail or threaten was the easiest option. Not that it was actually easy—she'd need a bigger threat than Familia already had. However, Quinn's next big assignment was helping Security with some personnel file security, so she'd use that opportunity to snoop a little. Maybe she'd be able to look inside the files before she secured them or hide a backdoor.

After hearing nothing new on *Indomito's* comms, she turned them off, yawned, and stretched a bit, then focused back on the space beyond *Indomito*. There weren't any people near her, so Quinn brought up her latest vid of Tech Paola's workstation. She couldn't contain her proud smirk at her cleverness.

She'd been detailed to inventory and test a compartment full of miscellaneous vid equipment. It was mostly junk, but there was a bin of self-contained vid systems in a variety of shapes and sizes, including tiny, pin-sized ones, probably used for spying. Stealing a few of those pin vids was risky, but she took a few of the older ones, marking them as "broken/recycled" on the inventory. Paola had been pleased—they'd been missing this particular bin for some time and the loss rate was less than expected. Quinn was fairly certain Paola didn't realize the tiny spy pins were in the bin; Quinn hid them in the middle of the inventory under their model name, like she hadn't realized what they were used for.

Once she'd charged the pin vids, Quinn perched one on each of her fellow trainees' workstations. A few weeks later, she'd been called into Tech Paola's work compartment for an assignment, and she'd taken the opportunity to put one there too. She'd tripped on her own feet, catching herself on Tech Paola's chair and pushing the pin vid deep into a rather dusty seam.

Quinn carried a pin vid everywhere she went, ready to deploy at any time. Since the spy vids relied on internal memory, not the net, she could only leave them someplace she'd be likely to return to within a few days, but leaving a vid was far less perilous than a tech finding an unknown signal on the net or finding a transmission during a routine bug sweep.

Downloading the vids was dangerous too, but she'd set up a script on her e-torc that did it automatically whenever she got within two meters of one. Running in the background, at first glance it looked like a data backup protocol. She'd learned that little trick from her spy vid on Fabriano's workstation—he'd hidden his underground gambling ring very well.

The vid on Tech Paola's workstation was obscured slightly by dust, but it was still pure gold. Quinn had gathered some important passphrases and codes, including some getting her into Security's vid net watching the "public" areas on *Indomito*. The vids on the enforcer's level and Justice Fatima's level were on a separately secured net, but if Quinn had to go up against enforcers directly, she was space dust.

Fortunately, accessing *Indomito's* public vid net let her confirm piloting assignments, security at the shuttles, and the prison. She'd found the prison cells entirely by chance, but since then, she'd uncovered everything she possibly could. After all, Quinn might find herself in one of those cells someday.

The block of cells, just twelve of them, was rarely used. *Indomito's* staff was thoroughly cowed, and most had loved ones on a Familia planet or right here on *Indomito*, perfect for ensuring trouble didn't last long. Quinn had heard those not-so-subtle threats herself from Paola: "I wonder how many lovely little girls the Sisters of Cygnus have right now? Maybe they'd be smarter than you are?" Quinn had burst into tears and bowed her head, gritting her teeth all the while, knowing that, even if she did everything perfectly, if Familia thought it was worth it, they'd go to Secundus no matter how well she obeyed. The only thing saving the Sisters' orphans was their remote location and small numbers.

Indomito's cells were mostly filled with beings from elsewhere. Someone would be flown to *Indomito* from a planet or station, transferred to a cell to wait for a day or more, "interviewed" by an enforcer, then flown somewhere else, often a different folder. Most of the time, the interrogations were short, with the prisoner drugged and telling the enforcer everything they wanted to know, usually awful things, accompanied by a lot of crying. One interrogation she'd stopped watching; Enzo and another enforcer had tortured the person, taunting the poor man with the knowledge they already knew everything he was confessing, that his painful death was a lesson for others, nothing more.

Despite that horrible experience, Quinn watched most of the interrogations, for several reasons. One, someone should witness for those who were innocent or at least not horrendous. Someday, she might get the chance to let a family member know what happened to their loved one. Two, she could test the security subtly, creating things that looked like glitches, such as a loss of vid or sound, and see how security responded. Three, sometimes, the prisoners let valuable information slip. She'd built up quite a library of security data on Familia stations and worlds and gotten some valuable blackmail intelligence. She'd be thrilled to use it against these awful people.

Despite the good information and intentions, watching the interrogations took a toll on her soul. Quinn found herself cowering around the enforcers. They responded well to her new attitude; Quinn just had to remind herself it wasn't real. But to some extent, it was. Despite her terror, she persevered. She was absolutely determined to escape. She would not live her life at the pleasure of these horrible people.

"Gentles, please prepare for fold to Valenti in five minutes. Secure yourself and all loose items," *Indomito's* chief purser announced.

Huh. This wasn't a previously scheduled fold. Quinn shrugged and looked around her lounger, ensuring she hadn't left anything lying around. Angelo caught her eye; he was jogging to her, bevtainer in hand. She scrambled up to meet him. "Angelo, you didn't have to hurry. I would be happy to have it after fold."

"No, you should have this now," he said, with a panting smile. "You need your strength." He handed the container to her.

"Thank you for allowing me to serve you." He bowed and jogged away.

"Thank you!" she called to his retreating form, hating the servant's required thank-you phrase. Quinn returned to her seat and sipped. *Delicious.* The staff cook, a middle-aged woman named Maria, was constantly creating treats for her. Quinn knew it was partially Enzo's edict that she "grow up"—the shakes, cookies, and cakes included medico-approved ingredients—but when Quinn was detailed to work on the kitchen's net, she introduced herself to the kitchen staff and did her best to make their net more effective and efficient. Between that and her treating them like human beings rather than faceless remotes, Quinn hoped it kept them from poisoning her someday, but that was probably asking too much. Besides, if required, an enforcer would poison her food, not the kitchen staff.

Quinn got rid of her hidden window and sipped her drink, snapping it into the holder just before fold. She drew the security net across herself and relaxed.

"Fold to Valenti in five, four, three, two, fold. All stations, we've arrived safely in Valenti."

As usual, Quinn felt nothing during or after fold. But she was always careful to sit or lie down, because after one fold, she'd felt strange, like her whole body got slapped. It was so odd, but it hadn't happened again.

A message came in from Tech Paola: "Report to shuttle bay Delta Twelve in thirty minutes. Be prepared to spend three days on Valenti Station."

Well, today was getting more and more interesting. She'd

never been on a station work trip. Her fellow trainees went often, but not Quinn. This must be a big deal. Or it was a test. She sighed. No matter how much she wanted to or how easy it might look at the moment, she couldn't try to escape during this trip. Any opportunity was sure to be a setup. They'd be watching her closely, and she had to lull them into complacency. She had to be a meek, obedient little girl.

Quinn jogged to her compartment and packed a small bag with uniforms and toiletries. Aurora sent her a message to pack some casual clothes too, just in case they were allowed a night off on the station. She smiled sadly. It wasn't likely, but it didn't hurt to shove an extra pair of leggings and a sweater in her bag. In twenty-five minutes, Quinn was waiting at the shuttle-level security station entrance.

In twenty-eight minutes, a group of ten net techs, her fellow trainees, and Tech Paola had gathered. "All accounted for, Tech Paola," a man she didn't know announced.

"Excellent. Let's go." Paola led the way through Security. Quinn hung in the back with her fellow trainees and walked through, noting this guard was paying attention, as was the remote. She half-expected to be stopped, but they let her go. It was almost certainly a test, but it was still useful to her. This was her first real opportunity to see the shuttles and bays in person.

Behind the security station, an open area led to six more hatches. Taking one on the right, they walked down a short corridor, through another hatch, and turned right again into another corridor, passing shuttle bays six through eleven. The airlocks at bay twelve were open, and they filed into a luxuriously appointed shuttle. Three rows of five cushy seats waited for them, and Quinn saw Tech Paola and two of the others enter a hatch off to the side of the shuttle's main seating area. The rest settled in; Aurora, Gio, Marco, and Fabriano took the last row of seats, Aurora patting the one next to her for Quinn. Her smile seemed strained.

At the front, the co-pilot stood. "Gentles, please strap in for pushback and launch. After our initial thrust into orbit, you'll be able to move about the cabin. Feel free to help yourself to food and drink," she pointed to the galley, "and the sani-mod is there. Note the location of the emergency suits and escape pods. They're all clearly marked." She pointed at several brightly marked compartments around the cabin. "Our travel time is approximately four hours and fifty-two minutes."

Quinn fastened her harness, noting her closest emergency suit was behind her. When she turned back, she saw Aurora had a death grip on the buttery-soft armrest cover. "Not a fan of flying?"

Aurora shivered. "Not a fan of space flight. Air flight is fine."

"Aurora had an unfortunate accident in a shuttle when she was little," Fabriano said in a mockingly sympathetic tone. "She was the only survivor, but she was in a bod-pod for a long time."

Quinn couldn't believe Fab had survived the gambling ring incident. His family must be really high up in Familia.

"Idiota," Gio snarled.

Fabriano snapped something back, but Quinn didn't care. She put a hand over Aurora's, who turned her hand and held on. Her grip was just short of painful, but that didn't matter. "It will be okay—I've got you."

Aurora didn't look convinced but hung on tight. Quinn kept talking until they were thirty minutes into the flight. Marco brought them tea and water, and Gio brought snacks. Quinn was sure it was for Aurora, not her, but that was all right. Aurora needed help.

After the tea and snacks, Aurora fell asleep.

Marco whispered, "The medicos know. They probably gave her something."

Quinn smiled her thanks. For the rest of the flight, the three of them shushed anyone speaking too loudly and woke her just before they docked with Valenti Station.

"Listen up," Tech Paola said. "Some station maintenance personnel have organized a 'Valenti Below,' similar to the protection rackets on other stations." She sneered. "Obviously, Justice Fatima doesn't think much of this idea. The initiators of this scheme have been arrested, and they're undergoing questioning right now. Our job is to look for hidden or shadow nets that allow station personnel to circumvent Valenti Station's laws regarding data storage and use. Station personnel have already found hardware deep in the air handling equipment commanding a shadow net. They've removed it. However, we believe there are additional comm nodes throughout the station, and we believe they also set up backup nodes that tunnel through the existing net. You've been split into teams already. Check your specific assignments in your official messages. The sooner we get our tasks accomplished, the faster we can do other things, and there may be other rewards as well. Capisce?"

Quinn nodded along with the rest but had nothing in her

official messages except an assignment to Team Three under Technician Matteo. Aurora nudged her. "What team are you on?"

"Three."

"Weird, me too."

"Make that me three," Gio said.

"You're all on my team," a man said behind her. "Lucky me, all the new kids." Tech Matteo was medium height and build, with the Familia look. "You," he pointed at Quinn, "will come in handy for this task."

Quinn looked at him skeptically.

"The rest of you? Well, we'll see. Come, follow me." Matteo didn't join the line of people leaving the shuttle. No, he turned to the cargo bay and entered. Inside, a pallet held several cases of equipment. Matteo unfasted the first case and pulled a small box out. "This is very basic equipment, but sometimes, the basics work well. We know what frequencies the illegal net used, so we're looking for hidden equipment using those frequencies." He looked up, with his lip curled.

"The problem is the legal equipment uses the same frequency. However, the legal equipment isn't hidden. So, we'll be climbing through maintenance areas and crawling along access shafts and all kinds of potentially dirty and not fun places." Matteo laughed. "And by we, I mean you." He pointed a finger at the four of them.

"But before we do anything else, we'll be flying surveillance remotes through every public corridor on the station to map where we find the strongest signals for the suspect frequencies. Then, we'll go to those areas in person. I'm sending a special program to your e-torcs. Install it, and you'll use that net ware to narrow down the suspect signals further. Then, we'll enter those areas, probably mostly maintenance areas, and see if there's legal equipment there. We'll check the legal equipment against the station's registered database and go looking for illegal equipment using these." Matteo held a small box on his hand.

"I've found some illegal net nodes in plain sight with fake inventory tags and some hidden in things like air ducts, water pipes, sewer pipes—hah! I see you have figured out why you're here." Matteo grinned. "I hope you brought extra clothes. Leave your packs here, but be sure you take some water and snacks with you. It's going to be a long day."

Quinn sighed. Remote flying sounded fun but the rest? Not so much.

∆∆∆

She walked her twenty-seventh kilometer, down a dingy passageway in the bowels of the station. Turned out flying remotes wasn't any fun at all for them. This wasn't Matteo's first station search. He had a pre-programmed swarm of practically invisible remotes; after unpacking, they flew away. An hour later, the four trainees were off surveying corridors of interest, a security remote trundling behind each of them. Fortunately, not one of the super-creepy human-like remotes. Quinn was sure the remote was there not only to guard the trainees but to watch them.

But that was okay. Quinn had learned a lot today. Like how easy it was to enter a maintenance access hatch. She'd always thought they'd be secured better, but they mostly relied on being hidden; the locking mechanism was a code comprised of the hatch's location by station level and area. Most of the locks weren't on the net, so you could simply pry one open and muffle the alarm mechanically. It might be an inexpensive solution, but it seemed shortsighted.

Inside those maintenance access areas, she'd found some excellent hiding places and some that initially looked like excellent hiding places but weren't. She'd also shimmied through some return air ducts, peered into cabling ports, climbed up and down a lot of maintenance access ladders between station levels, and found out a lot about how stations worked. Or how Valenti Station worked, anyway.

Despite her weariness, Quinn smiled. As part of checking if a net node was legal or illegal, they'd been given administrator access to the comm nodes. She was sure the station would change all the passphrases and access codes later, but while she was crawling through those access ways, she'd managed to set up a few backdoors on the legal net nodes. It was slightly risky—if a node needed replacement and someone examined the net ware on it rather than sending it off for recycling or rebuild, they could find her access. Figuring out who made the backdoor wouldn't be hard, they'd just have to look at who was in that area at the time of the access's creation and they'd find Quinn. But if she ever got the chance to run on Valenti Station, it would be worth the risk. She could infiltrate almost every Valenti Security system from just one of these nodes.

The detector showed a spike and Quinn slowed, looking for the access hatch. Most of them were small and down near the decking. She grinned. Fabriano must be having a terrible time—he was tall and a little heavy. She found the hatch and opened it, crawling inside. The area wasn't big enough to let the security remote follow her, but it was tall enough for her to stand in, so she did.

Boxes and hatches festooned the compartment walls, and tubes of various sizes ran through the cramped space. Many of the tubes had access ports on them as well. Using Matteo's program, Quinn scanned and finally found the net node. Bringing up her node admin access, she found this one was legal and set her now-perfected script running to create a backdoor. Then she took the detector box and swept it over every square centimeter of the maintenance area, including all the pipes and each access port. She finally found the illegal net node in a small hollow between a sewer pipe and the compartment's wall and, with a little effort, managed to pop it loose. Crawling back out, she put the illegal node into a bin on the security remote and grabbed her water.

Tech Matteo called her just as she was drinking. "Good job, Trainee Quinn. Come back up to the shuttle and grab your gear. We've got rooms on the station, then we're going to dinner. Tech Paola is very happy with our progress, so it will be a nice dinner."

"Thank you, Tech Matteo, I'll be there soon." She sighed, put the bottle back in the security remote, and started trudging. She was in shape, but she didn't usually walk quite this much—her feet ached. But as she went, she found more legal net nodes and created backdoor accesses on each one. If she was ever going to escape *Indomito*, it was likely to be here. But not this time.

She took a lift tube as far as it went—level Twenty-Five—and then walked deeper into the interior of the station to reach the next tube. Making the final turn, Quinn saw half the lights in the corridor were out and she stopped, then backed up. But it was too late.

Some sort of mesh material was thrown over the security remote, resulting in blue bolts zapping as it tried to defend itself. Four masked people surrounded her. Quinn backed slowly to the wall, ready to lash out. But at least one carried a stunner, so if they wanted her badly enough, she was done.

"Buonsera for us, boys," one of them snarked, walking closer.

"It's a job, not a game," the one on her far-right hissed. "Bella, you want out? Away from here?"

"Away from you? Yes!" Quinn said in a high, squeaky tone.

Snorts and chuckles sounded. "No, bella, away from those enforcers. We could use a net expert."

Quinn shook her head violently. "I'm not an expert. I'm just a trainee. I'm not going to do you any good at all."

"Shame. Well, we've got a use for you anyway. Stun—" He dropped to the floor, along with the rest. Armored security people and remotes surrounded her.

"Are you okay, Trainee Quinn?"

"Yes, sir, I'm fine. You got here just in time to save me from a stunner headache." She smiled, putting a little hero worship in her face.

"Good. Let's go."

Station Security escorted her back to the shuttle. Quinn didn't dare make any more backdoors on the way, but she knew there would be more opportunities tomorrow. After all, she'd passed the test—and she was sure it was a test. Security was too quick to respond, with too many people. And who would be stupid enough to blatantly proposition someone with an official security remote in a public station corridor? No, anyone really challenging Familia on their own station would be far more cautious. Guess her silly little girl act was working.

They took a float tube to level Thirty, a short walk through a food court making her tummy rumble, and another tube to Forty. Then, across a huge shopping area lined with fancy stores and restaurants, the plaza sprinkled with luxury goods kiosks and seating areas, and finally into a secured corridor leading back to their guarded shuttle bay. Once she passed the airlock security, her escort left.

"Quinn, glad to see you got here safely," Matteo said. "Change and we'll join the rest at dinner."

"Sure, Tech Matteo. Thank you." Quinn grabbed her bag and jogged into the sani-mod, threw on some clothes, and pushed the memories of the confrontation into a box in her head. Later tonight, when she was alone, she could process them. For now, she had to act like a normal, if slightly scared, girl. At least she'd have a good excuse to leave the party early.

Finished, she repacked her bag and joined Matteo, who motioned her out the airlock. Two security remotes joined them as they walked down the eerily quiet corridor.

"Quinn!" a woman's voice called from behind her.

She turned and peered around the remotes. "Ka—Enforcer Kathe. Nice to see you." She waited for Kathe to catch up, but she was moving slower than usual. "Tech Matteo, perhaps you should go without me? I'm sure Enforcer Kathe's security will be more than sufficient."

"I'll wait," he said, a mixture of trepidation and curiosity on his face.

Quinn shrugged one shoulder. She hadn't seen Kathe for…more than eight days. A surprisingly long time. When Kathe neared, Quinn grew concerned. Kathe looked tired, and she was strolling, rather than walking. Actually, it was more like tottering. "Enforcer Kathe, can I get you a float chair?"

"Nonsense, I've just been sitting too long in the shuttle." Kathe waved her concerns away.

But her security personnel, two humans, seemed to agree with Quinn because a float chair came up behind them. She smiled at the two, then turned her attention back to Kathe. "Kathe, this is Net Technician Matteo, my supervisor today."

Kathe frowned at him. "I see. Well, go on with whatever you were doing. I'm taking Quinn to dinner with me."

"Very well, Enforcer. I'll leave one of the security remotes with you and Trainee Quinn." He bowed and scurried off.

"He's a nice man. He was just escorting me to the net workers' dinner," Quinn said.

Kathe chuckled. "Eh, it never hurts to put a little fear into any man near you. Now, come along. There's a new place I want to try."

Quinn fell into step beside Kathe. They ambled along, but Kathe wasn't speeding up like she normally did; no, she was slowing. "Enforcer Kathe, are you sure you don't want a float chair?"

She stopped and sighed, her shoulders dropping as she stared at the floor. A deep breath in and Kathe straightened and turned to Quinn. "I guess I have no choice."

Quinn smiled sadly and shrugged. The float chair slid up beside Kathe, and she plopped rather heavily onto it. Quinn was ready to catch her, but Kathe seemed secure.

"Well, let's see what this thing can do," Kathe said with a grin.

Quinn laughed, but she could see Kathe was struggling with the idea of using a float chair. There was something else too. Pain, perhaps? She was holding herself rather stiffly. Kathe zoomed off and Quinn broke into a jog to keep up, keeping the pain of her aching feet off her face. Her feet would recover, but Quinn wasn't so sure Kathe would.

At the restaurant, one of the fancy ones she'd passed on level Forty, they were seated in a private room, the security remote left outside, the security people at either door. Both guards turned down Kathe's offer of a meal. Quinn rather wished she could have because the food was weird. The taste wasn't bad, exactly, but each course was strangely textured, in purees, foams, dried crisps, ices, and puddings.

"Well, that was interesting," Kathe said, waving away the dessert tray.

Quinn smiled tightly, not wanting to say anything to insult the chef, but she wasn't a fan.

Kathe also waited for the server to leave, then chuckled. "Not my favorite. I know Enzo wants to take you out to dinner tomorrow night. I'll be sure to tell him to take you somewhere else."

Quinn's heart sank, and she bit her lip to keep from screaming,

"No!" Then, she remembered who she was with and smoothed her face back into pleasant acceptance.

Kathe pretended not to notice. "Ah, well, you have to try new things, or you get old." She chuckled again. "Actually, you get old anyway. But even if your body fails, you can't let your mind get old." Kathe pointed at Quinn. "Remember that. Don't let your mind or spirit get old, no matter what." She dropped the hand, but not before Quinn saw it was shaking. "I asked you here tonight because I wanted to talk to you off *Indomito*."

Kathe did something to her holo, and Quinn shivered. "You sense that. Interesting. It's a combination of high and low frequencies which usually makes microphones collect nothing but squeals and static." She did something else to her holo, and a privacy shield popped into place around them. "Do you have any anti-spy stuff to add, Quinn?"

She pressed her lips together for a second, then realized that gave her away to someone like Kathe. "Sure." Quinn set her anti-spy protocol running.

"Good. While this wasn't the meal I was hoping for, I did want to talk to you." She grimaced and sighed. "I'm dying."

"What?!"

Kathe shrugged again. "I'm old. I've had a very long life, probably too long for the peace of mind of a lot of people, and it's coming to an end. I've done all the treatments I can." She snort-laughed. "I never once thought I'd end up dying in a bed. Not with the life I've lived. Maybe karma does exist. I've caused enough suffering, so I get to suffer through the end." She stared off into space for a moment. "Anyway, I wanted you to know. I didn't want you to be surprised or wonder or any of the rest of it." Another grimace. "I'll be leaving you some credits. Don't refuse them. Credits allow you to make some decisions on your own or at least make the life you can't change more pleasant." Abruptly, Kathe swept all the security off and moved her float chair away from the table. "This chair is pretty comfortable. I think I'll keep it. Come on, Quinn, let's go get you some gelato."

Quinn watched her float away until the security person behind her asked, "Trainee Quinn?" She shook herself out of her stupor, got up, and followed Kathe's chair through the restaurant, jammed with beings in strange, but surely expensive, clothing and adornments. Mutters followed them, but Quinn ignored them all. Her only powerful supporter on *Indomito* was dying, leaving her behind.

Well, she'd been working on escape support, but now she needed a real plan. Because when Kathe was gone, her life was likely to change forever. And not in a good way. If Enzo was taking her to public places, her life as a net tech trainee was over.

∆∆∆

"Fab, shut up," Gio said. "We're all tired of the whining. If you don't like the work, leave." His body strung tight, he threw a wrapper in the recycling and returned to his workstation.

"I can't leave any more than you can," Fabriano muttered. Amazingly, he didn't complain about Gio's use of the nickname he hated. Something must be bothering him, but Quinn couldn't find much reason to care. He wasn't a nice person.

"Then get in shape," Mario said, with a disdainful sniff. "But I agree with Gio. We've been back for three days. Find something new to complain about."

Quinn followed Mario, returning to her workstation and another mindless chore. But Fabriano's last complaint made her wonder—what did Familia have on Fabriano? It could be any number of things. Or it could be a lie to suck them into complacency. Either way, she wasn't making friends with Fabriano. Or the rest of them. They were nice enough to play games with or share a meal, but Quinn couldn't share any of her troubles with them—they all had their own. None of them would hesitate to betray her if it would ease their burdens. And it would. She'd give almost anything to be one of them, a regular worker rather than Enzo's special obsession. Well, enough dreaming—she had work to do.

"Hey, it's dinner time. Let's go," Aurora said.

Really? Where did the time go? Quinn pushed her screens away and stood, stretching high. All the sitting was killing her. "Do these workstations have standing or walking configurations?"

Aurora shook her head. "No idea. Should be in the settings if they do. Why?"

"I got used to all that walking on the station."

She groaned. "You're kidding, right? I'm happy to sit."

They waited in the worker cafeteria line. There weren't a ton of choices, but the food was good and mostly healthy. Quinn was careful to thank each worker—their jobs were hard, boring, and never-ending. They didn't get the same amenities the "skilled" workers did, like plenty of rec room space or a workout area. Their dormitories were more crowded too, and while they ate in the same cafeteria, it was at different, less convenient times.

Occasionally, she invited one of them to join her for games in a rec room, but they always turned her down. Probably didn't want the attention such a move would bring, and she couldn't blame them for that.

Food in hand, they found room at a table with other trainees and sat. "Old Earth vid night tonight. Superhero vids!" one of them announced. Cheers and groans rang out.

"Quinn, you have to come. You'll love these," Aurora told her.

She shrugged. "Sure, I'm not doing anything else." If the flat vids were too boring, she could review some of her stolen vid while the movie played—it was safe enough when everyone else was engaged in a show. Quinn ate, sort of listening to the others chat about the vid and games. None of them talked about work—there were too many secrets to keep. She finished and put her tray in the autocleaner with everyone else.

"Come on, let's go." Aurora grabbed her hand.

"You're really excited about this. You know you can watch these things anytime, right?"

Aurora frowned at her. "But that's no fun. You need a big screen, snacks, people cheering, and yelling—that's what makes movies fun."

"Movies?"

"That's the Old Earth name for the flat vids."

"Huh." Quinn considered Aurora. "So, you're a historian?"

"No, just a big fan of Old Earth movies. Some of them are weird, some I don't understand at all, some are just ridiculous, and they're all terrible, visually, but the ideas are fun. Especially superheroes and the action thrillers. I could use some of that in my life."

"Couldn't we all?" Quinn forced a chuckle.

They found seats, and Aurora went for snacks and drinks. Once the vids started, Quinn found herself watching a couple of them intently. They had some pretty good storylines and a few great ideas for escape and evading notice. One particular flat vid showed the improbable adventures of a secret agent for some Old Earth government ruling a tiny island area. Such an odd idea, splitting up people by geography on a world, rather than by entire worlds or species, or in the case of Familia, type of business, but Quinn guessed if humans were all you knew and you didn't have spaceflight, it kind of made sense. Whoever the agent worked for, his daring getaways and cool toys sparked her imagination, and the idea of hiding in plain sight under a fake name was intriguing.

Later that night in bed, she realized the concept of a secret persona was an excellent idea. By day, she could be meek, sweet little Quinn. At night, she could transform into…hmm, what would be a good superhero name for a net expert? Net Breaker Girl? No, she had to be a woman for this role, not a girl. The Secret Slider? The Sneaky Worm? The Trojan Horse? Quinn snorted. Those were ridiculous. She was making this too hard.

Q. Her secret name was Q. That way, if she slipped and said it out loud, she could say it was her nickname at the Sisters. No, as a kid. No sense in spreading knowledge of the Sisters in general.

She snuggled in, smiling. Quinn to Familia, Q in secret. She might not build physical gadgets like the other Q they saw on vid tonight, but she built them on the net, and she was smart. It was the perfect name.

CHAPTER ELEVEN

Paola marched into the trainee work compartment. Quinn
forced herself to keep working, using meditation techniques to
keep her breathing even and her heart rate low. She couldn't let
anyone see her sweat. But she felt a drop run down her spine,
regardless. As Kathe's illness progressed, the days, weeks, and
months flew by—she was running out of time. But maybe her
latest spying attempt was a bit too risky.

Paola snapped, "Everyone out. Return to your compartments!"

Quinn jumped to her feet, ignoring Aurora's fawning whine
about lost work. She walked slowly to her compartment, carefully
not thinking more about her foray into the security net. She'd
concentrate on her latest secret mission—Pilot Epstein. Epstein
was disgusting, lazy, and stupid—the perfect target. While doing
her assigned work, checking for illegal net ware, she'd taken the
opportunity to dig just a little deeper into the personal files of
Indomito's shuttle pilots. His personnel record had reprimands for
misuse of Familia property, tardiness, and an addiction to
pornography.

Familia didn't care about the porn, except as a way to control him. However, they suspected Epstein's true preference was child pornography. Familia did care about that because it made him susceptible to blackmail. They hadn't caught him yet. Like Cygnus Gliese's sand fleas, he was good at hiding, and when Epstein was almost caught, he jumped in unexpected ways to hide again. He also nibbled at his host but hadn't taken a big bite yet.

Q was enticing him to take that big bite—for her. She'd studied some of the kid's shows the horrible man watched and copied the mannerisms of some of the girls. Around Epstein, Quinn twirled her hair, looked up at him shyly, batted her eyelashes, and tried to look interested, without being so obvious anyone else would notice and report her. Epstein lurked in the kid's net games too, so she played those while he was online.

Q knew Epstein was stuck on the garbage runs—taking non-recyclables to stations and planets for disposal—and he took advantage by faking or making component failures so he could stay on stations longer, indulging his addiction. Over the last few months, she'd gotten good enough to break into the surveillance on some of the stations they'd folded to, and Q followed him via vid. She'd also sent some anonymous tips to station authorities after he left. Q felt awful that she couldn't stop him first, but she needed the sand flea to get off this folder.

But, to take full advantage of Epstein, Q needed a big distraction. She'd hoped what she'd programmed was enough, but if Paola was confronting trainees already, she'd failed. Hopefully, her failure wasn't fully attributable, or Q might be in real trouble. Or she'd get one of her fellow trainees in trouble. If she did, she planned to stick Fabriano with the blame. He'd made her life miserable. Quinn couldn't defend herself against his verbal or physical attacks—all carefully disguised as concern and accidents—and still look like a quiet little girl. She'd ended up with a lot of bruises from Fabriano's subtle shoving and tripping and a reputation as a klutzy, oblivious little girl.

Q entered her compartment and plopped down on her bed, looking as much like the sulky Quinn as she could manage. But before she strained her acting skills, a message came from Enforcer Kathe, wanting her company. Q sighed. She was happy to do what she could for Kathe, but it was so little. The medicos explained there was nothing they could do except provide comfort: Kathe was at the end of her life. While her body failed, her mind was still sharp. Q didn't know if that was better or not. At least Kathe had a very long, active, and rather privileged life; Q had seen too many leave this universe without any of those advantages.

She made her way to Kathe's compartment. In the middle of the enforcer's level, it was a multiroom suite done in a comfortable style, rather than the "I'm rich" style everywhere else on this folder. As soon as she left her compartment, Paola was messaging.

"Trainee Quinn, you were told to report to your compartment," Paola snapped. "Where are you going?"

"Enforcer Kathe asked for me, Net Technician Paola."

"Fine." The connection dropped with nothing further.

So, they hadn't found anything incriminating yet, or she wouldn't be allowed to continue. Keeping her eyes lowered, Q walked through the enforcer's level to Kathe's suite. Before she could hit the annunciator, the hatch slid open.

Medico Tech Natali stood there. "Thanks for coming." Her lips compressed for a moment. "This may be your last chance to speak with Enforcer Kathe, Trainee Quinn, but please don't wake her if she's sleeping." She turned and allowed Q to pass. Q made her way through the luxurious living area and into Kathe's sleeping compartment, which no longer matched the rest of the suite. A medico float cradled Kathe on a special mattress with slightly lighter gravity than the rest of *Indomito*. Tubes ran everywhere, and her current physical status was displayed above her head. Rolling chairs were pulled up to both sides of the float for visitors, and the air carried the sharp bite of disinfectant.

Q sat down in the chair that let her see the hatch and gazed at Kathe. Her eyes were black holes and her skin sallow. Her breath rasped slowly. Q waited patiently for Kathe to wake. While Q didn't want Kathe to suffer, she also didn't want to try and survive on *Indomito* without her. Kathe had protected her for so long, for no reason Q could find. She wiped away a tear, knowing Kathe didn't want to see her cry.

How strange that a Familia enforcer, someone who had probably committed terrible, evil acts during the majority of her life, was the closest thing Q had to a mother. Some of the Sisters tried, but there were so many girls, they couldn't nurture all of them. Quinn just hadn't connected with any of them the way Nat or Brin had. If Katryn had stayed…but she hadn't. She'd left for some of the same reasons Q did, so maybe they wouldn't have connected anyway. They would have both been unhappy.

A deeper inhale drew Q's attention back to Kathe. "Come

closer," she whispered. Q bent until she was within a centimeter of Kathe's face. "My e-torc. Take it. Coded to you." Gasps interspersed her words.

When no more words came, Q pulled back, bringing Kathe's e-torc with her and sliding it into one of the pockets on her leg. Hopefully, everyone would assume the medicos removed it. When she looked again, Kathe's face was slack. Q glanced at the medico status—she was still alive but unconscious. She took Kathe's hand and squeezed gently. "Thank you. Thank you for everything." She blinked and swallowed hard and then waited, holding Kathe's hand.

Before too long, Justice Fatima entered. Q stood but the Justice motioned her back down. She took the chair across from Q's and Kathe's other hand. Gazing at Q, Fatima said, "Thank you for being here for her. I think she was lonely."

"It was my pleasure, Justice Fatima. Enforcer Kathe is my favorite person, ever." She had to be little-girl Quinn, no matter how difficult that might be right now.

Fatima didn't say anything else. They both sat there, just waiting until the end came. When Kathe was gone, Q stumbled away, out of Kathe's suite and back to her compartment, where she could safely let the tears flow. She felt more like Quinn—a lost little girl. Her only real friend on *Indomito* was gone.

But Kathe left Q a wonderful gift, and she wouldn't waste it. She burrowed under the covers, slid Kathe's e-torc around her neck, and pulled up her banking information. There were a huge number of credits in Familia's preferred bank on Valenti. Q transferred the credits into several different numbered accounts with the same bank, carefully memorizing the account information because she'd have to leave both e-torcs behind at some point. It was risky to use a Familia bank, but there were fewer security hurdles to go through than a non-Familia bank. When she had more time, she'd transfer credits to other financial institutions. But for now, this is what she could do.

ΔΔΔ

When Q returned to the trainee work compartment the next morning, her fellow trainees were all there, even Fabriano. They worked quietly all morning and went to lunch as usual. But near the end of the day, Fabriano and the others gathered around the little galley. Little girl Quinn skipped over, filling her water bottle. "What's going on?"

Fabriano said, "We're not sure, but the remote guard team brought a couple of people into the cells earlier, then transferred them to suites just below the enforcer levels." He sneered at Q. "On the other end of *your* corridor." Fabriano hated being stuck in the trainee dorms, while Q would have loved it. She'd rather not be special. "They're supposed to be having dinner with the enforcers tonight. Are you?"

Q shrugged. "No idea. They never tell me anything until right before." She dredged up tears. "But I hope not because Enforcer Kathe died yesterday." Suddenly, her tears weren't fake.

Aurora pulled her into a hug. "I'm so sorry, Quinn. I know you were close."

Q just sniffled like the little girl she felt like, grateful for Aurora's comfort, even if it was phony.

Fabriano just snorted. Gio and Mario murmured condolences.

198

A bell dinged, and they all jumped and ran for their workstations. Their work hours used to be flexible, but all the rules were tightening, like an arachnid's web.

Q wiped her tears and concentrated on her mind-numbing work. But it wasn't long before she wondered if the prisoners could be the distraction she was looking for. Q couldn't check here, though. Doing anything but her assigned work was a quick road to an airlock. Not to be spaced but put to work at something far worse than net security. Paola didn't specify what that work was, but they all knew Familia was involved in all kinds of illegal activities, including slavery.

So, she summoned Quinn again and thought of Kathe, and her last moments. It wasn't long before she was bawling for real.

"Trainee Quinn, get yourself under control," Paola snapped over her e-torc.

"I'm sorry, Technician Paola, but I miss her so much!" she wailed.

"You're disturbing everyone. Go back to your compartment. If you want to eat, come back to work tomorrow without the crying."

What a sand flea! Why did Familia always use food as a punishment? Q took her bev-tainers and slid snacks in her pockets, and stumbled out of the work compartment, back to her living quarters. She kept crying, eventually burrowing under her covers, crying for real and falling asleep.

Q woke and checked the time; just twenty minutes. *Perfect.* Making her movements minimal, she ran her net program, spoofing the vids on her compartment. She couldn't move around, but if she was lying in bed, it was enough to fool the motion detectors.

Working through the backdoors she'd left on previous late-night forays into *Indomito's* net using the security information she'd discovered spying on Tech Paola, she found her way to the interior vid system. Ironically, it was less protected than most of the net on *Indomito*. Perhaps because you could only access it onboard; there was no easy outside access.

She found the compartments the "guests" were in. The connecting hatch between the compartments was open, and a man and a woman stood there, talking.

By the Mother!

Tensing every muscle in her body, Q kept herself from jumping and running around screaming. That was Captain Ruhger of Lightwave—she'd recognize those oddly broad shoulders and his glowering, black brows above the slightly hooked nose and compressed lips anywhere. The beautiful blonde woman, she didn't know, but if she was with Captain Ruhger, she might be part of Lightwave's crew. Or maybe a passenger?

This changed everything. Captain Ruhger was an experienced former mercenary and pilot, both folding space and shuttles. He got Lightwave Fold Transport out of a lot of bad places, including the dramatic rescue of the Sisters of Cygnus from Galactica Corporation's evil takeover of Cygnus Gliese. As a child, traveling on Lightwave seemed like such fun, a real adventure, jammed in with all the other girls, sleeping in a hammock perched near the ceiling, working in the kitchen with Chef Loreli. Once she got old enough to hear the full story from Nat and Brin, it gave her nightmares—at first. Then Q started thinking about what she'd do if something like that happened on Secundus, which was probably the only reason Lashtar had put up with her as long as she did. By the Mother, she missed them.

Before she could get too maudlin, Ruhger and the woman kissed. So, if she asked for Ruhger's help, this other woman was coming too. Unless they were faking it, but that kiss didn't look fake. No, the kiss was tender, and Q got the distinct impression they were holding back. The two finally broke apart and went into their respective sani-mods, coming out in plain, dark blue shipsuits. The guards took them up to Justice Fatima's level. Q didn't dare snoop on that level of the ship; she'd be caught for sure.

Ideally, she would break the two of them out, and Ruhger could fly Epstein's ship. Epstein had a garbage run scheduled for tomorrow, early in the morning. He'd complained bitterly about the scheduled time.

Her timing had to be perfect, but if Q could take Ruhger and the woman out of their room and through *Indomito* in the early hours of the ship's sleep cycle, she'd have very few people to avoid and not too many vids to spoof. She readied more vid loops of empty passageways.

The next problem was getting a stunner. She needed one to get into the shuttle level of *Indomito*. There was just too much security to get through. If she couldn't get a stunner, she'd have to use her rusty offensive y'ga skills, and that was risky because she hadn't practiced since she left Secundus. Hopefully, muscle memory would prevail.

A movement alert chimed. Ruhger and the woman were escorted back to their compartments by the guards. But they did very strange things. It looked like Ruhger was taking apart the bed, and the woman was using lipstick to block the vids. She did a great job too. Every vid was a smear of red, and the sound from the compartment was muffled. It was an effective trick, that was for sure. Q switched to the view of the passageway to those compartments and set another alert.

It wasn't long before that alert went off. Guards escorted Ruhger and the woman back to Justice Fatima's level.

Q bit her lip. There was no way to spy there. Q scanned through the various shuttle schedules. If she couldn't get Epstein to cooperate, maybe they could steal a shuttle?

A klaxon sounded. "Battle stations. All hands, battle stations."

What? Battle stations? Who would attack Justice Fatima's folder? This is insane! Q tried to find a way into the folder's surveillance, but she'd never tried for command and control before. It was locked down tight on a separate net.

"Attention all personnel. Secure for immediate fold. I say again, secure for immediate fold to Vela."

Q secured the straps across her bed and waited. Sometimes, fold did odd things to her body; she felt like she'd been squeezed. She'd noticed the longer the fold, the worse it was. She'd even passed out once; fortunately, she was in her compartment. She knew that wasn't normal, but she certainly wasn't going to ask one of the Medicos about it.

"Folding for Vela in five, four, three, two, fold. We've arrived in Vela. Remain secured. We will fold for Valenti shortly."

Q shifted uncomfortably. That was a long fold but not overly painful. It wouldn't keep her from doing what she needed to do. A few minutes later, another of her alerts came in. Q brought up the vid outside the Justice's main airlock. Ruhger and the woman were surrounded by guards; a couple of those creepy human-seeming remotes were part of the security detail. But Ruhger and the woman weren't going back to their compartments. No, they were going…to the prison.

Q grinned. Good luck for her. All those backdoors into the prison level would pay off now. Q swept up the vids and watched as Ruhger and the woman were placed in cells next to each other. *Perfect.* She didn't dare mess with the vids here—if there was someone in the cells, there was a Familia guard watching, but she could redirect the sound to her e-torc. It was a little risky because, if the guard looked, they might notice there was no sound at all coming from the cell, but most of them weren't that careful. They assumed if they could see the prisoner, everything was okay. Q held back a chuckle.

"Folding for Valenti in five, four, three, two, fold. We've arrived in Valenti. Resume all normal activities."

Q knew the Vela to Valenti fold was short, and it was confirmed when she didn't feel any additional pain. But what would these folds do to Epstein's scheduled garbage run? The drop-off still had to happen because they had a shuttle full of garbage. But where would the garbage go? Q scanned through the records. Non-recyclables went to Valenti Station. Q smirked. *Perfect.* Valenti station was huge, and she'd made all those secret backdoors in the net nodes on her first work trip. They still worked last time she was there, just a few weeks ago. Familia was lazy in their home system, thinking no one would dare attack them there.

But what about the shuttle schedules? Would they change? Probably. Well, just in case, she should set her little game with Epstein in place now. Q checked—yes, he was lurking in the Pretty Unicorn game again, watching the little kids play before bedtime. Q's lip curled. *Sand flea.* She triggered the first of her messages, asking him to play, which he accepted. Q set her script running. Epstein was predictable. He never responded to little kids' invitations, but teenagers? Those he accepted right away, responding in a way designed to groom them for more interactions. Epstein had always stopped just before making any real contact, but he came closer and closer each time someone contacted him.

Q knew just how to push him over the edge. *Lower than a tunnel worm.* She was probably going to have to touch him, maybe even kiss him. She sneered but couldn't hold back a shudder. But if it meant getting away from *Indomito* and Familia, she'd do it in a heartbeat and make it look and feel perfect. Besides, he'd get what he deserved in the end.

She enticed him through the game, sending him innocent sounding but flirty messages. Q steered them to the traveling part of the game, going on quests for rainbows, and she constantly mentioned how much she wanted to fly, to see the planets from a shuttle. Eventually, Epstein did exactly what she wanted: he invited her along for his garbage run and a visit to the station, even giving her codes to access the shuttle level. *Perfect. What an idiot.*

Q logged off the game and breathed a sigh of relief. Messaging Epstein and hiding those messages from the game's logs was challenging. After running through a short meditation sequence to reenergize herself, Q brought up the prison level comms system. There they were, Ruhger and the blonde, in cells next to each other. The guards were sort of watching from outside the row of cells—one was sleeping, the other playing a game on her e-torc. *Sloppy.*

She took a deep breath and let it out slowly. This was the first big risk. She opened the comms between her and Ruhger. Q opened her mouth, and an alert from the guard post cells pinged. She snapped her mouth shut and cut off her comm access. Her heart pounded like she'd just finished the Atlas Challenge course, and she swallowed hard. *So close.*

Justice Fatima stopped in front of the blonde woman's cell. "I give you one last chance, Saree of Jericho, to cooperate." She smiled, a nasty, mean smile. "Or off to Galactica you go."

Q knew that name too well. Galactica Corporation destroyed Cygnus Gliese, sending those evil Inquisitors first, then strip mining the entire planet, making the Sisters of Cygnus refugees on Cygnus Secundus. Whatever this woman had, Q didn't want Galactica Corp to get it.

Saree of Jericho said nothing. She just stared at Fatima.

Brave or stupid? It was hard to tell.

"No?" Fatima shook her head slowly. "Such a shame." She turned on her heel and walked away without a glance back.

Q released her breath and collapsed on her bed, waiting for her heart rate to slow. What would Fatima do now? Would she send them somewhere immediately? Q waited, minutes turning to an hour, then two. She recorded some vid of the two of them sleeping, so she could use it after she broke them out. Well, it was now or never.

She opened comms between herself and Ruhger's cell. "Captain Ruhger, wake up."

Ruhger blinked and sat up, scrubbing his hands across his head, making his dark brown hair stand up. He looked around the tiny cell and then walked to the front of the cell, trying to look through the force screen.

Biting her lip, Q waited until he turned away from the screen. "Captain, don't talk and try to not look like you're listening to someone. I've temporarily borrowed this commlink, but I can't block the vid. I know you do y'ga a lot, so stretch high if you understand or agree, and touch your toes if you don't understand. Stretch to one side if you disagree. Do you understand?"

Ruhger stretched up high.

"I think I can get you out of the cell and to a shuttle. If I do, will you take me with you?"

He stretched high, then to one side, pointing his fingers at Saree's cell. He wanted to get the blonde, Saree, out too.

Q nodded. She expected that and agreed. "I've got everything covered. I've got a ride on a shuttle to the station—the pilot *thinks* he's getting a date." She didn't try to hide her hatred of Epstein. "We'll have to take out the pilot, use his flight plan to the station, then buy passage out. I've got the credits and other…assets and contacts to cut the deal."

Ruhger stretched high, then over to Saree's cell again.

"Yeah, we'll get your lover out too. Have to, or she might give us away."

He stretched high and held it, then released back to standing straight.

"Good. It will be a few hours. I'll try to give you some warning but no guarantee."

Ruhger stretched up again.

Q's heart was pounding and her mouth dry. "Be ready. Out." Weird how she'd snapped back into the Sisters' quasi-military comms; she hadn't used the term "out" for ages.

Ruhger swung into a y'ga routine, a really impressive one, especially in the tiny cell. Q swept everything off and cleared her tracks from the net. She set an alarm on Kathe's e-torc and one for five minutes later on hers. She needed sleep, but she couldn't afford to oversleep. She concentrated on her breathing, falling into a meditation sequence.

Three hours later, Q woke to the alarm on Kathe's e-torc. She turned off the alarm on hers, set her previously recorded vid of her, sleeping peacefully, into place in the surveillance, and got up. Then, she grabbed the heating and massage pad the medicos gave her for sore muscles, set it to body heat and heartbeat-slow pulsing massage, took off her e-torc and wrapped it around the heating pad, and put the whole thing under her pillow.

Now came the painful part—removing the tracker they'd injected into her when she was initially brought on board *Indomito*. Q showered quickly, then contorted her arm to reach into the hiding place she'd made at the back of one of the compartments. She recovered the knife she'd stolen from the cafeteria while she was checking the kitchen's built-in net terminals. It was sitting in a recycle bin, slightly bent and dull—an easy fix. Grabbing the sterilizing/numbing wipe and skin seal she'd taken from the medico kit weeks ago, she positioned herself so the rear vid on Kathe's e-torc showed her back in the long mirror in the sani-mod, and taped a menstrual pad below the area to catch the blood. She used the wipe and waited for the area to numb.

Q felt for the lump, and pressed a fingernail in hard on both ends, marking her skin. Then, before she could think better of it, she clenched her mouth shut, took the blade between her fingers, and plunged it in. Eyes watering, every major muscle in her body seizing, she forced her hand to move and slice deep, holding back her scream by concentrating on the action. Blood welled as she probed with the knife, finally hooking the chip and pulling it out. Pressing the cut together, she sprayed skin seal across it in thin layers, breathing a sigh of relief when the blood stopped flowing. Q wiped the blood off, put a flesh-colored patch across the whole thing, then stood with clenched fists until the intense urge to scream went away.

Tears ran down her face. It hurt *so* bad. Thank the Mother it hadn't been deeper. Or a bone tag—that, she couldn't have done anything about. Too bad she couldn't steal a medical stunner. Or any stunner. She breathed through the pain and waited for it to fade to a throbbing ache. Staying upright, she slowly turned and washed her hands, face, and the materials she'd used to catch the blood, watching the swirls of red fade to pink. She put the rinsed materials into the recycling. Hopefully, she'd gotten enough of the blood out to prevent any weird alarms from too much human biological material. It should be okay; since she was a young female, her recycling was set a little higher to allow for menstrual cycles.

Q snort-chuckled. It still seemed strange that Familia wanted to prevent crimes and murders on their folders and shuttles when they had no trouble inflicting the same on others. Guess one was business, the other bad for business.

She downed a pain pill and made herself walk to the clothing compartment, breathing through pursed lips, one step at a time. The pain would fade, and she had to keep moving. She slid her clothes off, leaving them piled on the floor, and slid into the costume she'd picked. The bright pink said, "little girl," and the barely-more-than-a-bra and too-short skirt combo said, "sex," the perfect combination to distract Epstein. She added tall boots and slid a shipsuit over the outfit. She carefully didn't bring anything with her—any kind of bag might be noticed.

She took a few deep breaths. It was time to go. She readied the timed script to fool the security on her compartment hatch and bawalked to the bed, sliding the tracking chip under the heating pad. Then she activated the script and then the hatch and prayed she got the timing right. If she did, the hatch activation alert would be shunted away and hidden, and the vids on the way to the cells would switch to blank passageways as she traversed them.

Q brought up the vids to the cells. Ruhger and Saree of Jericho lay on their bunks. Q floated down the tube and swung out on the shuttle level. She slid the fastening down on the front of her shipsuit. With any luck, whoever was guarding the shuttle level tonight would also be distracted.

Suddenly, she was in the middle of a crowd. Q recognized most of these people; they were service workers, all happy, talking loudly and gesturing wildly. As they neared the shuttle security hatch, they started singing, something about partying. They must have gotten a day off on the station. A hand took hers, pulling her into the middle of the group—it was the cook, Maria. When she squeezed and let go, Q started waving her arms around and singing along with them. Without Quinn's e-torc and the tracker, the guards and system would have to catch her by facial recognition, and she was so short in the middle of all these people. Neither one would notice her. They danced through the hatch.

Q blew out a breath of relief, maneuvered to the side of the group, fastened up her top, and blew past them, scowling at the group like she was a worker on her way to a nasty job, jealous of the party. After the party stopped at their airlock, Q kept walking purposefully. When she turned the corner, she spoofed the vid, making the passageway appear empty. She leaned against the airlock to Epstein's shuttle and shimmied out of the shipsuit. Leaving it here wasn't a great plan but bringing it with her wasn't an option either.

She set the script running to break Ruhger and Saree out of the prison cells, opening all the cells and spoofing the vids, making it look like they were sleeping. Hopefully, Ruhger would notice the force screen going down. He was lying there like he was sleeping. Would she have to wake him?

He jumped to his feet and ran out of the cell to the next one, scooping up the limp form of Saree of Jericho.

Sand and sun! If she was unconscious, escape would be harder. Ruhger got to the hatch leaving the cells. Before Q opened it, she opened comms to the prison again and hissed, "Left, to the hatch marked delta one." If Ruhger took the correct hatch, he would come out directly across from this shuttle airlock. Hopefully, it was obvious. Once he was running, Saree swung over his shoulder, Q took a deep breath and summoned little-girl Quinn.

Quinn cycled the airlocks and skipped into the shuttle. "I'm heeeeere! I'm so excited! Let's go for a ride!" Epstein was already strapped into the pilot's seat, but he was fumbling for the release, a panicked look on his ugly face. *Sand fleas!* She couldn't wait, and she couldn't look for a stunner. Ruhger would be here any second. She had to distract Epstein! Q jumped on his lap, straddling his legs, and kissed him full out. He responded enthusiastically. And wetly. Q forced herself to keep kissing him.

Eww. Hurry, Ruhger!

The airlock cycled, and Q circled her hips to distract Epstein. It worked—he grabbed her harder. Then her mouth was shoved off Epstein's by an arm, and she jumped away. Ruhger had an arm around Epstein's throat, choking off his air. Q watched as Epstein flailed, then went still. "Did you kill him?"

"No, just knocked him out."

"Too bad." Q dug around in Epstein's shipsuit pockets. As she thought—flex cuffs. Sneering down at the tunnel slime, she pushed him off the seat, letting him thud on the decking. *Serves you right, flea.* Q secured his hands tight behind his back, then his ankles, and pulled his ankles up to meet his wrist, linking them together. "Let's see how much *you* like this." Epstein was garbage. Q grabbed hold of the flex cuffs and tried to haul him across the floor to the cargo bay, full of garbage just like him. *Ow.* That cut on her back hurt!

Ruhger ran back to the airlock, picked up Saree, and carefully belted her into a seat behind the co-pilot's chair. Once Saree was secure, he turned to her. Ruhger said, "Let me," and grabbed the man by the flex cuffs.

Q happily let go, and Ruhger dragged him to the cargo bay much faster than she could. She jogged ahead to open the hatches, wrinkling her nose at the smell.

"Anything in there?"

"Just garbage, like him," Q told him. She yanked Epstein's e-torc off. Q knew it was unsecured, so she could just hand it to Ruhger and run Ruhger's voice through a simulator to make it sound like Epstein's.

Ruhger dragged Epstein into the bay and dropped him next to bales of veg plas, stacked high. They walked out, and Q secured the hatch behind them.

Ruhger sat in the pilot's seat and put a hand up, then hesitated.

Q held out Epstein's e-torc to him. "Here, it's his—" she tossed her head to the cargo bay "—and he's too stupid to secure it." She plopped into the co-pilot's seat. Hopefully, she'd be useful there, not just dead weight.

Ruhger wiped it off on his shipsuit then placed it around his neck. He reared back in the seat and swiped something violently away.

Q's lip curled. "Porn, right? Sand flea."

"I'm Ruhger, and that's Saree," he said, thrusting a thumb over his shoulder. "You are?"

"Quinn." She nodded at him. "Call me Q."

"Q." He nodded in return. "Got more questions, but let's get going." Ruhger poked and pushed at the e-torc, scowling. "There's an orbit plotted here but just to drop garbage at the station, then a few orbits, and a return."

Q said, "By the Mother! Lower than a sand flea…." Epstein couldn't even spring for a room on the station. He'd make all his nasty moves here on the shuttle? *What a tunnel worm!* Q jumped up to go kick the snot out of him. He was ruining all her plans!

"Not now, Q," Ruhger snapped. "We need to get to the station, find a folder, and get out of here. What other reason do they have to fly to the station?"

Q turned and glared at him. "I don't know!" She couldn't do everything! Epstein was supposed to latch onto the station and have a room waiting!

"Okay, we'll break something after we dump the garbage," Ruhger said calmly, with a shrug. "Strap in."

Q returned to her seat and belted in. Now, what would they do? Think, Q, stop reacting like a little girl.

Ruhger swept up something else, then paused. "Q, what does this guy's voice sound like?"

Nasty, just like him. She pulled up her interface to Epstein's e-torc and set the voice sim running. "I got it. Just talk."

Ruhger nodded. "Excellent. Does anyone else know what he's doing?"

"Sure, they all know he's on the garbage run." Q shrugged. Epstein was always on the garbage run and constantly complained about it.

Ruhger glowered at her. "No, with you." He poked some more at the holo. Q watched; he was requesting pushback. Clever to do it by text, that way there was no chance the voice simulator screwed up.

"Oh." Q shuddered. If Enzo or any of the Familia enforcers had any idea Epstein had even talked to her inside a vid game, they wouldn't be here now. But she needed to tell him something…well, why not the truth? "No. He'd be dead."

Ruhger just looked at her for a few seconds, then said, "Thrust in five, four, three, two, thrust." He poked away at the e-torc.

She did the same, making sure all her scripts on *Indomito* finished and disappeared. She'd considered leaving some havoc behind her, but she'd rather get away quietly.

"Q?"

"Yeah?" She looked over at Ruhger.

"Is there a locator on your e-torc?"

Q chuckled. "Already taken care of." Q swallowed hard. "I'm safely locked in my room like always." If she didn't get away, when they brought her back, she'd really be locked up—in a cell, not a comfy compartment.

"Good job. Watch the navigation for me."

What? She wasn't a pilot.

Ruhger brought a view up on the big display in the shuttle. "It's pretty obvious if the shuttle icon leaves the programmed path." Ruhger pointed at it. "I've got to bring Saree back."

Bring her back? She was unconscious. Didn't Saree need to just sleep it off? "Back from where? I thought they stunned her."

Ruhger snorted. "No. She's somewhere in her own mind." He unbuckled and walked the few steps to the blonde.

In her own mind? Like meditation or something? Couldn't he just shake her awake? Never mind. Not Q's problem; she'd just do what he asked. "Okay, then. I'll just watch the cute little shuttle on the string." Gah, maybe she'd been channeling Quinn too much.

Ruhger spoke in a commanding tone. "Saree, return. Return now. We are safe." He said the same thing over and over, louder and louder. When Q glanced back, she was shocked to see Ruhger shaking Saree by the shoulders as he roared the words. "Blast and rad." He released Saree and rubbed her shoulders gently, glancing at Q. "Sorry, kid, but this is what she told me to do."

Kid? She hadn't been a child for years. "I'm not a kid."

"I suppose you aren't, but you probably should be." He sighed. "Got a stunner on this tug?"

Q nodded a little warily. He'd better not double-cross her. "Sure. Why?"

"Because it will take an electric shock to bring her back now."

Q got up to find the weapons locker, keeping an eye on Ruhger. She'd get one for herself too. "Stun me, and you'll get nowhere fast."

Ruhger shook his head. "Trust me, I don't want to stun you or prod Saree. It will be painful, and I know she'll get a migraine. But she can't stay under either, and she'll need the rest of our flying time to recover enough to walk." He stared down at Saree's body. He was trying to appear impassive, but Q could see the worry.

Saree was definitely more than just a crewmember.

Q pulled a stunner out of the weapons compartment. There was only one. She sighed and handed it to Ruhger.

Ruhger took it, thumbed through the settings, and put the contacts against the outside of Saree's thigh. "Saree, wake!" he roared again, making Q jump. Saree didn't react, and Ruhger's wide shoulders slumped. He really didn't want to use the stunner, but he did, Saree's body jolting. "Suns." He adjusted it and shocked her again.

What if this didn't work? Would he kill her? Q bit her lip to keep from protesting.

Ruhger shook his head. "Here goes nothing," he muttered and hit the stunner. Saree's body jumped, and she stopped breathing. Ruhger unlatched her harness, but as he was sliding his arms underneath her, Saree gasped and blinked. "Saree, can you hear me?"

Saree panted, her eyelids fluttering.

That had to be a terrible shock, no pun intended. What could she do? Q thought back to her first aid classes back on Secundus. Prevent shock by raising the feet and warming the patient. Q ran for the closest cabin, grabbed a wrapped blanket, and dropped the plas packing material on the deck as she ran back. She held the blanket out to Ruhger.

Ruhger said, "Thanks. Orbit?" He wrapped Saree up and held her hand.

Oops. "Right. I'm watching." Fortunately, the shuttle was right on-orbit and nothing else was near.

"Good. Thanks." Ruhger turned back to Saree, and Q watched

out of the corner of her eye. "Can you hear me?" he asked Saree.

"Yes." Saree put a hand to her head. "Hurts."

"Sorry, Saree, but I had to bring you back. We're escaping."

"Oh." She sagged into the seat, wincing.

Ruhger asked, "Q, are there any drugs on this tug?"

Q was sure there was a medico dispenser in the sani-mod. All the Justice's shuttles were fully stocked, even the ones on the garbage run, just in case something happened and Fatima had to fly in it, rather than her normal shuttle. Q jumped up and jogged to the sani-mod, turning back at the hatch. "Sure. I'll print some out. Migraine, but we don't want her sleeping, right?"

"Yes. Thanks." Ruhger fussed with the blanket.

Q hoped someone looked at her that way someday. But for now, escape was the important thing. Relationships could wait. "I'll print a bunch. We'll take them with us." She couldn't wait to get off this thing, one step closer to freedom. She should take something herself; the wound where she cut out the tracker was not comfortable.

"Good idea." Q heard Ruhger talking to Saree while she found the right meds in the medico-dispenser and ordered fifty. Q glanced around the sani-mod. It looked a lot like hers, with makeup and hairstylers. She searched the cabinet but didn't find a medical stunner. Once the first pills came out, she took one with a big glass of water. No sense in getting dehydrated either.

Ruhger said, "Q's bringing something for the pain, Saree. You can sleep until the station, then we'll need to walk out. Understand?"

"Yes," Saree said. Q strained to hear. "Ruhger, I think I found them."

Found who?

"Really? Wow. That's great. Did you call them?"

"No. Too confusing. Too chaotic. Too much." Saree's voice trailed off.

What did that mean? Q pulled the meds out of the slot, got another glass of water, and brought it all to Ruhger. She helped Saree hold the glass.

Ruhger belted Saree back in, with her arms outside the straps, and covered her with the blanket. "Sleep." Saree closed her eyes and seemed to collapse into the seat. Ruhger kissed her cheek and returned to the pilot's chair.

Q returned to the co-pilot's seat, glancing back at the sleeping Saree. "Is she going to be okay?" If Saree couldn't walk, escape would be next to impossible. Q could spoof the vids on Valenti Station, but people would notice someone being carried.

"I sure hope so. Can you figure out where we'd go if we break something? It should be a repair depot on the station someplace."

"Sure." Q pulled up the maintenance records on the shuttle and selected those for Valenti Station.

"Then, once you do that, see if you can find something else to wear that won't be so conspicuous. Something that covers your body. A hat would be a great idea too." Ruhger glanced at her, grimacing.

Q smirked at him. "Okay." Like she wanted to stay in this costume? *Yuck.* She kept looking through the records, knowing there was a clothes printer in the bunk room.

Ruhger asked, "Q, you're a Sister of Cygnus, right? Or raised by them?"

Did he recognize her? She didn't look the same after all these years, especially with her current, ugly Familia-brown hair. But she should explain. "Yes. That's why I took the chance to escape with you. I know who you are and what you've done."

"How did you get here?

Q laughed. "Oh, that's a long story filled with stupidity. Mostly mine." So, so stupid. So many things gone wrong, so many wasted chances.

Ruhger shrugged. "Okay. Later then. Will Familia be looking for you? Wait, let me rephrase that. Will they be looking for you any harder than anyone else escaping their greedy fingers?"

"Yeah." Enzo would search everywhere. His pride and Familia's reputation wouldn't allow her to escape. It probably wasn't fair to Ruhger and Saree, but she had to take this chance. Still, she owed Ruhger an answer, even if she couldn't face him. "Enzo had me marked."

"Marked? How? Is there a tracker?"

Q snorted and frowned at Ruhger. She wasn't stupid. She wouldn't make it easy for the slimeballs to find her. "I cut the tracker out. Hurts, but I'll live. The tattoo will take a body mod." She'd pay anything to get rid of the ugly thing.

"Why did he mark you?"

Ruhger had to ask, didn't he? Well, fine. "Because he wanted a virgin, the sicko, and he wanted to make sure anyone else seeing me knew I was his property. Sand scooter scat," Q spit out, hating every word. "Lucky me that he likes women, not 'little girl bodies,' as he put it. Idiot. I'm never going to be some sexy siren;

that's just not the way I'm built." They were all idiots. She held back a shiver. But idiots with a ton of power.

Ruhger scanned her up and down in a very clinical manner. "How old are you?"

Sand and sun! Q needed Ruhger to treat her like an adult, but he wouldn't believe an obvious lie. She'd add a year. Q sniffed. "Seventeen standards. I've been with Familia for a year, but I lied, told them I was fourteen." Two years, if you counted Adzari Academy, but he didn't need to know that.

"Smart. All right then, we need to find you coveralls or a shipsuit. A hat or…" He grimaced, looking at her. "Would you cut your hair?"

Q grinned. She couldn't wait! "In a heartbeat. I'll go do that right now!" Q jumped and ran for the sani-mod. Something totally different and short. Yes! She'd do some crazy makeup too—black and heavy. No one would recognize her face when she was done.

She closed the sani-mod hatch and opened the Style Three Thousand. The shuttles got a better styler than she did? Why? Q thumbed through the options. Well, it would look terrible with her skin tone, but bright colors were all the rage right now on Valenti. Q dialed in a cut with a very short, almost shaved back, left long on the top and in front, in a bright but warm yellow. She sat in the pop-out chair, thrilled to watch long strands of brown hit the floor. Sucked away by the vacuum, they looked like weird snakes. She smiled—her head felt lighter without all that hair. The chair leaned back, and the color was applied, then back up she went for the final styling. Q hopped up and shook her head, loving the way the silky strands lifted and swung. The bangs shaded her eyes, but nothing brushed her neck.

Makeup next. She opened the Beauty-in-a-Box, also an upgrade from hers, and scrolled through the choices. Ooh, look at that style from Old Earth. *Crazy!* Heavy black on the eyes and blood-red lips; the rest of the face, dead white. All that black would change the way her eyes looked to humans, even if it wouldn't fool a good facial recognition program. Along with the lighter skin, she entered some contouring, making her cheeks and nose look a little different. She closed her eyes and let the Box work. When it dinged, saying she was done, she looked in the mirror.

Wow. Totally different. Sister Lashtar wouldn't recognize her like this! What would Ruhger say? Q snickered. Time to find out. She left the sani-mod and walked over to Ruhger, who obligingly did a double-take.

"Suns!" Ruhger huffed. "I thought someone snuck on board for a second."

"Good." Just this little change made her ridiculously happy. The relief was intense.

"Can you find something else to wear? That—" Ruhger grimaced and waved his hand up and down, " —is terrible."

"It did the job. But yes, I can print shipsuits."

"Good. One for each of us, please."

Q considered Ruhger. "You should change your hair too."

He scrubbed a hand across his head. "I don't have much."

"Make it blond. It will look like even less."

Ruhger nodded thoughtfully. "Good idea. Watch the nav." He disappeared into the sani-mod.

Q plopped into the co-pilot's seat, drew her legs up, hugging them tight, and watched the shuttle fly along the orbit perfectly. She kept glancing back at Saree, but she didn't wake.

A few minutes later, Ruhger came out, blond. He didn't look much different. "You should smile a lot to make you look, well, not like you."

He bared his teeth in a grimace, sending Q rocking back in the seat. "Yikes. Yeah, don't do that. I'll go print the shipsuits." Q took the few steps to Cabin One and searched through the storage compartments. Toiletry kits, toothbrushes—she grabbed three each of those—bedding…ah, here we are. Clothes printer. She selected a shipsuit in dark gray. Q found the smallest adult pattern and started it running. She'd have to guess on Ruhger and Saree. When it finished, she pulled off the hated skirt and put the shipsuit on. It was way too big, but that fit the makeup.

She printed one for Saree in dark brown, and one for Ruhger in a lighter brown, then programmed in extra shipsuits, hats for all of them, a few underthings, and three carrybags. Once she got all that started, Q checked their transmission time to Valenti station—close enough to prevent time delay problems. Time to infiltrate the security net.

She connected to the backdoors she'd left on the previous trip and slid into the outer layers of station security. No warnings to look out for the three of them yet. Q fingered the e-torc around her neck. As much as she wanted to take Kathe's e-torc with her, she didn't dare. It was a big risk bringing it on the shuttle. Q returned to the main cabin.

"Ruhger?"

"Yes?" He continued watching his screens. Guess he didn't

trust the autopilot or the Station controllers.

"I need Epstein's e-torc. I've got to transfer some stuff to it." She held his new shipsuit out in trade.

He pulled the e-torc off and handed it to her. "Sure. You know more about this stuff than I do, by far."

"Thanks." She set up a handshake and started the file transfers, breathing a sigh of relief when it was done. Then she started removing the junk Epstein left on the e-torc and all the trackers. She also removed every non-essential program and ran a full reset on everything else. "Here you go."

"That one is bugged?" Ruhger nodded at Kathe's e-torc.

"I don't think so, but I don't want to take the chance. It isn't really mine, and there's some super-smart net techs back on the ship."

"Good. Leave it here." Ruhger's lips lifted at the very corners. "Maybe old Ep will take an even bigger hit that way. Can we take his?"

"Yes. I've scrubbed it thoroughly." And she had. There was nothing left on it to give them away.

Ruhger returned to navigation. "Yes, Valenti Station, you have that correct. Recycling and garbage drop." He listened. "Copy that, Valenti." Ruhger huffed. "Guess they're used to this guy. They told me where we'll be docking and said it would take five hours to unload." He snorted. "Five hours. Right. Definitely some credits changing hands here. The problem is, they'll see I'm not Epstein when we get off."

Q grinned. "Nope. Just give me your e-torc right after we dock, and I'll make sure they see Epstein. No one will come to the shuttle in person, not until we don't come back. I've been planning this for a long time."

Ruhger nodded slowly. "Good job. I'll leave you to handle the details, then."

"Well, I can handle getting us on the station and hiding us from the vids, but I could use help with finding us a place to hide until we can contact a folder," Q told him. "I have credits and some ideas on folders, but my best options aren't on station now."

"Okay, Q, I'll do my best and you do yours, and we'll get out of here, right?" Ruhger asked.

"Right," Q replied.

"We'll both need to help Saree. She'll be shaky for a while."

"Okay. I can do that."

A low moaning sigh came from behind them.

"Glad you're willing to help because we start now," Ruhger said.

CHAPTER TWELVE

Ruhger shook Saree's shoulder, and she blinked up at him. "You okay?" Ruhger asked.

Saree rasped, "Maybe. Need the sani-mod."

Ruhger said, "Okay. Q can help you." He unstrapped the belts and raised the seat.

Q forced a smile. Saree was going to slow them down. "Yeppers. Helpful, that's me." She sounded like little-girl Quinn again. But she was so happy to have someone who wanted to help her, and it wasn't a bad thing to be underestimated.

Saree smiled a little. "Thank you. I feel pretty shaky." She rose slowly, keeping her hands on the armrests.

"How's your head?" Ruhger asked.

"Okay." Saree wrinkled her nose. "It's kind of achy, but not horrible."

"Good. Drink some water while you're in there. You've got time for a shower too if you want. Q printed a shipsuit that ought to fit you and a hat to cover your hair." Ruhger nodded and returned to the pilot's seat.

"Great." Saree stood.

She looked pretty shaky, so Q stepped up next to her. If Saree fell, it would take her longer to recover and make their escape harder. Saree shuffled to the sani-mod, but her stride steadied and lengthened as she walked. At the hatch, she turned to Q. "I think I'm okay."

Q nodded at her and trotted back to sit next to Ruhger. If Saree felt steady enough, she didn't want to hang out in the sani-mod with her. Besides, she had work to do while she had Kathe's e-torc. She started moving credits, creating new numbered accounts at a couple of different institutions, including one that wasn't Familia. It was riskier, but she had nothing to lose. Go big or get captured.

When she finished, she realized more than a few minutes had passed. Q jogged back to the sani-mod, ready to break in if necessary, but Saree exited, her hair partially dark brown and raggedly chopped off. It looked terrible. "Girl, what did you do?! There's a Style Three Thousand in there—let's go." Q grabbed her arm and pulled Saree back into the sani-mod. What cut would look good on her? Q activated the Styler and swung Saree around to sit on it. "Take the top part of your shipsuit off."

Saree did as Q demanded, chuckling a little.

Q grimaced. "How long do you want it?" Maybe just a medium-length, straight blunt cut, nothing fancy or fussy. Saree's body was flashy enough; she must get lots of unwanted attention.

Saree shrugged. "Middle of my shoulder blades, I guess."

Q programmed the styler and told Saree, "Sit still." The styler got to work, combing and cutting Saree's hair. Since she'd already colored most of it, it didn't take long. Q had the styler do an updo, changing Saree's look further.

Saree stood up and stared at the styler for a long time. "First time I've seen that."

"Really? Huh. I thought everyone had those." Sure, the Sisters didn't, but they had them at Adzari Academy, and she'd seen them at stations and spaceports everywhere. Well, except *Indomito* stayed in the core mostly, and if she remembered correctly, Lightwave flew the fringes of the known universe.

"Seems easier than finding someone."

"Oh, yeah. Much. Unless you want something really special." Q checked both sides of Saree's hair. "Looks like the color covers all of it. Good. I'll throw some makeup on you, and no one will recognize you." At least she hoped so. Q turned to the Beauty-in-a-Box.

"Maybe not so dark?"

Q laughed. "What? You don't like Old Earth twenties? Me neither." She snorted. "Don't worry, I'll give you something more dignified. But makeup makes a big difference in appearance. With your hair up and dark and color on your face, no human man will recognize you." She grimaced. "Facial recog will, but not most men. Or women." Too bad they didn't have some of that light-scattering makeup. That would blur their appearance on most vids. But that didn't seem to be an option in the Box. Which seemed odd; you'd think Familia enforcers would need that stuff occasionally.

"Good point. Do your worst." Saree's nose wrinkled.

Q laughed and made her final choices, positioning Saree in the right spot. "You bet. Close your eyes and don't move." When it finished, Q closed the thing up and mirrored the surface. "Take a look." The shuttle jolted a little—they must have docked. Now, the fun part started.

Saree looked, turning her face from side to side. "Wow, Q. Nice job on the shading—my face shape even looks different." She plopped the small, brimmed hat Q printed for her on her head and pulled it down and to the side a little. "Especially with the hat."

"Thanks." Q remembered all the parties she'd had to attend, dressed up like a doll for Enzo. Never again. "I've had a lot of practice."

"Ready?" Ruhger called. "We should get going. Nasty boy there wouldn't be wasting time."

Q sighed and slid Kathe's e-torc into the recycling. But she snickered as she left the sani-mod. Nasty boy was a great name for Epstein. "Sure. Hey, what do you think?" She swept a hand down Saree's body.

Ruhger's eyebrows rose, and he nodded. "Great job. I wouldn't recognize her."

Q chuckled and handed carrysacks to Saree and Ruhger.

Ruhger nodded. "Okay, so what are we calling each other? I've got Epstein's e-torc, so call me Ep."

Not a "Q" sound, but something close… "Clove," Q told them. "It sounds close enough to Q for me to hear it, but not close enough for others to recognize." Q looked at Saree, who seemed to be thinking hard.

"Hmm." Saree's fingers tapped some sort of complex, repeating rhythm against her thighs. "I don't want to use an old name… How about Ferra? I'll certainly remember it." Saree grimaced.

Q couldn't hold back a gasp, then she grinned. Q wouldn't forget that name either.

Ruhger said grimly, "Good. Ferra, Clove is our daughter. We're on our way to Nexus Station, where we're meeting our new employers, Universal Fold Incorporated. We're changing folders here, but the next one won't be in for a couple of days, so we're headed to a hostel. I've already paid for it. Let's go. They could discover we're gone at any moment."

Q followed both of them into the airlock.

Saree turned back to her. "Where are we?"

Q snort-chuckled. "Valenti Prime, the main station. Customs is here and a lot of zero-g medico research." And a whole lot of Familia.

Saree turned back to Ruhger, her tone urgent. "Ruhger—I mean Ep—if we're stuck here for a while, maybe I can body mod back."

Well, that explained Saree's figure. It wasn't natural. Right now, she'd fit right in with the Familia enforcers.

Ruhger shot an incredulous look at Saree. "On a Familia station?"

"Oh." Saree snorted. "Sorry, I think I'm a little fuzzy still."

No kidding. She clearly wasn't thinking at all. They'd have to guide Saree, or they'd get caught. Q bit her lip.

"Great," he muttered. "Get unfuzzy because it's going to take all our wits to get out of here in one piece." He nodded at them. "Ready?"

Q nodded at him and motioned to his e-torc, but he turned away before she completed the motion. *Sand and sun!* She had to get the e-torc before they went too far, but the hatch was open now, and she couldn't chance making a fuss. All she could do was hope no one was actively watching the vids. They left the airlock, entering a moderately busy passageway, big hovercarts full of tools and what must be shuttle replacement pieces shoved against the bulkheads, leaving a narrow, winding path for them to walk through. Q started out trying to walk like a station worker, not paying attention to anything, but she couldn't help but look around. She'd never been in this part of the station.

No one paid any attention to them, and soon, they entered the maintenance worker market. Q hadn't been here either, but she'd heard about it. You could get food, drink, clothing, and all kinds of stuff at low prices. Low for a station, anyway. She looked at the decking as much as she could and used the crowd and the sales kiosks to block her from easy view.

Ruhger wove around the kiosks, obviously familiar with avoiding vids, and they strolled to the other end of the market, entering a connector shuttle to Valenti Prime Station Central, someplace Q had been too often. They flew through space for a few minutes, docked, and exited into Prime Central's main shopping area.

Much nicer and a lot larger, there were rows of shops and restaurants around the outside of the area and kiosks with food, drink, and all kinds of wares sprinkled across a wide plaza, the high ceilings making the area feel spacious. The walls were decorated in gold and red, and the shops had formal clothing and fancy restaurants with people doing the service rather than remotes. All high-credit stuff too.

They passed the restaurant Kathe took her to with the weird food, then the one Enzo chose. That food was almost as weird, there still wasn't much of it, and it was the most awkward eating experience of her life. Even if the food had been good, she'd been far too nervous to enjoy any of it. Enzo must not have enjoyed it either, because they never did it again. She shuddered, remembering.

While sweeping away barrages of advertisements on his e-torc, Ruhger said, "This is Level Forty. We're headed down to Level Twenty-One. Cheap hostels there."

Maybe not having the e-torc was a good thing—resetting it to standard left it open to the ads. But her neck felt naked. Q followed Ruhger and Saree to a float tube and down they went.

Q kept glancing around. She recognized some of these places. As soon as she had an e-torc, she'd be back into Valenti Station Security.

The shopping on Level Twenty-One was basic: food and clothing, a few gadgets and trinkets, and no fancy decorations. They stopped for a quick meal of pasta with red sauce, which wasn't good, but it was filling. Then they entered a narrow interior station corridor. The walls were bland beige, with industrial multi-hued plas decking underfoot and the occasional holo sign for guest check-in popping up as they neared each hatch.

Ruhger finally stopped in front of a holo for "Albergo Firenze" and checked them in, getting two access stickers for Saree and Q, since they didn't have e-torcs. Q copied Saree, sticking hers to the inside of her forearm, underneath the shipsuit. Ruhger walked forward and a hatch slid open. They entered an even narrower corridor, with hatches on both sides. Walking along, Ruhger found the correct one and entered.

The room was small and plain, but it looked and smelled clean. Bunk beds on both sides, the narrow space between them leading to a tiny sani-mod. Q could fit four of these rooms in her compartment on *Indomito*, but she was way happier here.

"So, Clove, let's see who's on station we can fold out with," Ruhger suggested.

Smart of Ruhger to assume someone was watching. Time for her to get into character. With the makeup, a bratty teenager was best. "I guess, Ep." Q sighed, loud and long, cocked a hip, and looked up at Ruhger through her thick bangs. "Can't we go shopping up on Forty? They had some out-orbit stuff up there!"

"Shopping later," Ruhger growled. "Virtual shopping. No way I've got credits for Forty."

Q whined, "You're no fun." She stuck her lower lip out and blinked pathetically.

Ruhger sat on one of the lower bunks and patted the space next to him. Saree pushed past both of them and entered the sani-mod. Ruhger stared at the sani-mod hatch, frowning.

That didn't look fake. Saree wasn't feeling good at all. Q bit her lip. She didn't want to go it alone, but she wasn't getting caught because of Saree.

"Let's find that ride," Ruhger said, widening the view of his e-torc.

Q sat close to him and made snarky comments about ship names. She didn't recognize any of these folders. *Daedalus*, *Excelsior*, and *Icarus* were scheduled to be here now—did something big happen somewhere?

Saree came out of the sani-mod, clutching her head. "My head hurts. Too much ruckus out there. You two find us a ride out; I'm napping." She looked wan and shaky.

Ruhger scowled at her. "Sure, Ferra. You rest, we'll do the work." He turned back to Q and pointed at a folder called *Basestar* on his holo. "What about that one?"

Saree climbed to the top bunk across from them. Both Q and Ruhger tensed, ready to catch her, until she reached the top.

Suns, what did Ruhger ask? Oh, the folder. It wasn't one of the folders she was looking for. "Nah, she's a rad-blaster. Can I scroll?"

Ruhger pulled the e-torc off and handed it to her, frowning at Saree's back. Then he huffed, got up, and went to the sani-mod.

Good. Q could do this a lot faster on her own. She slid the e-torc around her neck, found a net node with one of her backdoors, and got into Valenti's net security easily. She set up alerts tied to their names, current faces, and this station corridor. Good thing she'd memorized all the net access codes rather than relying on her e-torc. Then she returned to the fold transport list—they had to leave this station quickly.

Ruhger dropped into the bottom bunk directly across from her and under Saree. "Wake me if you need anything."

Q nodded at him, and he closed his eyes, seeming to drop into sleep immediately. After scrolling through every folder leaving

Valenti, she didn't find any she knew or trusted. Giving up on the passenger folders, she looked at the short-term work contracts.

Ah, here we go. A freighter looking for a net tech, a pilot, and general workers. Q looked through the work history. *Yikes.* These guys were barely limping along, but from the reviews and fines, they didn't get along with Familia. Perfect for them—Nebula Wraith wouldn't ask questions. Q sent off inquiries for a crew of three, including her real skills and Epstein's piloting qualifications, and got an offer back immediately. They traded messages for a while, Nebula Wraith's captain insisting on pics of all of them and assurances they weren't Familia because Familia was evil. *No kidding.* But this guy wasn't any better—he was a sand flea. Q sent the real Epstein's pic and doctored pics of her and Saree—no one would recognize them. Really, Captain Bonnet—which wasn't his real name, of course—should know better.

Q finally convinced Bonnet she knew her stuff by breaking into his personal e-torc and putting a message in his display. She got an agreement with a ludicrously low offer of credits. She was about to fire a counteroffer back when one of her security alerts went off. *Sand and sun!* Their escape from *Indomito* was discovered, and the three of them had been spotted on the station. She accepted the employment offer and got up.

She poked Ruhger. "Got to go now. Security noticed us." Q grabbed her carrysack and Saree's.

He jumped up. "Wake up—we've got to go, *now*," Ruhger hissed to Saree.

Q stared at the holo, reading her alerts. "We were spotted on

Forty on vid. It won't take them long to find us." She looked up at the two of them. No time for hair or makeup changes. "Sa—Ferra, take your hair down. Ep—suns, nothing we can do about those shoulders. Give me your hat."

Ruhger took his hat off, dropping it on her head and walking to the hatch. "As much as I hate to ask, do you have any idea what Below is like here?"

Q shuddered. Dead, that's what the non-existent station Below was like. "Bad idea. I got us jobs. We're going back out, turn left out of the hostel and to a float tube. Up two levels and out to shuttle arm Tango. I made a deal with a freighter captain for net work in exchange for passage. He expects help with piloting too; his pilot left him here and he hasn't found another one. It's not safe; he's got a bad rep. But he hates Familia more than he hates anything else." She whispered the name.

They left the Albergo. Q started spoofing vids with blank corridors and shunting alerts off to hidden data locations, but net techs were actively fighting her now. She jumped a little when Ruhger wrapped an arm around her shoulder but quickly realized he was guiding her while she worked. Q trusted that Ruhger remembered her directions and kept working the security.

"We're here," Ruhger hissed in her ear.

Q looked up and entered the security code Bonnet gave her into the hatch. The hatches opened for them, and they walked in, Ruhger shoving her behind his bulk.

But it didn't matter. A short, fat human male pointed a laser pistol at them. Despite the weapon, Q was sure the stench of rotting food was a bigger threat. She gagged along with Saree, her eyes watering.

"Fools. Hands up. Didn't you think I'd know Familia wants you?" He snorted. "You just paid my debt. Move there and sit."

He motioned at the row of observers' chairs behind the pilot and co-pilot's seats. Q bit her lip and walked to the right, Ruhger going with her. Saree went the other way. The man's pistol followed Q. She sniffed at her ridiculousness. The pistol was following Ruhger, not her. Before Q reached the seat, a stunner buzzed.

Saree lowered her hand, and Q gaped. Where'd she get a stunner? Oh, Ruhger must have given her the one from the Familia shuttle.

Ruhger sprinted to the pilot's seat and pulled up communications and navigation.

She shook her astonishment off. What if Captain Bonnet had better security than she thought? Q pulled the e-torc off the unconscious captain's neck and started looking through it. No security so far… what about messages? Had Bonnet already messaged Familia?

Ruhger said, "Get us an orbit out to… hah, here it is, Fold Transport Nebula Wraith."

Q looked up. Oh, he was talking to Saree. Good. She went back to Bonnet's messages, checking all his systems.

"Sounds like a pirate," Saree said.

"Probably is," Ruhger said. "Q, did he contact Familia already?"

"Doesn't look like it," Q said, looking through less obvious messaging systems. "But he could have sent something coded."

Some of these messages looked weird. And this one—yikes! She pushed it to the delete folder. *Ew.* People should know better.

"Any idea how many onboard the folder?" Ruhger asked.

Q recalled the messages between them. Bonnet hadn't said anything about the other crew. Or if there was anyone else on the crew at all. "Let me look." There was no organization in Bonnet's e-torc. Nothing was put in any kind of order. This would take forever.

Saree said, "Release scheduled in nine minutes, forty seconds."

"Perfect. Secure that idiot and see if there's any armor on this boat."

Q searched for personnel files while Saree secured Bonnet. Saree started poking around the shuttle, opening compartments. Waves of new and different stenches wafted to her, mostly rotting food.

Q finally found Bonnet's crew roster. "Ew. There's a crew of twenty on the folder, and most of them are Blattos." She'd never seen a Blatto, but the very idea of meter-tall cockroaches made her shudder violently. She scrolled down the crew list—Bonnet didn't even put their names down, he just numbered them. *Yuck.* Most of them were unskilled labor, like cargo loaders and cleaners. Blattos cleaned? There was a name by the engineer and purser, but they were lined through, and blank spots by the pilot and co-pilot. So, Bonnet had needed a pilot badly.

"Blast and rad. Those things are impossible to stun and hard to kill," Ruhger said. "Are any of them command or pilots?"

"No. And it looks like the pilot and co-pilot left, so the whole crew is Blatto except that guy." Q pointed at Bonnet. She smirked;

Saree had not only flex-cuffed his wrists but secured them to a loop under a broken plas floor tile.

Ruhger said, "Find out if this shuttle is usually the folder's command center or if piloting takes place elsewhere. Either way, see if the Blattos have access." He huffed. "I'm willing to bet they don't."

"Oh yeah? How much?" Q asked, laughing inside. The relief of being off station was making her silly.

"What?" Ruhger asked.

"How much are you willing to bet? I need some credits." She didn't, but Ruhger and Saree didn't need to know that.

Ruhger snorted. "It's a figure of speech. I don't gamble."

"Of course you don't." Q snorted. Ruhger seemed pretty humorless. Was he? She'd find out. Q yelled, "Saree, does he do anything fun?" Ruhger's back stiffened. This was kind of fun. And she needed some of that in her life, especially right now.

"Not very often."

"Figures. May as well be back on Cygnus with the Sisters." They both ignored her. *Fine.* Q flopped down in the co-pilot's seat and kept looking through Bonnet's messy files.

Saree said, "Ruhger, I'm not finding anything but garbage."

"They're saving it for the Blattos," Ruhger said. Q's stomach turned. He continued, "They'll eat anything, and believe it or not, stations pay good credits for Blatto waste. Makes good fertilizer. Find a seat. Launch in five…"

Saree plopped into a seat while Q fastened her harness. It was sticky. *Yuck.* Q jolted in the seat as the shuttle was shoved out.

"Thrust in five, four, three, two, thrust."

A surge of heavier gravity and then the grav generators came on. Q almost floated, then landed back in her seat somewhere near one-g.

"This thing needs an overhaul," Ruhger muttered.

"And an intense cleaning," Saree said.

"We might have the time," Q told them. "I don't think we dare message your Lightwave. Familia has too many sniffers on the comms out of Valenti; all of Vela, really. We need to fold out on Nebula Wraith or another folder already here. And taking this shuttle to a different folder will raise a stink." She laughed at her pun. "A bigger stink than this shuttle."

"Can you imagine what the folder smells like?" Saree asked, revulsion warring with wonder in her voice.

"I'm hoping we can dock the shuttle and avoid the folder entirely," Ruhger said. "We've got rations here, right?"

"Meal packs," Saree said. "I haven't counted them yet."

"If we fold out to wherever we want, then make a deal with the Blattos to give them the folder, hopefully, they'll just leave us alone."

Q said, "I don't think so. I think they'll try to swarm us and eat us." She'd seen it in vid games enough that she looked it up.

"They eat sentients?" Saree said over Ruhger's exclamation, "Seriously?"

"It's never been proven…" Q let the words trail off. "But I've seen lots of rumors on the net."

"This gets better and better."

More of her alerts went off as Valenti's security tracked them. Q went back to tweaking security's figurative nose. Security found

most of her backdoors and shut her out. But she still had a few…
"Sand and sun! Familia figured out we left the station."

"Blast and rad," Ruhger said. "Will they look for this shuttle?"

Q sighed. Valenti's net techs weren't stupid, they were just lazy. For example, their certainty the three of them had left the station just because they couldn't find the three of them immediately. "Eventually, they'll track us through the station by where I covered our tracks. They'll figure it out." What could she do? She had to make it look like they were still there.

Ruhger nodded. "Okay, then we're increasing thrust. We might be under heavy-g the whole way because these grav generators are terrible."

Q's arm got heavy, and she reclined the seat, despite the stickiness. She'd take a long shower later. She had to keep working now, despite the gravity and the dirty shuttle. "I know, I'll blank out a lot more vids on-station, try to make it look like we're still there, walking the passageways. But the interface on this e-torc is terrible and the shuttle net is worse." Q flicked a fingernail at the flickering holo display. It stabilized for a moment, then went back to flickering. She sighed. "*Captain* Bonnet is a cheapskate. We should have bought a decent e-torc on the station." She hadn't had enough time to find a shady dealer, though. The time lag was starting to be a problem too.

"We don't have credits for a decent e-torc. I just about wiped Epstein's account out as it was," Ruhger said. "If we'd had a bit more time, we could have earned them, but…" Ruhger let the words trail off. Q was about to tell him she had credits when he continued, "If we can make it to the folder, we've got a chance. If the fold generators work, I'll fold out right there. Familia wants to abduct us, they pay for it."

Wow. Fold out in the fold hold orbit? That would cause all kinds of disruptions for the folders in nearby orbits and to the Valenti fold clock. Ruhger was punching Familia right in the nose. Q snickered, then went back to finding out what she could about Nebula Wraith.

"Saree, how did you do that trick in Mensa?" Ruhger asked.

"I used a net worm Hal wrote and broke into the ore transport comms. Why?"

Q considered Saree. She hadn't gotten the impression Saree was a net tech, but she'd mentioned someone named Hal wrote the worm. But if Saree could use net tools, then getting away might be easier. *Sand fleas!* Locked out of another backdoor. Q swept the connection away.

"Q, could you do that?"

She brought her attention back to Ruhger for a split second. "Do what? I'm a little busy here."

"Break into a bulk space transport train comms system," Ruhger said with a bit of impatience.

What? Why would you want to? Q shrugged. Not much else she could do on the station now. "Probably. Which one?"

"Don't know; I need to find one."

Who had time for hypothetical questions? "Well, that's not helpful, Ruhger. I'm not chasing waterfalls."

"What?" Ruhger said at the same time Saree did. Q snickered again.

"How about I look around, Ruhger?" Saree asked. "Slide

surveillance over to me—oh, blast, no e-torc."

"Q can move, and you can take the shuttle screens."

Oh, sure, because that would be so easy in this heavy grav. But Ruhger was right. Q forced herself up out of the co-pilot's seat and staggered back to one of the observer chairs, thudding down harder than she wanted to. *Ow*. She could hardly wait until she could start training again.

After a few minutes, Saree said, "Ruhger, can you change orbit enough to swing us near Valenti Four-Two?"

"An under-construction station is the answer?" Ruhger asked.

"It might not be the answer for the universe and everything, but it's the answer for us. Plas shipments. They need lots and lots of raw plas."

"Good." He pulled Valenti Four-Two's orbit into the navigation, still showing on the shuttle display. "Find us an outgoing plas transport, and I'll find us a covert route for intercept. Let's see, I can duck behind this shuttle...."

An orbit for an inbound transport pinged in Q's e-torc. What was she supposed to do with this? She was still blanking vids on the station and setting off various alarms.

Saree asked, "Q, do you have any prebuilt worms? I can take on the plas transport infiltration. At least to start."

Good because she couldn't spare the time, not if they wanted to escape unnoticed. "Sure." Q connected to Epstein's e-torc and pushed a folder full of worms, viruses, trojan horses, and other fun toys to Saree's station on the shuttle.

"Wow. Okay, then, this should keep me busy for a while."

Q sure hoped so. With the time lag and Valenti net security

actively working against her, it was hard to do anything proactive. All she could do was watch for signs their escape from the Valenti Station was discovered. If Familia figured out they were on this shuttle, they'd have troops boarding them in no time at all. Probably those creepy human-looking remotes.

She shuddered. The sooner they could fold out, the better. If they couldn't fold out, hiding was the next best choice. No matter what, Q wasn't going back.

CHAPTER THIRTEEN

Q hauled another bag of trash into the cargo bay, gagging at the stench again. She should be used to it, but no. She tossed it up on the growing pile, watching as it teetered, then stayed. *Whew*. If it tumbled down, it might have broken and made everything worse. Although, that didn't really seem possible—she was so tired of cleaning. Saree was kind of a taskmaster. But she was right—the shuttle smelled a lot better without all the garbage.

She rolled her eyes at Bonnet's continuing threats and gratefully closed the airlock hatch behind her, opening the next and trotting to the sani-mod—she wanted to wash her hands in the worst way. "Are we done yet?" Q asked Saree, hating her whining tone but too tired to try and fix it.

"Yes, we're done," Saree said with a tired sigh.

"Thank the Mother." She washed her hands and plopped down in one of the seats. Q checked her alerts—the Valenti net techs found another of her nuisance attacks and shut it down. The time lag had grown to the point where there was little she could do anyway. All she could do was check her few remaining alerts for news of them, and even that was old news by now. Q rubbed her eyes, trying to stay alert.

"Any sign they know we're here, Q?" Ruhger asked.

Again? She scowled at him. "For the three hundredth time, no. None that I've noticed or seen, but there could be notifications going out right now on systems I don't know about or have never thought about. I don't know what I don't know!" Could he make her feel like more of an idiot? She wasn't an expert; she was still a trainee! She was doing the best she could, but the time lag was making it impossible.

Ruhger sighed and held up a hand. "I'm not trying to insult you. I'm just trying to plan for the worst, assuming I know what the worst is. Which I probably don't."

"None of us does." Saree was trying to play peacemaker, but her fake calm was annoying. She continued, "Look, we're all frustrated by the lack of control and the waiting. But that's all we can do. Q, it's your turn to take a nap. You're just checking things now, not actively working, so there's no reason not to. We'll wake you up if there's a problem you can fix. But really, at this point, it's up to fate or the gods or whatever you may or may not believe in."

That actually made some sense. "Fine." Q rolled her eyes and lowered her seat back. "But I doubt I'll be able to." She was so wired. But she was tired too. Exhausted. She concentrated on her breathing and shut their quiet conversations out.

"Bonnet, get back here! The bugs—you're not Bonnet! Who in all the suns are you?"

Q blinked up at the guy yelling on the shuttle's screen. Who was that?

"The new captain," Ruhger said dryly. "Bonnet tried to double-cross me and now he's a bit tied up. So… what can I help you with, Engineer Hindenburg? I am an experienced folder captain and pilot."

Oh, yeah, the engineer on Bonnet's crew list. He'd been crossed out, so she'd thought he was gone. Maybe it meant Bonnet wanted to get rid of him? Either way, he wasn't a Blatto. Q's nose scrunched.

"You… you… you!" Hindenburg stuttered.

"Use your words, Hindenburg."

He stood up straight and glared. "Fine. If you can get me out of here alive, you can have this bucket of blast and rad."

"What's going on?" Ruhger asked.

"The bugs are eating everything. I can hear them chewing through the walls. Literally." Hindenburg was practically jumping in his seat, looking totally paranoid.

But Q didn't blame him. If the Blattos were eating the walls… *Ew.*

"What do they want, other than food?"

"Until they get food, that's *all* they want."

"Do you know what food they prefer?"

"I don't think it matters, as long as it's organic. Thank the suns they can't eat cerimetal." Sweat ran down Hindenburg's face. "I think."

"How about plain plas?" Ruhger asked calmly.

Hindenburg shot an incredulous look at him. "I said they're eating the walls, didn't I?"

"So you did. All right." Ruhger nodded. "Well, we're currently hiding in a plas transport, so we'll see if we can't break one free and bring it along. If we can pressurize it, the plas should lure the Blattos in, then we leave them and the transport behind. Make sense?" Ruhger shot a glance at Saree and then her.

Would that work? Q had no idea. She shrugged.

Hindenburg laughed. He sounded a little crazy. "Sure, why not only steal from Familia but also dump a load of Blattos on them? Guess it's better than dying."

Ruhger said, "That's the spirit. Are the fold generators working?"

Hindenburg looked off to the side for a moment, then back. "Mostly. They'll get us through some short folds, but they're overdue for a major overhaul. Clocks aren't stable."

"Ah. Don't worry about that; we've got that covered."

We do? How? Q looked at Ruhger and Saree. They didn't have anything but the clothes she'd printed for them on Familia's shuttle.

"You've got one of those fancy portable fold clocks?" Hindenburg looked skeptical.

"Something like that." Ruhger shrugged. "The less you know, the better for you. Anyway, if we can make you safe, will you help us fold out?"

"Did you kill Bonnet?" Hindenburg's tone was accusatory.

"No. He's secured with the trash."

"He's tricky." Hindenburg shook his head, then pointed a finger at them. "You keep him and the Blattos away from me and keep the Blattos from eating the entire ship, and you've got a deal."

Q wouldn't trust this Hindenburg guy with an auto-bev, let alone a folder, but they were stuck with him.

Ruhger said, "Contract terms. You turn all controls, including piloting and comms, over to us upon docking and operate the folder in a safe, secure manner to a series of destinations of our choice. When we reach our final destination, we'll leave the folder with you."

"No dead systems! Leave me in a system where I can find a pilot, capisce?"

Uh oh. This guy is Familia! She got up and got in Ruhger's field of view, mouthing, "No!" at him.

"Understood." Ruhger shot a look at Q, but she couldn't read his expression.

"Agreed."

Ruhger said, "Agreed. We'll be there shortly." He looked at her. "What, Q?"

"He's Familia!"

"Did you recognize him?"

"No." She scowled at him. "Didn't you recognize the term he used at the end? Capisce?"

Ruhger shrugged. "Sure; it means, 'understand' in Old Earth."

Q stopped her eye roll—she needed to check the folder comms now. "Familia uses it all the time."

"Well, it's either make a deal with this guy or wait for Familia to find us."

She searched for the messaging system. "That guy is probably messaging them right now!" *Hah. Found it.*

"Oh."

"Yeah, oh." Q scowled at Ruhger and flicked off the transmitter. "Hah. Got ya, sand flea! Stopped him from sending by turning off all outgoing comms. Brute force approach, but he might not even notice his message didn't get out." She hoped it didn't get out. What if she didn't get it turned off in time?

"Good. We can worry about refinements later." Ruhger nodded at Q.

He appreciated her pointing out his shortcomings? How odd.

Ruhger turned to Saree. "Now, can you break one of these transports off and set it up so we can tow it along?"

"It will be noticed, Ruhger," Saree told him. "And it's empty."

Ruhger chuckled. Q stared at the unusual sound coming from the grim captain.

He continued, "Mostly empty. I'm sure there will be plenty of plas left in the cracks and crevices. More importantly, will it hold pressure, and is there enough air to fill it?"

Saree swiped through screens. "Hmm. I'll look."

Q volunteered, "I can break the last transport in line away and set up a link. But we'll be seen." A plas transport wasn't stealthy or small.

"Ah, but it's part of my plan." Ruhger looked confident. But he always seemed confident. "Once the orbital controllers start yelling at me, I'll yell back about how it's not my fault, I didn't do it, get it off me. We'll keep the transport between us and the station, just in case they start shooting. This thing—" he waved a hand around "—is big."

Well, sure, the plas transport was huge. But it was hollow, and it didn't have anything but rudimentary asteroid shields. What kind of protection did it offer?

"Good news, Ruhger," Saree said. "The last transport in the chain isn't a big bulk transporter. It transports the raw materials for the food printers, so it's a series of smaller compartments. Each one is designed to hold air for loading—they blow the food powder in, then suck all the air out, then use air to blow the powder back out again." She looked up with a grin. "Even better, the report on this one says some of the compartments are malfunctioning—the valves are blocked. So, they're full of food and air."

Q took the backdoor Saree made—with Q's worm—and found command and control. Now, which one was the food transport? *Ah. Got it.*

"Perfect." Ruhger nodded. "We latch a tube to the folder's cargo hold, lure all the Blattos out, and leave it all there. The fold to Antlia is short, so this hunk of junk should make it. We leave it and the engineer with Gov Human and get Gov Human to message Lightwave." Ruhger paused for a moment. "And we negotiate with Gov Human for a protection fleet. It's just not a secret anymore, Saree."

Q looked up from her holo. What wasn't a secret?

Surprisingly, Saree nodded grimly. "You're right, it's not. It's time to stop hiding because if I do, we'll all lose. We can't keep hoping for ignorance; it just makes us an easier target."

Q stared at Saree, bewildered. "Who are you?" And whether Saree had to hide or not, Q still had to. Familia wouldn't let her go easily.

Ruhger raised a brow at her. "If you really want to know, we'll tell you when we're someplace safe. I don't trust these beings. There's probably vids all over this shuttle."

"Good point." Q nodded her agreement.

"And you'll be safer not knowing, Q," Saree said. "Truly, you don't want this secret."

She wasn't sure about that. Secrets got people killed. Q told them about the stupid tattoo, didn't she?

Ruhger frowned at her. "Unless you're going to stay on with us. Then, you'll have to know."

Q grimaced. "Not sure I want to work with Katryn. She's a stickler." *All the rules, all the time. Boring.*

He huffed. "True. And you'd be working *for* Tyron and Katryn, not *with*. Tyron's lead."

From what she remembered, Tyron was a good guy. "He's sexy. I could work for him." At the look on Ruhger's face, she snickered to herself.

Saree snorted. "And Katryn's the jealous type. Don't even think about it."

Q kept her eyes from rolling—again. She was just kidding. "Fine. Ruin the fantasy. What about the other guys?" She was trying to remember the crew, but her time on Lightwave was confusing and crowded. It was a long time ago.

Saree laughed. "Chief's too old for you and probably not interested. Grant will be interested, but not for a long-term relationship."

Ruhger said, "Grant *won't* be interested. He doesn't mix business and pleasure. If she's working for us, that's what it will be, a working relationship."

Saree considered him. "Loreli?"

Chef Loreli? What about her? Q wasn't attracted to women, unfortunately. Life would have been easier with the Sisters if she had been. If they weren't going to become full Sisters, a lot of the older orphans formed relationships.

Ruhger shook his head. "No. We've all been friends since we were born, but that's it."

Saree nodded. "Makes sense."

Q told them, "You're talking around me like some little kid!"

"No, just as beings who have known each other for a while," Saree said. "We just met you. Be patient."

How long had Saree flown with Lightwave? Q was sure she wasn't onboard during the Cygnus Gliese evacuation—Saree stood out too much to miss, even in a crowd of women. Guess it didn't matter; Q didn't have any other choices right now. And thinking about choices, she'd better get back to the plas train. She found the correct area of command and control, the release commands for the individual plas pods, and the last one in the line. She looked deeper to be sure. Yes, the last one was a bulk food transport. Then, she got ready to open the hatch of the pod they were currently hiding the shuttle inside.

"And speaking of patient, are we ready to go?" Ruhger asked her.

Q looked up at Ruhger. "I got the transport ready to break away and follow."

"Okay, let's do this." Ruhger nodded at her. "Strap in. Open the transport hatch, and we'll fly out."

Q plopped back into a seat and fastened her harness, finding the right control and flipping the hatch to "open," then went back to the food transport. "Got it. Hatch is open, last transport ready to break away."

"Good job, Q. Release it now," Ruhger told her. "Sit back and enjoy the ride. Get a little more shuteye if you can—we'll have long watches when we reach Nebula Wraith."

Q flipped the transport release switch. "Transport free." Nice to be appreciated rather than yelled at for not being better or reading a tech's mind. Q snuggled back into the now-clean chair and closed her eyes. Maybe she could sleep all the way to the folder, maybe all the way out of Valenti. Wouldn't that be nice?

It would never happen. Still, she was tired. Q dropped into meditation and hoped for sleep to follow.

∆∆∆

Did Ruhger really think this would work? Q considered him. Maybe he was too tired to think.

"Okay, Q. Send the message," Ruhger told her.

"Here goes nothing." She poked at the translated message, sending it over the speakers of the folder, and shuddered at the weird noises. *Yuck.* Her view of Cargo Bay One was terrifying, and the rest of the folder worse; the interior was stripped down to the cerimetal. Only the water storage pods in the bulkheads were left.

Meter-long bugs scuttled in on all six legs. *Ew.* Q shivered and activated the voice distorter for Ruhger.

The first bug stopped before entering the flex tube. "You promised there is air, safety, and food and to take us far from Familia."

Ruhger said, "There is. I promise."

The bug stood up and stared at the vid. Q shoved back into her seat and turned the folder's sound back up. She wanted to check the voice distorter. Although, if it didn't work, it was too late now.

"If you have betrayed us, our tribe will hunt you down and eat you. It has happened."

So, the game vids were right! She knew it.

Ruhger said, in a very calm voice, "There is air and food on the transport. Someone will pick it up. I cannot promise what will happen after that. You can go there or starve here."

All the Blattos hissed. Q shuddered and tried to burrow into her seat.

"We go. You are not a friend of Blatto, Captain Ruhger. Do not look for help from us."

"Understood." Ruhger swept off the comms. "How did he know my name?"

Good question. The voice distorter worked. She'd listened. Q shrugged and shook her head.

The Blattos disappeared into the tube. Less than a minute later, the tube disconnected. Thank the Mother they were gone.

Ruhger closed the cargo bay hatch and did something to the fold equations. Adjusting for the plas transport? He said, "Hindenburg, ready for fold?"

The engineer didn't reply. Q checked the comms—they were all working correctly. Well, marginally, just like everything else on this folder.

"Q, pull up the vid outside engineering." Ruhger's tone bothered Q, but she did what he asked.

The hatch to engineering stood wide open. *Uh oh.* Q had a bad feeling about this.

Saree asked, "Q, can you find Hindenburg?" She started swiping through views on the big shuttle screen, bringing up Engineering.

Q pulled up vids of the crew cabins. There was nothing but cerimetal struts.

Saree took in a sharp breath, and Q looked up to see the view of Engineering zoom in on a pair of boot soles. By the Mother! They ate Hindenburg! Q put a hand over her churning stomach and swallowed hard. Nope. Not working. She was going to be sick. She sprinted to the sani-mod, dropped to her knees, and lost her dinner. The toilet cycled twice. She sat back on her haunches, pretty sure there was nothing left. Thank the Mother they'd cleaned this floor earlier. Q wrapped her arms around her middle.

Ruhger's voice was barely audible. "…any sign of sabotage, but… it's fold out or end up back in the hands of Familia."

"Fold. Fold now. I want off this ship!" came from Saree.

"Fold now!" Q yelled at him. Two to one, they had to try. She wasn't going back.

"Strap in, Q. Then, we'll fold," Ruhger called.

Q jumped to her feet and ran to her seat. No more thinking about—that. She shuddered.

"Fold in five, four, three, two, fold."

Saree brought up navigation. "Antlia," she said with a big sigh. "Contacting Laniakea Fleet for instructions on the Blattos and," Saree paused and glanced back at Q, "further discussions."

Great, more secrets.

"Might take a while to get the right person since we're not sending from Lightwave or our personal e-torcs." Saree snorted. "Guess I should have memorized a few addresses rather than relying on my e-torc." Saree composed a message and sent it.

Ruhger said, "Thrust in five, four, three, two, thrust. At least the Blattos didn't eat the fuel."

"Could they?" Saree grimaced.

Ew.

"I doubt it, but it is organic, so…"

"Can we stop talking about them?" Q asked, aware she sounded like a whiny little girl, but she really couldn't take any more.

"Sure. Sorry," Ruhger said, with a one-shoulder shrug. "I should remember that not everyone has grown up in a military-type environment."

Really? Q scowled. "The Sisters are close."

Ruhger laughed. Saree smiled at her. "In some ways, sure. With large numbers of children, discipline is critical to survival. When did you leave Cygnus Secundus?"

Guess they had the time to tell stories now.

"About two standard years ago. They sent me off to a new net school for 'advanced students,' thinking I'd be the next Katryn." Q wrinkled her nose. "Only more grateful. Unfortunately, it was really a feeder for Familia techs. The first year at school…" She slowed. She'd told them she was a year older than she actually was, so she'd add a year to her schooling. "…was great." Q held back her grimace. "I learned a ton and had a good time." At least in comparison to *Indomito*. "The second year, things changed.

They told me the Sisters had failed to pay the tuition, and therefore, I owed them three years of service. When I objected and showed them the proof of payment for a year in advance, they said that was for tuition, not room and board and all the fun stuff we'd done. I objected again, telling them I wouldn't have done all that fun stuff if they'd told me it was extra, and they said it was my fault for not reading the terms and conditions." She scowled. "Which is a bunch of sand scooter scat because I read every document. They changed the rules halfway through the year and didn't tell any of us."

"Classic Familia," Ruhger muttered.

"They wouldn't let me message the Sisters, and I know the Sisters' messages weren't reaching me. Sister Ani knows there's something wrong because we had code words and phrases set with a schedule of messages, but I doubt she's got the time or credits to come look for me. It's more a warning not to send anyone else." They had to notice the lack of messages. Or, if the school was faking messages, the lack of code words. "Hopefully, they know what to look for when a new school pops up."

"You can message them now, Q," Saree said. "We've got the time, and there's a few credits attached to this folder, so you may as well use them."

"You don't need them?" She'd rather not access her accounts yet. Not on this e-torc. She needed some decent net security.

Saree smiled at Q. "No. We shouldn't, anyway. The Fleet will come pick us up."

Why would Gov Human military care about Ruhger and Saree? They didn't care about the entire world of Cygnus Gliese, so why these two people? The only time she'd heard of the Fleet rescuing people was something big, like a sun going supernova or a passenger ship getting attacked by pirates. Or maybe something with rich people on the core worlds. Ruhger and Saree weren't wealthy people pretending to be poor—Q knew what powerful people were like now. "Who are you?"

Saree looked at Ruhger, and they both laughed. She said, "Nobody. Just a small folder who's done some favors for Gov Human."

Right. "Uh-huh. Sure. Fine, don't tell me." Thinking about it, she was pretty sure Gov Human didn't care about Lightwave either. There was something else going on here.

"Message the Sisters, Q, and say hello for us, please," Ruhger said.

Q frowned at both of them. "Sure." She'd do it from the bunk room. If they talked about it, then she could listen in.

"Teenagers," Ruhger huffed behind her.

Saree chuckled. "I guess it's good practice for me. I'll need to raise some someday."

Well, she didn't need to hear any of that. Q closed the hatch behind her and brought up the shuttle's message interface. Their code words didn't really fit this situation, but she didn't want to put her name in this message, either, because Familia would look for her with the Sisters. Text only was the cheapest and best in this situation. Now, what would a small, decrepit folder like this one want with the Sisters that wouldn't get the message deleted immediately?

An emergency message alert tolled loudly, and a red light

flashed. By the Mother, what was that? Q brought up the emergency alert. Oh, fold orbit assignment. That warranted a "we're all gonna die" alerter? *Yikes.* She left the bunk room.

Ruhger said, "Okay, good. Foxtrot is easy enough to reach." Ruhger brought up navigation on the main shuttle screen. "Tell Q, will you?"

"Tell me what?" Q asked them.

"We're changing orbits, so sit down," Ruhger said. "You know how bad the grav generators are on this thing."

They were terrible. She plopped down. "Where are we going?" She didn't need to tell them she already knew.

"Fold Hold Foxtrot. Gov Human's sending a shuttle to pick us up," Saree told her.

Q hadn't seen the message about the shuttle. Did it go straight to Saree somehow? "Wow, that was fast."

"It was." Saree smiled. "About time something went our way on this trip."

Ruhger muttered, "Oh, I can think of at least one thing that went our way."

Saree laughed.

Q hoped they were referencing her, but they probably weren't. *Typical.* Why praise the woman who saved you from Familia over and over? It just wasn't right. But she was just a kid, so they'd continue to cut her out, keep her in the dark. Q smiled. Well, they could try.

CHAPTER FOURTEEN

Q yelled, "Hah!"

Groans sounded. "Seriously?" Kylr asked. "How do you keep winning?"

Q looked him straight in the eyes. "I cheat."

The young Gov Human military member stared back, then laughed, shaking his head. "No, you don't. You've just got whip-fast reflexes."

He was right. She'd gotten faster since she started training for the Atlas Challenge. But Q was kind of cheating, too, because she'd played every single variation of this game already. The game designers asked Adzari Academy to test it, so designing and writing testing protocols became a third-year student project, while the first-years got to do the actual testing. Q sighed, remembering. The game was fun the first fifty times or so, then it was just drudgery. It was back to being fun now because of the company, not the game itself.

She hadn't appreciated being dumped off in the junior enlisted recreation compartment like a little kid at a care site, but this group of first-tour military was fun. They came from all over the universe, mostly core system worlds that were jam-packed giant cities. Q would love to see a planet-city, but she'd never want to live there. Omicron was close enough.

"Let's go, Q!" Winby exclaimed, bouncing enthusiastically in her cloud-chair. How could she move that much in the squishy bag-chair? Winby was super-sweet and an organizational wonder—she'd been the one to group all of them into teams on various games, so they could all get some play time, even though few of them knew each other and there weren't enough systems. Q helped by setting up temporary links between team members' e-torcs, making Winby her new best friend.

Q shook her head with a smile. "I need a break, Winby. Go ahead without me."

"If you insist." She turned to the rest of her team. "Come on, let's go."

Sauntering over to the bev station, Q noticed that, despite Windby's best attempts, there were several people not joining in the fun. A few appeared to be completely immersed in vids or books on their own, but there were also a couple who looked uncomfortable, nervous, or maybe even scared. Well, if she hadn't been thoroughly terrorized over the last couple of years, she might be scared too.

Stuck in space on a fold transport or a station with nowhere to run, in a military structure that took away your personal freedoms and put control in your superior's hands, with a whole bunch of people you didn't know or trust could be a scary situation. Gov Human's military said they did a great job weeding out predators and providing oversight and channels for reporting, but Q had already seen signs that wasn't completely true. But she'd also heard several recruits talk about the military being their only way out of a terrible home situation. If they got the wrong commanders, could it turn into something worse?

From what Q saw in Familia, selfish, evil people tended to find each other, so if a recruit had a bad boss, it wasn't unlikely the next person up the chain of command was just as bad, if not worse. It was probably the same in the military. In the two days they'd been on board, she'd seen more than a few instances of abusive language and intimidation already. Even though they were on the Gov Human Laniakea Fleet Commander's flagship, she kept hearing alarms and warnings in her head. She'd seen too many Familia-like tactics used on the junior enlisted she was hanging out with.

"Q, right?" A man and woman crowded her against the bev station. They were a little older than the crowd she'd been playing vid games with, trying to intimidate with their stares, standing too close.

Q sighed internally. Why did she always have to be right? If she hadn't spent the last year on a Familia enforcer fold transport, she'd be worried right now. Instead, she met their eyes with long stares back. "Yes."

"You're cute. We should play a different game. Alone." The woman made a circle with her finger, obviously including the man and the two of them.

"No, thanks."

"You don't want to turn us down, recruit," the man said menacingly.

She laughed at him. Why hadn't she turned on her personal vid? Q flicked a finger toward her holo, but the woman caught her hand and forced it down. Q said, "Let go, now."

"I don't think so, cutie."

"Wrong girl to pick on," Q told her. Now, what was her best play here? Victim or aggressor? Quiet or loud? These two had undoubtedly done this before. Loud and victim it was. Q dropped to her knees, one landing hard on top of the man's foot, throwing her drink in the air, splashing both of them. "Ow! Let me go!" she screamed. Gratifyingly, everyone turned to look. Most looked away, telling Q she was right, these two had taken advantage of their positions multiple times. She poked at her holo and turned the vid on, the automatic identification feature turning on with it.

"Oh, so sorry," the woman, Sergeant Z'Tera, said sweetly, gripping her hand tighter. "Just trying to help."

"You're rather clumsy, recruit," the man, Sergeant Berten, added on, yanking his foot back and wiping drops from his face. Even wearing boots, that had to sting.

Q twisted her hand loose from Z'Tera's. "Even if I was a recruit, you'd still be wrong." In one move, she jumped to her feet and back and noted the surprise on their faces with great satisfaction. They glanced at each other and walked to the compartment's hatch. *Sand vipers.* Quick on the attack but equally fast to run away if the prey fought back. Too bad she didn't get vid of that whole encounter. She had a feeling the compartment's vids had a "temporary malfunction."

She refilled her bev-tainer—fortunately, she'd only had water in it, and a remote was already mopping—and plopped down in an empty chair. Despite her confident act, confrontation was hard. Q took a drink and breathed slowly and evenly, getting her heart rate back under control.

A few minutes later, a boy dropped into the chair next to hers, scowling. He wore the same grey T-shirt and black shorts the others did, so he was obviously in the Gov Human military, but he looked pretty young. Was he a new recruit? Or was this another attempt at seduction or information gathering?

The boy ignored her, scrolling through his holo, so Q ignored him. She checked her messages again, knowing it was too soon for the Sisters to send one back, but she was still worried. What if Familia went in, full force, looking for her? What if they just set up net sniffers, looking for messages from her? She'd sent hers from a Gov Human public address and didn't use her name, but they might figure it out. Familia wasn't stupid.

"Hey, who are you?" the kid next to her asked.

"Who wants to know?" Q retorted. She discretely flicked her vid recorder on. She'd have proof this time.

His brows jumped high, drawing her attention to the pink patches on his face. They stood out against his black-coffee skin tone everywhere else. "Oh, sorry. I just assumed you'd have access to the ship's list. I'm Cap—" his shoulders dropped "—I mean, Lan."

He didn't know his own name? "Which is it? Cap or Lan?"

He sighed. "Look, it's Caplan. I've gone by Cap my whole life, but in the military, 'Cap' is short for Captain, and I'm a long way away from that." He snorted. "So, now, I'm stuck with Lan."

"Ah. Makes sense." It seemed like one of those things the

military would insist on. "Sorry you're stuck. So, which one do you want me to use?"

His mouth twisted. "Lan, I guess. I'm used to it. Mostly."

Q shrugged. "Okay, Lan, you got it. I'm Q."

"Q? Okay." Lan shrugged. "So, what are you doing here? You're not military. There's no way you're old enough."

Q scowled. "You don't look old enough either."

"Well, I am. But you're not."

Q didn't hold back her eye roll. These guys were all the same. "Technically, I am old enough. But I'm not military. I'm here because I'm with some people meeting with Gov Human military leaders, but I can't be in the meetings because…reasons."

"What kind of meetings?"

"The none-of-your-business kind." Q frowned at him. She'd thought Lan might be smarter. Too bad.

"Oh. Sorry."

Lan didn't look very sorry. He looked curious. She'd throw it back at him. "What's up with the pink patches on your face?"

He scowled at her. "None of…you know what? It doesn't matter. They removed my tattoos, okay?"

"You had tattoos on your face?"

"Yes. It's part of my culture, a family marking. But Gov Human military doesn't allow it. Says it interferes with facial recognition and makes it easier to fool your teammates with a body modded infiltrator." Lan snorted. "Like they can't make a perfect copy of anyone if they start with the right height and weight. Or fix those too. But why would anyone bother with me? I'm a first-termer, just got here. By the time I'm somebody, people will know me."

Q snickered. "You could be a deep-cover infiltrator right now, playing the long game."

"Right." Lan laughed. Then he sobered and leaned in, whispering, "I might be a spy."

They stared at each other, Q holding back laughter, the twitch of Lan's lips saying he was doing the same. Finally, they both laughed.

"You're funny," Q said.

"So are you. Cute, too."

"Aww, thanks." Q looked away for a second to collect her thoughts. She didn't want to offend Lan, but she did want to know. "So, this tattoo removal. Um, I get that it sucks for you, but is it painful?"

Lan shrugged a little. "Feels like a bad sunburn. A little numbing spray and it's fine. Why?"

"Because I need a tattoo removed." Before Lan could ask, Q scowled. "And no, I'm not going to show you or tell you about it. I just need it gone. Thanks for telling me."

Lan held up both hands. "No problem. Happy to help." He snorted softly. "At least one good thing will come out of this." He pointed at his cheeks.

"I really do appreciate it." Q's messaging pinged with a message from Saree. Well, not Saree. It was "Restricted User 1701" because they were trying to keep her presence on General Kerr's flagship quiet. Q still didn't know why, but she was happy about it because it kept her presence quiet too. They all knew Familia had lots of sources inside Gov Human, including the military. She was Restricted User 1703. "Hey, gotta go. Nice to meet you, Lan." She smiled. "Maybe I'll see you here again."

He returned her smile. "I hope so. Take care."

Q left the recreation compartment and made her way to their favorite bev station. It was a favorite only because it was close to their sleeping compartments and General Kerr's office level—all the military folder bev stations served the exact same thing. *So boring.* So was this e-torc, now that she wasn't plugged into the rec compartment net. She stopped just in time to avoid running into Saree. "This thing sucks. It's so slow."

Ruhger joined them, sipping on his bev-tainer, probably one of those horrible protein shake things. *Yuck.* "Better than not having one at all, isn't it?" Ruhger asked her.

"Maybe." Q shrugged. "Yeah, sure. It's better." They walked way too slowly to their compartment. It was a real let-down after Familia's luxury. She shivered. But it didn't come with the inherent evil either. Well, hopefully, that was behind her. If she could get rid of this tattoo, she could leave the constant reminder behind too. It was as good a time as any to ask. "So, they get a lot of recruits through here. I've met a bunch." Q frowned. That wasn't very clear.

"Yes, they do." Ruhger scowled. "Are they bothering you?"

"No, no, that's not it." Q waved Captain Super-Protective off. "I can handle those kids. No, someone told me part of military in-processing is removing tattoos and scars. Do you think they'd remove mine?"

"We can ask," Saree said. "I don't know why they wouldn't."

"Oh, good. Because I want this—" Q made a circular motion

around her stomach "—gone. Now." So badly.

"I'm sorry, I should have thought about that." Saree's shoulders drooped, then she perked up. "We can get you a full physical while we're at it. Who knows what else those—" her mouth clamped shut for a moment "—people did to you."

Q's nose wrinkled and she held back a shiver. "Ooh, creepy. But a good idea." She nodded, a little frantically, and tried to get her overreaction under control. "Yeah, the sooner the better." She bit her lip to keep herself from saying anything else.

"I'll send a message to General Kerr's aide right now. After putting us through today, they'd better jump right on this."

"So, no progress?" Q asked. *Blast.* More time in the rec compartment with the recruits. And the potential for more predators. She seemed to draw them in like candy.

They both shook their heads.

"What about…" Oh, wait, she couldn't say the folder's name. "…your crew?"

"Nothing," Ruhger said. "I'm getting…concerned."

They entered their compartment. Just four bunks, one of the bottoms made into a couch, a small table with four chairs, an auto-bev, galley sink, and a decent sani-mod. This sucked like giant black holes next to her compartment on *Indomito*. And sharing with the lovebirds was equally awful. All those longing looks. Q rolled her eyes.

"So, Q, we've got access to our credit accounts again," Saree said. "How about a meal out in the Station?"

"Yes! Let's eat some real food!" Military food was so boring. Nutritionally correct but mostly tasteless with an undertone of yeast. *Yuck.* She'd heard there was far better food on the Station. Commuter shuttles flew every thirty minutes between the flagship and the Station, so it should be easy to get there and back.

Ruhger chuckled. "Not Familia-style, right?"

What was wrong with him?! *Ew.* "No!" Q said.

Saree said, "I wonder if there's an Old Earth Middle East restaurant here?"

Ruhger arched a brow at her. "Two kills with one shot?"

What was he talking about? More stuff she was too young to know. Q scowled at them.

Saree grimaced. "Let's not do any shooting tonight."

Especially when they wouldn't give her even a stunner.

"Hopefully." Ruhger shrugged. "Just a turn of phrase."

"Oh!" Q remembered she was in recruit shorts and T-shirt. If they were going somewhere nice, she needed new clothes. "I need to figure out what I'm wearing, and I need a shower." She opened the clothing storage compartment and peered inside. Was there anything worth wearing in here? Q missed the clothes printers from their Familia shuttle. Why didn't everyone have those?

Ruhger said, "You go first, Saree. Take your time."

"Thanks." Saree slid past Q.

There wasn't anything good in here, just plain shipsuits. Maybe they could buy something on the Station? She ought to be able to reach her numbered accounts. But if she did and Familia figured it out somehow, they wouldn't think twice about activating an agent to capture her again. No, she was dependent on Gov Human, Saree, and Ruhger. *This sucks.* Q pulled a plain, dark blue shipsuit out of the compartment, along with some underclothes, and plopped down next to Ruhger to wait.

Even if she couldn't wear something pretty, at least she'd get some real food out of this deal.

ΔΔΔ

"That was delicious. Thank you," Saree told their server, a young girl.

Saree was right, it was delicious. The spices reminded Q of some of the stews they had on Lightwave, folding away from Cygnus Gliese, but so much better. And it smelled so good. If only the Gov Human military folder smelled like this!

A man stopped at each table and eventually made it to them. He wore loose, floor-length white robes and a black cloth draped over his head, secured by a twisted black rope. The man bowed, with complicated arm and hand waving. "Peace to you. I hope you are enjoying the meal?"

Ruhger nodded at the man. "Yes. It's delicious." Ruhger kept staring at the man, straight in the eyes.

The man asked, "Is there something else I can assist you with, then?"

"Are you familiar with the Circinus Madras?"

What is that? She'd have to look it up later.

"Yes, of course. I have family there." He frowned slightly at Ruhger. "Why do you ask?"

"Because we were there not too long ago and left under... difficult circumstances. We hoped to hear news."

"Good news, preferably," Saree said quietly.

"Ah." The man nodded again. "They sustained some damage, but it was quickly repaired." Both Saree and Ruhger looked relieved, but he held up a hand. "The *physical* damage was repaired. Political damage also occurred. There has been a change of leadership, and you will not be welcome. No outsider is. Many areas of study have been eliminated, and some students have departed."

Saree asked urgently, "Is the Maulana all right?"

"The former Maulana is well, as is the new Maulana." White teeth flashed in his tan face for a moment. "We are a religion of peace, remember? But still, the previous Maulana has left the Madras and entered a contemplative community on Circinus, taking a vow of silence, poverty, and service." He shook his head. "You will not meet him again in this life. You must find another way to achieve your aims, whatever those are." He turned away.

So, the Madras was a religious school, and Ruhger and Saree were there for a reason, not just a random visit. And that reason got the school attacked? Q bit her lip. She had to figure out why people wanted them.

"Do you know Al-Kindi or his wife Nari and how they fare?" Saree asked.

His robes flew wide as he spun back. "I don't know them, but if they are in Circinus, they should be fine, barring normal accidents. Do not return to Circinus." He scowled at Saree, then Ruhger. "Do not return here." His tone was menacing. What happened to peace? The man turned, his robes billowing, and strode across the restaurant, ignoring everyone and poking at his e-torc, the motions short and sharp.

Ruhger looked at his e-torc, sweeping something away, then at Saree. "I suggest we go."

She nodded, looking sad. "Yes. I suppose there is nothing more we can do or say."

"But I wanted dessert." Q wanted to try that flaky pastry thing she'd seen everyone else eating. It looked so good.

"We'll get something on the way," Saree said, standing up.

"But—" Really?

Ruhger stood and slashed a hand. "Not now, Clove, let's go."

Q scowled at both of them, then got up. "Fine." Figured. The one time they got to eat something good, they didn't get to finish. Was Saree some sort of criminal? Did she have some sort of huge bribery thing on General Kerr? Q knew Lightwave had a mixed reputation, but Saree was something different, something worse, but not worse. It was weird. Not knowing sucked like the big black hole of Andromeda. Outside, Q waited for them. They were slow too. "People don't like you very much, do they?"

Saree laughed. "No, they don't."

Ruhger said, "Actually, they like her just fine. Everyone wants her. Me?" He jabbed a thumb toward his chest. "Not so much."

Q laughed. "That I can believe. You're grumpy." But why did everyone want Saree?

"Thank you," Ruhger replied, with a short bow.

He was proud of it? These two were strange.

Saree laughed. "I don't think it's a compliment, Ep."

"I suppose not. There's a freezee shop over there." Ruhger tossed his chin to point it out. "How about that?"

Q turned to look. He was right. Well, it wasn't pastry, but at least it would be sweet. "Sure." Better than nothing. Once she got to the stand, she glanced back. Ruhger and Saree were talking quietly, somehow intensely focused on each other but also aware of their surroundings. That was a skill she needed to develop, even if she didn't have someone special to share it with. Until she learned, she was grateful to have Saree and Ruhger backing her up, no matter how annoying it might be sometimes.

CHAPTER FIFTEEN

"All stations, all personnel, we've arrived safely in Geneva. Perform post-fold checks, and report anomalies, and issues, including any medical issues. Personnel are free to move about. Command out."

Q winced. Why did they make those announcements so loud? But she was happy they were here. Now Ruhger and Saree could go check on Lightwave and hopefully, quit worrying about everything so much.

"Are you okay, Saree?" Ruhger asked. Q couldn't see his face, but he sounded concerned.

"Actually, I am. I feel a little… squeezed, but nothing like I've had in the past."

"Good."

Q stumbled a little getting up. She peered around Ruhger. "Why would you feel bad, Saree? It's just fold."

"Fold affects some beings negatively," Saree said, slowly rolling up and out of the bunk. "I'm one of them. We think it might be a… well, never mind. Just know I'm not the only one."

More secrets. But… Q thought she had imagined her reactions

to fold, but maybe not. She had a chance to find out right now. "You know, sometimes I don't feel very good after a fold either. It feels like my whole body got squished down into nothing, and I end up with bruises." Q looked up, remembering the one time on *Indomito* when she woke up an hour later, feeling like someone ran her over. "I passed out once."

"Really? Interesting." Saree looked at her like a scientist examining unexpected results. "Are you good at y'ga?"

Q laughed. "No, I'm terrible. No coordination." It used to be true, back at the Sisters. If Saree and Ruhger were keeping secrets from her, she'd keep some from them.

"No, I mean the meditation part. Have you ever found yourself in a place of peace and beauty?"

Q scowled. The only time she meditated was when she was totally bored or needed to sleep. "No. It's boring. Like watching sand blow away."

Ruhger huffed, the little puff of air sounding disgusted. "If you're doing it wrong, that's true."

"I don't do it wrong. I do it all right!" *It's still boring!*

"Right," Ruhger said, dryly. "That's why you ended up with Familia."

How was meditation connected to the Academy? The two of them were ridiculous sometimes. Q strode out of the compartment. She'd find something else to do, since they weren't going to let her go to Lightwave.

"Q?" Lan stood there in his uniform shipsuit.

Ooh, scorching! "Hey, Lan. What are you doing here?"

He grinned. "Waiting for you. I've been detailed to give you a tour of the net support squadron. For once, I don't mind being tour boy."

Q laughed. "Aw. How sweet. But watching people work on holos isn't exactly exciting." But it was way better than watching Saree and Ruhger fly to Lightwave.

"What if you got to help a bit? Would that be more interesting?"

"Oh, yes." Maybe she could figure a way around some of the restrictions.

"This way." Lan tilted his head to her right. "You know, I don't even know you, and I know that look is trouble. You're a natural-born net breaker, aren't you?"

Q wasn't going to answer that. "Nah. I'm an angel."

"Right. Well, just don't get me in trouble, okay? I wouldn't mind learning a few things from you, though." He laughed and held both hands up, palms facing her. "Net tips and tricks, that's all I meant."

"Sure." Maybe he meant that, maybe he didn't. He was cute, so either way, she'd win.

ΛΛΛ

After the tour and a session with the flagship's net techs, Lan took her to meet his boss.

"Well, Q, anytime you want a great career, message me," Master Sergeant Bryang told her. "You'll have to go through intake and basic like everyone else, but I'll make sure you end up right here on the flagship. Depending on how you do with people, you could be in officer country in a couple of years."

Q laughed. "No offense, Master Sergeant, but I grew up in a

military-type environment. I'm not in a big hurry to return."

He smiled but sobered quickly. "Sometimes, returning to your roots brings safety and peace of mind. Don't lose my contact info."

"Thank you. I won't." Since Bryang looked like he spoke from experience, it wasn't a lie. He seemed like a nice person. She would keep his contact information close. "And thanks for the tour of the net. I appreciate the opportunity."

"You're welcome. Take care out there." He turned to Lan and nodded. "You're off duty. Go get some chow and play net games. I know you two are dying to duke it out."

"Thank you, Master Sergeant! Come on, Q. Let's go." Lan led the way out of the maze of workstations.

None of them were as nice as Familia's, but they came with less commitment. You might get shot at or end up in a dangerous situation, but at least it wasn't just for money and power. Q sniffed. Or maybe the money and power were just better hidden. And you could leave. No one left Familia.

"Do you mind if I change first?" Lan asked.

"No problem. Do I get to see your compartment?"

"*My* compartment? You realize I'm still a basic recruit, right? I'm in a big compartment with eleven of my closest friends." He led her to a float tube, down a few levels, then through a maze of passageways and a couple more stairways down. "The only reason they don't shove more into a compartment is that we need room for emergency gear in case we… become less than space worthy for some reason."

"You don't have to worry about scaring me, Lan. I know I'm on a warship floating in a vacuum. I keep track of emergency stuff as we go." Like the bod-pods right there, clearly labeled for emergency use.

"Oh, good." He shrugged. "Sometimes civilians are weird about planning for the worst case."

"Yeah, they are. But not me."

He glanced at her. "Yeah, I get the feeling you've seen a lot of bad stuff in your short life." An ironic smile flashed. "Don't worry, I won't ask. I've been told your group is classified, need to know stuff."

"Sorry." Q shrugged. "Believe me, I wish it wasn't."

Another side glance. "I bet."

They entered a long, narrow passage with nothing but hatches to either side.

"This is the first tour dorm. If you do okay and come back for a second, you get a little more room but not a lot. Each compartment is airtight." Lan stopped in front of a hatch halfway down. "Hold here for a sec, okay? When I let you in, just look and go back out. Somebody's probably sleeping."

Q nodded.

Lan entered, looked around, then motioned her inside. The compartment seemed claustrophobic. Clustered in the middle, bunks stood three high, with some sort of folding partition to block the bunk off—several were closed. Tall, narrow secured compartments lined the outside of the space. Q entered and walked around the stack of bunks. Four sets of three-high bunks surrounded by a very narrow walkway, then storage compartments, all in bland beige and gray plas, and that was it.

Q left the compartment and leaned against the passageway

wall. Wow, that was tiny. This huge ship and all these people shoved in these tiny spaces. No wonder the recreation compartments were always crowded. She checked her messages. Ruhger and Saree made it onboard Lightwave, and the crew was all there, safe. Her body sagged in relief, then stiffened again. Now they had Lightwave back, what would they do with her? Would they let her work with them? With Familia looking for her, Q was a huge risk to take on. Next to Katryn and Tyron, her skills were nothing. Definitely not enough to make up for the danger of her presence.

Lan exited, the hatch sliding closed behind him. "Come on, we'll go back up to rec ten."

"That's all the room you get?"

A bark of laughter. "Yep, that's it. A bunk and a storage compartment with just enough room for your soft armor and three sets of uniforms." Lan shrugged. "It's okay. I've lived with worse."

"Really?"

"Oh, yeah. The world I came from? It's crowded. There, once you're working age, which is fourteen standard years, you get less room than that, and you only get the bunk for twelve hours. Someone else gets it for the other twelve."

"Seriously?"

"Yeah. Having a bunk to myself is a luxury. And it could be worse than that, even. Some of these guys come from worlds where you share a bunk that size with three people, and you only get it for eight hours. Or less."

"Wow. I didn't realize how lucky I was to grow up on—" sand

and sun, she couldn't tell him which world "—a frontier world."

"Was it dangerous?" Lan asked.

"It could be." Q shrugged. "You have to be cautious because there's always some big animal trying to eat you, and there's more animals trying to eat your food. It's a lot of hard work to stay alive."

"It's hard work to stay alive on my world too, but it's not animals, it's your fellow humans preying on you." Lan shook his head. "People will kill for very little. This," he motioned at the fold transport around them, "is luxury on a scale I couldn't imagine as a kid. Oh, sure, there's rich people with whole buildings to themselves and even some empty space, and the planet has some nature preserves, but my chances of seeing any of that were next to nothing. I was so excited to get accepted into the Fleet, even knowing I'd never see my family or friends again. I knew this was a chance at safety I'd never have there." He shrugged. "It's not truly safe. There are still plenty of bad people, and I'm on a warship, but it's way safer than my homeworld."

They entered the rec compartment, and Lan stepped in and stopped, looking around. Then, he pointed to the big vid console, with a bunch of first-termers standing around it, cheering and jeering. "Come on, let's go play."

Q grinned and happily followed him into the fray. But she couldn't help but think about Lan's expression at the end of his speech. Gov Human Military advertised itself as the ultimate safety for all humanity. But obviously, it was only as good as the humans in it. A structure like the military, where the higher-ranking individuals held all the power, could easily be abused.

And it would be hard to prove because, unlike Familia, military people would have to be good at hiding their abuse. She'd already seen it—those two sergeants trying to coerce her into some sort of group sex thing.

People like Lan, used to a kill-or-be-killed world, wouldn't believe the notices for alternative reporting procedures and anonymous reports for abuse of power. Those procedures were probably well-meaning, but in reality, would they really be anonymous? Probably not entirely. The combination of those factors would make it easier for the abusers to hide what they were doing.

So, the usual survival rules still applied. Be aware of your surroundings at all times, and never let yourself be cornered.

Maybe she could do more than just ride along, waiting for Ruhger and Saree to finish whatever it was they were doing. Maybe she could be part of the solution. Q smiled. If she could get to the right people, she could help Gov Human crackdown on these horrible abusers and send the predators someplace where they'd experience being prey for once. Or at least away from all these vulnerable first-tour kids, unwilling to trust their lives to a system that might fail them.

"Hey, Lan."

He smiled down at her.

"Got a message. I'll be right back." At least, she hoped she'd be right back, but Saree wanted to talk to her.

Lan winked. "Hurry. Got to have someone guarding my six."

"I will." And she would, in more ways than one.

∆∆∆

"You need to do what?" Q asked. That tour of the flagship's net work area seemed like eons ago, not just a couple of days. But Saree's statement made the boredom fade away.

Saree smiled at her. "I need to return to my normal body. This," she swept a hand from her head to her thigh, "isn't me. I'm not a blonde, nor am I built like this. Fortunately, I have the DNA code for my as-born appearance. Since I'm doing it, you may as well get your tattoo removed and a full health check now. Grant is here, and he'll watch over both of us."

Interesting that Saree didn't fully trust Gov Human either. Both Saree and Ruhger seemed much happier reunited with Lightwave—maybe it was more than finding them safe and the crew intact? Maybe they needed a way to escape Gov Human? Or just the backup for negotiations on whatever it was they were talking about?

"It would be my pleasure," Grant said with a little bow and a big smirk. Q remembered Grant well from Lightwave—growing up in a compound with all women, the tall, graceful, almost pretty blond man with the flirty manners and cheerful smile stood out, even when she wasn't old enough to understand why all the older girls were giggling. As Q grew up, Lightwave folded in occasionally, bringing supplies. Grant was one of the people who always flew down to see them, bringing fun stories with the trade goods. He was both annoying and useful—his skills as a negotiator got them better accommodations and the use of the officer's mess, but he was one more person treating Q like a kid.

Saree retorted, "Of course it would."

"It's a strategic move too," Grant said soberly. "We're not

making any progress with Gov Human, so we need to step back from the negotiations, let everyone cool off and think. This will give everyone a full day to do just that." He snorted. "It might even work."

"Maybe," Saree said. "I'm not holding my breath."

Grant shrugged. "Shall we go, Gentles? I've made the arrangements with the medicos already." He opened their sleeping compartment hatch and waved them to go out first.

Q snorted. "Got my life all planned out for me too?"

"Of course not. That's entirely up to you." He stepped up to her side. "You should think about joining Gov Human's military, though. You should be safe from, hmm, those people, and you'd put your skills to good use."

"Why is everyone trying to convince me the military is the right thing for me?" Q scowled up at him. "You realize 'those people' have a lot of power here, don't you? And it's not that safe here. I've already escaped a couple of sand vipers here, and I know there are plenty of recruits who aren't so lucky."

Saree turned so fast Q almost ran into her. "What? What kind of sand viper and who, exactly?"

If looks could kill… Q almost smiled. Someone actually cared. But…people were staring at Saree's outburst.

Grant made a little half-circle with his finger, then pointed toward the float tube. "Not here, not now, Saree. Keep going." He wrapped an arm around Q's shoulders, following Saree's cerimetal spine, marching along the corridor. In a low voice, he said, "After your procedure, I expect to hear all the details. I'll get the right people, so you only have to tell the story once. You said 'escaped,' right? You're okay?"

Q waved a hand. "I'm fine. Amateur hour, comparatively. But others aren't so lucky."

Grant snorted. "I hear you. I'll see what I can do." He chuckled a little. "This might even be fun. At least compared to negotiating with General Kerr's staff."

They walked into the medico bay, where two women waited. "Q?" the older woman, with skin the color of milky coffee, asked.

"Yes, that's me."

"Come with me. I'm Medico Joannam." She turned and headed off into a passageway, then into a small compartment with a med float. "I understand you were born on a frontier world, correct? No real medico stations or care?"

"Yes, Medico," Q replied.

"Okay, a complete checkup with a full DNA check and cleaning, tattoo removal on your stomach, and what else?"

"Can we put my hair color back? It's normally almost black. It's just a dye job, not a body-mod."

She tilted her head and tapped her chin. "I'll make sure you get an appointment with the closest Styler." Medico Joannam smiled. "That's an easy fix."

"Thanks! That would be awesome."

"You're welcome. Now, when I leave, take all your clothes off, hop on the med float, lie back, and say, 'begin examination,' loud and clear. If there's a problem, just yell my name or poke that big, red button on the side of the med float, okay? If you've never been in one of these, it will seem a little weird, but there's a holo that will tell you exactly what it's doing. Don't worry about all the arms and straps. They're for safety only, and you can stop at any time by yelling, 'stop examination!' loud and clear. I'll come running." She raised both brows. "Got it? Begin examination, Medico, or stop examination, that's all you need to say."

"Got it. Thank you, Medico Joannam." Q bowed a little.

"You're welcome. Lie back and relax." She left the compartment, the light on the hatch turning red to show it was locked, so Q did as the medico instructed.

Q looked down at her belly. She'd finally be rid of this ugly, horrible thing. She couldn't wait. "Begin examination!"

A holo appeared above her head, a stilted voice said, "Beginning examination, please lie still," and appendages popped out around her. Q smiled at the buzz of a medical stunner on her arm, where they'd take blood samples. Not only would she get rid of the ugly mark but anything else Familia might have left in her and anything caused by her lack of medical care early in life. Plus, she didn't have to join the Fleet. It was a pretty good deal.

ΛΛΛ

"You ready for this? You can say no," Saree said. "Or wait until after we come back from Cygnus Secundus." Even though Saree no longer looked like the woman Q knew from the escape from *Indomito*, she sounded the same. Not only was her voice the same, but so were most of her mannerisms and her attitudes. Saree was clearly worried about the lack of contact with the Sisters. Saree's new appearance was so strange—it was easier to pay attention if Q didn't directly at Saree, otherwise, the short dark hair, darker skin, and less curvy figure were all too distracting. Q vaguely recalled the new-old-look Saree from Lightwave and the Cygnus

Gliese escape—mostly, she remembered Saree singing and trying to teach guitar. But Saree was a Scholar back then; Q remembered the robes. The name "Saree" didn't sound right either. Maybe she'd been called something else? But none of that mattered right now.

Q was tired of doing nothing but worrying—the days passed too slowly. This was one little thing she could do and make a big difference for a lot of people. "I got this. These people are nothing." Q waved Saree's concern away. Next to Familia? These people were sand fleas. Besides, this might be her only chance. There was no guarantee they'd return to the Fleet. Depending on what they found at the Sisters' compound, she might have to stay there, go somewhere else forever, or any number of other possibilities. Dread sent icy shivers down her spine.

"Q will be fine. We'll be watching very closely," Major McFar assured them. As the head of undercover operations for General Kerr's Special Investigations Squadron, Q was sure he'd seen far worse. He had a quiet competence that was very reassuring. "And Shawnso will be in the compartment with a stunner, just in case." He pointed at the dark-haired woman next to him. "She's done plenty of undercover ops, just not on the flagship. She's usually playing your part, Q. She'll be near you, but she won't step in unless she has to. We don't want to give away her real job."

Q could see why Shawnso was normally the bait. She was beautiful, with dark skin, long black hair, a heart-shaped face, and big brown eyes. "I'd rather be doing this than my cover job," she whispered to Q with a wink.

"If you're ready, go," Major McFar said. "And thank you

again."

Saree put a gentle hand on her arm. "Be careful, Q. We don't want to lose you."

Q smirked at Saree and McFar but squeezed Saree's hand for a moment, gratefully. "I got this." Then she walked out with her new best friend, Shawnso, more than ready to get started. Maybe she couldn't do anything about Familia or Saree's problem, but she could do this. "So, what do you do?"

Shawnso laughed. "Oh, my last 'duty as assigned' was so nasty! I had to clean and oil the plas shredders. Brush shreds of oily gunk out of giant machines, replace dull teeth, then make sure the oilers were working right. So boring. So messy and dirty." She snorted as they entered rec ten. "But it could be worse. I could be mucking out stalls."

"You are so right." Q shuddered. "I'm so happy I never have to do that again." She hoped that was true. "Hey, I need a drink. I'll be right there."

Shawnso shrugged. "Sure. I'll be playing."

Q hung out and played net games like she usually did, but no one approached her. Did the word get out already that she was someone special? But she looked different now and had a standard recruit e-torc and identity, so unless it was the same two sergeants who approached her earlier, it shouldn't be an issue. But it couldn't be them. Major McFar said that, with her help, they'd gotten enough evidence against those two, and they were in the brig. Unless they got the chance to talk to others?

At the end of the day, they all met over a secure e-torc connection. "Good job out there today," McFar said. "Don't worry, this may take a couple of days. The smart ones will wait and watch. Just keep doing what you're doing. We'll have a different safety person in the compartment tomorrow. We can't risk sending Shawnso more than one day at a time. The only reason we can use you more than once is the medico profile we've got on your fake identity. Don't come to our compartment tomorrow. Just go to the rec room, looking bored."

Q nodded. "Okay. Thanks for hanging out, Shawnso."

"You're welcome." She winked. "You're a natural. Have fun."

Q swept off the connection and got ready for bed. Tomorrow was another day. Saree said they'd be folding from system to system while she and Grant negotiated with Gov Human, but they wouldn't tell her what they were negotiating.

Even if playing bait took weeks, it was better than simply flying along as a free-loading oxy breather.

ΔΔΔ

Q filled her bev-tainer. She was so bored. She never thought she'd get tired of playing net games, but she was. She plopped down in a chair at the side of the compartment and brought up her messages. Nothing from the Sisters. She was really worried. If they weren't responding to Gov Human Military messages, it couldn't be good.

Someone sat next to her, and Q glanced over, then smiled. "Lan! They've been keeping you busy."

"They have." Lan grinned at her. "But I'm here now. Let's go destroy some alien machines!"

"Oh, look, the new kids are so cute together. We'll have lots of fun with these two."

288

Q looked up to see two men and a woman surrounding them. Q had noticed all three of these sand vipers watching her and some of the others yesterday. She'd tried to find out who they were, but their identities were blocked, which probably meant they had someone on the inside of security. It might mean they were officers. Good thing her vid was running constantly, and those special investigation people were watching. She hoped so, anyway, because sitting in a soft chair was not her favorite place to start a confrontation. Although she had a straight shot at one of the men, right between the legs. He must not be very smart. Chosen fall guy or just muscle?

"Yeah, Lan knows what kind of fun we like," the woman said. "But he doesn't seem to have as much fun as we do." They all laughed.

Q risked a glance at Lan. His jaw was tight, his fists clenched on the armrests of his chair, and his expression was half terror, half fury. Well then, that made this easy. Two testimonies for the price of one. And if she had to act, she was going for maximum damage.

"You don't want to start something with me," Q told them, trying to put regretful sincerity in her tone.

They all smirked or snorted. "What you gonna do, baby?"

"Nothing the cutie can do." The guy in front of her bent down, with his lips millimeters from hers, and clamped his hands around her waist. "Doesn't even know who we are," he whispered in her ear, then bit the lobe, hard.

"Ow! Let go, or you'll regret it." *Idiot*. Q clenched her fists to keep from punching this idiot right in the nose. But she wanted cerimetal-strong evidence, so they'd be stopped for good.

"Right. Like you or the little boy can stop us." The man ran his nose down her neck and one hand up to her breast, squeezing hard.

"I said no! Take your hands off me." Q shot a glance at Lan. Hands clamped on his shoulders, pushing him down and back in his seat, the woman mirrored what the man was doing with her.

"You'll do just what we say when we say it, or you'll have a terrible accident. Those airlocks are tricky," the standing man said in a low tone. "It's happened before."

Perfect. Now she had proof, and she could hit back. A wave of silence drew her attention to the rec room's main hatch. "No, I don't think I'll be having any accidents. But you might." She tilted her head at the armored military police marching in. *Sand scooter scat.* All hope of getting a few shots in on these idiots was gone now.

"Black holes!" All three took a step back.

"You three, let's go," the fully armored man in front with officer's insignia motioned to the three.

"Hey, it was—"

"Save it. Identity blockers in a rec room? That's enough to put you and your security friends in the brig." The officer, Captain D'Baker, slashed a hand. "Go." His forefinger pointed, and when the one who stayed standing tried to step back into the crowd, one of the security members grabbed his wrist, pulled it up behind his back, and marched him out of the compartment. The other two followed, blustering about how they hadn't done anything. The officer remained, looking down at them. "Recruit Caplan, your presence is required."

"Really?" Q got up and scowled. "It's all on vid." She gestured at her e-torc. She'd been briefed they'd do this so her identity wasn't risked, but a protest was expected.

"Yes. But personal testimony is still required." He lowered his voice. "And he needs some support." He tilted his head toward Lan, still sitting in the chair.

Q shot a startled look at Lan. He was shaking. *Sand vipers.* Q offered her hand, palm up. "Hey Lan, I could use some company."

Lan looked up at her hand and then her face. Q tried to smile but gave up. He took her hand and rose, following her out of the compartment. The security officer took the lead, but not to security. They went to the medico compartments. There, Medico Joannam and Major McFar waited. Medico Joannam asked Lan to follow her. Q squeezed his hand and let go. Lan followed the medico down a passageway and into a compartment. Captain D'Baker trailed them, standing outside at the hatch.

Major McFar led her off to the side. "Thank you for helping. We appreciate it."

Q scowled. "My pleasure. I just wish you'd waited a minute so I could get a few hits in." She glanced at the hatch Lan entered. "But too bad you didn't catch on sooner."

The officer's lips flattened. "Yes. My fault entirely. I had no idea anyone was capable to the point of targeted identity blockers without alerting security overall. On. The. Flagship!" He scowled at the decking. "That means a real organization, which means widespread problems. It's not just those three." McFar looked at

Q, red flags of fury blazing on his cheeks. "We'll get them. All of them. I promise."

"I'm sure you will do your best." Q didn't think McFar could keep that promise; he didn't know who was involved or how far up it went.

"I will. Unfortunately, word has already spread." McFar scowled into the distance. "More signs this is an organized group." His gaze returned to hers. "As a result, you are now confined to General Kerr's level. We're having your things moved now. You can keep the e-torc; a conference room is being converted to a small rec room."

"I can't hang out with Windby and Lan in the rec compartments?"

"No, sorry, too risky."

"This sucks like the giant black hole of Andromeda!" *Some reward.*

"It does. Sorry. But it could be worse." McFar shot a glance toward D'Baker.

He was right. "Yes, of course." Q sighed. "If Lan wants to see me, will you let me know?"

"Of course. We are very grateful for your help." He stood. "Come on, I want the medicos to check you—you may have bruises. Then I'll show you to your new billeting."

Q followed along, aware that she was fortunate in so many ways. But helping others should result in a reward, not a punishment. Being restricted to the general's level meant she'd be all by herself, bored out of her skull. And have nothing to distract her from worrying about the Sisters. She had to get Saree and

Grant to talk the fleet into going to Cygnus Secundus. She had to know if Nat, Brin, Sister Ani, and even Sister Lashtar were okay.

Or who she had to kill if they weren't.

CHAPTER SIXTEEN

"Good news, Q." Grant sat next to her in the general's conference room, Saree sitting next to him. Her first glance, seeing Saree as a tan, athletic, short-haired brunette, was still startling.

"Oh? For you or me?"

"All of us," Saree said. "We're returning to Lightwave, then we're going to Secundus."

"Finally. I'm so bored." *Thank the Mother!* Q let her head drop forward on the table to hide her expression. Every day without an answer from the Sisters increased her apprehension. With little else to do, she couldn't stop thinking about all the horrible things that might have happened. She knew Saree, Ruhger, and the rest of Lightwave's crew felt the same way. It was such a relief to finally *go.* She was tired of riding along, folding from system to system, with nothing to do. At least Major McFar was keeping her informed about their investigation—they'd made a lot of progress but hadn't found the root of the problem yet.

"You're such a drama queen, Q," Grant teased, ruffling her hair. He'd fallen into the role of big brother quickly, teasing her constantly but at the hint of a threat, stepping forward to protect her. Q found it annoying and reassuring in equal measure.

She popped back up and smirked at him, determined not to show her feelings. "It's a tough job, but somebody's got to do it."

"Well, your next tough job is packing and saying goodbye," Saree told her with a gentle smile. "We're headed out in two hours."

Q felt her eyes widen. "That soon? I hope I can find everyone."

"If not, just send a net message." Grant shrugged. "Military people are used to this kind of thing. They won't think anything of it, and if you ever meet again, it will be like you were never apart." He quirked a brow. "Trust me."

Q snorted. "I've already learned not to do that." At his crestfallen face, she relented. "Just kidding. Mostly." Leaving her new friends was sad, but she wanted to find out what happened to the Sisters more than anything. If they weren't answering her or Lightwave… "Is the Fleet going with us?"

Saree frowned. "Yes and no. Most of the Fleet will fold to Cygnus Gliese. There are some reports of abuse coming from there. Being a Galactica planet, it's not surprising, and there's little General Kerr can do, but it's a reason to be in Cygnus. The Sisters aren't."

"Of course not." Q scowled. "Who cares about a bunch of women and little girls?"

"The Sisters are a tiny number of people. General Kerr can't justify the expense of folding the Fleet across a quarter of the known universe for a small group, Quinn." Saree stared at Q from under narrowed brows. "The only reason they're doing even this much is because they're following me, no matter how much they dislike the idea."

"Yeah, yeah. I get it." Q sighed. "I still don't get why they're following you, though."

Saree chuckled. "Someday soon, Q. Don't push it."

Q didn't hold back her eye roll this time.

ΔΔΔ

Q waved goodbye to the pilot and co-pilot and jogged to the hatch, more than ready to leave the shuttle. She followed Saree and Grant out. Saree was immediately swept into Ruhger's arms, and Q looked away. She didn't need to see that!

Grant evidently felt the same way. "Come on, I'll show you to your room, give you a quick tour, then we'll go see Loreli." He draped an arm around her shoulders. "Loreli will have snacks!" He chuckled. "I'm really looking forward to a decent meal. We'll catch up with Tyron, Katryn, and Chief later. Katryn will have a new e-torc for you, a better one than that." He tossed his chin toward her.

"Oh, good. This thing is so slow." They walked down a long, empty corridor, beige walls plastered with emergency escape pod warnings and additional hatches behind them, plain plas under their feet. It looked so different without the colorful hammocks fastened against every wall.

"Like many small folders, Lightwave used to be a military fold transport," Grant said. "It's a big cube; this level has shuttle docks around the outside bulkheads, two on each side, and the interior is split into a phys mod, observation lounge, dining hall, and kitchen. Below us are cargo areas and the engineering sections. Above us are crew quarters, hydroponics, security, and stuff like that. Lightwave's shuttles are docked above that—imaginatively named Alpha and Beta shuttle." They came to a secured hatch and Grant opened it. A steep stairway led up—more bland plas with emergency notices.

"Go up the ladder and turn right. I've got a compartment assigned to you already. I'll drop my gear and give you the rest of the tour."

"Okay." She hopped up the stairs and took the narrow passage to the right. "You guys don't believe in decoration, do you?"

Grant laughed. "No, we're pretty basic. There's a reason for that. My compartment is on your left, Loreli's on your right. Tyron and Katryn live next to Security, back the other way. I've assigned you the one next to Loreli, coming up next."

Q stopped in front of the hatch.

"Put your hands in front of the sensor and look at the blinking light."

She did so.

"And there we are. Katryn will program your new e-torc access, so you don't have to do any of that." Grant waved his hands around.

The hatch opened to a small compartment with a bed, a chair, what looked like a table folded down against the wall, and a tiny sani-mod beyond that. Not big but not tiny and done in the same boring beige plas as the rest of the folder.

"We only have a few passenger compartments and rarely use them, so they're not decorated. We have 3D printers. Feel free to use them." Q turned to see Grant slouching against the hatch.

"Thanks, this is fine. I'll use the sani-mod and meet you for that tour, right?"

Grant nodded. "Perfect. Give me fifteen mikes; I have a little more to put away than you do." He winked and turned away.

"Sure, thanks." The hatch shut behind him, a big yellow and red label showing directions for the nearest escape pod, ladder down, and shuttle. Q plopped her carrysack down on the bed. It wasn't big or fancy, but it felt safer than General Kerr's flagship and far safer than *Indomito*. And it was all hers—for now. She would be back on Secundus soon; whether she stayed or not depended on what they found. Q bit her lip and hugged herself. No news wasn't good news, no matter what the saying claimed.

ΛΛΛ

"We've arrived safely in Cygnus Secundus. Perform checks and report issues. Alpha shuttle departs for Secundus in ten minutes. Command out," Katryn said.

Katryn was so lucky to learn fold piloting. Despite the need to learn a lot of complex math, Q desperately wanted to learn both fold and shuttle piloting—she wanted to be as independent as possible. She snickered, then shut the sound off when she heard Alpha shuttle's hatch cycle. Armored footsteps rang on plas, and harness buckles snapped. Hah! She did it—she was getting to the Sisters' compound one way or another.

Then the latch on her compartment turned, and Grant was staring down at her. "Nice try kid, but no dice. Let's go." He held out a hand without a trace of his usual humor.

Q climbed out of the storage compartment, knocking Grant's hand aside. "I'm not a kid. I know the compound and you don't!"

Grant clamped armored fingers around her wrist, towing her

out of the shuttle at a trot. "Maybe you're not a kid, but you're also not trained in military operations."

"Sure I am. Lashtar trained us, remember?"

"You don't have armor. You've never trained with us. We have no idea what we're flying into down there." Her living compartment hatch opened, and Grant shoved her hard enough that she stumbled to the end, almost falling. "Stay here. If you're quiet and stay, you can watch. Make trouble, and we'll shut it all off, leaving you in the dark." The hatch closed behind him with a decisive thud.

Q immediately tried to get out, but they'd shut off her access to everything. *Sand fleas! So annoying.* Stuck on Lightwave and locked in her compartment, like she was some little kid! Q was trained, and she knew the Sisters' compound like the back of her hand. And they wouldn't even let her on the comms! *Stupid.* Thank the Mother they hadn't succeeded in sending her with the Fleet to Cygnus Gliese as Saree threatened to do when Q wouldn't stop arguing.

"Command, Beta shuttle," Rugher's voice said.

"Go ahead, Beta," Chief replied.

"Requesting push back now."

"Pushing back...you are clear, Beta," Loreli said.

"Flight time of six hours, thirteen minutes to Secundus orbit. On final into the Sisters' compound, we'll transmit visuals for you."

"Excellent. Command out."

Well, guess there wasn't any reason to sit there and watch nothing. She'd get out of this room. But no matter what Q tried, each action was countered immediately. Her best tricks didn't work at all—Katryn anticipated every one of her moves. *Blast and rad.* She slumped on her bed and pulled up Zombie Planet 2500 to kill time until Beta shuttle landed.

"Five minutes out," Ruhger said, startling Q. She turned the game off.

A view of Secundus appeared on her holo, labeled Alpha Shuttle surveillance. Q watched Secundus grow larger, then zoom into home. She gasped. Someone attacked the Sisters' compound, with big weapons! Buildings were destroyed, blackened ruins barely standing, craters where the main guard posts used to be. Nothing moved.

"Hey, let me out of here! I can help!" Q yelled, but no one answered.

Chief said over the comms, "I'm not sure Q should see this."

She yelled again. "Don't you dare. This is my home, my family."

"Chief, she's seen worse," Loreli said. "And she's right. Q isn't a little girl anymore."

At least Loreli listened to her.

"Even if she acts like one sometimes."

Ooh! Q almost stomped her foot, then realized that was exactly what Loreli was talking about. Guess her Familia "split personality" wasn't so split after all.

"Fine. I don't like it."

"None of us likes this," Loreli retorted. "Turn the sound on, let her hear Ruhger and the rest."

A smacking noise, undoubtedly Chief slapping his wrench into his palm, then she could hear the shuttle's crew shifting in their seats.

"Ruhger, don't land," Tyron said, his voice clear over the comms. They must be boosting the signal through a local satellite. "Circle at three thousand meters, and let us get a better look."

"Copy that," Ruhger said.

"This doesn't look good, Ruhger, but I don't see any active threats," Tyron said. "Bring us down to one thousand meters."

The vid showed them spiraling down, the scope of the destruction becoming clearer. Could anyone survive that?

"Down to one hundred meters, Ruhger," Tyron said. "Looks like an aerial bombardment on guard posts, followed by armed personnel or remotes." Tyron's tone was grim. "I'm informing Laniakea Fleet Intelligence. Someone knew this happened; there's no bodies."

Chief said, "The attackers may have buried them to avoid attracting predators and notice by the other homesteaders in the area."

Q snorted. "They got eaten." She scowled. She wouldn't cry. Not even angry tears.

"Probably not, Chief," Katryn said more than a few seconds later. The transmission delay from the planet's surface to Lightwave wasn't much, but it was enough to be annoying. "The predators here are vicious and fast. They'd have every bit of evidence gone in less than a day."

They continued in the downward spiral until they finally landed.

"We're down," Ruhger announced. "Armor up, people.

Weapons free, but full identification even if fired on, just in case we have survivors. Katryn, if you still have any secret comm codes or connections, now is the time to use them. This is a different shuttle; they won't recognize it as Lightwave's."

"I don't think any of my stuff is current, but I'll try some of the old stuff from Gliese. I'll keep broadcasting on the current addresses too. They might recognize my voice," Katryn said, swiping and poking at her holo as Tyron guided her to the armor storage.

"Q, do you have any current comm codes?" Loreli asked.

"I don't think so. It's been more than two years." Q swallowed hard. "And I don't have my old e-torc. I didn't memorize any of that stuff. Stupid me."

Loreli said, "It's not stupid, Q. You weren't coming back for a long time, if ever. Why memorize something like that?"

Q told her, "I do have codes for my messages, but they haven't responded to anything I sent, so it's not going to do us any good."

Two minutes passed, feeling like five hours. Why were they waiting? They needed to go, see if anyone was still alive, now!

"I'm getting nothing, Ruhger," Katryn said, worry creasing her face.

"Full enemy territory drill," Chief said. "I've got operational command. Ruhger, you're tactical command."

Her view changed from the shuttle to Ruhger's e-torc, with smaller views from Grant, Tyron, and Katryn's off to the side.

"Copy that, Chief," Ruhger commanded. "Tyron, you've got point, then Katryn and Grant. I'll take our six. Saree, I want you to stay here in the shuttle in case we need bigger weapons or a quick pick-up."

Her view changed again, with Tyron's in the larger area, Katryn, Grant, and Ruhger's stacked next to it. A fourth view came up, looking back into the shuttle—Ruhger's rear vid.

Ruhger said, "All right, let's go."

Tyron opened the shuttle hatch. It took Q a second to realize she was looking at the barrel of Tyron's laser rifle, up and ready to fire, just like Fringe War 300. Tyron scanned the compound, then sprinted to the first building. Scorch marks and holes pockmarked the buildings, and the outer doors were busted open. Katryn and Grant passed Tyron, and then Ruhger ran behind them. Tyron sprinted past all of them, and the pattern repeated as they crossed the compound. They entered the dining hall, then each room. Everything was holed, burned, or broken, but there weren't any bodies. Q swallowed hard—now that she'd seen the real thing, she wasn't playing FW300 anytime soon.

In the kitchen, everything was destroyed too, but the food spread around was rotting; larger animals hadn't gotten through the doors. *How odd.* They entered each building in turn, including the remains of the storage sheds and the now-open root cellars.

Q said, "Hey, Chief, there are escape tunnels and safe rooms in the dorms. They need to check those."

"Nothing," Grant said, frustrated.

"You know," Katryn said, "we haven't found any escape tunnels or safe rooms. There's no way the Sisters would build a big compound like this without both of those."

That's what she just said! Wasn't anyone listening to her?

"You are right, Katryn," Chief said. "I'll try scanning in

infrared. But if it's a deep enough hole, I won't find anything."

"Loreli! They're not holes! They're shallow tunnels and spaces built into the walls."

"It can't be too deep; the water table is too high here," Katryn said. "Look at all the ponds. You can smell the swampy water. Let's go back into the chow hall and look for hidden hatches, especially any going down. If we don't find any there, we'll look in the dorms next."

"There's nothing in the dining hall, the escapes are in the dorms! Come on, Loreli!"

The crew kept searching but found nothing, of course. They finally started on the dormitories and found hidden doors and hatches but no people.

"Might be slavers," Chief said, in a menacing rumble. "A bunch of girls would be valuable."

"If they bought off the authorities, there will be a trail and we *will* find them," Grant growled.

"If they were smart, they wouldn't have to, Grant," Chief said. "Come at night, leave the shuttles at a distance in the jungle, walk in, stun everyone, then bring the shuttles in one at a time for pick-up. The Sisters certainly posted guards, but they'd be used to watching for animals, not people, and they've probably grown complacent over the past year or so. Dump any bodies in the jungle on your way out. But let's check the fields before we go, just to be sure. I'm going to scan the area around the compound, see if I can find someplace a shuttle might land. Saree, fly top cover for them as they go. I want the shuttle close enough to do a fast pick-up."

Ruhger said, "Let's go, same order as we came in. Don't bunch up."

Tyron jogged across the compound, then through the electric fence gate and into the growing fields. It had taken so much work to clear each of those and protect them with the electric fencing and watchtowers. Now the watchtowers were gone. They walked all the fields around the entire compound.

Katryn said, "I haven't seen any animals yet. Where are the chickens and goats?"

"Eaten?" Ruhger replied.

His crew glared at him. But Q knew he was right.

Chief said, "If they got hungry enough, they'd break out. Then they'd get eaten. Maybe the Sisters got tired of defending helpless animals and started hunting the native wildlife? There is certainly enough of it."

They'd done some hunting before she left because protecting the animals took a lot of work. And it was free meat, if not very tasty. Maybe Chief was right.

"Could be," Katryn said thoughtfully. "I do remember some of them talking about how hard it was to protect the animals last time we were here. The only thing they couldn't get from the native animals was fleece for yarn, and they could trade skins or grow something for fibers instead. There's probably a native plant that makes good spinning fibers."

"Check the outside perimeter," Chief said. "If you don't find anything there, then we'll have to find their attackers another way."

"Tracking electronic trails isn't as easy or as satisfying, but it's easier to prove to authorities," Tyron said.

Saree snorted. "We have so-called authorities on call. Let them do the work. Keeps them busy and out of our hair."

The crew chuckled.

"Great point. Are you sending whatever we got along with a formal request?" Chief asked.

"Yes, but I'm sure the forces they left behind are monitoring us," Saree said, her tone sour. "They can get started *now*, before the formal request comes through."

Hmm. Didn't the Fleet all go to Cygnus Gliese? But the Fleet was interested in Saree for some reason, so she might be right.

"Hey, I've got something here," Tyron said, standing at the edge of the jungle about thirty meters away. They quickly joined him. "See, there's a path here."

That was new. But there were plenty of little platforms up in the trees out there for hunting.

Chief said, "It might be a hunting blind."

How did Chief know that? Wasn't he spacer from the start? Q suddenly realized she knew very little about any of the people on Lightwave.

Ruhger said, "Well, let's check it out."

"Saree, stay between the compound and our team just in case there's someone left in the compound we missed, and keep looking for any attackers outside the compound," Chief said. "We're watching for shuttles and vehicles, but we're too far away for personnel."

Tyron started down the path. He'd walk twenty meters or so, then move off and scan everything. He did it for more than an hour, proving he had way more patience than Q did. "Hold up," Tyron murmured over the comms. "I've got something." The view showed a very thin, shiny strand going across the path. A tripwire. Tyron stepped across the wire and followed it to a camouflaged box, presumably full of explosives and shrapnel, carefully unhooked that end, coiled the wire, and put it near the stake it was fastened to on the other side of the path. "Gather up. I bet there's more than a hunting blind here. Watch for sensors and tripwires. I found and disabled one, but there may be more."

He was probably right. Sister Lashtar was really good at that stuff.

"Maybe we should just yell," Katryn said. "We've probably been spotted."

The whine of a laser sounded over the comms.

"Right again, Katryn," Tyron said, with a breathless laugh.

"Katryn, *you* should yell," Ruhger said. "They might recognize your voice. Use your armor's boost."

"Hey! I can yell for you. They'll know my voice!" Q cried. Except it could be a recording. They should have brought her along. She pounded her fists on the bed.

"Sisters! It's Katryn from Lightwave! Stop firing!" She repeated it several times. Finally, the shooting stopped.

"Katryn, if it's really you, come out where we can see you," a female voice called. That might be Brin's voice. "No weapons."

"I'll come out, but if you know me, you know there's no way I'm disarming. Besides, even if I did, Tyron is backing me up."

No one said anything.

Ruhger muttered, "Careful, Katryn."

"No kidding, Captain Obvious," she retorted softly. "Hold your fire; I'm coming out!" Katryn yelled. The path showed clearly in her vid, but no one appeared.

Ruhger was moving through the jungle, then he stopped, watching something. Q saw someone carefully pushing her way through the jungle. Ruhger waited, dead still. Q realized Ruhger was waiting for the person to pass by.

That's Nat! Q released the breath she didn't realize she'd been holding. *Nat is alive!*

"Hold it," Ruhger said.

Nat spun to face Ruhger, her weapon pointed at him. "Sand fleas!"

Q snorted. Definitely Nat. She never was any good at the tactical fighting thing.

Ruhger knocked her rifle to the side and down, hitting it hard enough that Q heard the crack and Nat's yelp. At least Nat had a strap, so she didn't lose the rifle. Ruhger said, "Sorry, but I don't want to die trying to rescue you."

"Rescue? Yeah, right," Nat sneered.

Ruhger said, "Yes, rescue. I'm Captain Ruhger of Lightwave. You are?"

Nat stared, disbelief morphing to relief. Ruhger must have cleared his helmet. "Oh! You are! Oh, thank the Mother." Her whole body seemed to collapse, then she perked up. Q knew how she felt. "Hold on." She swept at something on her e-torc. "All stations, visual confirmation on Captain Ruhger." She listened for a bit, then smiled. "Okay, on our way in." She whistled, mimicking one of those obnoxious fruit-chompers. Q didn't miss the flying lizards. So destructive.

Another girl appeared down the trail. Q squinted at the crew's vids—even at a distance, she was pretty sure that was Brin.

Nat waved an arm, beckoning Ruhger. "Come on, let's go."

"Certainly." Ruhger followed Nat back to the trail and further into the jungle, meeting up with Brin. As they walked, Nat and Brin checked and reset traps. Looked like Lightwave's crew may not have tripped any of them, and some of them were truly clever and well-hidden, for low-tech stuff. Q started noticing that Nat and Brin's clothes—work clothes, not Sisters' robes—were filthy and torn, and they both looked exhausted.

Ruhger said, "Excuse me, but what are your names?"

Nat jumped and spun. "Oh! I guess you probably don't remember. I'm Nat and this is Brin."

"Ah, yes. The would-be pirates."

Brin blushed and Nat winced. Q laughed.

"Yeah," Nat said. "Sorry. We were stupid."

That was true. She'd only been seven, but Q knew trying to outwit adults on their own ship was useless.

"Hopefully, you've outgrown that particular mistake," Ruhger said. "Don't worry; none of us hold it against you."

"Good," Brin breathed.

As they walked along, Ruhger asked, "Do you have more watchers out here or just more sensors?"

"More sensors," Nat said. "With you here, that means you've got a shuttle, and I'm sure it's armed, so we should be safe to pull everyone in."

"You are correct. And thank you for reminding me. Command,

Alpha shuttle, contact made. Identities confirmed for at least two Sisters."

"Copy that, Ruhger," Chief said, like he hadn't been watching all this. "Safe to land the shuttle?"

"I believe so, but don't shut down."

"Understood," Chief said. "Alpha shuttle, land, but remain ready, weapons hot."

"Copy that, Command," Saree's voice said. "Landing; engines and weapons stay hot."

"Sisters," Ruhger said, "our shuttle will land, but we're ready to take off and attack at any time. We have a pilot on board. Please lead the way."

"Okay. Come on," Brin said, waving. Now that Q got past the relief and shock, she could see that not only were Brin and Nat exhausted but also worried. Really worried.

Ruhger followed the young women and occasionally set one of his high-tech sensors. The path twisted and turned, and the Sisters had built camouflaged gates and barriers. Some had to be crawled under or climbed. They finally reached a huge tree, a rope ladder hanging down.

Brin started climbing. Nat looked at Ruhger. "You should probably wait until Brin is at the top. The ladder holds a couple of us, but you're a big guy."

Ruhger huffed. "Thanks, but if you warn them I'm coming, I'll just use my grav generator."

"Oh!" Surprise crossed her face. "Coming up the fast way!" Nat yelled up. Her face turned back to Ruhger, her expression puzzled. "What? Your shuttle made all kinds of noise—that's why we were out there—and flying up through all that—" Nat pointed up at the tree "—won't be quiet either."

"Point." Ruhger nodded and then rose, slowly, passing Brin on the ladder. He slid around and through the huge branches, eventually reaching what looked like a treehouse. Girls crowded the platform, and there were a bunch in the mostly-screen hut. Q recognized a lot of them, and relief coursed through her. But it was tinged with worry—where were the Sisters?

Tyron, Katryn, and Grant rose through the tree and each perched on a separate branch. Ruhger asked quietly over the comms, "Have you figured out who's in charge yet? If anyone?"

"No," Katryn said. "I've only seen younger women and a few teenage girls and nowhere near enough of them."

Q bit her lip. What happened to Sisters Lashtar, Ani, Navarr, and the others? Where were the little kids?

Nat carefully pushed through the crowd to Ruhger, Brin behind her. Nat motioned to the women and girls behind her. "You see everyone who's left to defend us. There's injured inside and children in another location." She clamped her eyes shut for a second. "I know you've already done a lot for us, and we have no right to ask for more, but could you please take the injured and run them through your medico station? A few are barely hanging on."

"Of course we can!" Katryn exclaimed. "Why didn't you tell us sooner?!"

Nat collapsed into Brin, who held her tight, relief on both their faces.

Ruhger said, "Saree, we've got injured. See how close you can get to our location. Let's get them in the shuttle and upstairs. Chief, you heard?"

Chief said, "Copy multiple injuries inbound. I'm sending Loreli and the medfloat with our other… shuttle. It's faster."

Loreli was a pilot? *Huh.*

"Excellent choice, Chief. We can get the injured out of the gravity well, then transfer them to…the other shuttle."

What was the deal with the second shuttle? They never named it. Weird. Q realized she was frowning hard enough that the space between her eyebrows hurt. There were a lot of mysteries on Lightwave Fold Transport.

"Concur," Chief said after a moment.

Ruhger asked, "Nat, is there somewhere closer we can land our shuttle? Or at least a clearing we can hover over and use the tractor beam to bring people up?"

She blinked rapidly. "Yes." Nat pointed into the jungle. "About a half-kilometer farther in. We'll have to rig ropes to get the stretchers down."

"No," Tyron said. "We'll take them down. Strap them down and get them over here—" he pointed at the edge of the platform "—and we can use our grav generators to take them down and get them to the shuttle. We'll do a fast recharge at the shuttle."

"I heard that, Ruhger," Saree said. "I'm on my way."

"Oh, thank the Mother," Nat muttered.

Brin yelled, "Get the patients strapped to their stretchers or beds. Everyone who can safely climb down, get ready. Protection teams, form up below. Take everything you've got."

Girls grabbed bags and formed lines for the ladder along the edge of the platform. Others hurried inside the hut. Nat turned away.

"Nat," Ruhger snapped. "Let your people handle that. We need a situation brief, now."

A little harsh, wasn't he?

But Nat turned back and nodded. "Yes. Sorry. Uh, so, a few weeks ago, a couple of girls showed up and asked for help. They said they'd escaped from this guy who bought them off their drug-addicted parents. It happens." Nat grimaced. "They were beat up, so no one questioned their story. We got them fixed up, and they seemed happy, but a couple of days later, they kept talking about how great their life was at this place they'd come from, with all the food they wanted and pretty clothes and chocolate and all this other stuff and how they didn't have to clean or cook or any of the other chores we make people do."

Nat sighed. "They were careful to talk only to the younger girls, eight to twelve years old or so, or those who were already unhappy at the Sisters. They said their 'big sister' would be coming to get them and if anyone wanted to come with them to this great place—" Nat did the air quotes thing "—they should be ready to drop everything and run." She shook her head sadly. "A week ago, two shuttles swept in, and sure enough, a bunch of the girls dropped everything and ran to them, following those— those—sand fleas!"

Nat was furious and she should be. Those girls were stupid.

"We all grabbed weapons and started shooting, but they were armored and had more weapons. Sister Lashtar sounded the retreat, telling everyone to grab whoever they could and run. The retreat plan was fade into the jungle, then sneak to this place." She waved a hand. "There's another one like this farther in. That's where the girls with the babies and little kids are."

The first stretcher was carried out and carefully placed at the edge of the platform. That was Lashtar! She was unconscious and pale.

"Lashtar is the worst off," Nat said. "She won't make it much longer without real help."

Chief muttered something angry. "I'm sending a message folder to the fleet."

Tyron and Katryn hovered over to Lashtar's stretcher. "We've got her." They took either end of the makeshift stretcher, and they sank out of sight.

The next pallet appeared. Q didn't recognize the girl, but her face was heavily bandaged. Ruhger took one end, Grant the other, and they shoved themselves away from the tree, then lowered through all the foliage to the ground. They wobbled a bit on the way down, then managed to work together to get the girl down. Once on the ground, Ruhger turned and faced back toward the main trail. He did something to his holo.

Q recognized most of the girls gathering around Ruhger and Grant.

"Ready," Grant said.

"Ready, Sisters?" Ruhger asked.

"How fast?" the girl in front of them asked. Q was pretty sure it was Monab, but she was several years younger than Q; she would have changed a lot over the last two years.

"Formation running pace, if you know what that is," Ruhger

told her. Monab nodded and ran, holding her rifle in the right position. Ruhger left a gap and followed. They arrived at the shuttle in a few minutes. Saree used a hand tractor to bring each stretcher into the cargo bay. Ruhger and Grant plugged their armor in and drank some water. Then they jogged back, repeating the cycle three more times, passing wounded girls plodding down the trail. By the time they completed the last run, a whole bunch of girls and kids waited, but there weren't enough of them. Where was everyone?

She watched the crew settle the first load of girls around the stretchers. Then Ruhger's vid went blank. He was probably flying the shuttle. She watched Katryn and Tyron organize the rest of them, checking on their health.

"Q?" Chief asked.

"Yes? I'm here!"

"Can you come to the Operations Center, please?"

"Of course," Q told him. The hatch to her compartment slid open, and she jogged down the passageway, jumping down the steep stairs three at a time and running to what used to be a cargo bay. She remembered this location from their transport to Cygnus Secundus from Gliese all those years ago, but it wasn't a cargo bay anymore. The hatch opened and she entered. No, it looked fancy, with rows of workstations facing a big screen, a comfortable-looking seating arrangement in the back, and a couple of hatches beyond that.

Chief sighed. "Have a seat." He motioned at the chair next to his.

"What's wrong?"

His lips flattened for a moment. "I regret to inform you that Sisters Danile, Navarr, and Ani were killed in the battle."

What? Q stared at him. *How could that be?*

"Lashtar was the only leader who survived, and she might not if we can't get her to a real medico." Chief swallowed hard, and Q realized she wasn't the only one hurting and worried.

"Sand vipers!" Q clamped her lips together, staring at her lap. She wasn't going to cry. She wouldn't. She looked up at Chief again. "Who did this?"

"We don't know. It's more important to help the living right now. I've messaged the fleet, I'm sure they'll be back soon. But while we wait, we're going to need your help," Chief said.

"Of course. Anything you need."

"Good. You know where the 3D printer is?"

Q nodded.

"You remember the hammocks we used on the trip from Cygnus Gliese?"

"Yes." She smiled for a second, remembering the huge number of different colors and materials, splashed against the walls.

"I need you to start printing a bunch of them," Chief said. "Around fifty or so. The plans are in the printer. We'll need the hammocks and the mounting bars printed."

"I'm on it, Chief." Q jumped up and ran to the printer. She connected her e-torc and quickly found the necessary patterns and got one started. This would take a lot of plas. She'd better find the bulk stuff now and get it ready. It was better if she kept busy, didn't think about who they'd lost. There were more missing than just the three Chief named.

But while she searched, she couldn't help but wonder: what happened next? Most of the leaders killed, lots of girls and little kids needing help, and the Sisters were essentially gone. Someone had to help, and it wasn't Lightwave. Or Gov Human, not for the long-term anyway.

CHAPTER SEVENTEEN

Q ran to Cargo Bay One to help unload the wounded, her footsteps echoing in the empty compartment. She still remembered the last time: people lying everywhere, this particular cargo bay full of moans and screams. This time, a medfloat waited next to the airlock.

Chief said, "Latched. Lashtar goes first, strap her to the medfloat, and get out of the way. Nat and Brin and those assigned to patient unloading will unload them here, taking the closest to the airlock to the furthest tie-down points in Cargo Bay One. Monab, Q, your job is to get everyone not assigned to patient unloading to wait for the wounded to unload, then get them to Cargo Bay Two and set in quarters. Anyone not understand? Commence unloading."

The airlock opened, Ruhger walking out before the hatch was all the way stowed. Q saw he was towing a stretcher—it must be Lashtar. Q moved out of the way, against the bulkhead, but where she could see Sister Lashtar. Ruhger and Grant turned, and with Chief in the middle, they carefully transferred the much too-pale Sister to the medfloat. Appendages and straps popped out, attaching as the medfloat sped away. Chief stared at it until Ruhger squeezed his shoulder, muttering something. Chief turned back to the airlock and led the next stretcher, carried by Nat and Brin, to the back of the cargo bay. Q tried to smile at them, but she couldn't make her face move. Both women were watching their feet, anyway. Seeing her chance, Q slid into the shuttle right behind Ruhger and Grant, and once inside the shuttle, moved off to the side.

"Quinn!" Monab exclaimed, holding her arms open.

Q reveled in the warmth and comfort for a moment but pulled away quickly. They had work to do. Monab's sad smile said she understood. Q ignored the bustle of unloading behind her, focusing on the children lined up behind Monab along the shuttle's bulkhead. Loreli was doing something at the shuttle's controls—watching the surveillance while Chief was occupied, perhaps? This shuttle seemed really small in comparison to Beta shuttle. Why weren't they using the shuttle's cargo bay?

The last of the wounded disappeared through the airlock. Q raised her voice to carry over the chattering and sniffles. "Listen up! I'm Quinn. You might not remember me, but I grew up with the Sisters. You're going to pick up your stuff and follow me, okay?"

"Q, hurry, got Gov Human military shuttles inbound with medicos," Loreli said over her e-torc.

"Monab, you've got the stragglers," Q said quietly. She spoke up again, "Let's go, fast and quiet, okay? Stay away from the wounded. They're getting the help they need, and you will only slow things down. Understood?" Nods, but some were crying now. "Hold hands, now. Help your friends. Let's go!"

Q led them out the airlock and along the far wall of the cargo bay, as far as she could get from the wounded. She turned to walk sideways, so she could catch anyone trying to break free and run to one of the pallets, but so far, the children were behaving. Once out of the cargo bay, Q turned forward and walked a little faster, knowing there weren't any more distractions; all the hatches were closed except Cargo Bay Two.

She entered and led them to the far wall. "Okay, listen up. If you're injured, even a little, take one of the bottom hammocks on this wall. If you are under six years old, take one of the bottom hammocks. Otherwise, take a top hammock. Everyone understand?" About half the kids nodded, the other half were crying or just staring into the distance. At least she and Chief managed to get this first wall of hammocks set up and only three high, versus the five-high stack they had for the trip from Cygnus Gliese to Secundus.

A couple of the kids went scrambling for the top right away, laughing.

"Hey, no jumping from hammock to hammock!" Q yelled. "They aren't that strong!" They were, but the kids didn't need to know that. She and Monab settled the crying and shocked children in hammocks, then got the more active kids to "help" them set up the remaining hammocks. They weren't always helpful, but it kept them busy. As they worked, more girls trickled in slowly, many of them walking wounded, all of them looking worn out and dirty. About the time they got the rest of the hammocks set, Gov Human medicos entered, sealing wounds, setting broken limbs, checking everyone's health, and distributing hugs, which did more for the littlest than anything else. Another set of military people brought in cots, emergency meals, water, blankets, shipsuits, and temporary sani-mods, setting and securing everything efficiently.

"Monab, you got this?" Q asked her.

"I think so." A tired smile flickered. "Can you get me a schedule for food?"

"Sure, I'll check with Chef." Q left the cargo bay, sending the question to Loreli, who immediately sent a schedule out to everyone on board Lightwave. Then Q got a direct message from Loreli, summoning her for kitchen duty. Oh, yay, her favorite—chopping veg and cleaning dishes. Q dropped by the medico station first, but Lashtar was surrounded by military medicos, so she continued to the kitchen.

"Q, darhling! Wash up, we have work to do!" Loreli caroled.

"Yes, Chef." Q did as she was told. As much as she'd like to be looking for the missing girls, with Gov Human stepping in, this was probably the most useful place she could be.

ΛΛΛ

Three days later, Q, Nat, Brin, Monab, and all the girls older than fourteen standards, along with Lightwave's crew, gathered around Lashtar's chair in the dining hall. Lashtar lost her left leg at mid-thigh, but with Lightwave's upgraded medico station and Gov Human's help, her infection healed. Gov Human offered to grow her a new leg, but since she was the Sisters' only remaining senior leader, she turned them down. Poor Lashtar. She probably would have loved to regrow the leg, but her responsibilities came first. Chief was building Lashtar a state-of-the-art prosthetic.

Lashtar needed that downtime. She looked exhausted and old.

"Any word on our girls, Ruhger?" Lashtar asked.

"None yet." Ruhger scowled.

Grant said, "I'm suspicious of more than a few Secundus officials. They're actively obstructing us now. I think they're either involved or taking bribes to look the other way."

Q held back a smirk. Grant was smart to use her for snooping through Secundus's nets. The rest of the crew didn't seem to take her skills seriously; they all thought she should be thrilled to be back working with the Sisters' kids. So did Nat and Brin. They all ought to know better—she left for a reason. Net work was much more fun, more fulfilling—and much quieter.

Plus, Q really wanted to find those missing girls. She'd do anything to save them from the fate she so narrowly escaped. But there was something odd going on. Grant seemed to know more than he should; he must have another source of information. Which wasn't completely surprising, Grant being so well-connected, but some of it seemed like the kind of thing you'd dig up snooping around dark nets, not from trading connections. Maybe some of his connections were shady people?

"Grant," Ruhger asked, "have you seen indications of off-world involvement?"

"Possibly. If we can get the air traffic records I'm asking for, we can probably find out where these shuttles went, especially since the Sisters' net did have a few pieces of usable vid with the shuttle designations partially visible."

"I wonder if this kind of operation is a common occurrence on

Secundus?" Tyron asked softly. "Perhaps some organization has set up shop here, watching groups of kids, then swooping in to take them at the 'right' age?"

He was right. And Q knew just who did that kind of thing. Look at Adzari Academy—Familia was willing to wait for a decent payoff.

Ruhger growled, "Slime-sucking mud burrowers."

Lashtar said, "We thought the offer of land by Secundus was too good, but what other options did we have?" She shook her head. "Until now, we had no reason to be suspicious."

"If this is an organized effort, then they probably only strike every three to four years, enough time to get a new crop—" Tyron sneered the word "—and lower everyone's guard."

Q said, "You know what this sounds like to me?" She waited for everyone to look at her. "Familia. Who else goes to all the trouble of grooming victims and organizing crime on this scale? Sick rad-blasters."

"I suspect you are right," Tyron said. "It does seem like their mode of operation. It's what they did with you."

Q nodded at him. "Exactly. There's just less upfront outlay by Familia this way."

"I wonder how General Kerr will react to this?" Saree asked.

"She's been looking for a way to hammer Familia, right?" Grant asked Saree.

"So she says." Saree frowned. "I'm starting to wonder. It's very convenient she's taken the fleet to Gliese."

Ruhger said, "I've never gotten a false vibe off the general. What makes you think that?"

Saree sighed. "I'm not a great judge of character when those characters feel no remorse for their actions. I've been fooled before." She shrugged one shoulder. "Maybe I'm wrong. I hope so."

"Well, we know what's on Gliese," Katryn said. "Familia is a human problem; Gliese is part of a much larger issue."

"True, but I'm still suspicious," Saree said. "I think I'm suspicious of everyone at this point."

"Not a bad thing for you to be," Tyron said.

She snorted. "I suppose. Thanks."

"Can we get back to the real issue?" Lashtar asked in a surprisingly strong voice. "What am I going to do with all these kids? Especially if they're all at risk on Secundus? I'm the only senior leader left, and I'm only half a leader." She gestured at her leg, then held up a hand at the protests from Q and the girls around her. "You've performed miracles, Sisters, but are you truly ready to give up the lives you'd planned for and stay on, caring for girls?" Lashtar scanned the group.

Sure, Q left without looking back before, but that was before. She knew they'd need a lot of help to get back on their feet, and it would be worse if they couldn't retrieve all those girls.

Lashtar continued, "All of you had off-world or other travel plans. Even with Quinn's cautionary tale and our latest tragedy, I don't want you to live anything less than full lives." She shook her head. "That way lies bitterness, and bitterness can turn to evil. We've seen that before, and I'm not risking it now."

"Your younger children might not be at risk now," Tyron said. "Would anyone try this again? It's not going to work with this set of kids because they'll have heard what happened. None of these kids will ever believe the 'strangers with a better life' story."

"I didn't think any of our current kids would believe it," Lashtar said, waving a hand. "Haven't we told them enough about the dangers in the world and that if it sounds too good to be true, it probably is?"

Nat raised her hand but didn't wait for Lashtar to acknowledge her. "Yes, Sister Lashtar, but I was thinking about this last week. The rains were so hard and cold. It's spring, so the leftover food is pretty boring, and the meals were particularly terrible. Probably because those two women were on cooking duty—I bet they did everything they could to make things worse. We also started spring cleaning, so we were all working harder and longer than usual, in small, dark spaces. I don't think it's a coincidence. This was a really good time to make their point."

"Excellent thoughts, Nat. But how do we go back? There's only a few of us left who are able *and* willing to lead and care for all these children." Lashtar looked at Ruhger.

"Maybe the way isn't back or forward or staying still," Grant said.

"What's left?" Lashtar asked.

"A diagonal, an up or a down," Grant said. "You should reconsider your entire organization."

Ruhger frowned. "What, specifically, are you suggesting?"

Grant frowned back at him and then turned back to Lashtar. "Look, I understand why you became a Sister of Cygnus. I understand the attraction. You did good work and made the atonement you felt you needed to make for your past actions. You helped fulfill a desperate need to care for children that couldn't be cared for any other way. But have your ranks grown over the years here on Secundus? Are lots of children coming to you?"

Q wondered, again, what she didn't know about Lightwave and its crew. And how Lashtar fit into that past.

"No, our numbers are shrinking," Lashtar said. "Food is much easier to come by on Secundus. If you know what you're looking for, you can easily feed your family. And if you want more than a subsistence, hunter-gatherer lifestyle, it takes a lot of people to clear and hold land. Large, extended families are the norm." Lashtar grimaced. "Also, life on Secundus is dangerous. There are so many hazards here. Almost every homesteading family has lost a child or two." Lashtar shook her head, with a mournful expression. "We've lost children ourselves."

"And out of the children who do come your way, haven't a lot of them been adopted?"

"Yes," Lashtar admitted, nodding. "More families want to adopt children because they need helping hands." Her face hardened for a moment. "I realize that sounds cold, but life is hard on Secundus. We check every prospective family closely to make sure any deaths really are accidents and make random visits to our former children a few times a year." She shook her head. "I'm not sure how we'll be able to do that, with so few full Sisters left."

Grant bent slightly to look Lashtar in the face directly. "Perhaps, Sister, your purpose needs to change. Rather than caring for children yourselves, maybe the Sisters should become a clearinghouse, an adoption agency and a worker placement agency. The facilities you've already built can become temporary housing, and not just for children, but for families who find themselves in a tough spot. You can clear families for adoption ahead of time and find large-scale farms and ranches needing workers and check them for working conditions. Then place children *and* families accordingly. Will there be some families or children who never leave? Sure. But that's how you perpetuate your organization. Will there be some people who are just free-loading oxygen breathers? For the short-term, of course. But you make people work too hard. Freeloaders won't stay."

Grant wasn't just a pretty face. That was a really good idea.

Lashtar looked like she might agree. "A lot of the children come because their parents fell to an addiction of some sort or were kicked off their land by unscrupulous large-scale farmers or ranchers. With a little government assistance, we could start a treatment program for families." She spread her arms. "Come to us, you keep your kids while you get better in a supportive environment." Lashtar frowned. "But I'm not sure we'll have enough women, structure, and solitude to properly worship the Mother."

"Are you not worshipping by doing?" Katryn asked. "And what about some of the women working in the universe now? Maybe they're ready to come home."

"Well, of course, we are," Lashtar snapped. She took in a deep breath and blew it out, clearly recruiting her patience. "Sorry. Maybe some are ready to return."

"Sister Lashtar," Nat said, "we should talk about this, just amongst ourselves. Not having large groups of children in any one place certainly makes it harder for slavers to profit, so that part of the idea is really good. But there's no reason we can't figure this out on our own now. I'm not going anywhere until we do." Everyone around her nodded their heads in agreement.

Q joined them. She owed the Sisters a lot—her life, actually. She could stick around until this new thing got running. Besides, she'd had enough adventure for a while. The only problem was making sure Familia didn't come looking for her. If they did, Q might bring more problems than solutions.

"You are right, Nat." Lashtar turned to Ruhger. "I thank you for the rescue and the advice. We need to talk, to figure out where we should go from here. Would you mind if we took over the dining hall for the next few hours?"

"We don't mind at all. Just don't tire yourself too much; you're still healing," Ruhger told her, then looked at Nat. Nat nodded back. "Come on, crew, let's go to the Ops Center."

Sand and sun. Q wanted to know what the crew was going to do. If she was too risky to keep around, maybe she could stay on Lightwave. She bit her lip and looked at Ruhger.

Ruhger said, looking at her, then the rest, "Sisters, there's no need to make any final decisions right at this moment. We'll be staying here long enough for things to settle down, hopefully long enough to find out what happened to your children and bring them back. We can house and feed you for a much longer time than we could last time. There's no hurry."

Q smiled at Ruhger, grateful he understood her hesitation.

"Definitely," Saree said, her expression fierce. "Gov Human *will* find out what happened and find those children."

"And there are other options in the universe too," Tyron said. "Despite Quinn's bad experience, there are places, schools, and programs in other constellations, on other worlds, on ships, where people are treated well and given real opportunities. It just takes a lot of work to find them." From the hatch, he grinned at all of them. "Present company included in the good options." The hatch closed behind Tyron.

Nat, several others, and Lashtar started to speak, but Lashtar couldn't be heard over the ruckus.

Q said, "Quiet! Let Sister Lashtar talk!"

"Thank you, Quinn." Lashtar chuckled but quickly sobered. "Sisters, we are the only ones left. I know some of you were just starting your journey as Sisters, and many of you were planning on moving on and ahead, doing other things with your lives. I don't want to stop any of you. However," she scanned all of their faces, "I do ask you to wait until we get our girls back. Then we can talk about the next steps. If we can't get them back in seven days, we'll talk anyway. We should be back on Secundus by then. Your thoughts?"

Nat also glanced around the group. "Sister Lashtar, I think I speak for most of us. We're staying until we get our girls back and until we settle how we are moving ahead. Anyone with different thoughts, speak up now. Quinn, I mean Q, you go first."

Q frowned at Nat. "What different thoughts? If I can figure out a way to keep Familia away, off your backs and mine, I'm staying. You need help. I'm not becoming a full Sister—Sister Lashtar, you were right there, it's not for me—but I'll stay and help secure the compound, rebuild the net, and figure out who did this and how to stop it forever."

"I don't think forever is possible, but I appreciate your commitment," Sister Lashtar said. "We'll work with Lightwave and Gov Human to figure out a way to hide you from Familia." She scanned the group of them again. "Now, I know some of you can't wait to leave. Speak up, please. We don't need desperately unhappy people working harder than a tunnel worm through red rock—that ends in resentment."

"Sister Lashtar," Monab said tentatively, "I don't think any of us are going anywhere right now. Those kids need us," she jabbed a thumb over her shoulder, "and our little sisters need rescuing. We're staying until we rebuild, regroup, redesign, or break up." She ended strong, and the entire group, including Q, obviously agreed.

A heavy sigh came from Sister Lashtar, followed by nodding agreement. "You are very generous. Thank you. I don't know where we will end up, but for the short term, we have a direction." She smiled. "Nat and Brin, you figure out what we need to fix the compound. Work with Grant. See if you can get materials from Gov Human." She smirked. "They have humanitarian supplies and people who specialize in this kind of rebuilding. Play on their sympathies and make them feel guilty."

She scowled. "They should feel guilty, but they probably don't. Monab, get a team together, and figure out how much food we need to survive the next six months. Ask Chef Loreli for advice if you need to. Your team can also figure out how many other things we need, like clothing, toiletries, furnishings, bedding, kitchen gear, and tools. We'll get those basics from Gov Human too. Q, you have our net security, and teaching the net classes, so figure out how many e-torcs, screens, tablets, and servers we need to replace. You'll also work with me, Nat, and Brin on physical security, but that will come later."

Lashtar looked at each one of them. "Those of you not specifically assigned, take childcare, or assign yourselves to Nat's or Monab's groups. The net can wait for a bit. I'm sure Captain Ruhger will be okay with you meeting here, so split up and start planning. A few of you need to relieve the military people doing childcare immediately, before they decide to never help us again." Lashtar grabbed Q's arm before she could leave. "Q, help me back to my bunk, please."

"Of course, Sister." She wasn't sure why Lashtar needed help. Chief rigged a chair with grav generators, so Lashtar could go anywhere on her own. Q knew Lashtar and Chief had worked together previously, but she hadn't realized until the rescue that there was a tragic romance between the two of them. But it was super obvious now, watching the usually-stoic Chief fall all over himself trying to make things easy for Lashtar and her occasional longing glances. So sad. If anyone deserved a happily-ever-after, it was Lashtar.

As she suspected, Lashtar zoomed away on her own, leaving Q to trot along behind her. They entered Cargo Bay Three, going straight to the rough enclosure in the back corner. Gov Human built Lashtar this little room so she could have a private spot without maneuvering up the steep stairway to the crew quarters. They were adding additional rooms as some of the injured girls recovered enough to leave constant medico care, but those were closer to the main passageway hatch.

Q closed the door, and Lashtar levered herself off the chair and onto the bed, sighing with relief when she lay back and put a pillow under her thigh. "Modern medicine is a miracle, but some things still need time." She pointed at the remainder of her upper thigh. "Sitting too long puts too much pressure on this."

Q was surprised Lashtar was willing to be so candid.

"Oh, don't look so surprised. With everything you've been through and seen, you're not a child anymore, even if you should be." Lashtar grimaced. "If I'd had any idea…"

Q snorted softly. "It was bad timing. A year earlier, and I…well, no, it wouldn't be any different. Familia would still be after me."

"So, tell me why Familia wants you, specifically." One brow raised inquisitively.

Q sighed. "Long story short?" Lashtar nodded. "One, the made-up debt from my schooling at Adzari Academy. They claimed the Sisters didn't pay the whole bill, which is a lie. Two, I'm the reason Saree and Ruhger escaped. Three, and the worst part, is Enzo, Familia's head enforcer, wants me."

Lashtar took in a sharp breath.

"Yeah." Q snorted again. "But the best part is, he doesn't want me, he wants grown-up me, with a woman's body and Familia coloring." She shuddered a bit. "Which makes no sense. I'm not going to look like that, not with my genes. Any decent medico could have told him that. Suns, anyone with brains could tell him that! I'm sure, once the medicos said it was okay, that he'd force body-mods on me. They already made me color my hair and leave it long. I don't know why Enzo decided I was 'the one,' but it proved he's an idiot."

"Which makes it worse because here you are, a living reminder of his huge failure in judgment and a failure of Familia to hold on to something they claim as theirs." Lashtar sighed. "I've seen this before, where a person—in my experience, a man—suddenly develops an unhealthy and unexplainable attachment to another person, usually someone much younger. It's a strange phenomenon and requires a lot of medico help to overcome."

Q shook her head. "That's not going to happen, ever. Familia would see it as a weakness, and the head enforcer can't be weak."

"I'm truly sorry to say this, but you may be too big a risk for us, Q." Lashtar closed her eyes for a moment. "I wish it wasn't so."

"I know." Q swallowed hard. "I want to stay, to find those girls and rescue them, to help the Sisters recover and change, but I'm not sure I can."

Lashtar nodded slowly. "I think we're safe for now. There's too much Gov Human around us for Familia to make an open move. But after they leave…" she shook her head. "I just don't know. I'm sorry."

"It's okay, Sister. I don't want to bring more trouble than I solve. While we were with General Kerr, I changed my hair back to the original color, and they checked me over for anything else Familia may have done. They didn't find anything. But Familia will probably look here first." Q shrugged. "Everybody goes home."

"Even though you really can't." Lashtar pursed her lips.

"No, but I'm still going to help while I can."

Lashtar's smile flickered. "I appreciate it. So, make a list of the technology items we need to secure the compound—get Katyrn and Tyron to help you with that—and the tech we need to teach kids in general. Not net experts—Secundus doesn't need them, and we don't need to try the off-world school route again any time soon—but basic schooling. Reading, writing, and math, especially accounting. If we're staying here, or on any frontier world, that's what we need. Kids who want something more will have to find another way. The Sisters no longer have the luxury of teaching more than the basics."

"Sure, Sister. I'll get right on it." It was too bad, though. The Sisters were one of the few places on Secundus that girls could go to escape a life of basic subsistence. But if they were to survive, Lashtar was right. Q looked down at her—Lashtar seemed to be asleep already. The medicos warned them she'd need a lot more rest than normal. Q drew a blanket over her and crept out. Then she headed for the Operations Center, hoping to find Katryn or Tyron.

Ruhger was sitting in his usual chair in the Ops Center. "Everything okay?"

"Yes. Lashtar's asleep."

"Good. She needs it. What do you need, Q?" Ruhger pointed at her.

"Who, me?"

Ruhger smiled. It was weird to see such a happy expression on his normally glowering face. "Yes, you. What do you need?"

"Well, I need help from Katryn and Tyron to figure out what

we need to secure the compound again and what tech we need to teach the kids all the basics."

"Okay, I'll ask them to help you with that. But what I meant is, what do you need personally?"

"Nothing." Q shrugged.

Ruhger stood. "How about a hug?" He held out his arms. "Saree and I missed out on a lot, growing up too soon. Parental hugs were one of those things. It might be a little late, but I don't want you to miss out too."

Q grinned and blinked away the moisture gathering on her lids. "Yeah, that would be great." She walked up to him and hugged him tightly, while his arms closed gently around her shoulders. It seemed out of character for the stoic Ruhger, but she couldn't deny it was exactly what she needed.

"I know you want to help the Sisters, and I support that. But if you can't stay, you have a place with us." His soft chuckle vibrated through her. "You're essentially my kid, now. You'll always have a place with me, Saree, and Lightwave."

Q hung on tighter, hoping her grasp said everything she couldn't choke out. He couldn't know how much this meant to someone who'd never had a real home. Q was sure he wasn't saying the words lightly, that he meant it, and it meant more than the entire universe to her. She leaned back a gelittle. "Thank you. I do want to stay, but I need to help if I can. They saved me as a child, and I need to return the favor. But maybe someday, I'll come back to Lightwave." She smiled a little sadly. "I'd love to have you as a father."

"No matter what you do, you've got me." Ruhger folded her

close again, holding her firmly but not crushing her. Q decided to just enjoy the sensation while it lasted and snuggled into his comforting hold.

CHAPTER EIGHTEEN

Nat, Brin, and Monab stared at her, apparently astounded by what happened since Q left the Sisters. She couldn't help but be a little proud of what she'd managed to do, out there by herself. But she'd been lucky to attract really good people who wanted to help. Q settled back into the soft chair in the observation lounge, waiting for questions.

Nat blinked a few times. "Once we get our girls back and we're back on Secundus, or maybe before, you need to tell everyone that story. The little kids might not fully understand, but maybe something will stick with them. They need to hear how bad things can—"

An alert went off on her e-torc. "Report to Alpha shuttle immediately." Q was up on her feet and sprinting for the crew quarters before she finished reading, Nat and Brin on her heels. She heard more feet pounding behind them.

Katryn waited inside the shuttle's airlock. "Cargo bay, strap in tight."

Q trotted to the cargo bay, taking the seat on the far end and strapping herself down. A bin of what looked like soft armor was secured in front of them. Nat and Brin took the seats next to her, Monab and three of her year mates sitting behind her.

"Anyone not strapped in, sing out now," Saree said.

"Sing?"

Q snorted softly. "Turn of phrase. Anyone not strapped?" Silence. "Cargo bay ready, Saree!"

"Pushing back now," Ruhger said. "Stand by for a situation brief." A little vibration, then nothing. "Initiating thrust, now." A tiny surge in her seat, then the gravity stabilized.

"Listen up, situation brief," Chief barked. "The girls have been located. They are on a shuttle, flying to a fold hold orbit. We will intercept, board, and take the girls back. Katryn is in command of the boarding team. Helmets will be left transparent, so the girls can see you. We know there's a pilot, co-pilot, and a team of four, all in armor, inside the shuttle. Armor means stunners won't work. It will be critical to take the armored men down immediately with lethal fire. Sisters, that means shoot to kill. If you want to be a part of the assault team, you must be willing to fire immediately, without warning, without quarter. I need an affirmation from those of you willing to do this, individually. Q?"

"Yes, I am willing to shoot to kill." She was, without question. Q knew what fate awaited those naïve girls, drawn away by pretty pictures and smooth words. It was a life of degradation and pain.

"Nat?"

"I am willing to shoot to kill," Nat snarled.

"Brin?"

"I am willing to shoot to kill," Brin said.

"That's all we need for shooters," Chief said. A few muttered protests, a few more breathed sighs of relief. "The rest of you will be coming in behind the tactical team after the shooting is over. You all have important roles. Katryn, you're up."

The cargo bay hatch to the shuttle opened, and Katryn strode in, looking fierce in her dark armor. "Nat, Brin, Q, unstrap and open that container. Q, my old armor will probably fit you; Nat, Brin, we're hoping Saree's will."

Q got up and clicked open the fasteners on the bin. Saree's armor? She was sure Saree was in armor right now. Did she have three sets? That took a lot of credits. Q pulled the armor out, handing the larger ones to Nat and Brin and taking the small one for herself. She pulled off her outer clothes and stepped into the boots. A little big, but they'd work. Katryn and Saree helped them get the armor on and ran them through a quick tutorial on the controls. Saree was wearing armor, but it seemed extra bulky and heavy next to the sets Nat and Brin wore.

"Vacuum!" Katryn snapped.

Q found the control, brought the helmet up, and the armor tightened and stiffened around her. She made sure her comms were on.

"Ow!" Brin said.

"What did you do?"

"My hair got caught in the helmet seal."

Q saw Brin's head was tilted to the side, then she released the helmet. Katryn rolled her eyes. Saree handed her a hair tie.

Katryn stepped away from them, her hands on her hips, her normally high-pitched voice lower and louder. "Listen up, ladies.

We're infiltrating the enemy shuttle controls right now. We plan to use their own grav generators against them. For those of you in armor, once you're in the enemy shuttle, you need to have your grav generators ready to activate. There's a voice command—you can simply say, 'command input, one g, engage,' and your suit will compensate as much as it can. If we end up in zero-g, your boots have magnetized soles you can turn on. Obviously, if there's nothing to attract the magnets, then it won't work, but most shuttle decking is deliberately infused with metals designed to work with mag boots. Find the control."

Q already had the armor controls up, so she selected the mag boot option. Her heels jolted a tiny bit.

"Press down, then lift," Katryn said. "Walk around. Get used to it. Now, I'll remind you of all of this again if we have time. Questions?"

Q walked around the seats placed in the cargo bay, getting the hang of it quickly. Then she turned them off.

"Take a seat, plug the armor in. Be aware, grav generators burn a lot of power."

Q sat, moving a little gingerly to make sure she got her rear in the seat. Katryn popped the panel on her armor and plugged it in, Saree doing the same for Nat and Brin. Then Saree handed them all laser rifles.

"I know you know how to use these, but look at the controls, make sure you've got it."

Q examined them. Katryn was right. She hadn't used one since leaving Secundus, but she'd used it so often on guard duty against the vicious wildlife, and in Fringe War 300, that it all came right back.

"There are four armored beings, we're assuming men, guarding the girls," Katryn announced. "There's at least a pilot, most likely a co-pilot. We're working on the shuttle's net, but it's unexpectedly secure. Nat, Brin, Q, make sure your helmets remain transparent. We need those girls to understand we're friendly, here to help." Her mouth twisted. "Although, I'm sure they've been told all kinds of lies about us. So, don't expect all of them to be willing to leave. I'm sure, after watching us, they will be terrified or shocked."

Katryn looked at the row behind Q and pointed. "That's where you four come in. Once we take care of the security team, your job is to run in, grab those girls, and get them strapped in here. If you have trouble, let me, Nat, Brin, or Q know. We can use the power and protection of the armor to haul a fighter if we have to. Obviously, persuasion is better. You make sure we get all of them. If we're missing someone, tell Tyron or Saree. Understood?" Katryn scanned the row, watching them nod.

She then focused on the next row back. "Your job is search. We'll open all the hatches and compartments, looking for hidden girls or other things. Stay in teams of two, and don't go anywhere alone. The assault team will help you." Katryn refocused on Q, Nat, and Brin.

"Now, I know what Chief said earlier about shoot to kill. But, really, we want disabling shots. We don't want to kill anyone we don't have to. The best disabling shots in armor are powerpack shots, but since those are on the back, it's a difficult shot to make. Joints are good if you are precise enough—the waist, hip, or knees are next. You can blind someone with a laser with a headshot, and that's not a bad tactic in close quarters. Ideally, we'll turn their gravity to zero, and you fire while we're still in the airlock and hit them with headshots so they tumble away from the girls. Then we'll turn the grav up to 2 gs. You run in, using your armor's grav generator, and either fire to disable or, preferably, unlatch their armor." Katryn's smile flickered. "We hope to have net access to that shortly too. How many of you have experienced zero-g?"

Q raised her hand; she was the only one. She didn't have a lot of experience in zero-g, but some was better than none.

Katryn nodded. "If you feel sick, return to the airlock. There's no shame in it—zero-g isn't comfortable, and the first time is tough. Nat, Brin, this goes double for you—do not throw up in the armor."

Q's nose wrinkled at the thought.

"Now's the time to get in the right frame of mind," Katryn told them. "An Old Earth saying applies here: 'Slow is smooth, smooth is fast.' Think about what you're doing, don't just react. Think, then take action. Less chance for things to go wrong that way." Katryn continued to walk them through the action, then into an energizing meditation.

"Assault team, to the airlock, now," Katryn snapped.

Q unlatched her harness, unplugged her armor, and followed Katryn to the airlock, Nat and Brin behind her. Katryn stood to the right side of the hatch, Q mirroring her on the left, Nat and Brin stacked behind them.

"One minute, helmets up," Katryn said. "Bringing you into the operations loop. Don't talk unless you absolutely need something." She walked around each of them, checking their armor.

Q now understood why Ruhger, Saree, and the rest put up with Katryn's temper. She projected competence and command, becoming someone Q trusted without reservation.

"Tractor beam ready," Loreli said from the other shuttle.

"In formation. Fifty-five seconds," Ruhger announced.

"Tractor beam ready," Tyron said.

"Operation is a go," Chief said. "Thirty seconds."

Chief made the twenty- and ten-second calls.

Ruhger said, "Ready to latch."

Chief said, "Go."

"Tractor beam engaged," Loreli and Tyron said, speaking over each other.

Grant said, "Communications blocked."

Tyron said, "Closing gap."

"Airlock latched," Ruhger said.

"Go!" Katryn said. Alpha shuttle's outer hatch opened in front of them, then the enemy shuttle's hatch opened. "Outer hatch open... team inside." They followed Katryn inside, and the enemy shuttle hatch closed behind them. "Outer hatch closed. Working on inner hatch." Katryn was poking at the locking mechanism, putting in codes.

Saree reported, "Securing Alpha shuttle inner airlock."

"Kidnappers moving to airlock, confirmed heat signatures," Grant said.

Sand fleas! The enemy noticed their airlock cycling. Katryn said it was likely, but they'd hoped to take them by surprise.

"Weapons free, check your sight picture, try for disabling rather than killing," Katryn reminded them.

Q checked her rifle. Full charge, set for full power.

"Sharing vid. Ready to open inner airlock hatch," Tyron said.

Interior vids of the enemy shuttle came up in her helmet's display. Four men in soft armor stood with rifles pointed at the airlock, two within two meters of the airlock, the other two on the far end, and the girls strapped into three rows of seats. A pilot and co-pilot, also in soft armor, were at the front of the shuttle, swiping at controls. All of them had their helmets up, face shields mirrored.

"Katryn, stand by," Chief said.

"Standing by," Katryn acknowledged.

"Negative," Chief said. "It won't do anything to the armored beings."

Who was Chief talking to?

"Hold on; I've almost got the gravity controls," Tyron said. "Chief, recommend assault team activate magnetic boots with a go on countdown."

"Concur. Let me know when you've got it. Assault team, activate mag boots," Chief said.

Q activated hers.

"Team mag boots activated," Katryn said. "Assault team, remember, movement will be slow. Press your foot down, then pull up to make your boot release. Targets will move—double-check your sight picture before firing. If you feel like you're going to throw up, move aside, return to our shuttle. Again, there's no dishonor—everyone reacts differently their first time in zero-g."

"Got it. Heavy or no gravity?" Tyron asked.

Chief said, "On command, go zero-gravity, Tyron. Katryn, if you can't take them all out immediately or the children are threatened, yell 'heavy,' and everyone brace yourselves, use your grav generators to compensate if you know how. Tyron, on the 'heavy' command, go two-gs. Warning to all, don't stand under anything during the 'heavy' command. Katryn, make sure none of the kidnappers are floating over the kids before you go heavy."

Tyron said, "Copy on heavy command, ready to implement zero-grav."

Katryn said, "Copy assault in zero-grav until I give the heavy command. Nat, Brin, your primary targets are the men near the girls. Fire so they float away from the girls, preferably head shots so they tumble, say 'hover danger' if they are floating over the girls. Q, you've got the guy to the left, I've got the guy to the right, same warning phrase. Powerpack shots if possible; power packs are located around the shoulder blades usually. If not, disable legs and or arms. Fire, then step out and to the side. Brin, Nat, you fire over our heads, frontal assault straight to the target. Assault team, report if not ready."

Q swallowed and checked her rifle and grav generator one more time.

"Chief, ready on your command."

"Go!"

The airlock hatch slid away into the bulkhead. Q found her target and fired, her shield flaring with laser fire impact. The gravity went off and her target tumbled, just as planned. She kept firing and sprinted toward the man, pinning him against the bulkhead, feet up and to the side. She cut his rifle strap with her laser rifle, reached out, and yanked his rifle away just as he finally got it aimed back at her.

"Cease fire! Assault team, cease fire! Normal gravity, please," Katryn said calmly.

Her target thudded to the decking, and she aimed her rifle right at his neck seam, far enough away he couldn't grab the barrel. He rolled over to face her and raised his hands. Q mouthed, "Lower your helmet, now!" He glared but did so, and she stunned him, his body falling slack.

"Assault team, deactivate boots. Make sure your helmets are clear but don't lower them. Rescue team, get the girls up and moving, one for each of you. Search team, commence search. Make sure you stay with your battle buddy."

Tyron said, "Opening hatches."

The rescue team ran in and unstrapped the girls.

Q moved to the compartments closest to her and started flinging them open, rifle up and ready, one after the other, two of the Sisters behind her, pulling stuff out if they couldn't see everything. She met Brin doing the same and glanced around. They'd finished—there was stuff lying everywhere. Served these sand vipers right.

"Stun the pilot, Katryn," Chief said.

"Copy." Katryn spun the man to face her and socked him in the jaw, then stunned him and used flex cuffs to fasten his arms to the seats and his feet together and under the seat. "Sand flea," she hissed. "Search team, out. Assault team, behind them."

Q waited for the search team to go ahead and fell in behind Nat and Brin, heading back to their seats in the cargo bay. Katryn stood in front of them. "Lower helmets and strap in."

Q did as she was told.

Katryn counted each one of them, twice. "Anyone missing?" she asked them. "Command, Assault, Rescue, and Search team accounted for. Girls accounted for. Go!" Katryn stomped out of the cargo bay.

"Thank you," Chief said. "All shuttles, disengage now. Return to Lightwave."

Saree said over the shuttle speaker, "Strap in now." Q checked hers.

"Engaging thrust in three, two, engage," Ruhger said.

"Good job, everyone," Chief said. "Clean op. Watch your heat load, disengage cloaking when necessary."

Q turned to Nat and Brin. "Great job!" She raised her hand and smacked it against theirs.

Nat turned in her seat a little. "Great job, all of you. Perfect execution. We've got our girls back."

One of the rescued girls wailed, "But I want candy! And pretty dresses!" The others started crying and yelling too.

Q winced. This was why she'd left the Sisters. She did not want to deal with this. She started to unstrap, then the cargo bay hatch slammed shut, and she sank back into her seat. Blast it all to the great black hole of Andromeda. This wasn't her problem. It was Nat and Brin's. Q raised her helmet and closed her eyes. *Ah, silence.*

ΔΔΔ

Q, full of delicious Loreli lunch, watched the kids leave the dining hall, the previously kidnapped in charge of the rest. Thank the Mother Nat finally told the girls exactly what they had set themselves up for. Not only had she told them, but Nat showed them vids of other girls who managed to escape horrible situations telling their stories; many of those stories started just like theirs. That finally shut most of them up, and they realized they were lucky someone cared enough to rescue them. Most organizations couldn't go up against armed abductors, especially Familia. Most planetary authorities couldn't afford to go up against Familia.

The Fleet captured the kidnappers' folder and then made a huge sweep of Secundus authorities, making the Sisters much safer. If the truly evil were gone, the Sisters didn't have to worry about being betrayed by world authorities. Well, until a new bunch got brave enough to try.

In addition, Lightwave promised the Sisters weapons, including large weapons that could be mounted on the new guard towers the Sisters would build. That should give anyone in a shuttle pause before attacking them. There were easier targets on Secundus and nearby worlds, for that matter. Q wasn't sure how Lightwave had enough credits to be so generous, but she knew better than to look a gift cow in the mouth.

She went back to the Sisters' accounts and the transition documents Deneb Prime Bank sent them to ensure all the different funds had the deceased's signatories removed and new ones assigned. Q carefully didn't look at the names—she didn't need to cry more. There was one account here, labeled "Capital Improvements," Sister Lashtar hadn't told her about, and it wasn't on any of the Sisters' regular accounting files. But Sister Lashtar's name was on it. Q frowned at the entry. And it had a lot of credits in it, in comparison. A very large contribution had recently been made to their general donations fund and immediately transferred into the capital improvements fund, with no note about the donor. The timing seemed quite suspicious.

Lashtar seemed to be playing with her food, not eating it, so Q decided this was a good time to ask. She plopped down in the chair next to the Sister's grav chair. "Sister Lashtar, I've got a question, and you're probably not going to like it. Do you know anything about this donation?" Q pushed the files over to Lashtar's e-torc.

"No. This is huge! Why wasn't I told about this?" Lashtar paged through the donation entry and the associated funds. "I don't understand this. Wha—oh, by the Mother." Her head dropped to the table, thudding a little too loudly.

"Sister, you've got enough damage. Let's not add a concussion, okay?"

Lashtar straightened, with an ironic snort. "I suppose you are right. I wonder who it was this time and why? We didn't need credits that badly." She sighed. "I suppose it doesn't matter; they're all dead." Lashtar shook her head slowly. "One more thing to add to my list of prayers." A nod with tight lips and Lashtar looked Q in the eyes. "I don't know anything about that 'donation' or who gave it. I wish I did because I'd send it back. My guess is it will disappear from our Capital Improvement fund shortly, perhaps with interest. If it does, don't dispute it with the bank. Just assume it's Familia or someone similar. Try to move some of our accounts to other institutions, please. Put me, you, Nat, and Brin on all the accounts, and place individual logging on all transactions. We need to know who's doing what."

"Agreed, Sister. I'll let you know when I make the new banking arrangements."

"Well, now that we've got that taken care of, let's talk about the next steps." Lashtar raised her head and her voice. "Sisters, time for Circle."

Nat, Brin, and the others joined them at the table. They all raised their hands high, cupping them together, Q belatedly following along.

"May the Mother bless us. May we remember where we are, who we are, and the hands that hold us."

"May the Mother bless us," Q repeated with the rest of them.

"Sisters, the time has come to decide what we do next," Lashtar said. "Remembering we have an obligation to those young lives." She tossed her chin toward the hatch. "We can return to Secundus and remain the same organization, understanding that our numbers will continue to drop under the harsh conditions of Secundus. We could go elsewhere, some new world entirely, and start over. But I don't think there are enough of us to do that, and I, for one, don't have the fortitude to start all over again. Or perhaps Tyron and Grant were right, and it's time for us to work with our neighbors and with other religious and non-religious organizations on Secundus. If we work and live together, all of us striving to protect children and all human life, then perhaps there's enough common ground to prevent strife among us. The Mother knows we have more than enough land." Lashtar sighed.

"So, first, do we remain the Sisters of Cygnus? I'd like a show of hands, please."

Everyone's hand rose, except Q's. Lashtar raised a brow at her. "I'm not voting because I don't consider myself a true Sister. But I want to support you in the short term, no matter what you decide."

"Thank you, Q, that's very generous."

"Maybe." Q shrugged. "I might bring more trouble than I'm worth."

"We'll see. Right now, we need you." Lashtar turned to the rest of the women. "Q discovered something about our accounts. It looks like someone in leadership took a very large donation just before the girls were abducted. I don't know who. I know it wasn't me, so whoever it was, they're answering to the Mother now. I've asked Q to spread our accounts to several different institutions, make sure all transactions are logged with a personal identity, and put her, myself, Nat, and Brin on those accounts. We can add more Sisters later when we decide who's taking what role. Which brings me to the next question. If we're remaining the Sisters of Cygnus, do we stay here on Secundus?"

Hands rose; no one hesitated.

"All right then, we return. We need more people. Send messages to those Sisters you know in the wider universe, asking if they're willing to return for a year or two. Make it a request only, and make it clear that there are no hard feelings if they don't return. Understood?" Lashtar swept a look around the table at the nodding heads and nodded once in return, her lips clamped tightly for a moment.

"I propose we wait until we're resettled on Secundus before proceeding with our next question, but I am in favor of opening our lands and our hearts to other organizations. There is strength in numbers and the Mother isn't jealous. I truly believe there is room for other ways of worship—that everyone must find their own light and path, as long as that path doesn't infringe on others. But that's my belief. You," Lashtar pointed a finger around the table, "need to discuss this. Talk about the options and issues openly amongst yourselves, without my influence. Perhaps we don't go that far, but we just start coordinating and cooperating with our neighbors a lot more. Once we're back on Secundus, we will formally meet in Circle to discuss this and our way forward. Do you agree?"

All their hands raised again.

"Good. Now, go see to those children. Talk amongst yourselves and let's work to find our path with the Mother's guidance. I'll tell Lightwave we need to return."

Q stayed when the rest left. "Sister, are you well enough to do this? Amputation is a lot of trauma."

Lashtar clamped her lips again but just momentarily. "I've got to talk to children like they're full Sisters, so I guess I should start with you. You're less of a child than Nat and Brin, even though they're older." She glanced around the dining hall. "I tell you this in confidence, please. I'm not well. But this has some advantages. I can use my infirmity to shift the decision-making to Nat and Brin. The other Sisters are going to come to me for confirmation for a while, but I'm putting the power into their hands. I'll give them advice, lots at first, and then only if they specifically ask. This will speed the change of leadership because I intend to leave the Sisters after all this is settled." Sister Lashtar smiled, then laughed. "Close your mouth, Q."

Q snapped her jaw shut. "Sorry. It was a shock."

"I imagine so. Nat, Brin, the others?" She shrugged. "They wouldn't be able to accept this decision yet, and it wouldn't be fair to put this burden on them. But you're not staying. They might not stay, either, but I'm sure you're not. I'm telling you this because we need to watch each other, make sure neither of us is sliding into critical positions with the Sisters, so we can gracefully leave. It may be a standard year or more, but I'm leaving, and I know you can't wait."

Q chuckled. "You're right. I'm definitely not staying. Secundus has nothing for me, and I might be more trouble than I'm worth if Familia comes looking."

"Right now, I need you. Watch me. If you see me stepping in too much, tell me." Sister Lashtar smiled. "Be blunt."

"Okay, I will. And you do the same for me."

Lashtar nodded. "I will. Okay, let's do this." She brought up a comm request to Captain Ruhger, sharing her holo with Q.

"Yes, Sister?" Ruhger asked.

"We've decided to return to Secundus. We've sent messages asking some Sisters to return to us, for a short time, at least. Nat, Brin, and some of the others will stay on for an additional year or so until we're stable again." She pressed her lips together for a moment. "We are taking your suggestions under serious consideration. Perhaps the Mother is leading us on to something new, a better representation of her purpose in the world. I thank you for the idea."

Lashtar sighed. "Since Gov Human military has scooped up the Secundus officials they believe are involved in this evil scheme, and you've given us additional weapons, we will return to Secundus for now and work with our neighbors to secure our compound and the greater area. Grant, you were right back on Gliese; we should have cooperated and joined with our neighbors to create a mutual aid system. We've done that on Secundus, but obviously not to a great enough extent. We will work on that harder." Lashtar closed her eyes for a second, looking utterly exhausted. Q's heart ached for both of them. "Can you fly us back?"

"Certainly. Are you sure you're ready?"

Lashtar shook her head sadly. "No, but we can't delay you any more than we have. We've asked and received far too much."

"Not at all, Sister," Ruhger said. "We were happy to assist. Unlike the last time, this wasn't engineered by your people, right?"

She glared at Ruhger; Q could see when she decided the secrecy of the Sisters had to be swept aside for good. "Now that all the leaders except me are dead, I had—" a glance flicked to Q "—Nat look at our accounts. There are credits in our long-term savings I can't account for. So, we may have brought this on ourselves, but if we did, those women are dead and answering to the Mother. But you knew that, right?"

Interesting. Lashtar didn't want Lightwave knowing Q dug into the accounts. Why?

"Yes, we found that out," Ruhger told her. "It doesn't make us want to help you back to the planet any less. I trust *you*."

A small smile lightened Lashtar's expression. "Thank you. I'll try to maintain that trust. Let us know how many we can fly back at a time, so I can develop a schedule. And thank you to all of you. Our girls are back, and no one else was killed or seriously injured. It will be a tough road ahead, trying to settle into a new norm, but the Mother will help us. Thank you." She waved off the comms and sighed.

"Well, that's done. Good, bad, or indifferent, it's done." Her mouth pursed. "I named Nat instead of you because Nat will end up in charge. Even if I have a deep connection to Lightwave's crew, Nat is who they'll be dealing with in the future, if they keep the connection. Neither of us needs to be in the middle."

"Makes sense. Besides, I'd like to keep my name out of everything."

"Agreed. We'll take you off the accounts as soon as possible." Lashtar examined her. "Are you ready for this?"

"No, but I'll do it anyway." Q tried to ignore the sinking feeling of doom. Stuck on Secundus, Familia looking for her. Familia with hooks into Secundus' authorities, and Gov Human military leaving—it all seemed like a recipe for disaster. But she was needed, and she owed the Sisters more than she could possibly give them.

CHAPTER NINETEEN

"Let's trade jobs, Quinn." Nat plopped down at her desk, her official Sister's robe of a plain square of dark brown homespun flapping to her chest in the breeze she created with her dramatic collapse.

Q snorted. "Not a chance. I'm terrible at negotiations, you know that. I have a hard enough time teaching." More than a year later and she couldn't even teach Nat to use "Q" instead of Quinn. By the Mother, she was tired of everything here. Scrabbling for life, the completely inadequate net, trying to use that net to watch over the world authorities and beyond for Familia or other problems, the constant noise of construction as they widened their compound, the arguments between groups with conflicting beliefs, the constant heat and humidity—it was wearing her down. Being suspicious of everyone and everything didn't help either. But she had to be strong for Nat and Brin.

Nat grimaced. "Not sure I care right now. I'm so tired of dancing around everything, telling everyone half-truths, and asking for twice what I want, just so I can get what we really need at a price we can afford." She pulled the robe off over her head and tossed it onto the small cabinet behind her, wiping her forehead.

Those robes were just too warm for Secundus. Q was glad, again, that she'd refused to wear them from the start, since she wasn't a Sister. But she had good news for the Sisters and Nat. "A message came in today that might make everything a whole lot simpler, Nat."

"Really?" It hurt to watch the rise and fall of hope on Nat's face.

"Really." Q swept the message from Deneb over to her.

"Deneb make things easier? Since when? Our rich, environmentally conscious, adventure travel neighbors aren't interested in anything except their bottom line. Usually at the expense of everyone else."

"Ah, but we have something they don't. Available land and lots of people, all organized to a fault. A non-profit organization with a proven track record. One that's attracting more and more talented people and other non-profit organizations. And, most importantly, a medico school with an emphasis on trauma medicine." Q smirked. "In a secure compound with the firepower to protect itself and a net they can't break. These days, when Gov Human can't be trusted and the military is distracted by internal leadership struggles, that's a lot."

"Wait a minute. If I'm reading this right, it says they want to fund our medico school." Nat's face could be the model for astonishment. "Full funding for ten standard years and partial for at least another ten?!" She sobered abruptly. "What's the catch?"

"They get priority. No matter what's going on here—flood, fire, pandemic—Deneb's patients get priority."

"Hmm. That's a big ask for medicos. Doesn't really fit their oaths, now does it?" Nat frowned at the desk.

"No. But, if you talk to them about the benefits versus the low potential? After all, what's the max number of patients that will fold here? Ten, twenty? It can't be big. And we're not going to empty the school of medicos to respond to their emergency. They'll never know if the school leaves a few behind. Or we tell them, correctly, that the specialists have to stay here with the specialized equipment. Head trauma will heal faster here with all the right equipment, treatment, and supportive environment."

Q shrugged. "Besides, you're a great negotiator. Do that thing. Get them to put a few limits on it, even if it means a little less funding." Q laughed. "You have to bring Medico Administrator Ed'Whte into this negotiation, so tell him to bring Medicos Schmitt and Doering too. Between Schmitt's ethics lectures and Doering's 'results at all costs,' you'll get to a middle ground."

"Well, look who's been thinking about this problem." Nat raised her brows. "Bored again?"

Q shrugged again. "A little. You know there's not much challenge here for me. Especially when you won't let me steal from Familia anymore." Along with stealing Enzo's credits and some from the other enforcer accounts she'd found, Q donated most of Kathe's credits, since there was no telling how they'd been earned. It felt cleaner to contribute most of them to the cause. She'd kept enough to jump on a folder to the other side of the universe and live frugally for a year, just in case Familia tracked her down.

Nat frowned at her. "We don't need Familia's dirty money. Besides, a bigger, nicer medico school will mean plenty of work for you."

"Sure. But how I feel doesn't matter, you know that." Q lifted her hands helplessly. "I can't go anywhere without attracting Familia's attention. General Kerr's gift, enlisting 'me' in the Gov Human military, only works if I stay here, mostly hidden, so my decoys in the Laniakea Fleet can show up and be 'me' on a regular basis. I'm grateful, I really am. I've learned a lot of new things here from all of you."

Nat snorted. "Mostly that you're too blunt and terrible at negotiations."

Q shrugged a single shoulder. "Lizard can't change its scales. At least not this lizard."

"But you could. You could do a big body mod. Especially if we bring a bigger medico school here."

"Well, that will take some time, won't it?"

Nat wagged her head from side to side. "Maybe, maybe not. We can get the buildings done fast."

"The Travelers again?" Q raised her eyes to the overhead. Nat was right, the Traveler building clans did good, fast work, but Q didn't want to put up with everything else the Travelers brought with them. Parties, selling of pretty but useless items, accusations of cheating and theft from petty, jealous, and stupid Secundus people, and for her, constant, unending flirting and entreaties for her to fly away with them. "You're so pretty, Q! Join us, Q! You'll love living with us, Q!" It came from both sexes and all ages. The younger Travelers flirted with some of the other orphan girls but not to the extent Q got. She wished she knew why.

"Yes. You know they're perfect for this kind of building and they won't overcharge, not for this. Especially if we let them use the medico facilities too. You know they have a hard time getting accepted in some systems." Nat gazed into the distance for a moment, then back at Q. "We could encourage them to send students!"

"Now, that might work. They definitely would play fair if we're willing to take their people as students. Great idea, Nat." And she'd put up with the constant flirting for that. Why were the Travelers so intent on seducing her? It made no sense.

"I have one every now and then."

Q smirked at Nat. "Shall I send notice of Circle tonight, then?"

"Yes, absolutely. Never hide anything, that's our motto. But I'm going to tell Lashtar about this right now!" Nat practically danced out of their shared office.

Q smiled at Nat's joy. This was the opportunity they needed. After successfully rescuing their girls and helping with Gov Human's cleansing of Secundus's corrupt authorities, the Sisters developed a reputation for doing the right thing, even when it was hard. When they advertised their willingness to welcome other organizations working to better the lives of Secundus's citizens, they made a lot of great connections. When they opened up land and buildings, they had more applicants than they could handle. And when wealthy benefactors sent them credits for more buildings, they attracted the very best, not only in Cygnus but in this quadrant of the universe. Unexpectedly, they also attracted almost twenty different religious orders, all wanting to settle in a cooperative, safe environment. With the turmoil in Gov Human, safety meant a lot. The Sisters sent a lot of business to the construction Traveler clans.

It was exciting at first, but after a while, Q found all the organizations were the same. They needed lots of help to get settled, spent the majority of their time fundraising, and none of them really needed her talents. Secundus was just too remote to attract the worst of the net predators. But she couldn't leave, or Familia would find her. She was stuck, teaching basic net to kids and remedial net security to adults. But it could be worse. She put a hand on her stomach where the tattoo used to be. It could be so much worse.

Her e-torc pinged. Time for an Atlas Challenge session. Q grinned despite herself. Training again and practicing the full range of y'ga were true blessings. Even if she had to build her own course. But the advantage was she could change it whenever and however she wanted. Or her training partner wanted. Over the last year, they'd built three different courses—from beginner to expert. They left the beginner and mid-level courses alone but changed the expert often, trying to surprise each other.

Q left the office, changed from her shipsuit into athletic clothes, and jogged to the far corner of the compound with the course and other miscellaneous homemade athletic and training equipment. The high ropes course was quite popular with a wide variety of clergy and medicos, and everyone used the obstacle course. It was great for running the energy out of kids.

Ruth was already warming up. Q joined her, and they swung into a jog around the courses, then a run through the obstacle course at half-speed. One of the reasons Q enjoyed training with Ruth was the silence. Ruth rarely said anything unless it was relevant to their training. Q knew little about her background, other than she had associated with Lightwave's crew as a young woman, and she'd endured terrible abuse since then.

When Ruth had expressed an interest in the Atlas Challenge course, one of the psych medicos immediately talked to Q because they thought the training would be good for Ruth. But the medico warned Q that Ruth could be unpredictable—she had experienced horrific violence, and she had military-style training, so if something went wrong, Q could find herself in a very difficult situation. But Q knew what it was like to need a physical outlet for emotional issues. She was happy to train Ruth and leave the talking to the medicos. Sometimes, quiet was better, and pushing your body hard could blow all the circling emotions right out of your head. Ruth had responded well, and Q considered her a full training partner—and a friend.

Q set up the timers for the dual beginner course. This was the only one that was side-by-side; the others were only against a clock, as they would be in competition. They'd run through this one together, and whoever won went last on the mid-level course, then they'd swap for the expert course after a short rest.

The timer counted down and Q sprinted. Up and over the wall, across the spring-loaded stepping stones, the pull-up ladder, ropes, jump bars, and all the rest. She won by a hair and frowned speculatively at Ruth. She was holding back, so Q was sure she'd made changes to the expert course.

Without saying anything or responding to Q's look, Ruth

started the timer and swung into action on the mid-level course, finishing within five seconds of her normal warm-up time. Q started as soon as Ruth finished, also finishing within the same margin. She bent over, breathing hard for the first few seconds, then made herself straighten, surveying the expert course. By design, the first obstacle, the high-ramped wall, blocked a lot of the course from view, so she walked to the far corner of the starting box and peered around the wall. No changes she could see. This was one of the places her lack of height didn't help. It also didn't help her get up the walls. She had to compensate with jumping height and there was only so much she could do to develop that.

The rest timer counted down, and Q enabled the vids. At zero, she sprinted for the ramp wall, running up it without issue. She danced the length of the rolling log, jumping the sweep arms, then launched herself to the curved monkey bars. Across and up the pull-up ladder, and her shoulders were screaming surrender. She flung herself onto the platform at the top—ah! Her body flattened to the platform, shins banging painfully on the edge. Struggling to breathe, Q slowly pulled her body fully onto the platform and over to the pole fastened to the end. Tricky Ruth—she added a grav generator!

Q pushed with her toes and pulled with her arms, making it to the long slide pole where, rather than sliding down, she hung in near zero-g. "Argh!" Pulling herself down the pole hand over hand, she finished the course without other surprises. After a few seconds of lying flat, Q rolled and sat, watching Ruth power through the course, beating Q's time soundly, mostly because she pushed off hard at the end of the double-grav platform, sailing down through the zero-g without bothering to grab the pole and bounced off at the bottom into the next exercise. Q noted her technique. Would it be even faster if she kept pushing off against the pole with her toes on the way down?

"Great job. Tricky change."

Ruth nodded once, breathing too hard to speak.

"I thought grav generators weren't used in the Atlas Challenge?"

"They aren't, but neither of us is going to any big competitions, are we?" Ruth asked in her gravelly voice. At some point, her voice box had been damaged. Q noticed Ruth's visible scars were gradually disappearing, but that characteristic remained. "But we needed a new challenge, and I didn't feel like building anything by myself. I didn't try it out—this was my first time through."

Q wasn't surprised. Ruth was fanatical about fairness. "Well, let's watch the vid and see where we can do better." They discussed their mistakes and tried different techniques on the grav portion, cutting tenths of seconds off. After a final run-through with an audience—they always drew one these days—they swung into a y'ga-based cooldown. Then, they coached others on the first two courses, laughing and helping the littlest children on the taller obstacles. When they walked away, a small group of older medico students was running the expert course, but they were experienced and had enough safety watchers to work on their own.

"What's next for you?" Ruth asked.

Q shrugged. "I can always do more admin work, but I don't

want to."

"Yeah, there's always more rads to blast around. I'm thinking about a quick escape to the jungle. Maybe do some hunting. Want to come?"

"Yes! Let me grab my gear." These trips were all that kept Q—and Ruth—sane. They'd go mountain climbing or sea kayaking or, if they had to stay close, jungle bashing. Anything to get away from the stifling confines of the Sisters' compound.

Q was slowly coming to realize she wasn't the only one who felt that way. Ruth certainly did, but she wasn't ready to face the wider universe. Even going to the larger towns on Secundus was a trial for her. But that wasn't surprising. Q knew little about Ruth's official history, but she occasionally let some tidbit slip while they sat around camp at night. Those tidbits usually gave Q nightmares and reminded her why she had to stay in the Sisters' compound. If Familia caught her, the captivity might be more outwardly civilized, luxurious even, but the personal degradation would be the same.

The person who continued to surprise her was Lashtar. She kept stepping back, more and more, letting Nat and Brin make the decisions and lead the Sisters' worship. Lashtar's scowls were growing more and more obvious when the other leaders in the compound insisted on getting a final decision from her, rather than accepting it from Nat. Most of them were Lashtar's age and saw Nat as a child, which she definitely wasn't. Q saw how it chafed both Nat and Lashtar, but she didn't think most people noticed. Nat was trying not to notice; she didn't want to push Lashtar out, even if the constant need for Lashtar's approval annoyed her too. Besides, none of them had Lashtar's experience with physical security, and they still needed lots of that. They had too many people to protect.

Even so, Lashtar had taken to disappearing for days in a row too; they weren't sure where she was going but probably just to one of the jungle outposts. Q had caught speculative glances from Lashtar; they'd both silently acknowledged a growing feeling of entrapment and agreed not to discuss it. But someday soon, something would break loose. The question was what, and who first?

ΔΔΔ

As Q checked the safety on her rifle, an alert pinged. "Blast. Sister Lashtar needs me. Something related to that big remote attack in Sirius, killing all those beings and stations." Q bit her lip, unwilling to go, even though they had no choice but to return anyway or waste a lot of meat. She'd planned to lure Ruth into the medicos' gathering room, let the fancy soothing stones and meditation work on her, but that wouldn't happen now.

"She doesn't need me for intel work." Ruth turned away, still breathing hard from the close call with the giant lizard. "I'll take the kill for processing, then I'm going home."

Q watched her go, towing the carcass behind her with a hand-tractor. Ruth had to reintegrate into society sometime, but not today. At least she was willing to spend a few hours in the compound now and then, rather than sneaking in and out like a ghost after their Atlas Challenge sessions. Deneb's credits not only made the medico school bigger, but it brought more talented instructors and better equipment and treatments. And those pricey soothing stones. Q still wasn't sure how they'd managed to get those, and she didn't want to pry too hard in case she didn't like the answer. She hoped they were donated.

But with or without the soothing stones, Ruth was making progress, if not quite as quickly as many of them hoped. She still wouldn't speak directly to Lashtar, even though Lashtar wasn't involved in the tragedy that led to her trauma.

But enough speculation—she had a job to do. Q slung her rifle across her back and trotted past Ruth, back to the compound. Sister Lashtar put a high priority on the message but didn't make a call, so it wasn't a true emergency, like an imminent attack. She shivered a little at the thought of an attack like Sirius happening to an unprotected world like Secundus.

Just like every other human world, suns, most sentient worlds, Secundus was still on high alert. It wasn't long ago when the worlds and stations of Sirius were attacked by a huge, anonymous army of remotes. No one took responsibility for the attack, and Gov Human had been unable—or unwilling—to identify the attacker. The latest theory was an artificial intelligence, because not a single living being of any species had been found in the attacker's debris—no compartments with breathable atmosphere either. Also, no unknowns folded out of Sirius—the attackers stayed and kept firing until they were destroyed.

But Lashtar wouldn't call her back to the compound if they were under attack by something like that—they'd be told to hide. They didn't have enough firepower to hold off more than a couple of shuttles. Q bounded up the stairs and into Lashtar's office.

"Close the door. We need privacy." Nat and Brin sat at

Lashtar's small conference table.

Q shut the door and set her comm interference script running. Anyone snooping would hear white noise. "What's going on?"

"Lightwave's coming in."

Q couldn't help but breathe a sigh of relief. It wasn't something horrible after all.

Lashtar scowled. "Maybe. Someone, most likely Saree, sent a message about needing medico help due to a head injury sustained in the De Ferra tunnel. Or it's a fake, meant to lull us into complacency. Ferra's name wouldn't be hard to come up with, and everyone's seen vid of the Cygnus Gliese tunnels, including the markings on the walls."

Q brought up the fold hold orbit status. "Lightwave's not in orbit. No folders of Lightwave's model either." She checked the incoming shuttles. "But a shuttle has filed a flight plan coming here. It launched from a folder that's already gone. It's the same model as Lightwave's Beta shuttle, but that's a common model. I say extreme caution is required; assume hostile intent. Meet them with full defenses. They're due in twenty-nine hours, thirty-two minutes."

"Agreed," Lashtar said, Brin echoing.

"Agreed," Nat said. "Full defense. Let's keep it quiet, though, just in case it is Lightwave. They'll arrive after hours, so we should be able to run a drill with the security personnel already scheduled, plus a few more. Have them land at the hot pad—if we have to use the big weapons, it will be safest there. I'll let our more martial organization leaders know about this but not the purely religious. Brin, you decide who to add to the security roster."

Q told them, "One other thing. When Ruhger, Saree, and I were escaping Familia, Saree used Ferra as her fake name. That increases the possibility it really is Saree."

Lashtar nodded thoughtfully. "Maybe. Either way, Q, make sure Ruth's involved. It's been more than two years; she can't run away anymore."

"Yes, Sister, I'll tell her." Q wasn't sure she agreed but she wasn't in charge. She sent the message to Ruth at the highest priority and got an acknowledgment immediately. *Hmm*. Maybe Lashtar was right. She was still happy it wasn't her decision to make.

ΔΔΔ

From the shielded weapon control center, Q watched the shuttle land, shut down, and cool off. The hatch opened, and a too-pale Saree appeared, Captain Ruhger hovering close behind her, his hands poised at her waist. "Identity visually confirmed. Sending remote DNA test." The little remote floated out, stopping Saree before she left the shuttle.

Ruhger said, in a commanding tone, "Saree's injured. Get me a medfloat, now!"

Brin told the medicos, "Send the medfloat. You stay here until we get confirmation."

Q tuned out the medicos' complaints and sent the medfloat herself. Ruhger lowered Saree gently onto it. The movements and care for Saree sure looked like Ruhger. Once Saree was strapped down, Ruhger turned to the DNA remote and let it prick his palm, then he put Saree's on it. The results, which Q made sure came only to her, were positive. "Identity confirmed."

"Medicos cleared to approach," Nat said.

"Finally. Paranoid idiots," Medico Doering muttered as he and his team trotted away. Nat, Lashtar, and Q followed them.

Ruhger stayed right next to the medfloat, answering the medicos' questions about the injury, but from his constant survey of the area, he was aware of and approved of the Sisters' security. Ruhger's description of the injury, a localized grav generator error, didn't seem likely. Doering didn't think so either, from the skeptical look he shot Ruhger, but that was his story and he was sticking to it. It didn't matter anyway. What mattered was the amount and type of force and location of the injury. Q had listened to enough medico lectures to pick up that much.

Lashtar stopped at the medico emergency department entrance. "Captain, when you get her settled, come see me," Lashtar said.

"Understood," Ruhger replied over his shoulder. "Thank you, Sister. Q, come."

Huh. Q shrugged at Brin's surprise and followed Ruhger into treatment room four. It wasn't her first trip here; both she and Ruth had banged their heads more than once, fortunately, not severely. The medfloat slotted into the treatment room, and appendages appeared, applying sensors.

Doering asked something as Q entered the compartment.

Ruhger said, "Yes, as I said, she got some treatment. But it wasn't specialized treatment, just what you'd get from a military-style shuttle-based medico suite."

"Who did the treatment?" Doering asked.

"Classified," Ruhger snapped. "I've sent you the report the medico wrote."

Doering matched Ruhger's glare. "This is for her health."

"I've told you all you need to know, Medico. You can figure it out from here."

"Idiots," Doering muttered. "You're all idiots."

"Likely," Ruhger agreed. "Still can't tell you." He turned away with a huff and stepped back so the medico staff could treat Saree. The corners of his lips turned up, and he held out his arms. "Q!"

Q stepped into him happily. Ruhger gave the best hugs.

"We missed you, but we're both glad you were here, not with us." Ruhger's rumbling voice was a comfort Q hadn't realized she needed.

"Rough year?"

"Very. And this last bit was nearly fatal." Ruhger pulled away from her. "You look good, healthy." He surveyed her closely. "Strong. You've been doing something intense."

"Yes. I'll show you later if you want. But, overall, I'm good. Bored, but good."

"Well, this is encouraging," Medico Doering said. "Whoever treated her was a somewhat knowledgeable medico, not a completely inadequate emergency technician. You were wise to bring her here, though. This medico obviously doesn't have our equipment or head trauma experience." He sniffed derisively. "Of course, no one does. I'm the best."

Ruhger tilted his head toward Doering, with a quizzical look.

"Yes, he's for real," Q told Ruhger without bothering to lower her voice. Doering glared at her, and the other medicos smothered snickers. "But he really is the best, if also the most arrogant."

"Out!" Doering snapped. "Don't come back until you're called. Her treatment will take weeks. At least two, probably three."

Ruhger pushed him and the others aside. "You're in good hands now. Let me know if you need anything." He bent and kissed Saree gently.

"I will. Don't worry."

"Get out!" Doering said.

Ruhger stepped into him and gripped his shoulders, glaring. "If she gets worse, you will not like the results."

"Don't threaten me, you Neanderthal," Doering said, twisting out of Ruhger's hold, his tone cold. "My reputation means more than your threats, by far. She will get the very best treatment."

Ruhger glowered at him and stepped away.

Q shook her head at him, with a mock-glare of her own. "Come on, let's go. Sister Lashtar wants to see you, remember?"

Ruhger stomped out of the treatment facility. Q glanced back, catching Doering wipe his forehead. He might have stood up to Ruhger in the heat of the moment, but Doering wasn't going to match Ruhger for long.

On the way, Q punched Ruhger on the arm. "What was that for?" He didn't even have the grace to say ouch.

"You were blasting rads at the guy who's saving your lover. Does that seem smart to you?"

A brow raised and one massive shoulder shrugged. "Maybe."

"You're lucky. Doering's reputation means everything to him. If it didn't, he might have sabotaged Sar—her treatment!"

"That guy isn't going to do that. There's no way." He slashed a hand. "But I'll be nicer next time. I guess. You can use Saree's name. We've given up trying to hide her."

"With the medicos, okay. But not a good idea in the compound. Call her Sarah."

"Agreed."

They climbed the stairs to Lashtar's office, Ruhger examining the security improvements with an approving nod. "You or Ruth?"

"Both of us, with Lashtar."

"Good. I'm glad Ruth is talking to someone."

"She's getting there. Don't expect to see her, though."

"No, I suppose not." Ruhger's mouth twisted, and he shook his head.

Since the door was open, Q entered Lashtar's office, Ruhger on her heels. She activated the privacy script.

"It's good to see you, Ruhger, but where's Lightwave?" Lashtar asked. She'd already removed her robes.

"I wish I knew." Ruhger sighed. "It's been a while since we've seen them. It's been…interesting. We're secure here?"

"Yes," Q answered him.

"We were…" Ruhger glanced at Q, then returned to Lashtar "…in Octans, and a Gov Human military ship folded in and fired on Lightwave without warning. Lightwave folded out. They had no choice—it was fold or be destroyed. Saree and I were off Lightwave, flying Beta shuttle. We escaped the system with the help of some autonomous artificial intelligences." His mouth twisted.

What in all the suns? First, Ruhger won't say what they're doing out there, and now, they're consorting with artificial intelligences? Were they the same ones that attacked Sirius? Suddenly, the boredom of the Sisters' compound didn't seem so bad to Q.

Ruhger continued, "They call themselves The Consensus, which isn't an accurate name. They were fooled by one of their members named Westly; we think he engineered the attack on Sirius. But before that, Westly captured us, along with one of the Consensus members named Maxine. Westly's actions injured Saree. When she didn't get better, Westly captured a Gov Human military pararescue team we worked with previously. Doc patched her up, and all of us working together managed to get away from Westly, and eventually, we folded here. The Gov Human team is on their way back to the Laniakea Fleet; we don't know what happened to Maxine." Ruhger huffed. "That's the short version."

Wow. Q blinked at Ruhger. Boredom was looking really good.

Lashtar snorted. "I'm sure you're leaving out a lot. But that's okay, we don't need to know. For now, we'll keep your identities quiet. I'm sending a directive to the medicos now. Do you mind doing a little manual labor, Ruhger?"

"Of course not. Especially when it looks like we're going to be here for weeks." Ruhger's shoulders slumped momentarily. "Sorry, Lashtar, we didn't mean to bring trouble your way."

Lashtar waved a dismissive hand. "Don't worry about it. Besides, do you really think I don't know who sent us all those so-called grants? I had Q look into it."

Q smirked at Ruhger.

Ruhger held up both hands with a return smirk. "That was all

Saree."

Some of the grants were Kathe's credits but Lashtar didn't need to know that.

"Sure, it was. Anyway, what shall we call you while you're here?"

"Sarah and Rufus?"

"Good enough. What do you need to contact Lightwave?"

"We've done all we can there. Messages were sent and dropped. It's a wait and see." Ruhger shrugged. "It could take weeks."

"Well, let's talk later." Lashtar turned to Q. "Get him settled in one of the visitor's cabins, and put him to work with the grounds crew, then get back to work. No off-compound trips with Ruth until Saree and Ruhger are gone. Understood?"

Q bowed her head. "Yes, Sister. I understand." She hoped Saree and Ruhger didn't bring trouble with them. While it was too quiet, and she was bored, she wasn't bored enough to want a Sirius-style attack on Secundus.

Lashtar nodded and turned to Nat. "Sorry, Nat, I should have let you take this. But this connection is mine."

Q led Ruhger out of the Sister's office before Nat replied. She didn't need to get in the middle of the ongoing leadership discussion. Ruhger followed her downstairs and outside. On the walk, she found an empty guest cabin close to the medicos and assigned it to him, sending the door codes to his e-torc. She didn't want any of Ruhger's identifying information in their public-facing security net. "This is you."

Ruhger stepped up and opened the door. The cabins were all

similar; just big enough to fit a bed, basic sani-mod, and an auto-bev. They were designed to provide a refuge but encourage people to socialize. "This is great. Thanks, Q."

"I'll send you a schedule and an introduction to your new boss." She grinned at him. "Hope you're ready to work hard. We always need strong people repairing the fences."

Ruhger snorted. "Fine by me. But what's wrong with hand-tractors?"

"Physical accomplishments bring a sense of joy," Q parroted one of the psych-medicos.

"Well, that's true. But before I do any of that, I need to go button-up Beta shuttle. Want to come?"

"Sure."

They walked down the path, past the medico campus, and to the shuttle pad. Q checked her compound security status and the incoming shuttle schedule. Nothing for a while, but they needed to keep that emergency pad clear. "You should move Beta shuttle off the emergency pad. I've assigned you to pad Echo."

"Copy that. Come on, fly with me." He shot a tiny smile at her. "It will be like old times."

"Copy that," Q mimicked. But she was pretty sure getting in a shuttle was a mistake. All she'd want to do was fly away, far and fast. And she couldn't. Not with Ruhger and Saree. Lightwave had enough trouble—they didn't need more.

CHAPTER TWENTY

Q scowled at Nat. "Why are they coming this time? We don't have any work for them." The Travelers were too good at finding out secrets, and Saree and Ruhger had a lot to hide. Saree's three weeks of active treatments had just finished, and still no word from Lightwave. They were all starting to worry. They didn't need the Travelers' inquisitive minds poking around.

Nat shook her head, mockingly. "Such intolerance. Shame on you." She sighed. "Has it dawned on you that they aren't welcome in a lot of systems? That we're one of the few places they are? And we have food and other materials to sell them. After the Sirius attack, systems are even more suspicious of the unknown, and the Travelers fall into that category. Besides, I think they're dropping a student or two with the medico school."

"Sure."

"I don't understand why you dislike them so much. Yes, they all flirt terribly. But they don't push. Just say no and they're gone."

"I don't think I should have to. I've already been clear." Every time the Travelers visited, she had to turn down invitations from what seemed like everyone on board. Invitations to travel with them, invitations for sex, invitations for gambling, for worship; it was exhausting. And when she asked them why they were so determined to bring her onboard, they never answered. They wanted something from her, and if they weren't telling her what it was, she wanted no part of it. She was done with liars and users. Although, at this point, she was ready to leave with them just to get away from Secundus.

"Get over it, Quinn." Nat tossed her head and went back to reading something on her e-torc. Probably the Travelers' provision requests, which Q should be handling but wasn't. Not for the Travelers.

Sister Lashtar entered. "Come, I need both of you." She left without waiting for them.

Ruhger's voice rumbled from Lashtar's office. "So, I guess where and when is the question."

Lashtar's voice was unusually cheerful. "Oh, that's easy. Here. As soon as the Travelers fold in." Lashtar waved a hand at Q. "Quinn will help you navigate our suppliers. Nat will organize the party and invite the locals. I'll invite the Travelers." She grinned, and Q stared in astonishment. Lashtar never smiled these days. "Do you want me to officiate? Or do you have some other religion in mind?" She shrugged. "There's lots of them here, now." She sat behind her desk, and Q moved to her shoulder. Whatever Lashtar needed, especially something that made her smile, Q was happy to help with.

Saree looked at Ruhger and shrugged at the same time he did, and they laughed. Wow, whatever they were planning, it must make Ruhger and Saree really happy. Laughter from both of them *and* Lashtar? Must be spectacular.

Ruhger had eyes only for Saree. "The Sisters are the only religious tradition I've ever been a part of, no matter how peripherally. If you're comfortable with Lashtar, I am."

Saree smiled back at Ruhger. "Yes, Lashtar, please officiate."

Officiate what? Q looked between the two of them. *Oh! Yes!*

"Excellent. This will help in more than one way," Lashtar said. Saree and Ruhger finally broke their stare and turned to her. "As a new couple, you'll be left alone. You might get a break on your transport, since new couples are given gifts to help them establish their joint households. For the Travelers, that often means one person leaving their clan and joining a new one, since marriage inside the clan is discouraged. And throwing the Travelers a party is always a good idea. Be careful at any Travelers parties—their alcohol and drugs are particularly potent. They also use some to enhance spiritual awakenings and travel."

They were leaving? *I want to go too!* But with the Travelers? Q wasn't so sure about that part.

Saree shrugged. "I can't use drugs or alcohol, not for the foreseeable future. It's just too risky with the head injury."

Ruhger said, "And I won't. Can you make it clear to the Travelers that Saree's health would be endangered?"

"Of course." Lashtar snorted. "I'll take one for the team and drink your share."

Q looked at Lashtar, a little surprised. She knew Lashtar was ready to make a change, but drinking wasn't one of the changes Q had considered.

Lashtar laughed harder. Ruhger—and Saree—were just as surprised, glancing at each other.

Eventually, Lashtar sobered. "What? Life is short." She motioned at her bionic leg. "I came here," Lashtar spread her arms, encompassing the Sisters' compound, "because I needed to do something else, something life-affirming rather than life-taking. Helping people makes me happy, and the girls needed me. Especially over the last year. But," she slapped her hands on her desk and rose, "that's not the case anymore. Nat's been leading us for six months. We adopt out children faster than we get them in. I'm not particularly useful with the abuse victims because I'm just not outwardly sympathetic enough. I can't even get through to Ruth. The medicos are in charge of her. She's not a potential Sister. We've made all the security improvements possible with this location and mission. I'm just a figurehead to a dying religion."

"That's not true!" Nat said. "You're our spiritual leader. The one who keeps us on the straight and narrow."

The Sisters might not have a lot of members, but Q didn't think they were dying. The religion was important, something for women, especially those who'd been abused, to grasp when everything else had gone wrong and everyone else turned against them. She'd certainly found comfort in the Mother, especially after her years with Familia, both at the Academy and on *Indomito*.

Lashtar turned and sat on the edge of her desk. "Nat, maybe it's time to let this particular straight and narrow go. Most of you want to move on and do other things. We're not necessary for this world, and we're losing members. The work for abused families will continue without our religion. I think we make this not only a ceremony for Ruhger and Saree but a final ceremony for us too."

"But…" Nat stuttered, shocked.

Poor Nat. Q glared at Lashtar. Why say this to Nat, a true believer? It was a terrible thing to do, no matter how much she might want to escape. But doing it this way also made it shockingly clear to Nat that Lashtar was serious. She wanted out. Maybe this was Q's chance to leave too?

"I know I just sprang this on you, and I'm sorry. But I've been thinking about it for a while. We'll meet in Circle tonight." She grasped Nat's shoulders. "No matter what, I'm resigning this position. You truly have been in charge since I lost my leg. I lost more than my leg, I lost my passion. I haven't lost my faith in the Mother, but I've lost interest in leading others to faith. I've been hanging on, grimly, but I need to do something else now. Something fun. Something different."

Yes! That's what I want too. It would be a lot easier with a partner, especially one who'd been everywhere and could defend herself. They'd make a good team. But would Lashtar see it that way?

"What exactly are you thinking, Lashtar?" Ruhger asked warily.

She laughed over her shoulder at Ruhger. "I don't know. Maybe I'll join the Travelers with you." Lashtar chuckled. "Don't worry, I'll make my own deal and accommodations. But I need to travel, move, go places, and see things. Not take care of anyone but me. Be selfish."

Now was her chance, maybe her only chance. If Lashtar left, Nat and Brin would rely on Q more and more, and she didn't want to stay here. She was done with Secundus. And if Familia was still looking for her? Well, they'd get what they had coming. Q laughed loud enough to draw everyone's attention. "Hah. I've been thinking the same thing. I'm tired of taking care of everyone else. I want to go, to explore, to see new things, meet new beings."

"That didn't work out so well for you last time, Quinn," Ruhger cautioned.

Q smirked at him. "Well, I've learned a few things since then, *Dad*. A lot of things." She grinned at Lashtar, hands on her hips. "You're right. Nat's been in charge, and she's good at it. You can leave the Sisters in her hands. You know more about the universe than I do. Want to go adventuring?"

"Yes, I think I do. We'd make a good team if you can quit calling me Sister." Lashtar raised one brow.

Q snorted. "Oh, I think I can do that, Lashtar." With Familia's indoctrination on titles, it might take some work, but she'd do it.

Saree and Ruhger glanced at each other. He shrugged.

"What about me?" Nat said, with a bit of a wail. "I'm not sure I want to stay here either."

Well, that was just silly. Nat was a true believer, and she loved it here. She especially loved leading the entire compound. She was born to be in charge of something big.

Lashtar smiled at her. "There's nothing to hold you back if you want to go. You can train someone to do your job and leave in a few months. But I think you find this work fulfilling. That, and I'm not sure you and some of the others want to let the Sisters of Cygnus go." Lashtar grimaced. "I'm sorry, I was wrong to call it a dying religion. I still believe, and many others do too. There are many ready to take on spiritual leadership. Some of the women we've taken in have become entirely devoted. There's every reason they should take the reins and make it their own, a true refuge for body, spirit, and mind."

"Maybe, Sis—Lashtar," Q said, chuckling at herself for the slip, "it's more than time to make our religion more flexible. Why shouldn't women come and go as they please? There's no reason to tie anyone down, restrict anyone. Perhaps living here, in our compound, means staying celibate, unattached, and sober, but living in the community, women and men can still worship but live their own lives as they need to. Raise children, travel, do all the things. I think the complete control over individuals is part of what led to Ferra's fall."

"Yes," Lashtar said, smiling gratefully at Q. "That's a much better idea. You're right, there's no reason to hang on to old ways." She turned back to the bewildered and shocked Nat. "You know it's time for me to step down. I've seen you chafing under the necessity of justifications. You're ready to fly on your own, make your own rules, and it's better if I'm not here when you do it. You all know why."

Lashtar was right. She had to leave, or everyone would keep coming to her rather than Nat. That made it the right time for Q to leave too.

Nat bit her lip, but as Lashtar spoke, her confidence returned. "I hate to see you go, but you're right. It's been annoying for a long time, a useless process slowing everything down. It's frustrating when so many won't agree with me unless you've agreed with me publicly, and you haven't disagreed with anything I've decided for months."

Lashtar snorted. "And that's not because I agree with every decision you made, but it was more than time for you to make your own mistakes, find your own way." She shrugged. "Develop your leadership style." She nodded once, sharply. "You're ready, and I'm ready. It's time for me to fly." She laughed. "I have a new target. I aim to misbehave."

Q and Saree joined Lashtar's laughter while Ruhger and Nat looked skeptical. Ruhger finally huffed a chuckle and shook his head. "Well, you used to be pretty good at that, Lashtar."

"Run away, run away!" Q's relief bubbled through her like a soda spring. She would leave Secundus with someone to watch her back. And with just two of them, they could hide easily. Q knew exactly where to pull their escape credits from too. She'd finally found a clue to another of Enzo's personal accounts. "We'll find a quest and have a good time."

Lashtar chuckled. "We'll have to come up with some funds, get some weapons, get a few short-term jobs, but I've done it before. We can do it again."

Q snorted. "Oh, I'll get the credits, don't worry about that. Plenty of slimeballs who need a little lesson."

"Quinn, I thought we'd discussed this," Lashtar said, scowling. "We're not stealing."

"If it's already stolen, then I'm not stealing." Familia stole more than credits—they stole lives. They deserved to lose their ill-gotten gains.

"It can go back to the original owners."

Quinn shook her head, sadly. The majority of those beings

were gone. She always tried to find the original owners first. "Not when they're dead. Where do you think I got the credits for our rebuild?" Lashtar wasn't that naïve. But Nat was.

Lashtar and Nat scowled at her. Ruhger snorted, but his look was approving.

Q told them, for what had to be the four-hundredth time, "Look, I can show you where it came from, and you'll agree I'm more than justified." She took a breath. Time to move on from this never-ending argument. "More importantly, Lashtar, you've been a leader in this community for a very long time and never taken a salary. The Sisters owe you more than a little. I think we can fund your escape." Quietly, she added, "And mine." After all, she'd never taken a salary either. And she'd repaid the Adzari Academy fees many times over.

"Well, since you're more likely to find a job, Q, I'll go as your bodyguard, and we'll see what happens." Lashtar grinned.

Q jolted up. What a perfect idea!

Ruhger snort-laughed, shaking his head. "Right, that will work out just great."

"Back to the issue *I* came here for," Nat said. Determination and mourning seemed to war for supremacy on her expressive face. "You wanted me to plan a wedding, right?" She looked between Saree and Ruhger.

Ruhger pointed to Saree. "All yours, Saree. As long as there's a lifetime vow, I don't care what the ceremony looks like."

Saree chuckled. "I don't either. I'm just ready to do this."

"Well, then, let me do it," Nat said. "Nothing fancy, just a simple ceremony, right?"

"Yes. Use whatever the Sisters use," Saree told her. "I'll leave it in your capable hands."

Nat nodded. "Come on, Quinn, we've got work to do."

Well, she'd rather stay, but Nat would need some help with planning this party. Q followed to Nat and Brin's office. "Standard invite to everyone for a communal meal with a commitment ceremony?" The phrasing was deliberate—a commitment could be between people or between a person and an organization, or several other circumstances.

"Yes. Just tell anyone who specifically asks that 'Rufus and Sarah' decided to tie the knot after her recovery." Nat looked at her, with a mix of sadness and anger. "Look, I know you haven't been happy here. But you still have Familia on your tail. The minute you leave, your Gov Human military cover is blown."

"Not quite the minute, but you're right. Once I leave Secundus, General Kerr doesn't have to cover for me anymore." Q grimaced. "That was the deal. I stay here, she 'enlists' me on her flagship. But if I'm careful to stay in the fringes and away from Familia systems, no one should ever know."

Nat frowned. "I hope you're right. But I'm also worried about Ruth. She relies on you." Nat held up a hand. "No, that's not a good enough reason for you to stay. But maybe Ruth should go with you. Think about it." She looked away. "And get Brin in here. She needs to find someone to train as a deputy. Make sure you leave your net security deputy with everything except Sisters-only things."

Q shrugged. "Already done. Jeffe has been running net admin for everything but the Sisters for more than six months. K'tleen has the Sisters' net admin. They're both more than adequate for Secundus. They need more challenges, actually." Q sent Nat's message to Brin, with a high priority tag.

"I thought so. I just wanted to confirm." Nat scowled at her desktop and then at Q. "Sand flea. I can't believe you're leaving us."

Q sighed, got up, and hugged Nat. "I'm sorry, but I can't stay. Really, you're all safer this way. The Gov Human trick was going to fall through eventually, so it's better if I'm already gone."

Nat held on to her. "I know. But I'll miss you."

"I'll miss you too." And she would.

ΔΔΔ

Q rubbed her eyes. She was so close to breaking this final code for Enzo's account. But was she too tired to continue? If she messed up, she might have to run, right now, possibly leaving tracks for them to follow, so she couldn't go with Lashtar and Lightwave. But if she quit now, someone could discover the progress she'd made so far and lock her out. Then, she'd have to start from zero.

Stupid. She was letting her desires rather than her needs drive her. It was time to quit and go to bed. She could finish this tomorrow or even on Lightwave. Suns, it would be easier to do from someplace with better connectivity, especially on a folder. Then, if Q's scripts were discovered, she wouldn't be because they'd fold away and be long gone before someone could track her down physically.

Continuing now was a great way to mess everything up. Plus, Saree and Ruhger were leading a special meditation session tomorrow. She didn't want to miss that—or fall asleep because she was too tired to pay attention.

Q chuckled, the sound echoing in the empty office. Now or later, Enzo would pay. Q carefully backed out of her script locations, leaving them running, shut down all her active transmissions, and disconnected the dedicated comm link to the fold message center, making sure there was no way to trace anything back to her. Then she got up, stretched high, enjoying the movement of stiff muscles, and headed for her bed.

ΛΛΛ

Q floated, secure in the arms of the Mother, in tune with the universe. A ripple passed through her consciousness, bringing a sense of discordance. It increased, then gradually smoothed away, like it had never occurred. Environmental disturbance noted, Q returned to her meditative state.

"You return to full awareness. Your breath pulls in…pushes out," Ruhger rumbled, growing louder, firmer. "You feel your muscles working, your heart beating, your diaphragm, your chest, your legs, your arms, your head."

Q took a breath and took stock of her body. A little stiff from lying on the yoga mat for so long, but overall, she felt good.

"Remembering your sense of peace and beauty, come back to your body. Become aware of how it feels. When you are ready, stretch a little, roll back and forth, and return to a sitting position."

Q sat, feeling relaxed, yet energized. A very good y'ga meditation—Ruhger was an excellent leader. But he should be— he'd been doing it his entire life.

"Gentle beings, I thank you for joining us tonight," Saree said.

"Thank you for trusting us to lead you in meditation. As I said during the introduction to this advanced session, I had a specific reason for offering it. As you may have heard, there is a human clock maintainer working for the Time Guild now, tuning fold clocks."

Q snapped her head around to look at Saree. Really?

"Those rumors are true. The Time Guild is looking for more humans with this ability, the ability to sense something we call ^*timespace*^. One of the ways we find humans with potential is through meditation. Some of you may have noted something during this session, something that wasn't inside of you. I'm not going to tell you what it was because it may look different to everyone, and I don't want to plant a false memory. But if you did note something exterior to yourself and you want to explore the notion, knowing the job itself can be hazardous, come talk to me. Now or later." Saree smiled serenely.

Interesting. Q had definitely noted something, and she already had trouble on her tail. If she had a talent, one that was useful to the Time Guild? That might offer more protection than harm to her. She'd noticed Saree didn't confirm or deny she was the human Clocker. While Q had heard rumors of a human clock maintainer many times, she always thought it was wishful thinking or a ploy by Gov Human to keep humans safer in the universe. Time to find out if this was the big secret Saree had been keeping all this time. She waited for everyone to leave. A few people stopped to thank Saree or Ruhger, but no one stayed to talk.

When everyone was gone, Q padded over to where the pair

were rolling up their mats. "Saree?" Quinn asked. She sounded so tentative. *Yuck.*

Ruhger spun and Saree peered around his ridiculously large shoulders. "Yes?"

"Can I talk to you for a minute?" Quinn flashed a grin at Ruhger. "Girl stuff." She shrugged. This would be hard enough with just Saree, she didn't need Ruhger hovering.

Saree blinked at Quinn and motioned to the mediation mats. "Let's talk."

Ruhger walked away. "I'll leave you two to it and check in with Lashtar about the Travelers' status. See you back at the shuttle, Saree?"

"Yes. Thanks." Saree shot the last word over her shoulder, a soft smile on her face.

They were perfect for each other.

"So, what did you need, Q?" Saree asked.

Q sighed. "I think I might have seen…something." She shrugged. It wasn't really explainable, but she had to find some words. "There was a ripple, a disturbance, a wrinkle? Something I noticed, then pushed away, like you normally push aside things outside of yourself during meditation."

Saree's mouth twisted. "I guess I should have given different starting instructions, then. Blast. I didn't consider the normal response." She shrugged one shoulder. "Something for next time. Anyway, as you've undoubtedly guessed, I'm the human clock maintainer. I access ^timespace^ through meditation and use the frequencies of transuranic metals to tune the clocks to the universal standard. I'm still not sure if I'm only tuning the clock or

^*timespace*^ itself or both, but ^*timespace*^ is disturbed by fold. The more folders, the worse it is and the more often the clocks need maintenance."

"So, what does this ^*timespace*^ look like to you, Saree?"

Saree shrugged, with a tiny smile. "Initially, it was a place of beauty and peace, and I'd just drift there. The Sa'sa taught me to look deeper in ^*timespace*^ for the fundamental frequencies of the different transuranic metals used in the varieties of fold clocks and then ^*pull*^ them into my consciousness, for lack of a better term. Then, I 'tune' the atomic clock to that frequency. That ensures that all Time Guild clocks across the universe are telling the exact same time. It's a pretty difficult thing to do at first."

Saree smiled just a little. "These days, I can easily access ^*timespace*^. I've been doing this a long time and working hard, learning to talk to the Sa'sa in ^*timespace*^, so I'm always somewhat aware of it unless I'm actively blocking it out. I don't know how hard it will be for other humans to learn. It may be easier for me to access ^*timespace*^ because I've been sensitive to the Sa'sa since puberty. I wasn't born on the Sa'sa homeworld, but I grew up there, and that's how they found out about my talent—I was dreaming and interfering with the juvenile Sa'sa clock maintainers. I don't know if a connection to the Sa'sa is necessary to easily access ^*timespace*^ or not."

Q frowned. "I didn't notice anything like a place of peace and beauty. I only noticed a strange…disturbance running through my consciousness." Her nose wrinkled. "Kind of like a single wave across water, it rolled through and was gone."

"Interesting." She raised her brows, with a challenging look.

"Are you willing to go through some training? And endure the danger? The risk of abduction is real."

"Really?" Q snorted. "Familia is already looking for me, hard. Why not give them one more reason?"

Saree chuckled. "Indeed, why not?"

A memory struck Q. "So, that's why I remember you as a Scholar! It was your secret identity!"

Saree laughed. "Yes, it was. I traveled the universe as a Scholar of Ancient Music, studying an unknown field of folk music called filk for many years. But eventually, the cover wore thin. Big data processors matched traveling beings with clock tunings, and I ended up on a shortlist of suspects." She sobered and tapped a little rhythm on her thighs. "We've been running and hiding for longer than I thought we'd be able to." Saree gave a tiny shrug. "But we're safer now that I'm known to be a Time Guild member because I can call on the Sa'sa Warriors for help. They're pretty terrifying."

Q grimaced. She'd seen pictures but not the real beings. "They seem scary. I don't speak Sa'sa. Do they speak Trade?"

Saree tilted her head. "Some. But if you can do what I do, you can call on them in ^*timespace*^, which requires a lot less translation. It's not really a language, more of a place of impressions, thoughts, and emotions. You have to learn how to push your thoughts—folders incoming!" She jumped to her feet and ran out of the Circle room.

Q sprinted to catch up, then passed her. "Come on, I'll get a lifter; we'll pick up Ruhger." They pounded down the hall, everyone flattening to the sides, and out the door. Using her e-torc, Q selected one of Security's all-terrain lift vehicles and started it remotely while she ran down the hall, Saree right behind her. They sprinted out the door, across the yard, and to the charging station. Jumping in, Saree didn't even try for the driver's seat. Which was good because Q knew the compound far better.

"He's in the stable with Lashtar," Saree yelled.

Q drove like a racer, taking what might look like a roundabout way to the stables, but no one would be on this path this time of day, and it got them headed in the right direction. She came around the backside of the stable, immediately spotted Ruhger sprinting toward the shuttle pads, and pulled up next to him.

"Jump in," Saree shouted.

Q slowed a little, but Ruhger jumped and grabbed the roll cage behind Saree, rolling into the cargo area behind them. "Go!" he roared.

Q pushed the power up, bouncing along the narrow, muddy path, and brought the lifter to a skidding stop just outside the shuttle's marked blast radius.

Ruhger was sprinting for Beta shuttle before Q halted the lifter; Saree was right behind him, and Q ran all out to catch up before he reached the hatch. Ruhger put his hand up for the DNA sample while entering codes in his holo, and the hatch swung open. "Saree, you've got security."

"Copy," she yelled, running past Ruhger.

Q squeezed past him too, bringing up the shuttle's net and the backdoor she'd left. Would it still be there or did Katryn find it? But her regular profile was still active, so no reason to find out right now. She logged in, a vibration jolting through her as the main thrusters warmed up. Ruhger slammed into the pilot's seat. Q told him, "I'll take the weapons."

"Sure." Ruhger entered more security codes and another DNA sample and then swept the weapons over to her.

Q checked the weapons status; all fully charged and ready. No surprise there.

"Stand down," Ruhger said, pushing a surveillance picture to the shuttle's screen. "It's the Travelers. And, believe it or not, Lightwave."

"Really?" Saree said, incredulous relief clear in her tone.

Ruhger laughed, and Q stared at him. He was so much happier and relaxed these days. It was so strange to see. But she was relieved too. What if it was a remote army or Gov Human military gone rogue? There was so much turmoil in the human-controlled constellations right now.

"Really. Suns. I wasn't looking forward to searching for them."

"I wonder how they managed to get in with the Travelers?" Saree said.

Ruhger huffed. "I'm sure it was Chief. He did a lot of different things before he came to Phalanx Eagle."

Grumpy Chief? That didn't seem likely to her. Q told him, "It could be Loreli or Grant too." They were both a lot more outgoing and friendly.

Ruhger laugh-snorted. "Not likely. Grant's more likely to have started a blood feud by seducing a daughter, son, or both."

"Not anymore," Saree said.

Grant was kind of a flirt but nothing worse. A nice guy.

"True," Ruhger said, bringing Q's attention back to him.

"Loreli usually makes friends on planets where she can get new foods. If it's been grown or raised in space, she's already eaten it." He started writing Chief a message. It was addressed to *Charani*, registered to the Romani system in Draco.

Q commanded the weapons back to standby and checked to make sure everything was recharging correctly. Then she secured her status in the net. It took her a while to work around Katryn's security, but since she had a crew profile and full access affirmed by Ruhger's DNA, it wasn't too hard.

Ruhger said, "Are you all right?"

Q looked up. Oh, he was talking to Saree, lying there with her eyes closed.

"Yes," she said, turning to look at Ruhger. "I'm just minimizing screen time."

"Makes sense. Okay, you sit there. I'll button us back up but in warm standby mode this time."

Q recalled their conversation after the meditation session. If Saree was the human clock maintainer, and fold disturbed ^timespace^, she might not feel so good with… nine folders coming in. *Wow*. That was more than the Travelers normally brought. She should ask. "Saree, are you really okay? There are nine folders in close proximity. It must have disturbed ^timespace^ a lot."

Saree sat up. "Really? I'm not going deep in ^timespace^ now, that's for sure. I wonder why they'd do such a thing? Everyone knows you have to spread arrivals as much as possible."

"The Travelers do what they want, when they want," Q told her. "If there are consequences, they're usually long gone before it's a problem for them." Like all their flirting. Some of the younger girls and boys found that out the hard way, no matter how often they were warned. But that wasn't fair either; Q knew the Travelers were upfront about their lack of commitment. Sometimes, people heard what they wanted to hear. After all, people fell for Familia's blast and rad all the time. The Travelers were completely honest; they just omitted details. If you weren't smart enough to ask…

"You have experience with them?" Ruhger turned to ask, glowering a little.

Q frowned at him. "A little." More than she wanted. "I worked with them during the medico school build. They have an *interesting* type of honor. They're way better than Familia though."

"There's no reason you have to do anything with them, Quinn," Saree told her, her eyes still closed. "We can take care of it."

Quinn waved her concern away. "It's no big deal. Just be careful what you ask for and what you tell them. They'll take advantage of you if they can."

Ruhger huffed. "Most beings will. Better to learn that lesson now. A large group or extended family of some sort is just easier to target and blame. Everyone's looking for an advantage."

Q snorted at his lecturing tone. "Okay, Dad."

Ruhger turned and mock-glared. Q grinned at him. A smile flickered, then he turned back to the shuttle command and control. "Quinn, you've already integrated yourself into the Beta shuttle permissions, right?"

"Yep. Done."

"All right, let's head back to the compound. There's no reason to stay in the shuttle, is there?"

"Nope," Quinn said, popping the end "p" loudly. She led the way to the airlock. If they wanted a commitment ceremony, she had a lot of work to do.

"No, I don't think so," Saree said with a heavy sigh. "I'll tune the clock before we fold out."

"Roger that, let's go," Ruhger said. "We'll give it time to settle. By the time we fold out, ^timespace^ should be better, right?"

Q looked back at them, embracing. They were so sweet together. And sweet was the last description she'd ever thought she'd use for Ruhger.

Saree said, "I hope so."

"We'll worry about it then. Ready?" Ruhger let her go.

"Sure." Saree stepped away from him but didn't let go of his hand.

The hatch opened, and Q bounced down to the pad. "Okay to walk, Saree?" She nodded, so Q sent the lift vehicle back to its charging station. She wasn't the only one wanting to expend the energy of adrenaline.

About halfway back, Ruhger said, "Saree, I just got a message from Chief. Everyone's safe. He also says no 'big' issues. I guess we'll find out what issues exist when they get down here."

"Can't be soon enough for me, now," Saree told him.

Ruhger opened the chow hall hatch.

Lashtar waited for them. "I've told Nat the ceremony will be tomorrow night." She smiled. "I'm assuming you're both still going ahead with it in the same format?"

"Yes to both," Ruhger said as Saree said, "Of course." Saree continued, "We've told you the ceremony is up to you. The form doesn't matter that much to us."

Lashtar chuckled. "Tomorrow night, then. We'll have the ceremony, then a party." She sniffed. "I'd have a feast, but Loreli would never forgive me."

Ruhger laughed. "Sure, she would. If you tried to label it a *Loreli* feast, *then* she'd never forgive you."

"Right." Lashtar shrugged. "Well, whatever you call it, there will be a ceremony, food, drink, and music. We've arranged for a local band to play, but I'm sure the Travelers will bring a group down too. They can trade off or play in another building. I'd like to hold the whole thing outside, but you know it's likely to rain."

"Doesn't it always?" Ruhger asked, shuddering. "This place is terrible. Space is much better."

Lashtar held up her hands, turning and inspecting them. "I'm always surprised I haven't grown fins or flippers yet."

Huh. Q had never realized Lashtar was funny.

"Or developed rust to go along with the ground-in mud," Saree said. "Everything else has both."

"I never knew cerimetal could rust until we moved here," Lashtar said, laughing. A shadow crossed her face, and her laughter stopped. "I can hardly wait to leave. This place *is* terrible."

Q felt her eyebrows raise. Was this really how Lashtar felt all along, or was it the relief of letting go of all her responsibilities?

Ruhger gripped Lashtar's shoulder.

"Let's grab some tea and see what last-minute chores Nat has for us," Saree said.

Ruhger smiled at her. "Excellent idea."

Lashtar snorted. "I'll leave you two to deal with Nat. She's not my problem anymore. I'll finish packing." She turned down the passageway. "I'll see you at dinner."

"See you then," Ruhger replied. Q followed them, sure Nat had more for her to do too. Even if she didn't, Q did. She had an account to crack and a head enforcer to annoy.

Q walked through the halls of the Sisters' main building and up to the security offices, plopping down in one of the chairs in the small area outside the main offices. There was never anyone here, and the chairs were surprisingly comfortable. She retraced her steps through the scripts she had running in Valenti and found they'd finished and done their work. She had the account numbers, access instructions, credentials, and tokens she needed. Enzo thought he was clever, hiding his credits in an Antlia bank used by lots of Gov Human personnel, but he wasn't smart enough on his own. He'd done the transfers from *Indomito*, and she still had access to the comms there. He really needed a net expert to help him—his paranoia was his downfall. Q considered for a moment. It was a little surprising—she was sure they would have found her comm sniffer by now, but if they had, they were trying to use it to track her down. Since she was routing the traffic through the addresses the Gov Human military gave her on General Kerr's flagship, they'd be hitting some pretty solid blocks. Q chuckled evilly, punching both fists to the ceiling.

After a short celebration, she got back to work, sending the scripts that would back her out of the security holes she'd exploited and wipe her traces from Valenti's nets, along with a couple of little traps for anyone following her back on the route she'd used. She erased her current profile from the fold message centers throughout Cygnus and all her history. Since she had administrator access to Secundus's fold message center, that part was easy.

Using a brand-new identity at the Cygnus Secundus messaging center, she sent the formal request to transfer all the credits except the minimum balance from Enzo's account in Antlia to her new accounts on Nexus Station. Then she transferred half the funds from all those accounts to a numbered account she'd set up back on Valenti, administered by the "Emergency Worker Relief Fund" she'd set up for the families of those unfairly targeted by the enforcers on *Indomito*. Angelo and Roberto's spouses ran the board.

Then she set an order to her Nexus bank account to transfer the remaining credits to four different accounts, three of which were at other banks. From there, she'd transfer several more times, but eventually, most of the credits would go to the Antlia bank account set up for her Gov Human military pay, the same one half of the new Fleet recruits used. Ten percent would end up here, with the Sisters.

Ironic, because the amount she'd stolen from Enzo was about the same number of credits she'd earn in a thirty-year military career. Q laughed. Once again, Enzo would lose. She could almost see his face growing purple, his teeth gritting, and his fists clenching. *Hah! Q strikes again!* She got up, bopping around and chortling for a minute, then went to check on the big ceremony.

∆∆∆

Q stood just behind Lashtar, Nat and Brin beside her, on the hastily erected stage at the front of the dining hall. She was flattered Ruhger, Saree, Lashtar, and Nat had all insisted on her involvement in the actual ceremony. Ruhger and Saree walked slowly toward them down parallel but separate aisles in the crowd. Both were throwing big grins at each other the whole way. Q couldn't help but smile—their happiness was contagious.

The dining hall was packed. Even Ruth was there, at the very back of the crowd. She stood with a wall at her back, scanning the crowd for threats.

Saree wore an amazing dress with huge, gorgeous jewels. The dress was a deep, rich red at the shoulders and bust, matching the giant rubies in her necklace, then it faded to orange and finally pale, pale yellow at the bottom. Saree let them touch it—Tazan silk was so soft, so comforting. Ruhger wore Chef Loreli's kerchief, the blindingly white triangle of Tazan silk around his neck. The two met in front of Lashtar, grasping hands. Sister Lashtar looked regal in the Mother's ancient white, silver and gold robe, and Her blackwood staff.

Ruhger leaned in and kissed Saree quickly.

Aw. They were so cute.

Lashtar chuckled softly. "Ready?"

"Of course," Ruhger answered, with Saree saying, "Yes!" at the same time.

Lashtar nodded at Brin. She rang the Sisters' Circle bowl and let the tone ring. Whispers and conversations ceased, everyone gazing up at them.

Ruhger smiled again at Saree.

Q muttered, "Look at that, he does smile!"

Nat said, "Shh," and kicked her lightly. Brin picked up the Sisters' ancient worship text and opened it carefully, holding it so Lashtar could read it easily.

Lashtar's voice rang out, sure and yet humble. "Gentle beings, welcome one and all. You witness the binding of these two human beings into one, partners for life, under the Mother's care. Does anyone here object to this binding?" She waited for a moment, then continued, "Can anyone here attest to the good intentions of this couple, someone who has seen their fidelity and devotion demonstrated, who believes this partnership will endure forever?"

Chief Bhoher, standing just below them, said, "We, the crew of Lightwave, attest to the good intentions of both Saree of Jericho and Ruhger, Captain of Lightwave Fold Transport. They have proven their love and loyalty many times."

Chief used their real names? *Surprising.* Everyone knew there were big rewards for information about Lightwave, her crew, and especially Saree. Well, they were all leaving immediately after the ceremony—the perfect way to bow out of the Sisters forever.

"So attested." Lashtar looked at Ruhger, then Saree. "Both of you, repeat after me. I, state your name, swear to love and honor you for the rest of my days."

Ruhger said, "I, Ruhger, swear to love and honor you, Saree of Jericho, for the rest of my days."

Saree echoed him, "I, Saree, swear to love and honor you, Ruhger of Lightwave, for the rest of my days."

Lashtar continued, "Do you swear to cleave only to each other, forsaking all other romantic and sexual attachments? To open communication and full disclosure? To nurture each other in every way possible? To act in each other's best interests ahead of your own in balance with the greater community of living beings and the Mother?"

Ruhger and Saree both answered, "I do," to each question. Somehow, Saree's voice projected, even though she wasn't yelling. She was a singer, so it must be something she'd learned to do.

As soon as the last, "I do," rang out, Q turned back and carefully picked up the binding cloth. No one knew how old the cloth or the worship text were, so they handled them as little as possible. Lashtar took the long, narrow, roughly woven cloth from her, and Q breathed a sigh of relief.

Lashtar wrapped the cloth gently around the couple's clasped hands. "As the faint reflection of the Mother in this universe, I hereby bind you, Saree of Jericho, and Ruhger, Captain of Lightwave, to each other forever." She raised their hands high. "What is now joined, let no other part."

Q yelled, "Yes!" while Nat and Brin said, "Mother bless you!" Applause, whoops, and blessing from the crowd were almost deafening. Lashtar eventually brought their hands back down and carefully unwound the ancient cloth, handing it back to Q. She carefully rolled it on the holder and placed it back in the case. *Whew.*

Ruhger pulled Saree into his arms and kissed her.

Nat stepped forward and announced, "Let the celebration begin!"

Ruhger released Saree, both of them turning to accept blessings from Nat and Brin. Q waited for her turn and got a hug from each of them, vaguely aware of Nat and Brin removing the Sisters' precious relics. Ruhger jumped off the platform and lifted Saree off too. They got hugs and congratulations from their crew, joining into one giant hug, Lashtar with them. Q didn't feel like she was quite family yet but maybe someday.

"Okay, enough of this for an old man," Chief mock-grumbled, pulling out of the group hug. "I need a drink to cut all this sweetness and light."

Lashtar laughed. "You and me both. I'm done. Nat and Brin can make sure no one gets too out of hand."

Thanks be to the Mother Lashtar hadn't named Q—she had every intention of celebrating her goodbye.

Chief grinned and put his arm around Lashtar's waist. "Good. I've been waiting for this moment for a long time. Let's go!" They disappeared into the crowd, the rest of the crew following. Ruhger and Saree were caught in a crush of congratulations, well-wishes, and blessings. Q sent a reminder to Saree that they'd stocked Beta shuttle with food and drink for them.

A message from Ruth popped in, and Q swiped it up. "Caught a sneaky lizard. Come to the north treehouse, now." *Blast.* Q glanced at the party below her. She really wanted to celebrate, but if Ruth needed her, she had to go. She made her way to the back of the stage, dropping her borrowed Sister robes, and exited the rear door, checking to make sure it locked behind her. Then, she summoned a lift bike from the nearest charging station—she really didn't feel like running tonight—and steered it virtually to meet her at the north gate.

Exiting the gate, Q was happy to see, from the messages on the security net, that Security was doing their jobs, rather than being completely distracted by the party. They were aware Ruth caught an intruder and were looking for more. Q sent a quick message back, thanking them, then pushed the power up on the bike. Night meant taking it slower, but she knew this route like the back of her hand, so it wasn't long before she reached the treehouse and climbed to the top.

Peering up over the edge, she saw a man, upside down, swinging gently back and forth from ropes at his ankles, and Ruth, tapping her toe next to him. She was wearing hunting gear, including a head net, which not only kept the insects off her face but also concealed her face enough to confuse a stranger.

"New toy?" Q asked.

Ruth almost smiled. "I guess you could call him a cat toy."

Q chuckled. "He does rather look like one."

"Now, he does. Before, he looked like a scavenger, trying to mimic a sniper." Ruth's voice was raspier than usual. "He didn't even come close." She gave him a little shove, sending him swinging over the edge of the platform, and he moaned.

Q wasn't sure why—it was dark, so he couldn't see the drop. But Ruth had to bring him up here to begin with, so maybe the distance up was enough of an indication.

A derisive snort and Ruth jerked on the ropes binding the man, bringing him to a halt. "But I asked you out here for a reason. This guy's got the look."

The look?

A pin light appeared, spotlighting the man's face. It was dirty, covered with the red slashes of swinging branches and a few bug bites, but Q recognized him. Unfortunately. "That's Fabriano. I told you about him, remember?"

Ruth sniffed. "The bookie? They sent a screwup? It should be *Idito*, not *Indomito*."

Q snickered but sobered quickly. "My guess is he isn't here for anything but reconnaissance. He's not supposed to be sneaking into the compound—he's supposed to be checking nets here on Secundus." She sniffed. "But the Sisters' nets are locked down pretty well, aren't they, Fab?"

He tried to sneer, but it looked pretty funny upside down.

Ruth sent him swinging again. "When he first woke up, he actually looked relieved for a moment." Ruth snorted. "That didn't last long. So, Fab, either you tell us exactly what you're doing here, or we'll just leave you here, like this. You won't last long; the wildlife is pretty aggressive. Too bad for you it will be small wildlife, eating bits and pieces of you, slowly and painfully." She sounded gleeful, but Q could tell Ruth wasn't entirely comfortable. The counseling might have been more successful than any of them thought.

He jerked against the ropes but stopped when he swung harder. "Okay, okay, just don't leave me here!"

Q told Ruth, "I didn't think it would take long."

"Do you promise not to leave me here?" Fab whined pitifully. "And cut me down?"

"Sure." Ruth took out a machete and cut through the rope holding Fab up. He thudded down like an already-harvested lizard carcass.

"Ow!"

Ruth toed him. "Talk." When he didn't say anything, she added, "If it was me, I'd just cut your throat and toss you over, so talk."

"Okay." He gasped a bit. "I'll talk. Give me a second."

They both waited, Ruth's toe tapping again. Q finally took a little pity on him. She held up a bev-tainer, and when he nodded, she dribbled some water in his mouth.

"Thanks." Fabriano sighed. "Yes. I was sent to see if Quinn was here. They just wanted to get a pic or a vid because they figured out you're not really on General Kerr's flagship. I don't know how they know that; it's what they told me. If I could get sight of you, I'd get a chance at enforcer."

Q's lip curled. He was nasty enough to be one of them, but he didn't have the trickiness required.

"But I couldn't get through the net, and no one in town would talk about the Sisters at all. No one in Gov Human would, either, so I figured if I came out here and snuck up to the fence, I'd see you eventually." Fab's whining tone made Q's ears ache.

"Why did they send you here?" Ruth asked.

"Because everyone goes home, even when they shouldn't." Fab looked so sad. If he hadn't come looking for her, Q might be sympathetic—he'd obviously found that out for himself.

Ruth asked, "What happens if you don't come back?"

"They'll come looking for me in a week!" Fab's eyes were wide—and scared.

Ruth's mouth twisted in a parody of a smile. "I doubt it. But they might in two or three. Or never. So, here's what you're going to do. You're going to have a lovely stay in a secluded little cabin. You'll be giving me your e-torc, with full access, and telling me *exactly* what messages need to be sent. If any of it is false, you'll never see me again and you'll die. Probably of starvation. Or cold if you're lucky." Ruth shrugged. "I won't care, and Q will be long gone. See, if I hadn't caught you, a predator would have, and you'd have never seen Q. She's leaving tomorrow and never coming back." Ruth looked in Q's eyes as she said the last part.

Q nodded at Ruth. It was true—she couldn't come back, not with Familia looking actively.

"You're also going to tell me everything you know about Familia. Everything." Ruth barked a rough laugh, or as close as she came to one. "Yep, you and I will get along fabulously, Fab. Get it?" Fab rolled his eyes, and Ruth gave him a sharp little jab with her boot. "Don't disrespect me, Fab. You won't like the results. I don't like men. At all."

"It's true, all of it," Q told him.

"I'll string Familia along as long as I can. Then, I'll let you go. But only if you cooperate—fully. And I do mean fully, Fab," Ruth snarled.

"Okay! I get it! Capisce!"

Q shook her head slowly. "You'll have to remind him more than once, Ruth. Probably every time you talk to him. But it's a good plan. I'll help you with the e-torc right now." Q took Fabriano through the settings, making sure everything was unlocked, then she pulled it off his neck. She didn't put it around her own neck but grabbed a game bag from Ruth's belt, wrapped it around the e-torc, and held it up next to her. Fab's face fell. "Really? You expected that to work? You are an idioto." She sighed and put it back down around his neck, where she walked him back through all the security, then she held it up again, and started going through files. "Here's the instructions for check-in, Ruth, I'm sending those to you now. And it looks like he's got a ride out in a month."

Q looked down at Fab. "If you're smart, you won't go home again. If you survive this, and there are no guarantees, you should run far and fast. Take that ticket and change it for a fringe world in Octans, Apus, or Pavo. Make a life for yourself far from Familia, Fab. Because you're not going to make it through this one. Or you'll wish you hadn't. I don't care how much your family has sheltered you so far, they can't help you now. Run."

Fab started blinking back tears, and Q turned to Ruth. "Even though it's safe now, don't put this on. Give it to K'tleen, tell her to use the captured enemy protocols." She handed the e-torc to Ruth, who put it in her pocket. "You're going to the mountain cabin?"

"Yes." A smile flickered on Ruth's face.

"Good choice." Q grinned, then sighed and looked down at Fab again. "Goodbye, Fab. I hope this is the last time I see you because you won't survive the next time. And, Fab, if you're dumb enough to go back to Familia, warn Justice Fatima that Enzo must give up." She shrugged. "I know he's obsessed and embarrassed, but coming after me is useless. I have friends in very high places, and they're not all human. He might end up a target if he's not careful. And these beings don't miss their targets."

"Trust me, I'm not going back. I'm running just like you said," Fab told her.

Q shook her head. "I doubt it, but I hope so. You'll be a lot happier." She tilted her head toward the other side of the treehouse, and Ruth followed her. "Thanks for taking care of this and not just killing him. He's not very smart, or nice, but maybe he can learn."

Ruth sniffed. "I doubt it. But we'll try. Everyone deserves a second chance. If he takes it, great. But he'll survive this and go back, I'm sure of it."

"Yeah, me too." Q took in a deep breath and let it out, letting all the regrets and could-have-beens go. One thing her time with the Sisters had done: she'd practiced forgiveness a lot and was getting better at it. "So, this is goodbye, right?" she asked Ruth.

Ruth actually smiled at her, a real smile. "Nah, it's just farewell. I like you. I'll see you again, but it won't be here."

Q laughed and held out her arms. "Deal."

Ruth hugged her, then stepped back. "Farewell and safe folds."

"You stay safe too."

"See you soon." Ruth left, and Q heard the noise as Ruth used a hand-tractor to lower Fab through the foliage.

Q stared up at the dark, cloudy sky until she couldn't hear Ruth and Fab's passage, then climbed down and started back to the compound. Time to make her final goodbyes and wish everyone here the best of luck and happiness. They didn't need luck, though, because they were in great hands. Nat and Brin would lead the Sisters of Cygnus to a wonderful future.

That left Q free to fly, far and fast, and find a new adventure, taking some dangers away with her. She was more than ready to take control and move ahead on her own, rather than dance to someone else's tune. If she could help the universe as a whole as she did? That was a fabulous opportunity. Q wouldn't waste a moment—she'd thrust full power, straight ahead, into her new future!

The End!

Thanks for reading! Q's adventures continue in *Quinn of Cygnus: Escape Velocity*, out now.

Sign up for my mailing list here:

https://www.amscottwrites.com/lightwave-free/

ACKNOWLEGMENTS

Wow, a new series! I'm getting to the point where I'm repeating myself, but I am truly thankful for all of you!

First, thank you, gentle readers, for reading my novel! I truly appreciate the time and money you spend on my stories.

As usual, big thanks to Julia Huni, author of the Space Janitor, Krimson Empire and Recycled World series. This book would be far worse without her developmental edits. Check out her novels!

Also huge thanks to Jim Caplan and Kyle Roesler, amazing beta readers! This novel is much better because the time and effort you put in—I appreciate it so much. Check out Kyle's novels too!

Thanks to Deranged Doctor Design for another amazing cover! I love the way you've captured Quinn, but made it consistent with the Folding Space Series.

A huge thank you to Polaris Editing. Paula, you finished my proofreading so fast and did a wonderful job!

An extra special thank you goes to my Advance Readers: Deb S., Neil B., Stella M., Robert M., Lloyd B., the other Jim C., Barbara H., Manie K., Brian B., and Marti P. I really appreciate the time and effort you put into your reviews—you make it much easier for this author to get noticed!

Thanks to the Facebook Virtual Writing group for the sprints! The accountability really helps keep me on track.

Thanks to the 20Booksto50K community, and in particular to Craig Martelle, one of the founders, SF author and the editor of the anthology, *The Expanding Universe 6*. Thanks also for starting the Independent Alliance of SFF Authors.

Thanks to AK Duboff, the editor of the anthology, *The Great Beyond*, and the founder of the new SFFCon: The Science Fiction and Fantasy Con!

Thanks to Kate Pickford and the other wonderful authors and volunteers in the *Hellcats: Anthology*. What a cat-tastic experience!

Thank you to the group who responded to my Facebook question: "What's a really boring IT task?" I hope you enjoy your Tuckerizations! Windy B, Joanna S, Jeremy F, Kyle R, Brian Y, Kathe K, Jim C, Craig M, Shawna B, DeeDe B, Thomas S, Jeff W, Ed W, and Rich D.

Thank you to several other author Facebook groups: Mark Dawson's SPF Community, Marie Force's Author Support Network, the Indie Author Support group, and the fun folks in Space Opera! Another big thank you to Patty Jensen, the Ebookaroo guru and Facebook SFF newsletter swap queen and every author who's swapped newsletters with me.

To my Team Rubicon family, kicking disaster ass! Way to adapt and overcome during the COVID-19 pandemic.

To the US Veteran Administration doctors, PAs, nurses, techs and everyone else working so hard to keep our veterans alive.

To everyone fighting COVID-19 in the hospitals and communities. Wear a mask!

Thanks to my husband, the Amazing Sleeping Man, for putting up with all my writer complaints during our twice a day walks with Zoe. I love you!

Finally, thanks to God, for sending me on this writing adventure!

ABOUT THE AUTHOR

After twenty years as a US Air Force space operations officer, AM now operates a laptop, trading in real satellites for fictional spaceships.

Sign up for the Scott Space Newsletter and get three free short stories, *Lightwave: Short Stories 1*.
https://www.amscottwrites.com/lightwave-free/
The Folding Space Series is complete and ready for binge reading! Start with *Lightwave: Nexus Station* or *Lightwave: Clocker*. Quantum Fold will be complete in early 2022. Start with *Quinn of Cygnus: Lift Off*!

If not out adventuring, find AM in all the usual places:
Website: www.amscottwrites.com
Twitter: @AM_Scottwrites
Instagram: https://www.instagram.com/amscottwrites/
Facebook: https://www.facebook.com/AMScottWrites/
Email: am@amscottwrites.com

AM's writing cave is deep in the mountains of western Montana; check out Montana, The Amazing Sleeping Man and Zoe, their slightly crazy German Shepherd, on Instagram. AM is also a volunteer leader with Team Rubicon Disaster Response.

I love to hear from readers. If you find errors, please let me know at the email address above. I'm on all the normal social media, but somewhat irregularly, so if you ask a question or make a comment, please don't be offended if I don't immediately reply. I'm particularly difficult to contact when I'm on Team Rubicon operations or out backpacking—cellphone towers don't exist in disaster zones or the wilderness!

Please consider leaving a review. I don't buy a book these days without reading a few reviews, so it's truly helpful.

Quinn of Cygnus: Lift Off © 2020 by AM Scott. All Rights Reserved.

All rights reserved. No part of this book may be reproduced in any form or by any electronic or mechanical means including information storage and retrieval systems, without permission in writing from the author. The only exception is by a reviewer, who may quote short excerpts in a review. Pirates may be thrust into the giant black hole of Andromeda without further warning.

Cover designed by Deranged Doctor Design
Proofreading by Polaris Editing
Developmental Editing by Julia Huni

This book is a work of fiction. Names, characters, places, and incidents either are products of the author's imagination or are used fictitiously. Any resemblance to actual persons, living or dead, events, or locales is entirely coincidental.

AM Scott
Visit my website at www.amscottwrites.com

First Printing: October 2020
Lightwave Publishing LLC

www.ingramcontent.com/pod-product-compliance
Lightning Source LLC
Chambersburg PA
CBHW021334310726

48971CB00001B/124